Finding Jacob

Chris Coad Taylor

Also by

Chris Coad Taylor

Novels
Secrets of Havenridge
A Havenridge Mystery Novel

The Rainbow Murders
Amber Novels of Ybor Book One

Saffron's Place
Amber Novels of Ybor Book 2

Return of Evil
Release date TBA

Finding Jacob

Chris Coad Taylor

JoHazel Publishing
Land O'Lakes, Florida

Published by: JoHazel Publishing
Land O Lakes, Florida 34639

For permissions:
JoHazel Publishing
email:publisher@johazelpublishing.com
Attention: Permissions Coordinator

Bulk Orders: Special discounts are available on quantity
purchases by book clubs, corporations, associations, and others.
For details, contact the publisher at the email address above.

Prologue

THE WEDDING-1987

As I watched my brother in the gazebo of my backyard preparing to pledge his love for his bride, Leann, my heart filled with joy. My entire being was at peace.

Things were so different now from two years earlier. Back then, I had thought peace would never be part of my life ever again. I had been lost and filled with despair without my daughter in my life, but it was my brother who pulled me out of the hollow that had imprisoned me.

Now, I'm content. My loneliness has been lifted. Looking at the yard filled with wedding guests, I'm happy.

Across the yard, the caterers were busy arranging food trays. The fragrance of young love once again filled the air. The old Victorian house from the Brewer estate that I bought was bright again. Bitter moments of the past faded from my mind as I imagined Mabel Brewer happily in love and sneaking out of the back door of the house to meet her lover. Once I had questioned the mystery surrounding Blue Lake and the two lovers. I thought perhaps it had been a made-up fairytale of a powerful family invented by the wild imagination of the people in town. I too had questioned if the rumors were false until I found the old letters hidden in the house.

After my brother's bride had shown me a letter written by her great uncle, it confirmed the Blue Lake lovers did exist. The letter pledged his love, saying that he would return home to his beloved Mabel, the last Brewer who had lived in the house that I now owned. The

1

fairytale romance about Mabel Brewer was true. And my brother's bride, Leann, helped put the missing pieces together.

The conversation Leann and I had before coming downstairs to join the rest of the bridal party in the gazebo echoed in my mind. "Please help find out what happened to my uncle and why he disappeared without a trace. I need to know why he didn't return for Mabel and bring her home as he said he would in the letter." I'm still a bit in shock. My mind raced with thoughts about Mabel, Jacob, and Leann's request to solve the seventy-year-old mystery.

"Do you take this woman to be your wife?" The minister's voice pierced my rambling thoughts, pushing me back into the present. My brother's blue eyes gazed at his wife-to-be.

Focus on this moment! Today was all about new beginnings and a wedding. Old mysteries can wait, the present is about my brother and his bride pledging their love to each other forever.

The two lovers of the past needed to remain in the shadows. *Mabel and Jacob's mystery will stay unsolved for a little while longer.* I scolded myself but a chill flowed over me as if a ghost had touched my arm. Was Mabel here as another couple recites wedding vows that had been forbidden for her?

"Does anyone here hold reason that these two not be wed?" the minister said. "Speak now or forev . . . er—"

"No!" A troubled voice cried out. "No, no, no."

A hush fell over the crowd as they turned to look toward Gladys, who sat in the third row on the groom's side. Her eyes widened as she saw the wedding party and guests frozen, watching her.

Gladys's face flushed crimson as she popped up from her chair. She smiled and waved a lavender flowered handkerchief at the bride and groom who stood dumbfounded. "Oh, not you," she said sheepishly.

She pointed toward the right side of the yard. "It's the cake." Two caterers were carrying the wedding cake out to a garden table.

"It can't be in the sun. The frosting will melt." Gladys flapped her handkerchief toward the bride and groom again. "You two go right along with the ceremony." She moved, inching her way past guests, out of the row. "I'll take care of the cake." Once free of the row of chairs, she marched down the aisle and off toward the table.

A combination of sighs and chuckles filled the air. The scene helped corral my run-away thoughts of the past. The people of Havenridge were unique. The town had a magical presence and it seemed like nothing bad ever could happen there. The powerful charm overflowed onto my brother, which led him to find his beautiful bride. New beginnings weren't just for my brother. This town had taken the darkness away from my life and had given me an appetite to live again. Now, I too, had a new beginning with a purpose—to *find Jacob*, Mabel Brewer's secret lover.

The Promise

ONE MONTH AFTER THE WEDDING

Leann was convinced that Mabel's secret lover had been her late great uncle Jacob, but she couldn't prove it. Nor could she prove that Jacob meant what he wrote to her relatives so long ago.

I was confident I could unravel the Havenridge mystery. Between my uncanny skills for reading people, which was getting better each day, and my best friend, Betsy's love of history along with her know-how for research, we made a good team. We could do it, and change rumors and myths that had lived for decades about secret lovers into proven documented facts. That would give Leann the proof to restore her uncle's honor and good name to the remaining family members.

The dark mysteries of the Brewer family were the type of material that great books were written from, or so I thought. Self-determined, I had convinced every person in Havenridge to believe that I could write a book about the town and the Brewers. But one month into my task as the great American author, my confidence wasn't as strong. Nor was I so sure what I wanted.

Sitting at my kitchen table, I picked the check in front of me up. Imprinted near the top left edge was the name TopHat Publishing Company. On the *payable to* line was my name, Stephanie Oliver. My fingers skimmed over the Manhattan City Bank check. The dollar box held the number eight, with three zeroes following. A check of this size put my neck on the preverbal chopping block. Talk wasn't good enough anymore, I had to produce. Action was required.

The people of Havenridge had their tales about Mabel Brewer and her ironhanded father, Cain Brewer. Maybe it was just that, tales about a spinster schoolteacher who in her younger years had a steamy love affair with a mysterious stranger who was passing through town. It had been the early nineteen hundreds, the perfect setting to seed a rumor of love and mystery. What could be better to spin a tale than a drifter coming into town, and months later, disappearing in the darkness of night? It had all the right elements: love, a powerful and controlling father—and secrets.

I stared at the check. *What if there isn't any story? What then? If I track down Leann's Uncle Jacob and he just drifted on to live a life of nothingness, I'll have nothing to write.* The warning, "be careful what you wish for," came to mind.

Truth tends to be slanted, depending on whose truth it is. Was it even possible to trace back to the truth? Leann's family had their own interpretation. They thought of Jacob as the black sheep of the family. He had never amounted to anything in their minds nor did he ever do what he promised. Leann was set on proving them wrong.

On the other hand, the town of Havenridge had its own truth. They saw Mabel's father, Cain Brewer, as evil. In their eyes, Cain had been a person who would stop at nothing to gain control of anything and anyone, even his daughter. The letters I found revealed the Brewer family lived a tragic life. Cain believed that he was cursed and that his daughter's destiny was doomed. That was Cain's truth. *What truth should I believe?*

The evidence that I had uncovered confirmed Jacob and Mabel Brewer were secret lovers, but I needed more for Leann and my publisher. Restless souls of the past pressed heavily on my shoulders. There were so many counting on me to deliver.

Could I change the tarnished character of Leann's uncle? How could I prove Jacob Thompson had been an honorable man? I put the check down and went to retrieve the platter of sandwiches and the pitcher of iced tea from the refrigerator. Leann and Steve would be here shortly. I would soon know whether I would be cashing that check.

I rubbed my throbbing temples. *What if I find evidence about Jacob and it's not good?* I had to face that it was possible. Leann begged me to search for answers and suggested I write a book about my findings. However, I wondered if she had considered the ramifications if my findings were bad. Or considered that they might even be horrible. Once I cashed the check, I would be committed to writing whatever I found.

"Sometimes the past is best left in the past," I mumbled. Publishing a book could unlock a Pandora's box for Leann. My writing a book had seemed surreal and far into the future, but now that future was crashing down on me.

The Beginning or The End

Little was known about Jacob after he left Havenridge and in the years leading up to his death. The letters and the journal that I had uncovered established that Jacob and Mabel Brewer were secret lovers, but that wasn't enough. I needed more for Leann and my publisher. What little I had surely wasn't going to put the souls of the past to rest.

Some in Havenridge who had grown up hearing the stories about a secret love affair and forbidden love held tight to the romantic stories gossiped about for years. Still, others dismissed the tales as no more than appealing ghost stories. I knew the truth. The legend was real. Jacob Thompson was not a ghost but a live, skin-and-bones man. My confident self had vowed to unravel the mystery of Jacob and Mabel's story and write the real history.

Leann was banking that her Uncle Jacob's reputation would be vindicated. I hoped that I wouldn't disappoint her. However, there was so much more at stake than just making Leann happy. The Brewer love story had been part of the town's history. What if there was no love story? With no truth backing me, I couldn't write a book of lies. If I failed to produce a sellable book, I'd have to answer to TopHat, possibly in court. If they pursued a civil action for breach of contract. What then? Jail?

I needed to decide if I'd go forward with my investigation, and sign with the publisher, which would mean that I have a contractual commitment. I had to consider all the possible consequences, whatever they might be—and—I needed to have Leann's approval before making my decision to move ahead.

The table was ready. The tea and sandwiches were out. I gathered napkins and glasses, placing them next to the tea pitcher. My nervousness about talking to Leann mounted with every minute. When I found Cain Brewer's journal and the letters, Steve had not yet met Leann. The only people involved were ghosts of the past.

I wrung my hands, pacing, too anxious to sit. I looked around the kitchen. Everything had the illusion of perfection. The old wood floor, now refurbished, glowed with a rich sheen that harmonized with the new, cheery wallpaper I had hung. Both were labor-intense jobs, but worth the long hours it took. The old Brewer house no longer reflected a dilapidated house lost to age. It reflected me, not the Brewer family. It was my home, where my brother and his wife came to visit. My home was a happy one. Could a curse of sadness that once lived inside the walls of this house be rekindled by my decision today?

I walked into the living room yelling at myself, "Get a grip, Stephanie. This is not a Twilight Zone episode. Just wait until you speak to Leann before freaking out!"

Becoming a published author was a dream come true. It gave me purpose and direction. In my excitement, I signed the contract without thinking about how it would open Leann's family history to the world. There was a clause in the contract allowing me to change my mind within three days of signing, and there was only one day left.

"Steph, we're here." I jumped when I heard my brother's voice through the screen door. *I hope he didn't hear me talking to myself. He'll think that I've lost it again.*

"Coming," I said, as I hurried to the door. Steve deserved happiness. *I'm fine. I can handle it, whatever that is, author or no author.* As I approached the screen door, I saw Steve on my porch kissing his new bride.

"Should I go away and come back later?"

Leann pushed back from Steve, looking sheepishly at me. "Oh. Hi Stephanie."

I opened the screen door and LeAnn strolled past me into the house, her face a shade of hot pink. My brother chuckled and said with a devilish twinkle in his eye, "Just two old married people groping each other."

Leann turned back and scolded, "Steve! That's terrible." She turned a deeper shade of rose as she took a seat on the couch. "Stephanie, we brought the wedding pictures. I can't believe it took a whole month to get them from the photographer. I also got the honeymoon pictures developed and brought them, too."

Four envelopes and three albums filled her arms. She bent forward, toppling the contents onto the coffee table. "I'm wildly spending your brother's money. I bought two albums for us and one for you."

Steve interjected, "It's not my money. It's *our* money now."

Of course, that brought on giggles from both of them. Why is it that love changes the most intelligent adults into blushing, babbling idiots?

Leann picked up one of the albums and thrust it forward. "This one is for you. It's our thank you for letting us have the wedding in your backyard gazebo."

After we looked through all the pictures—twice, I stood and said, "Let's go in the kitchen. I made some sandwiches. I've some news to share."

At the kitchen table, Leann and Steve sat mute, waiting while I took small bites of an egg salad sandwich. The folded check seemed to pulse an irritating glow that only I could see.

Steve broke the silence, "Well, what's the news?"

I took a deep breath and exhaled. "I really wanted to get Leann's okay about something I've done."

I picked up the check, unfolded it, and slid it forward. "I've been offered a contract to write a book about Mabel and your Uncle Jacob. They paid me an advance. I have only one day left to change my mind."

"Change your mind, Steph, why?" Steve asked.

I ignored him.

"Leann, I signed a contract but I can get out of it." I pointed to the check. "Should I cash it?"

"This is wonderful news," Leann said as she picked up the check and studied it. "But why would you ask for my permission?"

"You need to think about this, Leann. I've only scratched the surface about your great uncle. I may find out things you might not want to know. It might not be a fairytale romance like the one we think. Or the truth could be bad. The things that your family thinks about your Uncle Jacob may be right, that he was a wanderer with no redeeming qualities. You need to be sure because after accepting this check, I'll have to write whatever I find."

Leann's happy look diminished into a serious expression. "All my life, my family would talk trash about my Uncle Jacob. They didn't even know him. I hated it. Actually, my great-grandmother was the only relative alive who had ever known him personally. When I was older, my relatives, the elder ones, would whisper about me having Jacob's wandering soul. I traveled, which was not what young women were supposed to do, according to their old thinking. I didn't fit into their well-mannered box. A respectful girl was to be married and thinking about children. But I was thirty and still single. Not *normal.*"

"That's changed now," Steve said. "They can find someone else to whisper about."

Leann paused, touching Steve's hand. "I know." She smiled, then turned back to me. "Whenever we had family parties, I was the center of gossip. They said I was just like Jacob, inherited his bad genes."

Leann's eyes welled with tears. "They didn't know I heard them. But I did. My family is not bad, but they're old fashioned and have a certain way of thinking. Like if a girl doesn't get married in her twenties, there is something wrong with her, since she can't get a husband. I wasn't ready to get married then. I liked traveling, like Uncle Jacob. Add to that, I'm an artist, which only gave more fuel for their gossip and concerns. My family still thinks the only right choice for a woman is marriage, and if that doesn't happen, then she could choose to be a nurse or teacher. Well, I didn't follow any of those paths. That didn't make me damaged goods! And it didn't make Jacob bad because he didn't fall into step either."

Leann looked at Steve and smiled. "I found my true love, and maybe—just maybe—my Uncle Jacob found his love. She squared her shoulders, straightened herself in the chair. "Either way, I want to know. Even if Jacob wasn't good, or kind and less honorable than I believe. Maybe he did something awful, maybe he was irresponsible, even a womanizer, but I'm ready to find out."

She pushed the check forward. "Cash it, Stephanie. Find out what happened to Jacob. To hide the truth can only bring harm."

Sleepless

I had tossed and turned all night, drifting in and out of sleep. Stress of any kind always resulted in sleepless nights for me. I turned over on my back and stared at the ceiling. I must have been crazy to think I could unravel the mystery of what happened to Jacob.

Two and a half months had gone by since getting Leann's approval to cash that check from the publisher, and I was no closer to knowing where Jacob had disappeared to or why he hadn't returned to Mabel. The only new bit of information I had attained was three more names of cities that had no record of Jacob Thompson's existence.

Turning over on my left side, I laid still, thinking. Betsy and I had mapped out a thirty-mile radius around Havenridge to target our search. Our theory was that in the early nineteen hundreds, if a man were to travel seeking work or was just wanting to move on to another town, it was more than likely that he wouldn't go far. We sent out dozens and dozens of requests to city halls, old churches, and medical facilities inquiring about a wanderer named Jacob, and the result was zilch. Nothing. It seemed like Leann's great uncle disappeared without a trace.

It was no use. I threw the sheets back and sat up, dangling my feet over the side of the bed. I wasn't going to sleep. Awake since three a.m., and now my clock sitting on the nightstand read 6:30. It was best to get up, but no one ever said Stephanie Oliver was a morning person. After pulling on the terrycloth robe from the foot of the bed, I headed downstairs to make coffee.

In the kitchen, I put last night's dinner dishes away while I waited for the coffee to perk. My frustration mounted like the coffee. "Why do I have to be so sure of myself? Think I can move mountains!" I exclaimed as I poured a cup of Joe. As if my scolding would make anything different but I couldn't help it. "I should go back to the quiet, insecure little mouse of a woman I was when Daniel and I were married. *That* Stephanie would never have convinced anyone to give her money to write a book."

Of course, I didn't really want that again. It took almost a year for me to "find myself" after Daniel and I were divorced. Havenridge and the Brewer secrets helped me crawl my way back to the *real* Stephanie I had once been. Whether it was an angel, or maybe Mabel's spirit, that guided me to find the hidden space inside my living room closet, the contents found inside gave me a new purpose in life. The letters, Cain Brewer's journal, and the old Brewer Bible saved my sanity. Yes, I wanted desperately to trace back the Brewer history to get answers for Leann and myself. However, whether I could solve the mystery or not, I'd never go back to mousy Stephanie.

Still, in my heart, failure wasn't an option. TopHat and Leann, not to mention the entire town of Havenridge, were counting on me to find answers about Jacob and write this book. Even Mabel Brewer's spirit seemed to be waiting for me to find out why Jacob never came back to her.

I rubbed my temples. Leann's words played in my head; *I need to know what happened to Jacob.*

I grabbed my coffee cup and went into the living room and sat down at the desk. The stack of mail from the last two towns in our thirty-mile target group lay there. The answers were all the same: "In regards to your inquiry of Jacob Thompson. Our search found no records in our offices."

My search included death certificates recorded at city halls and those recorded at the capital; names on land sales and public sales as in automobile, truck, farm equipment, horse and livestock, and large purchases or sales of agricultural products, all turned up nothing. Betsy and I had checked the logs between the years of 1900-1980 per each search.

I opened the drawer and pulled out my journal. The lesson I learned from this whole endeavor was that history should be documented—good or bad. It is vital for future generations. With pen in hand, I wrote today's entry.

Entry: March 1988

To the contrary of what the people of Havenridge believed, Mabel Brewer and her family were not cursed. I believe this with my whole heart. It is a falsehood, fed by fear and superstition. Undying rumors from people of a small town with nothing better to do than to invent stories and pass them on from one generation to another.

Perhaps it was preordained that Mabel lived the life of a lonely spinster. I don't know, but was she cursed? Absolutely not! However, Mabel's father, Cain Brewer, did believe that his daughter was cursed with an infected bloodline starting as far back as his wife's mother. He lived his entire life waiting for Mabel's insanity to surface just like his poor wife, Hanna.

Yes, Mabel's mother did go insane. Yes, there was a family history, the records prove both Mabel's mother and grandmother lived in an institution and died there. Nevertheless, I refused to believe blood is tainted. Shame and ignorance led Cain Brewer to fabricate a story to cover up the fact that his wife was locked away in an asylum in Milledgeville.

With all the Brewers deceased, Cain's lie that his wife died in a faraway hospital from pneumonia still lives on today. Bringing the truth to the surface seems unlikely to happen; however, I'll continue to document what I find, along with my thoughts about this history.

The ironic thing is that believing in tainted blood and that it would be inherited, Cain destroyed the happiness that could have been for his daughter. Cain's hidden journal and letters confirm that Mabel and Jacob Thompson's unhappiness was not destiny–but man-made.

I stopped writing and put my pen down. "What happened to you, Jacob? Where did you go?"

The Brewer family had so many secrets. Poor Mabel died alone, never knowing why the love of her life didn't return for her. The history of the Brewer family was an abomination. Jacob was a missing piece to the dreadful puzzle of a family and their unhappiness. *Could the truth be lost forever and buried with Jacob?*

Digging up answers to what happened seventy years ago was a monumental task. It seemed as if Jacob had evaporated into thin air. Firsthand witnesses, who knew young Mabel or Jacob, were nonexistent. I only found one exception: the old man, Clarence Swain, who lived on the edge of town. However, his memory was selective.

I put my head in my hands, feeling defeated. "How can I tell Leann I need to stop the search?"

And Havenridge? The eyes of the town were watching me. "They want answers. They'll demand answers–and a book!"

My publishing a book about their town was the biggest thing that had hit this small town in years. A book about the legendary lovers of Havenridge was all the people had been talking about for months. Then there was TopHat Publishing. How was I going to tell them that I hadn't uncovered anything? I was at a dead end.

Standing, I started to pace around the room. It had become a typical response to the stress of my new career as an author. I laughed. *An author who can't write!*

What was I going to do? Wringing my hands together hard, as if it would force information out of my pores, I moved around the room.

"Think, Stephanie, think. There must be somewhere else to look. I can't give up. What will I tell Phyllis? Look, I know you got me a great deal with the publisher and convinced them to give me, an unknown author, an eight thousand dollar advance, but I just cannot deliver. Oh and by the way, I spent all but six hundred dollars of the advance money. So sorry. *Right. That'll work.*"

The phone rang, making me jump. I swiftly grabbed the receiver.

"Hello."

"Stephanie, what's going on?" It was Phyllis. "I expected to hear from you with a progress report."

"Oh, I've been busy." An eerie feeling swept over me. Could Phyllis have read my mind? Maybe she had an agent's sixth sense that told her I was a fraud. Did she sense that only twenty-five pages had been written?

"Sorry," I said, trying to sound sincere.

"Well, I hope you are gaining a lot of ground, kiddo because my ass is on the line."

"R-r-right. I was just writing something now."

"Good. I really pushed Doug at TopHat to take a chance with you, you know. My reputation is at stake."

Just what I needed to hear.

I rolled my eyes and blurted out, "Don't worry. I have it covered."

"You'd better."

"Uh, you know Phyllis, I was thinking. . . . uh . . . maybe the story would be better if I focused on how Cain Brewer almost single-handedly built the town of Havenridge. You know, I could write about his power in these parts, instead of writing about his daughter Mabel. She *really* didn't do anything."

"What! Are you crazy? Everyone in town knows about Cain Brewer. It won't sell. Mysterious love stories sell."

I heard a short pause and then the sound of Phyllis' cigarette lighter clicking. I recognized the sound of her blowing out a long exhale of smoke. The mental picture was so vivid; it was Phyllis' M.O., especially in stressful situations. The routine always the same, like when the publisher made us "sweat it out," as Phyllis called it. Phyllis and I had waited weeks to hear from TopHat about a book contract. Each time I spoke to Phyllis to see if she'd heard anything the scenario played out the same—the pause—cigarette—lighter click—the blowing smoke sound.

"Look," Phyllis said finally. "It is either you solve the mystery about Mabel's secret lover, the one she would sneak away to this Blue Lake to see, or the book deal is canceled. Then you'll have to return the advance money and you're through as an author. Sooo, unless you find Jacob Thompson's remains buried in the Brewers' backyard, there will be no changes to the story concept. Got it?"

"Got it."

"TopHat expects to see at least one hundred and fifty pages of the first draft in less than two weeks. You better have made significant progress on the manuscript."

"Okay."

"Okay? Why are you still talking? Get cracking," Phyllis bellowed. "I've got to go now."

A loud click followed and Phyllis was gone.

"Well, that went well." *Boy, I've done it this time. I'm going to let everyone down.* I couldn't even ease the spirit of poor Mabel Brewer. Like everyone else, she's probably in limbo, waiting for me to find out why Jacob didn't come back for her.

I chewed at the side of my nail, thinking. "The advance is almost gone," I mumbled. "America doesn't have a debtors' prison, but I wonder if they can put you in jail for not producing the goods promised in a contract?"

My head pounded and I paced some more. *Think.* My pacing probably would only result in wearing a groove in the wood floor of my living room. One more thing ruined by my actions.

I stopped so quickly that I stumbled. "Blue Lake! Yes, that's it," I yelled. I needed to check out the old shack at Blue Lake. Jacob homesteaded the place back when he lived in Havenridge.

Why didn't I think of it before?

The old shack was still standing—boarded up, overgrown by weeds and underbrush—but still standing. Stories were that no one had been inside for years, untouched since Jacob left. Maybe he left something behind, a clue where he was traveling to look for work.

One clue was all I needed. I had to get inside that shack.

Abandoned

I grabbed my car keys and headed for the door. My business partner Betsy had closed the store last night, which meant I needed to open today but not until ten o'clock. It was early and I had plenty of time to walk down the path adjacent my property to Blue Lake before leaving to go to work.

After locking the front door, I decided to take the crowbar from the trunk of my car. I would need it to pry open the door of the abandoned shack. No doubt the wood would be petrified solid after all these years and the door would be difficult to open.

When I bought my house from Mabel's estate, the land around Blue Lake was no longer part of the Brewer property. Originally, Cain Brewer owned all the land around Blue Lake plus a vast amount of other property in the county. He had been wealthy beyond imagination at the time, and with money comes power. His only surviving heir was his daughter Mabel. It seems that she met with a lawyer, hired him, and named him executor of a trust fund, which gave thousands of dollars every year for improvements to the town. The only stipulation was that Blue Lake never be developed or changed in any way. Additionally, the old shack had to remain on the land—untouched. To ensure no one would ever disturb the old building, her estate would continue paying the taxes on the land for forty years after her death. There was a clause that revoked all monies to the town if any of her wishes in the will pertaining to Blue Lake were broken.

I received a survey of the property and its boundaries when I bought the Brewer house. The trust involving Blue Lake was spelled out in the paperwork that I received at the closing. If not for Mabel's money-hold on the town, the county would've condemned and demolished the shack years ago. If I were to get caught breaking into the shack, and the town lost the trust money—I would probably be lynched by the townspeople. So I couldn't get caught, that was all there was to it.

Just a quick look around. In and out, it'll take less than ten minutes.

There had to be some clues in that shack. I hurried to my car as I rationalized that Mabel would want me to investigate. After all, I wasn't out to violate memories. I wanted to prove that her love story was real. Mabel believed in Jacob's love but so many thought it was a rumor or something made up by a lonely old woman. It had to be true, why else would Mabel have gone to such lengths to preserve the old shack?

I opened the trunk and reached in for the crowbar but before retrieving it a noise of an approaching vehicle on the long gravel driveway caught my attention. Peering around the open trunk, I saw a sheriff's patrol car approaching, with Deputy Rick Stafford behind the wheel.

He pulled up in front of my parked car, turned off the motor, and waved. Emerging from the car he called out, "Morning, Miss Stephanie."

I froze, feeling like the cat caught with the canary in her mouth. My heart seemed to have stopped for a moment but I snapped out of it by telling myself that he couldn't have known what I was about to do. I waved back.

Just act natural. I slowly removed my grip from the crowbar and pulled the trunk down as he sauntered toward me.

"Good morning, Rick."

The gravel crunched with each of his steps, reminding me of the beating heart in Edgar Allan Poe's story, *The Tell-Tale Heart*.

"Rick, what are you doing out here?" I tried to act casual. "Is there trouble?"

"Huh? Oh, no." He took his hat off, paused, and stood there with a big Cheshire Cat grin on his round face.

"Hope you aren't on official business," I said. "Did someone complain that I was driving too fast through town again? You know I'm always running late, but since the last time you stopped me, I've been trying hard not to—"

"Oh no, I wouldn't come out here for that." He spun his hat in his hands and stood there silent—smiling.

"Well?" I prompted.

"Well, I sorta need your help."

Rick was somewhat of a displaced citizen of Havenridge, much the same as me. We both didn't blend in. The curse of the outsiders. The older townspeople considered only third generations as real "Havenridgers," leaving the rest of us marked as outsiders.

Rick was born here and third generation, but his parents left town when he was six months old, which I guess voided his generational status. However, shortly after Rick finished college, his parents were killed in a car crash and he returned to Havenridge to find his roots. Not long after Rick's return, the deputy of the town had a sudden heart attack and died. None of the citizens of the town could spare time away from their farms, so Rick was appointed the position by default, so to speak.

"You see, Stephanie," Rick said, digging his heel into the ground and chipping at the gravel. His huge size gave the image of a big plow horse stamping its hoof. "Folks in town have been up in arms about passing travelers camping out at Blue Lake."

"Oh, Blue Lake. Campers, huh? But, I thought only people who have grown up here knew about Blue Lake. It's so hidden and all. There's just that little path leading back there."

"Yeah, sorta." He scratched his head and gave a big sigh. "Remember a few months back, the Boy Scouts cleaned the highway that circles around onto this road here?" He pointed behind him. "Well, that road winds around on the other side of the lake. They didn't know it was within a one-mile radius of the lake, which was a requirement of the no involvement area, as stated in the Brewer trust."

"Oh boy, that's not good," I said.

"No. I'll bet the lawyer wasn't happy, 'cause now anyone driving by can see the lake, but he let it slide. Picking up trash didn't technically violate the trust fund regulations. But now, I've received calls from townsfolk saying they witnessed cars parked on the side of the grass. People have seen strangers pitching tents and building campfires. There's going to be trouble if anyone goes wandering back by the shack . . ."

"And everyone expects you to run off the campers."

"Yup. People are afraid of losing the Brewer money for the town, and I don't blame them," Rick said as his frown deepened.

"I can see your dilemma," I said. "And?"

"And, I thought you could help. If I post a "No Trespassing" sign, then I'd have to arrest anyone near the lake, even Havenridgers. People still take walks out there. So, I was thinking . . . do you think you could keep an eye out for any strangers and give me a call whenever you see someone hanging out or pitching a tent?"

"Sure, but I don't see how. I never really drive on the other side of the lake."

"Don't have to. You should have a clear view from your upstairs window on the east side. You'll see a little clearing before the shack, and the highway isn't that far. It should be in view."

"Guess you're right." I glanced at the trunk. "I'll keep my eyes open for trouble."

Time was slipping by and I needed Rick to leave. Country folks seem to linger so, and I wasn't sure how much country was in Rick. Maybe he needed a nudge. "Is there anything else I can do for you, Rick?"

"Nope. Have a good day." Rick turned, got into his patrol car and backed down the drive, leaving a cloud of dust as he pulled away.

Thank goodness. I thought he would never leave. I opened the trunk and grabbed the crowbar. If I don't get locked up for spending the advance money from TopHat and not delivering a finished book, I just might go to jail for breaking-and-entering the old shack. So I better get a move on and not get caught. *I have no other options. I have to get into that shack.*

I headed down the path to Blue Lake, with the crowbar in hand and determination on my mind.

Blue Lake

Although Clarence Swain couldn't remember the name of the drifter that supposedly had been Mabel's secret lover, he said the man had homesteaded the old shack at Blue Lake. That's where Mabel and the drifter would meet. I was certain now that drifter was Leann's uncle Jacob. Not having much money and moving from town to town, drifters usually packed light since they traveled on foot back then. Any items Jacob acquired while staying here in Havenridge might have gotten left behind in the shack. Maybe he left a clue to where he was heading. I was grasping at straws, but I needed to give it a shot. *What could I lose?*

When I reached the dwelling, I was grateful to have brought the crowbar with me, because the house was barely visible. Wisteria had engulfed most of the small wooden building with a mass of lavender blossoms and snarled woody branches. I would have to pry my way through the twisted mess. The vine had climbed up and across the rusted metal roof, and a blanket of blossoms and twigs filled in between the thicker limbs.

I noticed that the growth of brown and lavender with traces of light green leaves disappeared midway across the rooftop into a black hole. The weight of the plant must have caused the roof to cave in.

I pried the crowbar between the twisted branches, systemically working my way through. After twenty minutes, I had managed to clear away an area that revealed a dilapidated door. After the third try of shoving at the door, which moisture and age had swollen shut almost permanently, the stubborn thing gave way. The door opened about five inches, barely enough room for me to squeeze through.

Once inside, the stale air attacked my lungs, causing me to cough and gag. I caught my breath and scanned the sparse room. It had only the bare living necessities. In the far corner, a plain wooden bedframe stood, and a thin, striped mattress still on it. The mattress—I called it that with reservations, since its thickness of four inches barely qualified it as a mattress—was dirty and tattered and hanging halfway through the rope straps that served to hold the antiquated bedding in place. It had a huge rip in the material with the stuffing stretched out in lumps. Probably raccoons or some kind of woodland creature had scavenged it and carried some of the material to their nest. *Far away and not in here, I hope.*

On the opposite side of the room stood another bed frame, but it stood tall with three single-size beds stacked on top of each other, bunk-bed style. It looked the right size for children. More than likely, Cain Brewer let a sharecropper's family live in the building at one time.

A small table took up most of the rest of the floor space. A kerosene lamp stood on top and three chairs sat around it. Inside the large opening nearby, was a fireplace for cooking. A black pot hung on a hook. The pot looked like it was made of iron—or maybe it was just black from soot. A thick log above served as a mantel. A forgotten tobacco pipe lay in the center of the mantel. It was like whoever lived there just picked up and walked out the door, leaving everything where it lay, frozen in time.

Interestingly, the walls were adorned with wallpaper, a dainty flowered pattern. They appeared to have been dark rose color originally but now had a yellow cast, making the color more of a dirty peach. I wondered if Mabel's mother added the homey touch. Although the dwelling was modest, it did look . . . comfortable.

If Mabel's father had known that this sweet little abode served as his daughter's secret rendezvous location, there would've been hell to pay. *No, Cain Brewer definitely didn't know about the love nest.* If he had, this place would have been destroyed years ago.

I owned the Brewer family house, slept in the room where Mabel had been born, and now I stood here where she secretly met her lover. Shivers went up my spine. Although my intentions were to honor Mabel, for the first time I felt like an intruder. What if Cain Brewer's perception was right? No one in town knew anything about the drifter who lived in this old shack. Maybe Mabel did need to be protected. Was Jacob honorable? *Should he have been trusted with an innocent young girl?* My mind raced with the possibilities.

"It's weird," I mumbled. "Mabel setting up that trust to keep an old abandoned shack standing, fifty years after a lover left her."

I looked around the dusty room, which was void of any personal items—except for the pipe. I walked over to the mantel and picked it up. "Mabel having the lawyer pay the taxes and watch over this old shack for the next forty years, it's not just weird, it's. . . crazy."

Feeling the old pipe in my hand, the smoothness of the worn curve of it, I wondered, *Could this have been Jacob's?* If so, why wouldn't he take it with him? My eyes searched the room again, but for what? Why did I feel such a bond with a dead woman? That alone was a bit crazy in itself. Of course, there was the promise I had made to Leann—and my contractual responsibility, but it was as if I had a duty to uncover the Brewers' dark secrets for Mabel. An insanity gene, was that dark enough to keep it a secret? It seemed enough for Cain Brewer. But that old way of thinking was wrong, and it had to stop. *To hide the truth can only bring harm.*

I searched around the room for a clue. I did believe Jacob loved Mabel.

"Mabel, I promise I will find out what happened to him," I called out as if she could hear me. "If I have to walk on hot coals to do it, but I need help." I called out, again, "Mabel. . . .Jacob. . . . Help me."

Maybe I *was* violating their memories. Tears filled my eyes. That's when I saw it. A small glitz, a sparkle caught by a sliver of a sunbeam seeping through the open part of the roof. I blinked my eyes to clear away the tears, but it was gone. A small breeze squeezed through the cracked wall to my right, and dust particles shone in the sunbeam.

There was no evidence of any rich possessions, but Mabel and Jacob's love occupied the room like a treasure chest full of gold. The only thing that was important, or real, was their love. Years could not kill it. Death could not kill it. It still lived here in this shack.

If only there was more light. I went over to a branch protruding down from the roof and pulled on it, hoping to clear a bigger hole for the sun to get through. Dirt, branches, and pieces of wisteria petals rained down lavender as the bright sun streamed in. Turning around, I crouched down on the floor, looking for the sparkle again—nothing.

When I sat back on my heels, a beam of sunlight shot across the floor from the newly expanded roof opening and a small sparkle shone through the slit in the floorboard. Lying flat, I peered into the slit in the floor. The floor planks would have to come up. Something was beneath it.

"I'm sorry Mabel, but I have to break up the floor." I grabbed the crowbar, stuck it in a knothole in the wood, and pushed. The crowbar slipped and the floor stayed intact. Angry, I swung the crowbar down hard, making only a dent in the wood. Placing the claw end between the planks again, I pushed and bits of dry wood chipped away. I had to get the floor pulled up to see what was lost underneath.

Touching the Past

On my fifth try, parts of the floor broke away like pieces of gigantic brittle toothpicks. Still, most of them remained. Although the morning air was cool, I had to wipe sweat from my eyes. I worked to pry up two wide planks. Underneath laid a half-inch space in the moist dirt. Something scurried into the safe darkness that remained uncovered. Since I had not brought a flashlight, and I hate bugs, I took the crowbar and stirred the dirt, hoping to see what the sunbeam had caught.

I knew I had not imagined it, something had sparkled. It had to be small to have slipped through the crack in the first place. Just then, the crowbar scraped against something. The weight of the crowbar seemed to push whatever it was deeper into the dirt. I'd have to reach in to get it. I wiggled my fingers to survey the dirt until I felt a roundish object, cold-like metal buried from the world for years.

As I pulled up a flat disc-shaped object, a chain dangled from it. It was oval in shape. It was a vintage-looking woman's locket. *Mabel's?* I pressed the catch, but it wouldn't budge. It would probably open once it was cleaned. I put the locket in my pants pocket. Perhaps it could have a picture of Mabel—or maybe Jacob.

Placing the planks back into place, I headed outside. The tangled branches and twisted stems of the wisteria that I had pulled away lay in a pile next to the shack. My hands ached with cuts and long scratches that covered my arms from breaking the wisteria away from the building. The last thing I wanted to do was to have to tackle the plant again. Once I had loved the beautiful lavender flowering plants growing in the area, but now I possessed a hatred for them. In Florida, we had hibiscus bushes. Their soft leaves and stems of the tropical plant could be snapped easily by hand without any bodily injuries. I grabbed some twisted wisteria and piled them against the house so it would look undisturbed.

By the time I reached my house, I only had time to shower before leaving for the store. Once ready to leave, I paused and picked up the phone, and dialed Betsy. While it was ringing, I carefully wrapped the locket in a handkerchief. Betsy answered by the third ring.

"Betsy, could you come into the store early? I have something to show you and I need your help."

"Of course, what is it? Did you get information back about Jacob?"

"No, the last courthouse answered back, saying there were no records of a Jacob Thompson. The same as the others said. But, I do have something I found and I want to show you. Can we talk about it when you get to the store?"

"Of course, I'll be there around eleven."

Havenridge was one of the last small towns that still had phone lines that were connected to each other—the famous old-time "party" line. With Mabel's trust money available for town improvements, I felt it wasn't as much resistance to modernizing but holding onto being able to listen in on neighbors' conversations. It seemed to be the most popular pastime. I knew better than to talk to Betsy on the phone about any news regarding Mabel Brewer or Jacob. Whatever I might say would spread from person to person in town faster than the plague.

Rhythms of Havenridge

The waking of downtown Havenridge was slow and steady, like time-lapse photography of a flower unfolding in the morning sunrise. Shopkeepers opened store doors and moved about inside, getting ready for the day's business. As I drove, I realized how right everything in my life had become. Discovering Havenridge. Meeting Sarah and Betsy, and becoming good friends. When Sarah decided to move away and sell the general store, it seemed natural for Betsy and me to buy it. The store purchase was my final and ultimate act of setting down roots. As a store owner, I had become another spoke in the wheel of the town. Yes, everything seemed so right, like fate was leading me every step of the way.

I continued down Main Street and waved to Mister Healy, who was sweeping the front sidewalk of his barbershop. Three doors down, Annie's new neon "Open" sign glowed in the window of Yesterdaze Ice Cream Parlor. It had made history as the first neon sign in town. When she announced at the town meeting that she ordered it from Savannah, it became the topic of the month about town. All the other stores, ours included, had hand-printed cardboard signs that read "open" on one side and "closed" on the other.

At least talk of Annie's sign gave me some relief from the persistent inquiries about my book from everyone. It was nice to have people interested, but it did become somewhat tiresome.

I drove down the alley to park at the back of the store building. The Trenton twin boys passed me, feverishly pedaling their bikes toward the direction of the school—late as usual. After unlocking the door, I hurried to turn the lights on and open the front door. When I pulled the A-frame sign outside with our posting of the tea of the month, I heard a familiar voice from somewhere behind me.

"Yoo-hoo."

"Oh, yeah. That's right, it's Wednesday," I muttered. "Church shopping day." I turned around and saw the familiar lace hankie flapping in the air as she hurried down the sidewalk. "Hello, Miss Gladys," I said when she reached me.

"Oh, my," she said, fanning herself and breathing heavily. Gladys was always hurrying. Carrying thirty pounds more weight than she needed, she was constantly out of breath. "You're late opening, Stephanie. I already had a long chat with Annie and thought I'd have to come back for my shopping after I opened the church office."

If Gladys didn't make a point to stop and check on every person's whereabouts, she probably wouldn't have to hurry like she always does, but then that wouldn't be Gladys.

"Now, Miss Gladys, you know I don't open any earlier than ten o'clock."

"Yes, dear, that's why I was concerned when you weren't here by 10:05." She pushed past me and marched into the store.

"I'm sorry to cause you concern, Miss Gladys." There was no sense arguing, she believed that punctuality was a virtue and welcomed every opportunity to tell me so.

"I have so much to do at the church today, no time to waste." She plopped her huge leather purse on the counter and rummaged through it. "Now where's my shopping list? I know it's in here somewhere."

"Of course it's in there," I muttered.

"What, dear?"

"Nothing, Miss Gladys," I said, and smiled. She makes a new list every week with the same five items on it. *Coffee, one small package of tea napkins, one box of chocolate chip cookies, one box of vanilla wafers, and one pint of half-and-half,* I thought to myself, making sure this time they didn't slip through my lips.

"I have the Pastor's sermon to type." Her entire face was buried inside of her purse but the muffled words escaped. "I must hurry. The Pastor says he can read his longhand; however, a typed copy is proper."

Gladys' face popped up out of the purse like a Jack-in-the-Box with her hand up, waving a typed list with five items on it. "Here it is," she said, shoving it at me. Then she walked over and took a seat at the small table in the reading area of the store. The Great Hunt for the Missing List proved to be exhausting, no doubt.

"Like I said," Gladys continued, "I don't have a lot of time to waste since I have to type Pastor's sermon—it's my job. I must stay busy. You know, *Idle hands are the Devil's workshop.* What is your tea of the month, dear?"

"Black Currant."

"Black Currant? I haven't tasted that one yet."

"Can I get you a cup to go, Miss Gladys?"

"To go? Oh my, that would be so impolite of me, wouldn't it? I can make time to have a cup with you, dear. I'll wait while you put the tea kettle on."

I left, like a good little girl, to put the kettle on and clung to the hope that she wouldn't stay long. The beckoning locket would have to wait. When I returned with two cups and the teapot, Gladys had her eyes closed. I could hear the ever-so-faint sound of snoring.

"Here we are Miss Gladys," I said softly to alert her before placing the tray on the table. She would be embarrassed if I had startled her abruptly. Gladys would never admit that she could possibly doze off during daylight hours.

"Good, I don't have time to waste. Must be leaving soon. However, I did want to ask you, dear . . . how is the book coming along about our town? Did you dig up the truth about that horrible Cain Brewer?"

"The truth is, Miss Gladys, Cain Brewer's only crime was that he was not very pleasant."

"Not pleasant? My dear, he was a tyrant. Everyone knows that he raised his poor daughter Mabel to be afraid of her own shadow. No telling what went on in that house. Cain Brewer was evil."

Gladys leaned in close toward me and lowered her voice. "People say Mabel had herself a boyfriend. Probably Cain ran him off; you know Mabel died an old maid. Something just wasn't right in the Brewer house. Hear tell, Cain's wife left and never returned just like Mabel's boyfriend. That is if he, Mabel's beau that is, even existed. Crazy, crazy, crazy."

Gladys paused and put some sugar cubes into her cup. Six, to be exact. Then she started stirring. Tic, tic, tic, the spoon sounded as the tea swirled. "No telling what went on when Cain Brewer was involved." Gladys paused, tapping her spoon on the edge of the cup, and pausing to take a sip of tea before she continued her gossiping. "Hear tell Mabel was a little wild. But her father ruled with an iron hand."

"Things were very different then, Miss Gladys. All fathers kept close watch over their daughters. I'm sure he did his best and loved Mabel."

Gladys shook her head and made a clicking sound with her tongue, "Tsk-tsk," to mark her final disapproval.

I hate that sound. Gladys only knew Mabel as her sixth-grade English teacher. That's how most people in town knew her. My temper was starting to get the better of me so I figured I'd start to gather the church order. Maybe she would take the hint, finish her tea, pay for her order, and leave. Pastor Bob must have the patience of Job, working alongside her. *Better him than me, that's for sure.*

I picked up a handbasket and placed a box of vanilla wafers and a box of chocolate chip cookies in it, and headed toward the paper products aisle as Gladys continued babbling on.

"Stephanie, you don't know. Cain Brewer wouldn't stand for any shenanigans from his daughter. The story is the boy, the one Mabel was carrying on with . . . the story is that he up and disappeared. Cain probably did away with that boy called Jac—" Gladys stopped in mid-sentence. "Stephanie!"

She put her teacup down and cleared her throat with a loud, "Ah-hem," and called out to me in a raised voice, "Where are you going?"

"I'm getting the things on your shopping list."

"Well, stop moving about. It's distracting. Come here and sit."

"But . . ."

"Your tea is getting cold." Gladys stared at me defying me to argue.

She caught me. "But I thought you were in a hurry."

Gladys sat there in silence, waiting.

"Well, all right," I said and I went and sat down.

She dabbed her handkerchief across her forehead, blotting up small beads of perspiration. "As I was saying, people said he just moved on. Mark my words, that poor Jacob boy is probably buried outside of the shack where he lived. The one at Blue Lake, near the Brewer house—I mean your house, dear."

"Gladys, I'm sure that's just handed-down gossip from people who don't have anything better to do in life. It must've been very hard for Cain Brewer, having a small child to raise and no one to help him. Plus, he had to maintain one of the largest cotton farms in the area. He probably didn't have time to win any personality contests."

"Well, Stephanie, I am just telling you what is known and accepted as truth by the people who have lived in Havenridge for years. People who've been here longer than you. People here know things."

Oh boy, here we go, with the, *I don't know because I am not from around here.* What is it about this town, only recognizing a Havenridge pedigree?

Gladys was not used to having someone talk back to her. She was turning an angry shade of red. I almost expected to see steam come out of her ears any minute now.

"I don't gossip, Stephanie Oliver!" she said straightening up in her chair. "If that's what you're implying."

Uh oh. Now I've insulted her.

Gladys quickly swallowed her tea and placed the cup down. She huffed toward the front of the store.

"Gladys, wait."

"Good day, Stephanie." She hurried through the door.

"But, your church order." It was too late. She can move quickly when she sets her mind to it. "Come again," I said to the empty doorway.

Opening the Locket

I gathered up the cups and teapot and took them to the back. After washing and drying them, I heard the front door chime. *Maybe she's back. I do hate it when I lose my temper. Gladys is a good soul.*

I hurried out front to find Betsy putting her purse under the counter where the cash register sat.

"Oh, it's you."

"Nice to see you, too," she answered.

"Sorry, I didn't mean it like that. Gladys was here. She left rather upset with me."

"Stephanie, why do you let her get under your skin?"

I shrugged. An answer to Betsy's question most likely would never be known. I liked Gladys—truly. However, she had the uncanny knack of pushing my buttons. I hurried over to my purse. "I can't wait to show you what I found. I think it may have belonged to Mabel."

"Oh, really?" Betsy put on a pair of oversized plastic reading glasses and took the locket from my open hand. Her nimble fingers gently unwrapped it.

"What do think?" I asked. "Do you think it's old?"

"Well, my grandmother had a locket made similar to this. The type of filigree engraving on this one looks almost identical to hers. If I had to guess, this probably is from that same time period—or earlier. That would make it eighty or a hundred years old. Where did you get it?"

"I found it under the floor. It must have slipped through and been lost for years."

"In your house?"

"No, not at home." I hesitated for a moment. "I found it in the shack at Blue Lake."

Betsy stiffened and then turned to me. "You said inside the shack?"

"Yes. Now, Betsy, don't get that look on your face. No one saw me. Really. I was careful."

What I thought was a disapproval look, turned into a smile that spread across her face.

"I love it," Betsy said. "You have guts. All of my friends and I used to imagine going inside that shack when we were growing up. Of course, we were too chicken to do it."

Betsy turned back to her examination of the locket. "There's a hinge. Did you open it? Was there anything inside?"

"Dunno, I couldn't get it open. Maybe a knife would work."

"A knife could damage it. We don't want that, not if we can help it. What we need is some oil."

We had some cooking oil back in the kitchen, leftover from baking cookies for an event we had held the previous month. After retrieving it, Betsy applied a few drops to the hinge. While waiting for the oil to seep in and loosen things, she gingerly brushed the edges with a soft cloth. Bits of dirt and encrusted grains of what looked like rust clung to the white cloth. With the precision of a surgeon, Betsy manipulated a thin razor blade she'd got from the storeroom, and slid it into the seam of the locket. Eureka, the locket opened like magic.

"You've done it!" I cheered.

Inside, a small piece of folded, yellowed tissue lay wedged into the well of the locket.

"Stephanie," Betsy said as she wiped her hands. "You pull it out carefully and unwrap it. My fingers might still have some oil on them."

The locket was rather large, about an inch in diameter. Betsy said that must've been the style of the times. Her grandmother's locket had been oversized, too. The aged tissue cracked in pieces, falling apart as I unfolded it and a black leggy substance fell out onto the counter.

"What is that?" I remarked.

"Hair," Betsy said. "It's hair."

"Yuck. Why would Mabel keep hair in there?"

"Think about it, Stephanie. We still keep hair, strands of hair tied with ribbon, slipped in a baby book. Is that repulsive?"

"Well, no. It's kind of precious." I felt sad, sad for Mabel, and well just sad. "I guess a lock of hair can turn into something valuable, especially when there's nothing else to hold on to."

"You understand more about Mabel than you realize. Keeping a lock of hair was more popular during the turn of the century since back then, there were fewer ways to preserve memories of loved ones. Women kept the hair of husbands who had to leave because of war or travel far to get work. Some women kept the hair in lockets."

Betsy pinched together the black strands, placing them in her palm. "If a woman had a lock of hair from a secret lover, wearing the locket under her clothing would avoid any interrogations from a domineering person in her life."

"Like Cain Brewer."

"Exactly."

"I can't believe it. We really have Jacob's hair," I said. This discovery renewed my strength to search for answers about the Brewers and find out why Jacob never returned for Mabel. It was as if the truth was beckoning us from the grave.

Truth or Rumors

The possibility had always existed that Jacob was a cad and never intended to come back for Mabel. Searching the variety of records available from so long ago proved somewhat unreliable. Either the official papers were destroyed by age, by fire (like one courthouse replied back to me), or records didn't even exist in the first place. Therefore, a certain amount of guesswork by me was required to keep moving forward. All my efforts lately seemed to be a leap of faith that I would ever find out what happened to Jacob.

Still, I had to remember to keep an unbiased and open mind and not be influenced by the romantic notions of a long-lost love story. Leann's wisdom echoed in my mind, "To hide the truth can only bring harm." Whatever I wrote about Mabel and Jacob had to be proven. Unfortunately, my long, hard research seemed to have only scratched the surface. I feared there was a great deal of work ahead before I could write my book.

Funny how so many things can influence others. When I bought the old Brewer house, little did I expect that it would link me to the past and change my life. The Brewer family's secrets not only gave me a writing job; it gave me a purpose and restored something lost inside of me—a zest for living which filled my days again.

It was time to get serious. I looked at Betsy. Her face was serious and focused. It was so much more than a love of history for her. She respected the people from the past and cared about them. Until now, I played the role of female sleuth, unraveling a mystery about abstract people. Everything was so surreal as if I were reading a Nancy Drew novel. The locket snapped me back to reality. Jacob Thompson was real. Very real.

"I have an old photograph of Jacob that Leann gave me," I told Betsy. "It's in my purse, I'll get it."

I returned with the black and white photo and handed it to Betsy. "It's in pretty bad shape. It's yellowing with age and cracking but you can see Jacob well. He's the man in the middle with the hammer. Leann said he was kind of a *jack-of-all-trades*."

Betsy took the photo. "Well, it's nice to have a face to go with the name." She examined the picture. "Jacob might have chosen where to travel by wherever work would be available. Remember when we spoke to Clarence about Mabel? He said the stranger she was seeing came to Havenridge looking for work and did odd jobs for Cain Brewer. That's probably how he met Mabel." Betsy looked hard at the picture. "He's quite handsome isn't he?"

"Yeah, I can see why Mabel was infatuated with him, with looks like that." I moved closer and looked over Betsy's shoulder. "You know, now that I look closer, that wall the men are repairing looks like it could be the storage shed near the pear trees in my backyard. It's hard to tell since only part of the building is in the picture. At least Jacob's face is clear. You can tell his hair was very dark. Leanne told me relatives said Jacob's hair was coal black—just like her father's hair." I picked the hair up to examine it again.

"You can't get any blacker than that," Betsy said, not taking her eyes off of the picture. "His eyes look light. Probably blue or green."

"Leann seemed to remember her grandmother saying Jacob's eyes were ice blue." I stared at the old photo. Jacob's clothes were worn and his face held deep lines. But his eyes were not cold with the bitterness of a hard life as he stared into the camera lens. Jacob's eyes were tender and soft as if he understood the world. "My grandmother would've called eyes like those *old-soul eyes*."

"I haven't heard that term used in years," Betsy said.

"You've heard that saying before?"

"Oh, yes."

I was amazed. "The first time my grandmother said it to me, I was around six years old. She commented that a neighbor had 'old soul eyes.' When I asked her to explain, she answered that some people live more in one lifetime than others do. I didn't understand then, but I'm starting to now." Jacob's life as a drifter opened the world to him.

"It's much more than that," Betsy said. "Some people believe 'old souls' have lived before and are connected to the universe on a different plane, and that they feel things. Some think they possess a sixth sense and can see into the future."

Could he have sensed tragedy in his future? The evidence gathered so far indicated that Jacob had been happy once, just like Mabel. However, Cain's journal showed me that the world was unjust. Some people's happiness is taken away from them for no good reason. Was that what I saw in Jacob's eyes? Did he know that happiness would be denied to him? The thought made my stomach sour.

Betsy looked down at the bits of yellowed paper on the counter. "Stephanie, there's writing on the paper that the hair was wrapped in." With her finger, she pushed around the paper bits like puzzle pieces. The parts came together, revealing a penned message.

To Mabel, you possess my heart, Jacob.

Dread washed over me as Gladys' words came back to me.

"Stephanie, what's the matter? You look upset."

"In the mail yesterday, I got an answer from the last courthouse request we made. They had no records of Jacob Thompson. They checked land and property sales—everything—no court records anywhere. No death certificate, either. Nothing."

"Then we'll just have to broaden our search radius. He had to have gone somewhere. We'll find something eventually. His death must be recorded somewhere."

"Unless . . . ."

"Unless, what?"

"Something Gladys said has me thinking. It might be why we can't find anything."

"What did the busybody say this time?"

"It's a crazy theory. Probably only vicious gossip." I sighed and rubbed my forehead. "Cain Brewer's situation was desperate, right? He was positive insanity ran in Mabel's bloodline. That's why he didn't want her to marry. Not to anyone."

"Okay. So?"

"Gladys said people thought Cain murdered Jacob and buried him somewhere on his property, like around Blue Lake."

"What? Cain Brewer was a controlling man—but murder? That's something most people are not capable of doing."

"Right, but . . . think about it. Maybe he found out about Jacob and Mabel's meeting at Blue Lake. He could've confronted Jacob. If Jacob told him of his plans to go away to find work so he could return and ask for Mabel's hand in marriage . . . well, that could've pushed Cain over the edge. He might have panicked and killed Jacob. We read in Cain's journal how fearful he was that Mabel would marry someday and bear children. The tainted bloodline thing. No one would question a drifter's sudden disappearance. No sheriff snooping around to find a body. No body—no death certificate."

"It could happen. A doctor has to sign and send in papers for a death certificate to be recorded." Betsy spoke in a low voice, more as if talking to herself.

"We've checked courthouses—how many? A dozen? Two? We've hit dead ends every step of the way. It's as if Jacob Thompson never existed. There's no death certificate—anywhere."

"Exactly what did Gladys say? Did she offer any facts to back up her murder theory? Did she actually use the word murder?"

"Her words were that Cain probably 'did away with him.' Gladys said there has been speculation for years. Said he probably killed Jacob in a fit of rage."

We sat in silence, while thoughts of murder, deceit, and violence hung thick in the air like toxic pollution from a nearby incinerator.

"Clarence told us," I said, "that Cain had a reputation of having an uncontrollable temper."

"That's right, and Gladys has a very active imagination," Betsy snapped back. "Gladys and people like her are one of the reasons Clarence decided to withdraw from the community and live like an old hermit in his cabin outside of town."

"Yeah, he's an eccentric," I said. "But let's focus on Jacob and Cain Brewer right now. You have two men, who loved Mabel but wanted completely different things for her. The stakes were high. Both were protective and determined men. They were used to having their own way. Cain because he's, well, Cain Brewer and very dominant. And Jacob was used to marching to a different drummer and not answering to anyone. Add to the mixture that one has a raging temper and POW! You have all the right elements for an explosion."

"Like two mountain goats butting heads," Betsy said.

"What I can't understand in this scenario is, why someone wouldn't go to the sheriff if there was suspicion of a crime?" Betsy didn't answer me. She had a frown on her face "Betsy? The whole town wouldn't have kept quiet, right? They hated Cain Brewer."

A few moments passed until she answered. "In small towns, everyone knows everything about their neighbors, they'll gossip, but there are unspoken boundaries. Family business is private, many secrets are kept."

"So, you think it's possible that the reason we can't find any death records for Jacob Thompson, could be that Cain Brewer murdered him?" I felt Cain's love for Mabel in his writing. I didn't believe he was capable of murder but I had to face the possibility.

Betsy's eyebrows squeezed together as she frowned. "People here are God-fearing people. People in Havenridge have respect for the law. A family business is one thing but the line is drawn when it comes to murder.

This is the Bible belt, for goodness' sake. Gladys can't be right."

The one thing I had learned about Betsy was that she focused on details. She hated loose ends; all the *i*'s had to be dotted and the *t*'s had to be crossed before she would let something go. Betsy wasn't finished with Gladys's murder theory.

"What?" I prompted her.

"At the turn of the century, justice was different than it is now. Justice was rough around the edges, but people had a loyalty of sorts. My dad told me once about a town, not far from here, in another county. He said a group of the KKK lynched four men back in the 20s or 30s. The whole town knew about it. The next day the black family cut the men down, took the bodies to the black cemetery, and buried them. No one spoke about the incident after that and nothing else was done."

"I can't believe it. The sheriff didn't arrest anyone?"

"No," Betsy answered. "Dad said the sheriff was a Night Hawk, that's what the Klan called their head of security. The Klan is family-driven; normally if one family member is in the Klan, then you can bet the whole family is. The sheriff's father and his three brothers were Klansmen. At least, that was what Dad had heard."

"Nice tradition. How did your father know about it?"

"Word travels. I still hear about things happening every now and then."

"But Jacob wasn't a Negro. What does that have to do with him?"

"Who knows the reasons people use to justify their actions? Or actions not taken. According to the Bible, a father is head of the family. That might be enough excuse to turn a blind eye. Same as not doing anything about a lynching."

"Lovely! So kill someone and bury him in the backyard, and no one does anything?" I touched the paper with Jacob's vow of love. "Betsy, do you know people who are in the Klan?"

"Oh dear, no! What Dad talked about was a long time ago. In another county, around Bakersmith and Harwine."

I got goosebumps when I asked the next questions. "Are there Klan members in Havenridge?"

"Not in Havenridge. There's no Klan here. People here are good."

"I'm relieved to hear that. I mean, I couldn't imagine Gladys in a white pointed hood."

Betsy began to laugh, which made me start laughing, too. Soon we were laughing uncontrollably as we held our sides and tears rolled down our cheeks. After I regained my composure, I said, "I think we can scratch out the murder theory and widen our search radius to towns that Jacob might have traveled to find work."

"Sounds like a plan."

New Evidence About Hanna

It was five fifteen and Betsy had left for home. I wrapped up the locket and put it safely away in my purse. I wondered if all authors had similar experiences and suffered from being discouraged about writing.

What I'd heard about an author's life, the glamour, the travel to exotic places, the recognition from the general public, I sure hadn't experienced any of that. Breaking into a dirty, crumbling shack, while fearing the police would catch and arrest me, was absolutely not glamorous.

Was everyone's writing journey difficult? I didn't mind paying my dues; however, the battle scars were wearisome. Finding the locket restored my confidence that I had at the beginning when I had boldly contacted the local newspaper about signing a publishing deal with TopHat.

As the saying goes, *be careful what you wish for*. The interview I gave to the paper piqued others' interest. At the very beginning, news about my book and my research on the Brewers had spread like locusts invading a cornfield. After that, the paper had asked if I would write a weekly column, which was when the phone calls began. At first, I had thought the calls could be useful, but then reality set in almost immediately.

I was trapped in a nightmare wish of stardom. The paper's coverage went to surrounding towns and people called from Tifton, Bakersfield, and Milledgeville. The plague bestowed on me was nobody's fault but my own.

"Are you the author writing about the Brewers?" they would ask. Their commentary about Cain Brewer ran the gamut from that his love of money had blackened his soul to suggesting that he was the devil himself. Although lately the calls had seemed to lessen over the last few weeks, and for that I was grateful.

I hoped that finding the locket would be a turning point in my writing research. My stomach made an unsettling noise. Glancing at the clock, I saw there was just enough time to eat the dinner I'd brought from home before the evening crowd hit the store. They came in every night between six-thirty and seven thirty. Not to buy, no buying was done on shopping evenings for the people in Havenridge. They all were creatures of habit. Shortly after dinnertime, they would stop in to see what we had new in the store—every night. They'd talk for a few minutes, and then leave. I guess in a small town, there's not much else to do other than visit downtown after the dinner hour.

I had just sat down with my food and took the first bite when the phone rang. I swallowed and answered. "Stephanie and Betsy's Tea Room and Gifts," I said, wiping my mouth. "How may I help you?"

On the other end of the phone, a woman asked if I was Miss Oliver, the one who was writing a book.

Ugh, not now. I wanted to eat my meal and relish the peace of mind that came after Betsy and I had dismissed Gladys' murder in Havenridge theory. *Why can't I have five lousy minutes!* No gossip. No dead bodies. Not even images of poor Mabel sitting waiting for Jacob. I took a deep cleansing breath and answered, "Yes, this is Miss Oliver."

I ordered myself to be positive. *Think happy thoughts and put a smile in your voice.* It probably was a customer wanting to know this month's tea special.

"The Miss Oliver who writes the column in Havenridge Press?"

A customer calling? Not a chance! What was it about small towns that made good people turn obnoxious? When I first started writing at the paper, the editor inserted small sub-headlines before each of my weekly columns. She said it was to pump up interest. Her overly dramatic wordings bordered on outright lies. The worst one was a play on words that read: MS. OLIVER LITERARY DIGS UP SKELETONS IN HAVENRIDGE. I had hoped the calls generated by those pesky lines starting my columns had now been a thing of past, but apparently, that was only a figment of my imagination.

"Yes, this is Miss Oliver, the author and shop owner," I said through clenched teeth. "How may I help you? Would you like to hear what our tea of the month is?"

"Tea?" said a confused sounding voice from the other end of the phone.

I waited through the silence from the other end.

Then the voice answered, "Oh, no, my mother has important information for you."

"Very well, who am I speaking to?" My happy voice now gone, I didn't even care to hide my irritation.

"I'm sorry to call you at your place of business, but it's vital. We must meet with you. It's about the Brewer family." The woman continued blabbing away, ignoring my question, and not giving me her name. *Obviously, it's another person who needs excitement in her life.*

She paused and asked once more, "You are the author, right?"

"Yes."

I wondered how many authors she thought lived in Havenridge. The town's population was a whopping 1375. I was about to hang up on her but thought better of it. As a store owner and an author, I needed to maintain a good relationship with the public.

The woman on the other end of the line rambled on about reading my articles to her mother. How they brought back memories to her. First Gladys and now this woman, what more did I have to look forward to before closing time?

She paused to take a breath and I interjected. "I'm sorry, Miss . . . uh . . . Who am I talking to?" I had reached the limit of my patience.

"I apologize. My name is Miss Hamilton. I'm calling from Milledgeville."

"Miss Hamilton, I have a shop to attend to . . ."

"Please, I implore you to hear me out. My mother has been talking about Hanna Brewer. Her husband was Cain Brewer and his power stretched farther than Havenridge."

"Miss Hamilton, I don't have time to listen to idle gossip about the Brewer family history. Cain Brewer and his daughter led a quiet life. It is as simple as that."

"Perhaps you have not heard all the facts, Miss Oliver." Her voice took on a firm tone. "There is more than what can be seen on the surface. I think my mother can help you. She has information about Hanna Brewer."

"I'm sorry, but your mother must be mistaken. Hanna Brewer's last living relative was her daughter, Mabel. Mabel died three years ago at ninety-eight years old.

Mabel's mother would be one hundred and eighteen years old if she were still living. The Hanna Brewer your mother is talking about being friends with must be a different Hanna Brewer."

"Miss Oliver, you misunderstood me. I said my mother had information about Hanna. Not that she was friends with her. It is imperative you talk to my mother before it's too late. She knows things about Hanna and secrets that nobody else knows about. You must come to Milledgeville immediately."

"If you are speaking about the mental hospital in Milledgeville where Hanna Brewer was a patient, I'm aware of it."

Cain's journal entries wrote about Hanna's confinement and the insanity that began with her mother, Josephine. Two generations of insanity were what convinced him about the tainted bloodline. It was all there in his journal.

"I contacted the hospital in Milledgeville," I said. "I've obtained copies of Hanna Brewer's records. I'm seeking information about a man who Mabel Brewer was connected with by the name of Jacob Thompson. Medical facts about Hanna Brewer are not necessary for my book. I don't think private family matters need to be printed. Therefore, your mother has nothing to say that I need to hear. Thank you. I do appreciate your call but I must go now."

"Wait! Those records are wrong. You are looking in the wrong places and my mother said Hanna knew about Mabel's beau."

This whole conversation was bizarre. How could hospital records be wrong? Of course, small towns were a new experience for me. And yes, this area of the country had its own set of rules that people followed. Sure, babies were born at home by midwives, but hospitals and professional doctors kept accurate records.

"My mother," Miss Hamilton continued, "She keeps saying it is time to tell. Says she has kept the secret for too many years. Families need to know the truth."

"The truth about what?"

The woman was talking in circles but the crazy thing was, she had piqued my interest. All the Brewers were dead. Clarence Swain was the last person in town who knew Mabel in her younger years and he had told me everything he knew. If this woman's mother knew something else, I needed her.

"What does your mother mean, families need to know?" I asked. "What families?"

I wasn't going to get roped into trusting in false information from a well-intentioned person who believed whatever her mother told her. I had heard about the road to Hell being paved by good intentions.

"I don't know what families she's talking about but it is so very important to her." Her voice quivered. It sounded like she could be trying to camouflage the sound of crying. "My mother keeps saying she needs to 'right a wrong.' She's an old woman, Miss Oliver, and she is terrified she's going to die because someone wants to stop her from talking to you. She insists she must talk to you before it is too late."

She got me with the "terrified," not to mention that this old woman thought talking to me might stop her death, so I crumbled. "Okay, I'll talk to her. Put her on the phone."

"She won't talk on the phone. She's afraid that certain people might be listening in, and if they find out what she knows . . . . She needs your help. Now, she's even afraid to take her medicine or go to sleep. Please, can you come here? I'm begging you."

"Where in Milledgeville are you?"

"My mother is on the outskirts of town, on Sinclair Lake."

"I've got a store to run. That's a long drive. Why would anyone want to hurt your mother just to keep her from talking about the past?"

"I don't know. And frankly, I really don't care. My mother was a nurse and has taken care of others all her life. Now *she* needs help. I promised her I'd help her and convince you to come."

She sounded so desperate. I couldn't refuse. I wondered if her information could have anything to do with Jacob. I wrote down the address and agreed to drive to Milledgeville tomorrow. It was my day off. I said I'd be there before noon.

"Thank you, Miss Oliver. Your visit just may keep me from losing my mother."

House on Lake Sinclair

While driving to Milledgeville, I figured that I could talk to Peggy Hamilton's mother, Sadie, and be back on the road no later than five o'clock. Peggy said her mother had known Mabel; if that was true then maybe she could shed some light on where Jacob had disappeared to so very long ago.

My directions led me a few miles out of Milledgeville's city limits. The scenic drive with the giant live oak trees and the occasional pink dogwood growing wild along the highway should have calmed me, but it didn't. I was anxious to get a solid lead. Still, doubt crept back into my mind. Perhaps I couldn't unlock the mystery surrounding Jacob. I wondered how historians trace back generations to people who had been dead for hundreds of years. At least I had Clarence's testimony, but there were so many huge gaps. All my hopes hinged on Sadie.

A little bit before 1 p.m., I turned down a dirt road identified as Pleasant Lane. It turned out to be a private driveway lined by cedar trees. I followed it to the end, where a pale yellow house sat, nestled comfortably in the middle of a well-manicured yard. It was very different from the modern ranch-style homes of Florida. The large, wrap-around veranda gave it a welcoming, southern Georgia look. Conveniently spaced around on the front porch were a dozen or more red rocking chairs. Baskets of white geraniums hung from the surrounding overhead beams. I almost expected a young Antebellum lady to breeze out in a hoop skirt and a wide-brimmed hat, holding a mint julep. A sign adorned with hand-painted Magnolia blossoms hung from a chain with the name: Magnolia Breezes Boarding House.

I parked and went inside to a small foyer. To the left, a woman dressed in a white uniform sat behind a petite writing desk, paging through a magazine. The nameplate with the word "Receptionist" on it had been wedged tightly in front of a ceramic pot of African violets. A pink princess-style phone sat on the opposite corner of the desk.

The woman looked up and smiled. "Oh, you must be Miss Oliver." Before I could answer she said, "Sadie and Peggy have been waiting for you. I'll show you the way."

We entered a large, bright room, with at least a dozen windows. The ivy-patterned wallpaper gave a garden-like atmosphere to the room. "Moon River" quietly played in the background as a television to the left side of the room blared. Five elderly women huddled around as Bob Barker of the "Price is Right" game show asked the price of an item. The woman with lavender-gray hair called out, "Five dollars and thirty-five cents."

"You're crazy, Esther!" a woman sitting next to her argued. "It's at least ten dollars."

We walked past a table where two men were playing checkers. One paused, a hand in midair over a red checker, as both men turned to watch us. I heard one of them say, "She must be Sadie's visitor."

I shook my head in disbelief. *Did they send out a memo or what?*

At the far wall, two women sat on a white wicker settee. One appeared to be dozing and the other, a rather large woman with flaming red hair, looked my way. She struggled to stand. Once on her feet, she hurried over to me and extended her hand. "You must be Miss Oliver. I'm Peggy. You don't know how glad I am that you agreed to come."

"Please call me Stephanie."

She looked over her shoulder briefly and then said in a low voice, "Mother refused to go to the dining room for lunch for fear she would miss you."

Nice, now I've made an old woman go hungry.

"I'm sorry I got delayed getting on the road. She should've eaten and not waited for me."

"I know. But she's gotten so stubborn in her old age. Has to have things done her way. She never used to be unyielding."

I followed Peggy over to the frail-looking woman. Her white hair was neatly combed into perfectly formed waves. A single strand of ivory pearls bordered the neckline of her navy blue dress. She sat with her hands together, fingers interlocked. The aged hands rested in her lap, with every fold of her skirt in place. I imagined that Mabel Brewer probably would have dressed similarly, ever so proper and ladylike.

"Mother." Peggy gently touched the older woman's arm. "Miss Oliver is here to see you."

The woman's eyelids popped open.

"Remember?" Peggy said. "She's the author you wanted to talk to from Havenridge."

"Of course, I remember. We were just talking about her, weren't we? I'm old but I still have full faculty of my memory."

She looked at me and motioned a withered hand for me to sit. I took a seat in an overstuffed chair next to the settee where Peggy joined her mother.

"Please forgive my daughter," the older woman said. "Sometimes she thinks old age turns a person stupid." She brushed her wrinkle-free skirt as if to smooth it. Then she looked up again and said, "Miss Oliver, it's a pleasure to meet you."

"Thank you."

"Oh, dear me," the white-haired woman replied, "I have been rude. I didn't properly introduce myself. I'm Mrs. Sadie Campbell. You, my dear, can call me Sadie. My daughter was five when I married my second husband and he died before he could adopt Peggy. Therefore, we have different last names. Nevertheless, we are mother and daughter." She patted Peggy's hand. "It doesn't seem fair, me marrying twice and my daughter never finding a husband."

"Mother, please." Peggy seemed to shrink before my eyes. I guess there's no age limit on a parent's ability to embarrass their child.

Sadie looked at Peggy, "If you could just lose a little weight, dear. You are still young enough to find a husband—you are such a pretty girl."

"Mother, Miss Oliver is . . ."

"Stephanie," I interjected.

"Yes, Stephanie," Peggy replied. "She doesn't need to hear about me. She has come a long way to talk to you about the Brewers."

Despite Sadie's slightly blunt evaluation of her daughter's weight, she had a tender and gentle manner that showed through. Peggy, although obviously embarrassed, didn't seem angry. Sadie's eyes lit up every time she glanced over to her daughter. Both of the women appeared very devoted to each other. They were genuine. I liked them immediately.

"Sadie," I said. "You said that Mabel Brewer took care of you when you were a baby?"

"Yes, she did. Although, she wasn't but a child herself. My mother was ill, you see, and father had his hands full. Besides, fathers didn't care for babies back then. That was the job for mothers or siblings—if they were sisters, that is."

Sadie went on, speaking of her childhood with amazing clarity as if she were telling me about last week's events, instead of over eighty years ago. Her descriptions of Havenridge and the people were accurate, too. She knew about small towns, and her account of the eccentric ways of their people matched things that Betsy had told me or that I had observed myself. Sadie even remembered Clarence Swain when I mentioned him.

"Clarence couldn't tell me much about Mabel when she was younger. He told me a lot about her father, Cain Brewer."

"Oh, yes, I remember Mister Brewer. He was very strict. I was scared of him. That is, when I got older and Mabel took me along with her to the house so she could do her chores."

Sadie told me that she had been born in Havenridge. Her father worked for Cain Brewer's father as a young boy. After Sadie's father married his high school sweetheart, they bought five acres of land and raised cotton. Right after Sadie was born, her mother contracted TB. That's why her father hired Mabel to help take care of Sadie. Mabel was only ten years old at the time. Sadie filled in many of the gaps for me. I couldn't help but wonder if she moved away from Havenridge early on, how she could provide any information about Jacob. Then I found out.

"We grew up together, Mabel and me." Sadie continued with her recollections. "Mabel was mother and sister to me. We were very close and stayed in contact with each other—until Mabel passed away. I do miss her dearly."

A concerned look came over Peggy's face as she touched Sadie's hand and said, "Mother, I think we've talked long enough."

No! I thought. *I have only been here for twenty minutes.* I hated my selfishness but I needed more information.

"It's probably a good idea to take a little nap," Peggy insisted." You're getting tired."

"I know when I'm tired." Sadie's voice changed to a firm and harsh tone. "Or when I need a nap! If you are bored, why don't you go play checkers with the men? Or go home. I'm not finished talking."

I truly didn't want to cause Sadie to get mad at Peggy; however, she could take a nap later. "When did you move away from Havenridge, Sadie?" I prodded. "You said Mabel wrote to you. What did she write about?"

Sadie smoothed her skirt again and looked at me. "I was six when my father and I moved to Milledgeville. Mabel had begun teaching at the school in Havenridge—sixth grade. Mother passed away in the fall before our move. I think father decided to leave because of the emptiness that mother's passing brought to our house. Too many memories of her being sick. He cared for mother for so long. He was completely devoted to her. He must have been lost after she passed."

"Mom," Peggy said. "I'm sure he was thinking of you. He probably knew there would be more opportunities for you in a larger town like Milledgeville."

"Maybe, but back then, children didn't ask a parent why they were moving. I don't know why we moved. We just did."

Peggy looked at me and added, "Mother went to nursing school in Milledgeville. Most women didn't have careers back then. Right, Mom?"

"Yes, you either got married and had children, or became a teacher, or you could be a nurse. Mabel became a teacher."

"But you stayed in touch with Mabel by writing her?" I asked.

Peggy watched her mother with worry. I could see Sadie was growing tired and her hands were shaking as she fingered a lace handkerchief.

"After nursing school graduation, mother worked at the hospital in Milledgeville. That's where she met my father. He was a doctor."

"Is that when you learned about Hanna Brewer's stay in the mental ward?" I asked. "I know Cain Brewer kept that she was institutionalized from Mable. Records say Hanna Brewer died here in Milledgeville."

"No. No. No!" Sadie shook her head repeatedly. Her agitation was building every second. "I keep telling everyone. Hanna Brewer did not die in the Milledgeville asylum."

"But the records," I stammered.

"Mother, you're getting yourself upset," Peggy said. "You need to go lie down."

"That poor woman," Sadie said. "She died in that horrible, horrible place. It was a Hell on earth. I didn't believe it existed at first. My dear husband assured me that no doctor would let such a place exist."

"What place?" I asked.

"He was wrong—it did exist." Sadie started to cry. "Years later, I learned that the stories about the Lost Fifty were true. I told that Chicago reporter who came to town. But they made him stop writing about them. You must help the Lost Fifty find peace. You must."

Peggy gave me a quick, worried glance and reached out to touch her mother's shaking hands. Sadie's gnarled fingers bent at the knuckles and twisted in an unnatural horizontal position. "Mother, you shouldn't talk about the Lost Fifty, it only upsets you."

The fragile, old woman snapped her hand away from Peggy. "Don't tell me what to talk about. Leave me alone." Sadie's voice shrilled as she strained to push herself up from the settee. Her eyes widened as she looked at Peggy. "Who are you?"

"Mother, please," Peggy said, reaching out for her.

"Did they send you here to shut me up?" Sadie's voice trembled and her face contorted. She straightened up, holding herself rigid for a second before her back gave out and slumped down into a bent-over position again. "Well, you won't stop me! I have proof. I have the newspaper clipping. You didn't think I was smart enough to hide it from you, did you? But I did . . . I did!"

Peggy stood, reaching out to Sadie.

The frail woman stepped back, nearly falling. "Stay away from me. Stay away!" Sadie screamed.

A nurse rushed over at lightning speed. "Sadie, calm down," she said. "What's the matter?"

"Nothing, as long as you keep this woman away from me." She pointed an accusing finger at Peggy, and then, pushed past the nurse. "I have to get something for Miss Oliver. I'll be right back," Then she disappeared down the hallway.

Peggy and the nurse spoke privately. I overheard Peggy telling the nurse to let Sadie be, that she would be fine, probably would forget about why she had left by the time she got to her room. Then the nurse left.

"I'm sorry, Peggy. I didn't know," I said. "It was my fault, I shouldn't have pushed her."

"No, if it wasn't the Lost Fifty, it would've been something else," Peggy said. "This morning she seemed well. I thought she would be okay for your visit. I thought seeing you would help." Peggy collapsed on the couch and buried her face into her hands, sobbing. "I'm losing my mother."

Holding onto Time

I sat still, while Peggy cried. I didn't know what to say or do. So I just sat and kept quiet.

What had happened? Sadie was a clear-thinking, intelligent woman, and then within seconds, she changed, right before my eyes.

Peggy retrieved a handkerchief from her pocket and dabbed her tears. She pushed back a lock of hair, squared her shoulders, and turned toward me with petitioning eyes. "I am so sorry you had to experience that, Stephanie."

"Don't worry about it," I mumbled awkwardly. I had driven her mother into—what—a mental meltdown? And now, Peggy was apologizing to me? I would sit for a minute or two, then I'd give some kind of lame excuse and leave. A quick exit would be best for all.

"Honestly," Peggy said, pausing to take out a handkerchief to wipe her nose, and then she shoved the handkerchief back into her dress pocket. "I thought that my mother would be *with* me longer this time."

Oh, no, don't do that. Don't apologize to me again.

"My mother suffers from some kind of dementia, or Alzheimer's. The doctors haven't determined which one because of her varied symptoms. There are the typical periods of forgetfulness found with Alzheimer's, but then, the vivid hallucinations are found with a particular type of dementia. She imagines things, like the Lost Fifty. That's when she becomes highly agitated, like what you just observed."

Or when an idiot like me probes her for information and gets her upset. I lowered my head to avoid eye contact with her.

Peggy touched my hand. I sheepishly looked up at her. She smiled. "She's afraid," Peggy continued. "She believes that someone wants to hurt her. Unfortunately, sometimes that someone is me—in her mind. I never know how the day will unfold. I've been seeing her slip away, little by little. Reading the column about your book seemed to help at first."

"I'm sorry for what you're going through. But there's no need for you to explain to me. Really."

Peggy kept talking like I hadn't said anything. "She is really a very caring woman—that's the strongest quality of my mother. When I first started to read your articles about Havenridge, it seemed to be something for her to grasp onto and her thinking sharpened. But it wasn't long after that, whenever I read to her, she became extremely upset. Especially when there were things about the Brewers or Mabel in it. Eventually, I stopped bringing in the paper. I made up excuses like I forgot it, or it got thrown away by accident. But that only made matters worse. Then she started rambling on about the Lost Fifty. How she had failed them. That she had to try one last time and make someone listen. I thought if she spoke to you it would help ease her mind. Even if it was a fantasy, I had to try to help her."

Sadie had pieces to my puzzle, I just knew it. The problem was they were scrambled, lost in her mind.

"She started talking about the Lost Fifty after listening to my articles?"

Peggy nodded her head. "That's right,"

"Maybe her Lost Fifty are real. Some kind of group," I said. "Maybe the Lost Fifty are connected to Mabel Brewer or her family."

"Maybe. Reading about Mabel seemed to be a trigger for her to start talking about them. She would repeat over and over that someone needed to expose the real truth."

Leann's words echoed in my mind. *To hide the truth can only bring harm.*

"Peggy, Sadie's memories and the details she spoke about today were so accurate. Up until. . ." I stopped, not wanting to cause any more grief.

I hated to interfere, but maybe Sadie *was* remembering something real. If no one believed her that would certainly be a reason to get agitated. She might be ill but not delusional.

"There's an elderly man named Clarence Swain," I explained. "He was born and raised in Havenridge. I've spoken to him about Mabel and the Brewers. Some of the things that Sadie spoke about, Clarence talked about, too. What if the Lost Fifty did exist?"

Peggy's brow furrowed as she shook her head. "I never agreed with the doctors when they said she was suffering from hallucinations, not at first. She gave such specifics and recalled the smallest details. Her memories seemed so clear. It just didn't seem possible that she could grasp so many things with so much accuracy, and then mistakenly imagine others."

Peggy's passive demeanor morphed into assertiveness. Her tone took on a determined firmness. "What she's remembering must be real!" Her stiff stature slackened. "But then, she's so aggressive, right to a point of being violent at times."

She looked directly in my eyes as if to make me believe her, "That's not my mother. She's nurturing by nature. The doctors just don't know her. They must be wrong."

Doctors only go by experiences that they have with the average patient. Sadie by no means appeared average in any way to me.

"It's as if mom's mind is like a big house containing everything about her life behind various doors and windows. When one of them opens, I see my mother in ways I have never been able to see her before. I'm discovering my mother, the person that co-workers, patients, and friends knew. The hard part is when she doesn't know me and calls me Mabel. I'm ashamed to say, I find I'm jealous of the bond she had with Mabel."

"Think, Peggy, could there be something in Sadie's past that would've put her in danger? Maybe when one of those doors you described opens and that's when she becomes frightened. Her anger is a defensive reaction."

"She was a nurse, how dangerous could that be? A devoted nurse. She seemed more dedicated to her patients than being part of my life. I don't remember her ever attending any of my school events because she was at the hospital all the time." Peggy gave a small smile. "We only became close in recent years—after I moved back here. I actually don't know much about my mother's life except that she was always going to battle for someone. Everyone would come to her for help. People called her 'Fearless Sadie.'"

We sat silent for what seemed like an eternity. It seemed hopeless. I was about to make up an excuse for a hasty exit when Peggy's eyes widened. "Wait, I do remember something," she said. "Several years ago, I received a very odd call. I lived in Hawkinsville, Georgia at the time. Mom never called after ten o'clock. It was late, almost 2 a.m. when the phone woke me from a dead sleep. I answered and Mom started talking immediately. She went right into telling me about making a decision. One that might cause a major disturbance in town."

"What was it?"

"She wouldn't say, just said that I needed to know certain things, in case she wasn't around. I was groggy. I listened to her insist that she had always tried to be a good nurse and a good mother." Peggy sighed. "I remember—good nurse, good mother—in that order. She rambled on about how the truth would come out and I needed to know about a safety deposit box that she had at the bank. It had important papers and I should get to them immediately if anything happened to her. My name was listed along with hers so I wouldn't have any trouble."

"What happened?"

"Nothing. She never spoke about it again. When I moved to Milledgeville, I asked about her safety deposit box and she claimed there was never any safety deposit box. Said I misunderstood."

"Maybe that was the start of her Alzheimer's?"

"Oh, no. That was years before I moved here. Even at the time that I moved to Milledgeville her mind was sharp, just as always. In fact, I couldn't understand why she had insisted I pull up stakes like that and come here. To be close to help if she needed me, was the only explanation she gave. My mother kept her diagnosis a secret at first until she couldn't explain away the spells of forgetfulness. You see, my mother, being a nurse, had been very aware of her prognosis. She wanted to save me from worry for as long as possible. As a nurse, she knew what was ahead, so early on while she was mentally capable, she made arrangements. Had her name put on the waiting list here and paid for five years in advance. Her doctor called me when her health deteriorated enough that it wasn't safe for her to live alone. That's how I learned about it. He gave me a letter mom had written explaining her condition and that it was time for me to insist on her moving to Magnolia Breezes. She wrote that it was best and she hadn't wanted to burden me until necessary. She even made funeral arrangements. Imagine that. Her doing all that so not to burden me."

Peggy glanced toward the empty hallway. "I would've taken care of her at my home but she played the mother card and told me no. I know now she always loved me, just in her own way. I would do anything for her."

Sadie's slender silhouette appeared at the end of the hallway. She moved toward us with a determined, steadfast stride and a paper in her hand. She stopped in front of me and waited until I focused on her.

"Good, you haven't left, Stephanie," she said in a strong voice. "I found the newspaper clipping. I hope you can do something about those poor people. I tried but they stopped me."

She thrust the paper forward. Sadie looked down at Peggy sitting on the couch. "Don't worry, Mabel. This nice Miss Oliver will help us. Once your mother is released, she will talk to your father about Jacob. We'll find him."

I took the aged newspaper from her. Halfway down, in big bold print was the headline:

MILLEDGEVILLE NURSE BLOWS THE WHISTLE ON MENTAL HOSPITAL ABUSE.

A New Door to the Past

A worried nurse came over to Sadie to calm her before there was another eruption. However, Sadie's agitation had completely diminished. Still, the nurse said she'd had enough excitement for the day and convinced her to go take a nap. Sadie and the nurse retreated down the hallway once again. Peggy and I remained speechless from the turn of events we just had experienced.

My hand trembled slightly as I held out the worn newspaper clipping. "Do you know anything about this?"

Peggy took it and read aloud. "Sources claimed misconduct at the Fleming Convalescent Hospital in Harwine. Accusations brought forward in a recent article led to an investigation of the century-old hospital." Peggy stopped. "This is the Milledgeville newspaper—it's over twenty years old."

"Did Sadie ever work at that hospital?"

"She worked here in Milledgeville, not Harwine, not that I know. But sometimes hospitals borrow staff nurses from neighboring towns. There's a registry. If there was a shortage or a particular need for extra medical personal then I suppose she could have, if that hospital had requested to borrow some staff nurses. It is possible, I just don't know. Stephanie, I've never seen this paper before. Mother never spoke about any investigation."

"Sadie could've been the reporter's source. Is there a byline?"

Peggy looked down at the paper. "Do you mean, who wrote it?"

"Yes."

"It says the reporter was a W. McCoy. If my mother saw something, if there had been patient abuse," Peggy pause for a second as if collecting her thoughts. "If that was so, then that would have been cause for her to start an all-out war. That must be the disturbance she spoke about that night on the phone to me. I thought her voice sounded worried but it wasn't worry—it was a sound of determination and anger."

"Does the article mention the Lost Fifty?"

Peggy's eyes moved quickly from side to side as she scanned the article. "Yes, here it is. 'For years rumors existed about a group of patients that were being abused at a nearby hospital. Area people who lived around Harwine had grown up hearing stories about patients who were institutionalized illegally or without medical reason. Parents used to tell children that if they weren't good, they would have them locked them up like the legendary Lost Fifty.'"

Peggy fingered the paper, separating it from another clipping. "There's another story—it's a retraction. The editor has added his personal apology. It says that the reporter William McCoy had worked for a Chicago newspaper and didn't follow proper procedures in checking the reliability of his sources. The editor pretty much throws him under the bus."

"If the investigation was squashed . . ." My words drifted as I thought out loud and tried to put the pieces together. "That could explain why Sadie never told you any more than what she did."

Peggy seemed to be lost in her thoughts and was not fully listening to my ramblings. "I bet someone got paid off. Mother would not have made a mistake of that magnitude. In this retraction, it claims that the newspaper was duped by a woman using a rumor as an instrument to receive her fifteen minutes of fame."

Peggy slammed the cushion with her fist, making me jump with surprise. She pushed the newspaper clipping toward me, waving it feverishly. "Fifteen minutes of fame! How dare they. If that reporter's unnamed source was my mother, then by golly, the Lost Fifty was not just a rumor. They were real!"

I took the paper from Peggy to look at the byline and searched for any information about where to locate the reporter. I had learned a while ago that if a story was important enough, an out-of-town reporter might track down information, maybe even come to the town where the story was happening, and write about it. His hometown paper would publish it, and the local paper could pick it up from the wire service of the Associated Press. The byline should have AP indicating it was not locally written. I wanted to know if this reporter named McCoy actually worked at the Milledgeville paper, or lived in Chicago. "We need to track down this reporter. There's got to be more to this."

"You better believe there's more to it," Peggy said. Her face was as red as her flaming hair. "My mother is not a lunatic. If she believed patients were being abused, I can guarantee she found proof. My mother may have trouble with remembering what day or year it is, but she's never been paranoid before. Someone killed the investigation, just like she says, and they were out to stop her."

Tracking Records

I agreed to stay the night in town. Sadie needed my help and I hoped that it was not too late to uncover some answers. Underneath the lies and the deception, there was a connection to Hanna Brewer and Harwine. Sadie was the only living link to the truth. She knew something that could lead me in the right direction. I just could feel it. As Peggy feared, I worried that like the old crumbling newspaper and the fading picture of Jacob, Sadie would soon vanish, along with the link to Mabel and the answers that were locked in the past. Sadie was retreating into a world that we could not enter.

Tomorrow after Sadie is rested, maybe she'll share something about Jacob. If only it was that easy and rest could cure her condition.

When I returned to the bed and breakfast, I called Betsy to ask her if she'd hold down the fort at the store another day. She told me not to worry and even suggested I consider staying another two or three days in case Sadie had some more lucid moments. The extra time would allow me to check about the old Fleming hospital in Harwine and see if it was still operational. Peggy had said Harwine was a rural town not too far away. Perhaps I could talk to the hospital staff and see if anyone could look up Hanna Brewer's records—that is if she had ever been a patient there. If I was lucky, maybe one of Hanna's therapy sessions would shed some light on things. If everything went well, the hospital was still there and the staff was receptive to help, I might find a way to get copies of any sessions or even get to read letters. They possibly could give me a clue about Jacob. Cain could have shared with Hanna his concerns about Mabel and Jacob. Of course, I was fantasizing, but why not? Jacob's existence *had* impacted the family in so many ways, there had to be more. I was grasping at straws, but straws were all I had right now.

I told Betsy that this McCoy reporter apparently had been in Chicago at one time but the headline didn't indicate the story was from there. "Do you think he might have returned there to work?" I asked Betsy. "I certainly can't afford to fly to Chicago."

"Don't jump to conclusions. A Chicago reporter wouldn't come down just to do one story on a mental hospital near Milledgeville," Betsy said. "But it does seem odd that they made a point to say he was a Chicago reporter."

"His name was on the original article and in the retraction; it said he worked for a newspaper in Chicago."

"Worked?" Betsy repeated. "It said worked, past tense? Sounds like he was a reporter for the Milledgeville paper and they were trying to deflect the guilt elsewhere. Citing the Chicago paper could've been a good excuse for the reporter's lack of checking his sources. The paper in Chicago trained him—not the local paper. Therefore, they were the scapegoat for the Milledgeville paper's erroneous story."

"But he would have to answer to the local paper's editor, plus you would think he certainly had to have some kind of training from the Milledgeville paper. At the very least, guidelines to follow."

"Doesn't matter," Betsy said. "Divert the attention, and push the blame elsewhere. That's how the game is played."

She continued to remind me how the people in Havenridge considered new people "outsiders" for years. The reporter could've easily been living in Milledgeville and writing for the local paper, but still, have been referred to as the Chicago reporter.

Betsy had a way of cutting through all the garbage and untangling the truth. She had been my rock through all these grueling months of investigation. Her theory made sense. I only hoped that McCoy was still living in Milledgeville and working for the local paper. I'd call the paper in the morning.

We said goodnight and hung up. I was beat, so I pulled out of the plastic bag the nightshirt that I had purchased at the college bookstore on the way to the bed and breakfast. The young girl who helped me with the purchase sounded like a transplant from South Carolina and had been very helpful. When I asked about the newspaper, she told me the local newspaper was not far from the campus. She even looked up the address in the phone book behind the counter and wrote it down for me, along with the phone number.

It felt good to get out of my clothes and slip into the oversized shirt that had a silk-screened Bobcat on the front, the college mascot. I turned off the small lamp that sat on a round table next to the bed and pulled the covers up to settle in for the night, but my mind still raced. Although it had been a very long day, I mentally went over my plans once more before sleep beckoned me. First thing in the morning, I'd call the local newspaper. Instead of inquiring about archived papers like I had intended to, now having this new evidence from Sadie, I'd ask if they had a reporter named William McCoy.

The next morning the sunlight pierced through the lace curtains, waking me bright and early. I felt refreshed. The bed in my room at the Antebellum Inn was so comfortable I was tempted to sleep longer, but I was determined today would provide new hope and new direction for my search. After all, luck had gotten me this far; I had met Sadie and had gotten a room for the night. The innkeeper had told me that until an hour before I called, every room had been booked. However, the guest who had reserved my room called right before me and had canceled their reservations due to car trouble. Usually, the bed and breakfast was booked months ahead with visiting parents of college students at this time of year. The location of the inn on Columbia Street was ideal, located in historic downtown Milledgeville and just a short walk to the college. Yes, I think luck was starting to turn for the better for me.

I dressed and quickly went downstairs to the dining room. The buffet had an array of breakfast choices from fruit to steaming hot trays of scrambled eggs and bacon. I fixed a plate of a little bit of everything. The aroma made me realize I was starving. I had skipped dinner the night before.

After taking a seat near the window, a mature woman with salt and pepper colored hair entered the room. She filled a plate of fruit, a bagel with cream cheese, and after pouring a cup of hot tea, she walked over toward my table. "Do you mind if I join you?"

"Not at all, please do," I said with a smile. "I hate eating alone."

She introduced herself and explained that she had moved away eight years prior and was in town for a large family reunion. Our conversation soon led to why I was in town. I mentioned I was doing research for a book and planned to contact the newspaper about the old article that raised the abuse question of the mental hospital in Harwine.

Suddenly her pleasant demeanor turned nasty. She remembered the newspaper article, and said with disdain in her voice that she knew "that McCoy reporter."

What is about me? I seem to agitate everyone I come in contact with here.

"He should've let sleeping dogs lie," she said, frowning. "Turned things dark with that article of his!"

"You remember reading it?"

"Most certainly." She huffed and then sipped her tea.

"What do you mean, turned things dark?"

She looked hard at me, not speaking.

I chose to keep my mouth shut.

She blotted the corners of her mouth. "Well."

Gotcha! Can't help but to continue with the gossip.

"Story like that snowballs with all kinds of speculation," she said. "People started wondering about the hospital here in Milledgeville. It raised suspicion and tainted the reputation of all good hospitals. Why the local newspaper didn't fire him right there on the spot, I'll never understand."

"So, he's still writing for the paper?" I asked.

She didn't say anything, just sat there glaring at me.

Oh, no. I better be careful.

"Where did you say you were from?" she asked with an untrusting tone.

I figured that I needed to use Betsy's soft-handed style, instead of my usual Stephanie's blunt style.

"Havenridge. I moved back to restore dear Mabel's, that's Mabel Brewer, old homestead. You probably have heard of the Brewer family, Mabel was Cain's only daughter. Well, she must have tried to keep up the house, but when you're in your nineties, things don't get repaired like they should. Not that poor, dear Mabel didn't do her best."

Maybe if she gets in her mind that I'm related to the Brewers, she might be a little more positive. Third-generation thing. I paused to take a sip of my beverage, while she eyed me in silence.

"Now I'm trying to see if there might have been a distant relative who moved to these parts, possibly had been a patient at the . . ." I paused and then leaned in and lowered my voice. "The asylum in Harwine." *Lord forgive me for implying that I'm in the family but it's just a small white lie. It's for Mabel and Jacob.*

"You own the Brewer home?"

"Yes. I'm just here for a day or two. Trying to find out some things about the family."

She seemed to relax her body and smiled at me before saying, "You should check our hospital here first, dear. Maybe your family member was a patient in Milledgeville, if the good Lord was watching over them, that is. I guess you could talk to that reporter, William McCoy. He really shook things up. He might have some useful information if your, uh, if who you're looking for was a patient in Harwine."

"I suppose so. She was a great aunt of dear Mabel, God rest her soul."

She glanced at her watch and gasped. "Oh, no. I need to get on my way." She gave her apologies and wished me luck in my search as she rushed out.

Amazing. I can use Betsy's style, too. I felt a little Nancy Drew-like. It gave me a sense of power. Thanks to my breakfast companion, I knew the W. McCoy was William McCoy and he still worked at the newspaper. Today definitely was looking good after all.

I dialed the paper's number on the phone in the parlor and asked if the reporter William McCoy was working. I was immediately put on hold, but about a minute later a man answered.

"Bill McCoy, how can I help you?"

I explained the reason for my call. He wasn't very eager to talk to me. "The story is dead. Didn't you read the retraction?"

"Yes," I answered. However, I explained that I still wanted to talk to him. Finally, after a great deal of persuasion, he agreed to meet me at the student center at Georgia College.

"Okay, I'll give you ten minutes. I'll meet you at 2 o'clock," he said. Before hanging up he added, "I'll be wearing a blue shirt."

I arrived five minutes early and took a seat near the door. Minutes later, a tall, young-looking man with pockmarked skin walked in wearing blue. Eager—too eager, I started to get up. A dark-haired girl pushed past me and threw her arms around his neck. Together they walked by, laughing and talking. *I should've known–he was too young.* As if no one else would be wearing a blue shirt.

I sat again and waited until ten after two. Obviously, I had been stood up for our two o'clock appointment. I guess my good luck streak was finished. I wondered if Nancy Drew ever got discouraged. It seemed like feeling disheartened had become my norm.

As I was standing to leave, in walked a slightly older man with a rumpled blue shirt and carrying a briefcase. He scanned the room. When he saw me, he briskly approached my table.

"Miss Oliver?"

"Yes."

"I'm sorry I'm late. My editor stopped me as I was leaving."

He took a seat across from me with no other explanations, and pulled a paper out of the briefcase, placed it on the table, and pushed it toward me.

"I was able to get a back copy from our files. I remember the article you asked about very well. It almost got me fired. I had just moved from Chicago, and this was the second job I had ever worked. I had worked at a small wannabe newspaper in Chicago, not the Tribune that the Milledgeville paper assumed, but I didn't correct them. It seemed to impress people here, and I was hired.

"People looked up to me like I knew things about reporting, and it gave me a big head. I was too stupid to know any better than to play along. I tried reporting on some local stories and had to interview people. I knew I was in big trouble when I couldn't get a single person in town to give me the time of day. So to prove myself, I jumped on the Harwine story with both feet without checking my sources. Breaking a big headline story about a century-old hospital and its atrocities in the backwoods of Georgia was a dream come true. I honestly thought I might be up for a Pulitzer. Instead of ace cub reporter, the impression I made was big city idiot. I'm still trying to live it down after twenty years."

"So, Harwine. Where *is* that?" I played dumb, hoping my newfound easy-going style could work again.

"That's the point. It's this little spot of land. Most folks living there don't have indoor plumbing, even now. They keep to themselves. I told my editor that I spoke to a nurse who confirmed the story. And the asylum *did* exist."

He raked his fingers through his hair and let out a heavy breath. "I had checked the capital—there was a licensed hospital and the MD listed as a director. I was under a deadline so I turned in the story. Figured I'd drive out there and speak to someone after we went to print to tie up the loose ends."

"Did you get to talk to a doctor out there?"

"Are you kidding? Fleming Convalescent Hospital was there, all right. The building is still there even now. Only after the story hit, suddenly there was a quick change of ownership to a Phillip Andrew Reed."

"So, why didn't you talk to him?"

"I did. He said the place was not operating as a hospital anymore. When I called the woman back that I spoke to originally at the capital, the public records identified it as a multi-family dwelling. The listing was a boarding house and that makes all the difference in the world. Boarding houses don't fall under any regulations. None of the state's departments enforce or inspect boarding houses."

"So what?" I said. "The abuse was when it was a hospital; therefore, why not pursue the story?"

"Phillip Andrew Reed is a scary man, especially when you're a reporter with no proof. He declared I had no story and threatened to sue me and the paper."

"What about the families living around the area? Did you talk to any of them?"

He shook his head. "Those folks don't like to talk to outsiders. Especially someone like me, who was wearing clothes that screamed *city slicker*. One man shot at me!"

"What about the nurse?"

"Someone filed a complaint about the nurse four days after the article ran. That discredited her. And with that . . . my source and my story went up in smoke."

"That's absurd. Four days after the story ran. Didn't anyone see through that?"

"Didn't matter."

"Why not a surprise inspection? Then they could find the deplorable conditions."

"It wasn't a hospital—not anymore. No one to call for an inspection."

"What if I can get more information and . . . "

He held one hand up to halt me. "Miss Oliver, I have no doubt that what I wrote was true. But unless you can get a past patient—or Fleming himself to confess to the allegations, then you have nothing."

"But..."

McCoy stood, signaling the end to our conversation. "I'm sorry. I can't help you. Even if you get the Governor of Georgia himself, I still can't help you. I can't risk my job. I got married, again, last year. My wife is eight months pregnant, and that's scary enough at my age. I brought the information on the transfer of names on the property. I'm not getting back into this old battle. Maybe the paperwork will help you but that's all I can do."

He reached back into his briefcase and pulled out a manila folder, from which he produced a two-inch-thick stack of papers attached at the top with a large binder clip.

"Here. This is what I gathered while I was under the gun and it still didn't save my ass. Even after years of me kissing butt, my boss continues to hate me. He'd love to find a way to fire me. My only saving grace was that the attorneys representing the paper told them that if I was fired it would imply an admission of guilt and would be as damning as a headline that read, *Local newspaper knew reporter fabricated story.* My job is secure, as long as I don't open this Pandora's Box again."

"But if we could prove that the story was right . . ."

"No. I can't help you. I've stuck my neck out already by making those copies. You're on your own."

With that, he turned and walked away.

I picked up the stack of paper. The top paper was an official-looking document with an imprinted state seal. It read:

Deed of Property

Lot 14328, rural acre A-80045, Rockaway County, Harwine Township

Grantor: J. T. Fleming III   Grantee: Phillip Andrew Reed

I felt a bit defeated. There was no more hospital to investigate. Any abuse was gone, the same as Hanna and Jacob. I didn't know how I was going to do it but I had to find J.T. Fleming III. It was my only hope.

J. T Fleming

Betsy agreed that I had to locate J.T. Fleming. He would be the only link to answers about Hanna, unless relatives of other past patients started to drop out of the sky to testify. However, it would be more likely it would rain gold coins.

Tracking answers about Jacob required following any link, no matter how weak. I remembered a cousin of mine who was an electrician. He said troubleshooting a problem required patience to systematically check each wire. It would either lead to a connection (be a hotline) or you would find the break. Hanna's record might or might not give us answers but I wouldn't know until I tracked the lead to the end. Right now, Hanna was a connection and J.T. Fleming was my lead.

I hoped that Fleming still lived in Harwine, or at least in the same county, and hadn't moved out of Georgia after the sale of the hospital.

My trip to the public library to check phonebooks, old and new, only showed two Flemings in Harwine. The 1985 book listed a Wm. E. Fleming and a Robt. Fleming. I found a phone booth outside the library and called the number for William and got a disconnect message. Then I dialed the one for Robert Fleming. No answer. At least it was a working number. I would call again after six thirty tonight. That would give time for him to get home from a job, in case that was the reason for the no answer during the day.

I walked back inside the library and over to the information desk. "Excuse me. I was wondering if I could see some maps of the area."

The librarian didn't look up. She continued filing index cards in a box. Her nimble fingers moved quickly, sliding the last card into the tightly packed box. She gave a heavy sigh, then looked up. "Where do you want to go?"

"A city called Harwine," I answered.

"There's no city called Harwine around here."

"But, I know there is. There was even a hospital there," I explained.

She took her glasses off and rubbed the sides of her nose where there was indented, red skin at the spot her glasses had rested. When she stopped, she stared at me. "The Fleming Convalescent Hospital. I know about it."

Exasperated, I asked, "If it isn't in Harwine, then where?"

"Oh, it's in Harwine. Harwine Township, not a city. That hospital was about the only thing there . . . that and maybe a dozen or so small houses scattered within a few miles of one another."

I forgot that like Havenridge, as in most small towns around here, people are particular with how things were relayed to them. They all have their own way about doing things and most of the time that meant not offering any more than what is asked of them.

"Well, that is where I want to go," I said. Crazy I couldn't get used to small-town people. They were frustrating. "Do you have a map?"

"It's not like there are road signs out there. A map won't do you any good."

She asked me more questions. Like, why did I want to go out there? And, how did I know about the Fleming place? I fell back on my great aunt story—that she had stayed there while recovering from a nervous condition. Remembering to use the correct words and terms like nervous condition, which was the way people around here spoke. Their polite way of avoiding words like insane or crazy. Those less than polite words were reserved for private whispered conversations. Using the correct words equaled a country person, which equaled getting information, or at least it indicated someone was from around the area and wasn't an outsider.

"I can tell you how to get there," she said. Then the librarian proceeded to give directions to the Convalescent Hospital's location. She warned that if I was not expected, it might be best not to go snooping around in the area. I thanked her and decided she might be right, remembering what Bill McCoy said about having been shot at once.

Nevertheless, I had no choice. I had to track every possible lead down. If I could speak to Robert Fleming, he might be a relative of J.T., and maybe he would know how I could reach him. It could mean that I wouldn't need to go to Harwine. I would wait to call the number again back at the bed and breakfast tonight.

The Voices of the Lost Fifty

I used the phone in the parlor at the bed and breakfast because it was easier to jot down notes at the small desk in the corner. The houseguests would start trickling into the adjacent living room in thirty minutes for the traditional evening gathering, to enjoy a glass of port or sherry and conversation. Therefore, I had plenty of time for a private call. The phone rang six times before a man answered. His voice had a smooth sound, like a radio announcer's voice.

"Good evening," I said. "I am glad you answered, is this Mr. Robert Fleming?"

"There is no one here named Robert Fleming."

"But the phone book listed a Robert Fleming."

"My dear lady, you are mistaken. Goodbye."

"Wait, maybe you can help me." I explained who I was and that I was looking for J.T. Fleming. "I was hoping perhaps you were a relative and knew where I could find him?"

"I'm J.T. Fleming. The phone listing is R-O-B-T period, which is an abbreviation for Roberta, not Robert. The phone is listed to Roberta Fleming, my late wife. I never bothered to change the listing. What can I do for you, Madam?"

I apologized for my mistake about the listing and expressed my condolences. Then I explained that I was looking for a long lost relative and had been told by my grandmother before she died that my great-aunt Hanna may have been a patient at the Fleming Convalescent Hospital. Another white lie. They were starting to add up.

J.T. Fleming said the J was for John and I could call him John. A pleasant surprise, since I've been receiving the cold shoulder from most everyone I'd been in contact with so far. He was very cordial and by the time we concluded our conversation he had invited me to come out the next day to speak more about my search.

I must say that I felt a bit guilty by lying to him. However, what I had learned over the last two years living in Havenridge was that sometimes it was better to offer people what they are comfortable hearing than the truth. So since family was more important than life itself in these parts, I would stick with my dear great aunt Hanna story. I left out my questions about why records of Hanna Brewer's existence seemed to have mysteriously disappeared after her being committed, and also, I didn't mention that nothing had been recorded about her moving to Harwine. If I was looking for answers about the wife of a man whose only virtue was money and power, then I would get nowhere.

John stated in a matter-of-fact voice, "Fleming Convalescent Hospital is still in business." Then he proceeded to give me directions to come out for a meeting.

I interrupted him, "Hospital? I understood it wasn't a hospital anymore."

"Yes, Yes. That's right, Miss Oliver. It is not *officially a hospital* because we do not prescribe medicine, we only dispense it."

He continued to say that he still owned the property. The sale to his stepson was yet another legality of words. "It's all rather confusing, as laws can be, and regulations can get hung up if one uses improper words. My stepson explained it to me. It was much easier when I was the director; there were not so many regulations and legal mumbo-jumbo back then." He sighed. "So much has changed."

"So it's your stepson who is the director?"

"Well, mostly. I am the person that has to sign the documents. My stepson handles the rest of the legal things. Thank goodness. I'm too old to have all that paperwork to deal with, and having to keep track of everything. Oh, by the way, Miss Oliver, the new name is Harwine Boarding House. You will see a sign about a half mile after you turn down the dirt road that I told you about."

I thanked him and we hung up. Something didn't feel right. *John's dear old stepson handles everything, except for signing his name to things?*

Something sure smelled fishy to me. I wanted to see what someone local thought about John Fleming. And I only knew one person that I could trust around here. I grabbed the phone and dialed Peggy Hamilton's number.

Harwine

I had been driving for forty minutes. The last vehicle that had passed me was a rusty old pickup truck about thirty or forty miles back. Outside my side window were bushes encased in kudzu, a vine-like plant running rampant in Georgia. Its growth coiled around the trees, climbing toward their tops. It reminded me of the cocooned people in that old black and white movie. I wondered how long it would be before the trees would disappear altogether. Ahead of me stretched what seemed to be an endless length of blacktop.

When I spoke to John Fleming on the phone, he said my drive would take close to an hour. Once I passed an old burned-out barn on the left side of the road, I needed to watch for a green mailbox ahead, on the right. There would be a dirt driveway leading into the trees, which I was to take.

When I shared this information with Peggy, she insisted on calling her friend Max. She promptly called me back after speaking to him and said he would meet me along the way. Max urged her not to let me go alone. Max would wait at the green mailbox and if I got there before him, I was not to venture down the driveway alone. Peggy assured me I'd be safe with Max Baker at my side.

"He'll be driving a white work van with ladders hooked on the side," Peggy told me. "He paints houses for a living and is a good man. You'll have no trouble as long as Max is with you as backup."

"All right, but I don't expect any trouble. John Fleming invited me."

"That doesn't matter. Max said Harwine is a strange place. He had a helper that worked for him some time back that knew about the area and he told Max things that even made him uneasy . . . and Max isn't afraid of anything or anyone," Peggy said. He had insisted that she convince Stephanie to have him go along with her, *for her own protection* were his very words.

"Max won't interfere, Stephanie," Peggy said. "He won't go in with you when you go inside to meet Mr. Fleming. He said he'll wait in his van."

Something told me that Peggy's Max Baker knew things about Harwine that I didn't want to know. Instinct urged me to accept Peggy's suggestion to have her friend accompany me; therefore, I didn't argue any further. Another thing I noticed, Peggy's tone had softened when she spoke of Max Baker. My guess was that Sadie should not have worried so much about her daughter being lonely. Even though Peggy hadn't married, I would bet she had a man in her life and I would soon meet him.

Why Peggy chose not to share with her mother about Max, I don't know. Maybe it was her way to hold onto her independence and keep her own personal space during her mother's all-consuming final days. Whatever the reason Peggy had for keeping Max Baker private was none of my business. I knew what it was like to have loved ones force their own insecurities onto you about being a single woman. The cookie-cutter married life is not in the cards for everyone. Happiness doesn't necessarily require a fairytale happily-ever-after ending. I've grown to understand that a woman who chooses the less-traveled path in life is not necessarily hopelessly unhappy, or lonely.

Just ahead, I noticed the white van parked near the green mailbox. A burly looking man stood next to it. I slowed down and turned into the driveway. As I rolled my window down, the man, who wore paint-spattered overall advanced to my car. He looked over six-feet-tall and had a kind-looking face. His beard was full but neatly trimmed.

"Stephanie?"

"Yes," I answered. He reminded me of some of the charming and ruggedly handsome frontiersmen in old western movies. He threw a half-smoked cigarette down on the ground and put it out with his foot.

"Peggy said you would be driving a blue car. Look, I'm here if you need me, that's all. When you go inside, I'll wait in the van. You know, Peggy was right to call me. In these parts, there's nobody around for miles. Anything could happen to a woman alone. There won't be any funny business as long as I'm with you, I guarantee it."

"I really think there's nothing to worry about, I was invited." These last two years had been a struggle for me to regain my independence; however, I'd grown very comfortable flying solo. Still, I confessed, "Even so, I do feel better with you here. Thank you."

We drove down the dirt road about a mile back into the thick and unkempt landscape of underbrush and trees. It seemed more like a walking path than a road, which led to a heavily wooded area. The path forked to the left and we kept straight for a few yards more. A flock of crows bolted out from the brush, flying straight toward my car as if they were on a Kamikaze mission. I slammed on my brakes to avoid the birds crashing into my windshield.

Once they flew away, I could see beyond where Max's van was. I saw a house. It was large, had pillars in the front, and peeling paint on most of the building. I drove around the van and parked in front. Max pulled over to the side and parked in a less conspicuous area under a nearby oak tree. It resembled a giant dark octopus with clumps of Spanish moss that hung down from the long, tentacle-like branches.

I walked over to the van. "I might be a while," I said.

"Take your time. I have the morning paper."

It was hard to believe that the inside of the house was in worse condition than the outside. Peeling paint around the ceiling and small dark patches of mold in the corners gave the interior a gloomy and melancholy appearance. A stench of sickness hung in the air, an odor that Sadie's nursing home did not have. A woman seated at a desk in a small room to my left called out to me that if I was here for Mr. Fleming, his office was down the hallway—first door on the right.

My footsteps echoed on the linoleum floor as I went down the hall. At the first open door on the right, I saw a distinguished elderly man sitting behind a massive mahogany desk. I entered.

"Miss Oliver, I assume." As he stood, he extended his hand and then motioned to a chair facing his desk. "Please take a seat."

We spoke for a short time. I asked about Hanna and he said he knew of her. "I thought she had no family. That is what the records showed."

His voice lowered as if speaking to himself in a melancholy tone. "None of them had family. There was no one for them."

"What? That's not true, Mr. Fleming. Hanna Brewer had a husband."

"Miss Oliver, let me explain a bit of history for you. This place has been in my family for years, my grandfather and great grandfather opened it up many, many years ago. You see my grandfather . . . ." His voice trailed off and he sat in silence for a second before continuing.

"It was a different time. They didn't understand mental illness back then." He spoke in an undertone, almost as if speaking to himself.

He cleared his throat and looked directly at me and continued. "At least, that has comforted me all these years. I am so sorry for what went on here in the past. My grandfather wasn't like me. He was a cruel, selfish man and there was no one to stop him. With no family on the outside, the patients were at his mercy. They made him rich."

"Who, the patients?" I asked.

"I'm afraid so. Maybe I can rectify some of his deeds today."

"Was Hanna Brewer one of the patients?"

"Yes. You see, there were fifty patients that my family took into the hospital—because of the overcrowding in the Milledgeville hospital. The doctors there were glad for our help. My grandfather, and my great-grandfather, who was still living, agreed to take the ones that the doctors thought could be cured. Your poor aunt, Hanna Brewer, she was not supposed to be part of the transfer because the Milledgeville doctors thought she was incurable."

"So why did she come here?" I asked.

"I'm not exactly sure. The records are incomplete. However, my family came into a large sum of money right before the transfer. I don't know the reason for the large payment. Perhaps there's a connection between Hanna Brewer's transfer and that substantial money deposit into the family account."

"Did the other transferred patients get well? Were they released?"

"Well Miss Oliver, that is what a newspaper reporter questioned several years ago. He wanted proof if any patient had ever been cured, or released from here. His accusations were that the patients he named, "The Lost Fifty," were never treated properly and were abused. He claimed that many of the patients should have been released but weren't."

"I understand that the newspaper retracted that article."

"They were forced to because of my stepson. He halted any investigation by bringing in a pricey lawyer. The one he hired was very good at his job. He knew how to twist the facts. Phillip, my stepson, doesn't want me to talk about it to anyone."

"Why? You're talking about patients from over a hundred years back. You're not responsible."

"Phillip says it would hurt us financially. He thinks the families of our guests . . . that's what he wants me to call our patients. The families of our guests would pull them out of here if a scandal got out about the past. It has nothing to do with us now, I told him. My stepson says it doesn't matter. It was the Fleming family that did the abuse and we still run this place."

John stopped speaking. He fidgeted with things on his desk, like straightening a perfectly stacked pile of papers. I waited as difficult as it were to watch. He clearly was deeply distraught.

Seconds passed and I said, "Please go on," I needed to keep him talking.

"We take care of our guests," he mumbled defensively.

"Of course, you take care of your pa . . . uh, guests," I said.

I was here not to accuse him of any wrongdoing; I assured him that he mustn't feel guilty about the past. That would be the best approach if I was to get any information from him. However, I couldn't help to think that if the condition of the place was any indication of how he or his stepson took care of their guests, they weren't doing a very good job even today.

"I don't care what my stepson says. Fifty people, lost in time, existed here and it's time to give them back their identity and let them rest in peace. That's why I asked you to come, it is my duty to set things right."

His words echoed what Sadie said a day earlier. Souls from the past were reaching out, calling for recognition.

"Miss Oliver, there are other buildings on the property. We have over one hundred acres. There is a smaller house that has been used as storage for years. You would have passed it on your way in. It's tucked into thick brush and trees, just off the road leading here. You may have not noticed it.

"The Lost Fifty came here—the strong patients—the ones who could've been treated. Because of my relatives, those patients didn't get the help they deserved. My grandfathers realized that they could be hard workers. Workers who weren't required to receive pay for that work."

"John, are you telling me that they were treated like slaves?" I thought about Cain Brewer. Could it have been Cain's money that allowed Hanna's transfer? Was he buying treatment for her, hoping to save her, or wanting to lock her away for good? But his journal read like a tragic love story. Maybe the Brewers *were* cursed.

"Slaves? No, not slaves but valuable assets. The women made clothing or cooked. The men worked the fields or did the heavy work needed. They performed jobs and had skills that if others had performed would have received substantial compensation for, but not patients under a doctor's care."

"Didn't the hospital in Milledgeville require a follow-up report on the patients' status on recovery or an update on their condition?"

"Oh yes, but those reports to the doctors in Milledgeville were false. Milledgeville doctors received reports that some patients had taken a turn for the worse. They needed to remain here for their safety and to receive treatment. Others, falsified death certificates were filed. At that time, illness was spreading across the county. Many people in the area lost family members. No one questioned deaths at hospitals. Who would question a death certificate signed by a doctor?"

Cain could've been notified that Hanna died. "My aunt, Hanna Brewer—she never went back to Milledgeville, did she?"

"No, Miss Oliver." He hung his head and avoided making eye contact. "She must have gotten well enough to be a *valuable asset*. None of the well patients, who were named by one of the staff as the Lost Fifty, ever left. Whether patients recovered their sanity, or not, they were all condemned to stay here." His voice cracked as he said, "Trapped in life and forgotten in death."

Why would the newspaper stop their investigation when they found out? Money. Everything has a price, even people.

The already small and delicately built man in front of me seemed to shrink even more in stature as he purged his family's secret. John pulled a white handkerchief from his pocket, removed his wire-rimmed glasses, and wiped his eyes. He put his glasses back on, pushed his handkerchief back in his pocket, and spoke in a soft, determined voice. "Miss Oliver, you need to come with me."

I followed him out of his office. He spoke and walked rapidly down the hallway. "In the storage building are the suitcases that the Lost Fifty brought with them. They have been there for as long as I can remember. I first saw them when I was around six years old. I was exploring and I got a whipping for going in where I was forbidden to go."

When we got outside, he told me to follow him in my car. He also urged me that time was of the essence because his stepson was due back very soon.

Max followed in his van. We drove back to where the road forked, cut across a field that was thick with bushes and weeds until we reached an opening into a meadow of high grass. Off in the distance sat an old brick building with vines growing on its walls. The three of us parked.

John Fleming stepped out of his car and walked over to me. "If you want, Miss Oliver, you can take all the suitcases. That is, if you think there may be other relatives out there besides you. Maybe you can find them."

Max stepped out of his van and approached us.

Fleming looked at Max as he spoke to me. "Best to have your friend pull his van around to the back of the building. There's a back door he can use."

John reached in his pocket, pulled out a key, and rushed toward the front door.

Max returned to his van and pulled around to the back. I told him we needed to hurry because we'd probably be stopped getting the things out of the building. I joined John as he unlocked the door. It creaked open, reminding me of the noise old joints make after a lengthy stay at rest.

There inside, wooden shelves lined both sides of the room. On the shelves were rows and rows of ancient suitcases, some brown, some golden, others black There were some stylish leather ones; however, most were old battered black ones with string wrapped around the outside to hold them together and keep the contents safely inside. *So many.*

The cases filled the shelves of the small room. Each revealed a different personality. *The owners' history–locked away from the world.* Tags hung from the handles of each case with only a number marked on them for identification. Aged yellow cards nailed to the wooden-frame shelving were marked A through W. Suitcases and bags–the last evidence of discarded lives from so long ago.

Race to Grab History

John crossed the room to the back door and unlocked it. As he turned the knob and pushed—nothing happened. He leaned his shoulder against the door and pushed harder. I vaguely noticed his difficulty because I was awestruck by the vision around me. My eyes scanned the room. First looking in front of me, and then to my right, and finally to my left. There were row after row of shelves, crammed full with dust-ridden bags and timeworn valises. I could only imagine the contents, surviving evidence that the Lost Fifty did exist.

"Miss Oliver, please," John cried out. "I don't have the strength. Come help me open this door, it's stuck. *Please*, we must hurry."

I raced to help, on the count of three we shoved together and the door flung open. Sunlight streamed in from behind a giant shadowed figure outside.

"Max, hurry," I said, shielding my eyes from the sun. "Get the suitcases off the shelves and put them in your van. Start at the rows marked "A" and "B.""

Max charged past me, moving with the determination of a mother elephant going after her young.

"There's no time to waste. Mr. Fleming's stepson might try to stop us."

What I suspected to be the smell of mold assaulted my nose. Stagnant air, mixed with whatever mold spores now floated around us, made me nauseous. The room's decaying condition showed a few holes in the walls exposing the outside light, either from the elements of neglect and weather, or perhaps from mice gnawing in for shelter.

John started coughing and grabbed his handkerchief from his pocket. "I . . . I'm sorry, I have to get some fresh air," he said, before staggering through the front doorway.

I joined Max at the shelves. He had one suitcase in his left hand and another under his arm as he grabbed for a tweed-patterned case with brown straps with his free hand. "Stephanie, get that brown bag there." He pointed with his chin. "Put it under my right arm."

Moving quickly, I grabbed it and did as instructed. "Max, there must be over a hundred bags and boxes here. They have been stored all these years, waiting to be claimed. No one cared enough even to get rid of them, they weren't even given the same attention of trash that someone would take away. It's so sad."

"Who do they belong to?" Max asked.

I realized he didn't know anything that John Fleming had told me inside his office. "Patients," I answered.

Even without knowing, Max hadn't hesitated to act with speed when I called on him. Peggy was right. Max Baker was a good man.

"These suitcases have been locked away for years. Eighty years, maybe some for as long as a hundred years. The belongings of patients put here and forgotten, the same as the people were forgotten. John—that is, Mr. Fleming—said they've been here as long as he can remember."

"I sure hope they have what you're looking for," Max said as he hurried out. He called back over his shoulder. "How many do you need me to pack?"

I had two more bags in my hands and paused to look at the shelves. The bags held answers to the past. "All of them!"

Max hurried out. Seconds later he returned, and said over his shoulder as we passed each other, "It's going to take time to get all of them."

"I know, but we can't leave any of them."

Returning, I grabbed two more suitcases; dust puffed up and floated down. I gagged. Time being of the essence, I hurried out to the van, coughing.

We packed case after case. With the heat, the air quality of the building, and no hint of a breeze, we couldn't keep this pace up for long.

Max took out a blue-checkered handkerchief and wiped the sweat from his forehead. "How much time do we have?"

"I'm not sure. I'll go out front and ask John if he has any idea how much longer we might have left. I really should check on him anyway, he didn't look well."

I passed the empty shelf marked with the letter B. The closer I got to the front door, the louder I heard John's voice. He sounded upset and it seemed as if he were arguing with someone. I went outside and saw a slender man in a gray suit. Behind him, a flashy red car parked askew with the driver's door left open. The man's face tightened into a twisted expression as he narrowed his eyes, raging with incoherent screams at John.

"John?" I interrupted.

John turned. He had a look of fear in his eyes. "Miss Oliver, I . . ."

"Who the hell is she?" The man flashed a seething look my way and then turned back to John. "Why did you bring her out here? You stupid . . . old man, I told you not to talk to anyone! You don't have to do anything, just sign the admission forms and keep your mouth shut."

"I'm Stephanie Oliver," I said, and moved closer to the arrogant man. "May I ask, who are *you?*"

"I am Phillip Andrew Reed, and you madam, are trespassing."

"I most certainly am not. I was invited by Mr. Fleming."

I hated to put poor John in the middle of things. Reed may be a bully, but he didn't scare me. I had experience with bullies and most of the time they didn't know how to handle someone who stood up to them.

"Well, Miss Oliver, my stepfather has no authority to invite you onto this property. I own this place. And now, little lady . . . ." he grabbed me by the arm and proceeded to drag me toward my car. "You will get in your car and leave."

I pulled my arm free. He turned and I glanced back at John who stood paralyzed in place as if he might turn into a pillar of salt if he moved.

"You, Mr. Reed, will not touch me again or I'll bring charges against you."

"Have it your way. You have exactly three minutes to get off my property or . . ."

"What's going on here?" Max's voice boomed as he charged toward us.

John's stepson turned and backed up as he saw the massive man advancing toward him. "You stop right there!" Reed yelled and pointed a shaky finger at Max. "I'll call the police and have you all arrested."

I shook my head at Max. He paused as I mouthed, *just go.* I nodded an okay and pointed my chin toward the house. Silently I begged; please get the van out with the suitcases we have now. Then I gave a pleading look and mouthed, *I'm okay–go now.*

Max stood planted like an immovable tree for seconds, and then said, "Remember that you're dealing with a lady." He turned and exited through the building.

Reed frowned and gave a double take in my direction, where I stood unmoving. I heard the sound of Max's van engine start. Reed gave a big sigh and shook his head. Then the painter's work van drove out from behind the house and disappeared, with dirt flying up in a dust trail behind it.

"Yellowbelly," Reed said and laughed. "Your friend appears smarter then you are, Miss Oliver. My dear stepfather does not have legal authority to invite you onto this property. I am the owner and I will have you arrested for trespassing if you do not leave immediately. Do I make myself clear?"

"I'll leave, but you haven't heard the last of this." I walked leisurely to my car. I was buying time for Max to get off the property. Once in my car, I leaned my head out of my open window and looked toward John. "Mr. Fleming, will you be all right? Do you want to come with me?"

"I'm fine, Miss Oliver." John's brows pinched together, his eyes seemed to plead for my quiet retreat. Then he looked down toward the ground, avoiding further eye contact. "I'm so sorry for my stepson's rudeness."

"Oh, please spare me the dramatics." Reed spat. "My stepfather is a stupid old man. Just like the old buzzards, he calls our guests." He waved his hand dismissively at me as if to shoo me away. "Now get off my property and don't come back." Then he turned on his heels and headed toward the shack. "Law around here allows me to shoot trespassers, Miss Oliver. You've been warned."

Reed won this battle, but it wasn't over. I hated leaving poor John. It was obvious he was terrified of his stepson. When I looked in my rearview mirror, Reed had disappeared into the shack. I had seen men like him before; they manipulated the law to better suit themselves. With Reed, he probably used the fine details of the law to line his pocket with others' misfortune.

Before turning at the fork, I glanced back in the mirror and saw Reed race out of the shack and over to John, waving his fists at him. John cowered. Reed must've found the empty shelves. He kicked the dirt before getting into his car, leaving John standing in front of the dilapidated building. Reed's shiny car sped in my direction.

I pushed down on my accelerator but my tires spun in the soft dirt, and my car started to fishtail. I slowed to get control. "Just come after me, mister, and try something. You'll be the one that goes to jail," I muttered, watching Reed's car in my mirror. I made it to the green mailbox, turned onto the highway, and peeled out. Seconds later, the flashy red car chasing me stopped in defeat at the end of the path at the highway's edge.

Six miles down the road, I saw the white van in the grassy shoulder with Max standing next to it, waiting for me.

Secrets Shared

Max said that once we entered Milledgeville city limits we should split up. If Reed changed his mind and chose to follow us, he couldn't go in two different directions. I needed to drive on to the bed and breakfast and stay there for a few hours. That way it would look as if I was there for the night. Later on, I could come over to Peggy's house, and Max would be waiting there. We could look over the suitcases then.

Max claimed that he had run across people like Reed. Although he was certain Reed would be trouble, he didn't think Reed would have the nerve to follow us into Milledgeville.

"People like Reed are more likely to hire 'goombahs' to do his dirty work of following and making more threats," Max had said. "Trust me, this fight is not over. He needs time to gather his men."

I was afraid Max was right. We might have just won this battle, but it wasn't over. Besides, there were suitcases left behind and I wasn't about to leave them there.

Max also said that he thought it was a sure bet that we had a major war ahead of us. Then he added that the eyes of Harwine could reach far past its country roads. His warning made me shiver. I had no experience with backwoods people and their unwritten law of revenge. I drove on, hoping I would be able to stay alert and be able to recognize something suspicious. A shadow of uncertainty in my mind left me wondering if I might not be cut out for the fight. Over the last year, I had grown comfortable with Havenridge's naïve ways, as if there was no possibility of danger lurking. Sometimes in the morning, I would find I had forgotten to lock my front door the night before. I knew now that it couldn't happen anymore.

Max's word echoed in my mind. Goombahs. I had never heard the word before, nevertheless, I got the point. No doubt, Reed would continue to project the image of respectability on the surface, while he'd enlist his not so respectable associates—goombahs—to stop me and any investigation.

Before Max and I split up I voiced my concern about him. "Certainly Phillip Reed or his people wouldn't be sleazy enough to physically attack a woman, but you, that could be a different story. Even though you're a big man, Max, they could force your truck off the road and jump you when you get out. If they have knives or guns . . ." I stopped, not wanting to think about that scenario.

"Don't worry." Max grinned and then chuckled. "I hit six feet a little before my twelfth birthday. I've had a lot of experience with fellas picking fights with me. Back when I was in grammar school, everyone wanted to be the guy that took down the biggest kid in school. I hated fighting. Wasn't raised to use my size to settle arguments—but others saw me as a challenge."

He paused and ran his fingers through his thick hair. "You see, Stephanie, the older I got, the harder it was to avoid confrontation. I got a reputation for not fighting, so the challenge became kinda like an unofficial school competition. Everyone had illusions of being the fella that knocked out big, bad Baker. Go figure. Not fighting made every guy in town want to fight me even more."

He shook his head and chuckled. "So, the long and the short of it is—I know how to take care of myself if need be. I can fight. Don't worry." Before he got back in his truck, he added, "I also know how to ditch someone following me."

We had stopped two miles past the city limit sign for our conversation. I felt better knowing that he had another side of him other than big and pleasant. Even though I felt bad for his past experiences with having to defend himself with the violent part of the world, it gave me reassurance that he knew how to deal with it. We split up and agreed to meet back at Peggy's house sometime after seven thirty. Max said he was making dinner for Peggy, or Peg, as he affectionately referred to her. He said he didn't know how to cook small; so there would be plenty and I needed to come hungry. After dinner, we could discuss what to do about the suitcases.

AT THE BED AND BREAKFAST.

When I got to my room, I realized the day's events had taken a toll on me. Exhausted and keyed up at the same time, the threats from John's stepson whirled in my mind and made me cringe. Phillip Andrew Reed was a vile and contemptible man. Nothing like John.

I stretched out on the bed to be comfortable, grabbed the phone and dialed Betsy's number back home. I needed the comfort of her unwavering, calm nature. Betsy had been part of this almost since I found Cain Brewer's journal. She always helped me center myself, besides all her other help, like getting Clarence to talk and share about Mabel. Without Betsy, Clarence would never have spoken to me. From the first time I drove into

Havenridge, Betsy had become my rock to lean on, even before we bought Sarah's store and became partners.

After ten minutes, I had finished telling her about Reed and everything that had happened.

"Sounds like Harwine people are exactly the way the rumors claim. They're not at all like Havenridge folks. There's real danger out there, Stephanie."

"Tell me about it. I'm glad Max was there." I realized that my nerves were calmed but my rage remained, coursing through me whenever I thought about Reed.

"Betsy, there were seventy-five, maybe even a hundred suitcases, still in that old building on the property. I'd sure like to get my hands on all of them. I don't think an invitation from John Fleming is going to work for us again. Do you have any ideas?"

There was a moment of silence, while Betsy was clearly running options through her mind. "I have a friend in the Historical Society in Milledgeville. Doris. I'll call her. Maybe someone in the society has come up against something like this before. Doris has friends in high places with a lot of influence. She might be able to shed some light on what we need to do. After all, Reed possesses items of historical value."

"Thanks. It's worth a try. However, the Historical Society probably doesn't have the legal authority to seize personal property—or to even go on private land."

"If she can't help, I think you better hope that you'll find something about Jacob Thompson with Hanna Brewer's belongings." Betsy was always positive. Nevertheless, she was above all else truthful, and saw things realistically. I figured she was right about Hanna's suitcase being our last hope. "You might not have any other chance to discover where he went to after Havenridge."

"That's if Hanna's belongings are in Max's van."

Before hanging up, we both decided I needed to stay at least one more night in Milledgeville and find out what was concealed in those suitcases. I placed the phone in its cradle.

I rolled over on my side on the bed and close my eyes. *I'm so tired. I'll just close my eyes for a few minutes.*

EVENING 7:15 PM

When I woke the room was semi-dark. I bolted up and noticed the time glowing from the small clock on the round table next to the bed.

"I can't believe I slept so long."

Plenty of time had passed since leaving Max. It certainly must be safe for me to leave for Peggy's house without any possibility of being followed.

If I hurried, I still could make it by seven thirty. Max said he didn't expect Peggy until around eight thirty but I should come early for dinner. Peggy always stayed until Sadie was settled down for the night so there was no need to wait for her before we ate. Besides, some of the nights that were more difficult with Sadie, Peggy would stay even later. Max said that those nights, she would come home totally drained and too tired to eat.

I pulled in the driveway at seven thirty on the nose. The house was medium size and displayed a conservative look with neatly trimmed ligustrum hedges around the perimeter. I rang the doorbell and heard Max's familiar voice call out that he would be there in a minute. When the door opened, he was standing with a spoon in his hand and an apron around his waist.

"Perfect timing. Hope you're hungry. I made stew."

"Actually, I am famished."

In the kitchen, Max dished out two heaping bowls and set them on a small oak table across from the stove. He grabbed a bowl of biscuits out of the oven before returning to the table.

"This looks great," I said as we both took a seat. "Are those homemade biscuits?"

"Absolutely. My mother raised me right. She said a man should know how to cook for himself."

"I think I would like your mother."

"Yeah, that's what Peggy said when we first met. Peg hates cooking. Mother passed away five years before Peg and I met."

Max and I were halfway through our meal before he asked, "So Stephanie, not that it's any of my business—but what's the story about Harwine and those suitcases?"

"Well, it's not that complicated. Two and a half years ago, I moved from Orlando, Florida to Havenridge. I bought an old Victorian house that belonged to a family named Brewer."

"Brewer," Max said inquisitively. "Peg said you were talking to her mom about someone named Mabel Brewer. Said Sadie had grown up with her."

"Apparently so. Mabel watched Sadie when she was a baby. Later on, Sadie and Mabel became close friends and kept in touch right up until Mabel died a few years ago."

Max grabbed another biscuit. Then he lifted the bowl, holding it out toward me. "Have another biscuit, Stephanie?"

"I've had two already," I said sheepishly as I took another. "They're irresistible. You'll spoil me."

Max smiled and blushed, then looked down at his stew, and moved it around with his spoon. "You know, Peg said Sadie had become every agitated after she read to her about this Mabel Brewer in the Havenridge newspaper. It seemed like there was nothing she could do to calm her down. Peg hoped your visit would help set her mother at ease again."

"I feel bad about that. I wanted my visit to help—not just for me but for Peggy's mother. I like Peggy, really. Sadie, too. Sadie must have been quite a strong woman before . . . you know . . . the dementia."

"Yeah. Hear tell she finished nursing school, worked, and raised Peg when it was frowned upon for a woman to continue working after having a child."

"That must be where Peggy gets her compassion from—she is very good with Sadie."

"It's been difficult on Peg," Max said, wiping his mouth. "Sometimes Sadie doesn't recognize her. Those days are the hardest. Peg comes home and doesn't want to talk. She just wants to be alone. So, I stay at my house and do my woodworking. I'm making a standing jewelry chest for Peg's birthday. It's next month."

"Sounds lovely. How did you and Peggy meet?"

"She called me about putting in new kitchen cabinets. It was in the heat of summer and I usually try not to take on any outside house painting jobs then. For at least three or four months, I do carpentry work. Well, after everything was finished and Peg had her new kitchen, we got to talking and Peg said she didn't even like to cook."

He gave a deep hefty laugh. "I asked her why remodel a kitchen if she doesn't cook? She answered that she just thought the house needed it. One thing led to another, and I offered to cook her one of my famous gourmet dinners. I make a mean rack of lamb with a pineapple sage sauce. We declared the kitchen "cook-worthy" and have been together ever since."

"I guess it's not only women who find their way to a person's heart by cooking a good meal," I said. That brought a broad smile to Max's face. "You two seem so right for each other."

"We are. You know, not everyone understands our relationship. People want to have a marriage certificate to validate a couple's commitment to each other. Her neighbors don't understand why we both keep separate houses. That seems to stick in their craw. I'd like to have a place of our own together—but—whatever makes Peg happy. That's the only thing that's important to me."

I finished my stew as Max dished out another bowl for himself. When he returned to the table he asked, "What about you?" He pointed at my hand. "You don't have a ring on your finger. You have a man in your life?"

"No. I was married once, but things didn't work out. We were mismatched."

"Best to find out before kids," Max said. "Children need both parents."

"Daniel and I had a daughter."

"Oh. Sorry. I can really put my foot in my mouth. She lives with her dad?"

"No. Lily died when she was six. An allergic reaction to a medication. After that, I realized that Daniel and I never should've been together. Daniel's a good man, though. We're divorced now and he remarried last year. They're right for each other. She's a doctor, too. They think alike—it's a perfect match."

We sat quietly for a few minutes before Max asked, "So, what's the big mystery about Mabel Brewer?"

I took a deep breath and then exhaled. "Well, most people don't think there is any mystery. Mabel was a schoolteacher, the proper old spinster. Just about everyone in Havenridge was either her student or she taught their children at one time or another. She died a few years back at ninety-eight years old. I found out things about her—and the Brewer history—that were kept secret from the people in town."

"That's a hard thing to do in a small town," Max said. "People know more than they might want to share."

"Boy, you've got that right. But with the Brewer secret, it was different. Shortly after moving into the old Brewer house, I found a crawl space—more like a hole in the wall with a door. I stumbled onto it when I was putting some boxes in a closet. This compartment or hiding space, I really don't know what to call it, was in the back of a closet and not very noticeable. The wood was stained, almost as if to camouflage it and there was no door handle, just an indentation in the wood in order to pull it open."

"Whew," Max blew out a deep breath. "Yeah, these old houses have all kinds of hiding places in them. Especially old farmhouses. It's crazy that country folks, who don't lock their doors, are the most suspicious group of people you'll ever find. Always hiding things away . . . like they have anything worth stealing!"

"True. I mean about being suspicious. I never met people so secretive, especially toward new people. "

"Oh, you noticed that, huh." Max chuckled. "So, what was hidden in the space?"

"An old family Bible, papers . . . some records of cotton sales, and sale documents of a few farm horses. And a journal and some unopened letters to Mabel. They were tied with string. That was the start of my search for the truth. Mabel never got those letters."

"Who were they from?" Max asked.

"A man named Jacob, a secret lover that Mabel had, only he wasn't that secret. Mabel's father knew about him and intercepted the letters."

"Man! Why do people think they know what's best for everyone else?"

"Well, he was her father and wanted to protect her. Anyway, there's this man I spoke with in Havenridge, Clarence Swain. He knew Mabel when she was young and free-spirited. Seems she sowed some wild oats back then, so to speak. Clarence confirmed Mabel had a secret lover and that she would have rendezvouses with this stranger. I know now that his name was Jacob and I thought Sadie might know something about him, maybe even might know what happened to him."

"No offense, Stephanie but seems like you're going to a lot of trouble just because you found some old letters."

"It's not just the letters. The uncanny thing is that my brother met my neighbor in Havenridge, her name is Leann, and they fell in love and got married. Well, turns out the reason Leann had moved to town was that Jacob, Mabel's lover, was Leann's deceased great uncle. She was trying to track down information about him but she hit a dead-end sometime after she bought a house in Havenridge. She lived next to me and that's how we all met."

"So it's more like a family connection for you?" Max said.

"I guess, all I know is that I feel an intense bond with Mabel. And now, I've made a commitment to my sister-in-law to find where her uncle Jacob went to. He seemed to disappear completely."

I didn't need to share about the publishing contract and me writing a book. Max was great; however, my new motto was to give out info on a "need-to-know basis." I suppose some of the small-town ways had rubbed off on me.

"Wow. So you're helping your sister-in-law track down her family history? What a great story. What luck she married your brother and you found those letters."

"Yeah."

Max didn't need to know how much I felt obligated to Mabel, a dead woman. He would think I was crazy. Heck, I couldn't explain why that from the very beginning I felt a strong connection to Mabel. All I knew was that Mabel had been all alone, with no one on her side. She must have felt abandoned, hopeless, the same way I had felt not so long ago. Lost in darkness. When I found the letters and Cain's Journal, it gave me something to focus my way out of my darkness. How could Max understand that?

"How is Jacob connected to Harwine and the suitcases?" Max asked between bites of stew. "It's a long way from Havenridge."

"Not Jacob. Mabel's mother is connected. I'd never have made the connection if not for Sadie. You see, I wrote about the Brewer family in the Havenridge newspaper, and Peggy called me after reading them. Sadie knew about Hanna Brewer being institutionalized in Milledgeville and then transferred to the asylum in Harwine. Sadie is positive that Hanna was one of the people known as the Lost Fifty."

"Well, you have become quite the detective. But how will tracking down Hanna tell you anything about Jacob?'

"I have nowhere else to go. I hope somehow Hanna found out about Jacob. Her husband, Mabel's father, kept it a secret that his wife was alive. He didn't want anyone to know his wife went insane. Although he did write her faithfully, at least at first, according to his journal."

"Even nowadays people don't want to share that with others. Look at how Joe Kennedy handled his daughter Rosemary's mental retardation. If rich people like the Kennedys are ashamed of family, just think how simple country folks must feel about insanity."

"I'm learning to understand their thinking. However, it makes it very hard to decipher between truth, rumors, and lies. Over the years, there have been some fantastic stories about the Brewers. Mabel's father, Cain, was not liked. He had money and power, which does not fit well with people who don't have either one. When Hanna took ill, Cain's money made it possible to send her away and tell people she was being treated for consumption. When she didn't get better, he said Hanna died. That way he kept the shame of mental illness a secret."

"Just like Joe Kennedy wanted with Rosemary," Max said. "I remember a rhyme the kids around here would chant because of the mental hospital that is just outside of town. I don't remember all of it but it went something like *'if you're not good . . . they'll send you Milledgeville'* . . . *something, something . . . . And there you'll stay the rest of your days.'* That was the gist of it but it did rhyme, like that one about Lizzie Borden taking an ax and giving her mother forty whacks. Except I can remember the Borden rhyme completely, not the one about Milledgeville. Guess living here made the Milledgeville rhyme much scarier. I hated that rhyme. It was just mean. Even the parents would threaten children who misbehaved that they would be sent away to Milledgeville.

"But they didn't *really* send children there, did they?"

"Who knows, I tried to be good," Max answered. We sat in silence. Then he said, "You know a hundred years ago it was easy to lock someone up in the asylums. I understand that husbands could send their wives away for not obeying them. The doctors would approve the paperwork to commit a wife just on the husband's word alone that she needed to be committed."

"That's awful." I hated even thinking about the subject. A sudden flush of goosebumps went up my arm. "Things were so different then. I'm glad I didn't live at that time. There was so much unknown back then, especially mental illness."

"I'm glad Sadie was able to give you information," Max said, then gave me a sheepish look. "But I have to be honest, I'm sorry this whole thing got started. I was the one who suggested to Peg to get that paper mailed to her and read it to her mother. The stories about the Brewers seemed to accelerate Sadie's dementia. Every day she slips deeper into the past and stays there longer. Peg is losing her mother more every day."

Max Baker was a complex man. He had class, intelligence, and I could tell was completely head-over-heels in love with Peggy.

We picked up the dishes. Max said he would unload the suitcases from his van once the kitchen was cleaned up. He said that he didn't want Peggy to come home to dirty dishes. So he washed and I dried.

When we finished, Max set out a new bowl, a bread plate, and a sparkling stemmed goblet on the table for Peggy.

Then the front door opened and we heard Peggy call out, "I'm home. Something smells good."

Claiming Identities

"How did things go in Harwine?" Peggy asked.

"You were right, things got very sticky," I said. "It was very fortunate Max was with me."

Peggy sat down on the blue flowered sofa and took off her shoes. As we talked, Max disappeared from the room, returning shortly with a pair of fluffy pink slippers in his hand and gave them to Peggy.

Max tried to encourage Peggy to go into the kitchen and eat but his efforts were in vain.

She said, "Today was one of mother's bad days. I'm too exhausted to eat." Max stood behind her listening and nodding while he rubbed her shoulders.

Peggy explained that Sadie was herself, alert, knew what year it was, and recognized her. "Mother was very short-tempered today and annoyed at me."

She frowned and continued to explain. "It's strange, Stephanie, sometimes the times when her illness is *not* affecting her, those days can be the worst. She can be very angry, at me and at everything in general. I think it is because on those days she realizes what's ahead of her."

Peggy patted Max's hand. "Come sit down, dear." She picked up a box from the coffee table, opened it, and grabbed a chocolate candy from inside.

"Stephanie, I'm sorry to go on like this," she said as she nibbled on a chocolate. "Were you able to get some information on Hanna Brewer or about the Lost Fifty that mother talks about?"

"Yes."

Max and I told about her about Mr. Fleming and his vile son-in-law. I recounted all the details of the day, praising Max's uncanny insight on how to handle things.

"It was nothing," Max said. "Any country boy knows how to handle someone like Reed."

"Still, that doesn't make it any less dangerous," Peggy argued.

"It's only dangerous if you're naïve to the backwoods ways and how the good ol' boys play," he insisted.

Peggy grabbed another chocolate and popped it in her mouth. "Exactly." She placed her hand in front of her mouth so she could continue chewing and talking at the same time. "Stephanie isn't experienced about the type of people who live in Harwine."

I could see why Peggy was not wasting away from skipping dinners. "All I know," I interjected, "is that I'm grateful that you were there, Max. If Peggy hadn't called you, I wouldn't have gotten so many suitcases."

"Suitcases?" Peggy said as she grabbed another candy.

Max and I explained that Reed had threatened us at the storage building. By the time we finished telling her about our adventure, the previously full chocolate box was empty.

"Stephanie, why don't you and Max go out to the van and bring in the suitcases? It's all right with me if you want to leave them in my guest bedroom until you decide what to do with them. I'm going to lay down here and rest my eyes while you two are busy unloading them."

Max and I headed to the kitchen, but before we got to the door I glanced back at the sofa. Peggy appeared to be already asleep. On the coffee table was the open box, and inside scattered about were the crumbled candy wrappers.

Max had parked his van between the house and the front of a detached garage so anyone passing by wouldn't see it. He slid open the side door behind the driver's seat, revealing a mass of aged luggage. "I tried to get as many as I could before we were thrown off the property."

After unloading all of the cases from the van, we counted eighteen small travel-size suitcases, ten large ones (slightly smaller than a steamer-style trunk), and five small satchels. I felt a rush of optimism and promise that I hadn't felt for so long.

I also had a feeling of anticipation as I surveyed the collection. "We did good, Max. Can you imagine having the only evidence of your existence left to fit in one or two small suitcases? How could someone be so heartless to conceal knowledge of those poor people? Phillip Andrew Reed is an evil man!"

"Evil is hard to fight." Max appeared steadfast and unshaken by the day's events. I admired his strength. Although in the last year I had regained my fortitude that had faded over the years, still every day was a battle to stay strong and to regain my past self.

Would I ever be that strong person again? I didn't know the answer. I did know that I had been a confident person and that was the person needed for the job ahead of me now. Still, Reed didn't scare me. Funny, I felt the most powerful in the face of danger, like today. It was the quiet moments, those times of solitude that tested me, those times were when I weakened and became unsure of myself.

"There has to be a way to fight Reed," I said with a surge of the fighter, my old self, in me. "I don't know how, but I will find a way. We will get the rest of those suitcases. The Lost Fifty are not lost anymore."

"Even if who you are looking for isn't part of the Lost Fifty?" asked Max.

"Absolutely! I've never backed down from a fight and I won't now." I turned over a tag on a gray suitcase in front of me, Rebecca Adams. The next one read, Cyril Abraham. "Max, did you get *any* suitcases in section B?"

"Almost all of them. There weren't many in section A."

"Did you see a tag with the name Brewer?"

"I didn't read the tags, I was in too much of a hurry but I'm sure if there was one for Brewer, it must be here."

Shivers came over me when I thought about the discovery we had made. If Mabel's mother had been committed to the asylum, it would be a long shot that she knew about Jacob, and even a longer shot that she knew where he went.

Max and I continued looking, calling the names out as we searched. "Cecil Brown, Evelyn Ackerman, Agnes Bales."

No Brewer. *How could it be? All this and nothing?* My optimism slowly drained and an overwhelming sense of defeat replaced it.

"Pay dirt!" Max yelled. "This leather suitcase is marked, H. Brewer. What was Mabel's mother's first name?"

"Hanna."

My hands trembled as I pushed the tarnished clasp. "It won't open. It must be locked."

"I'll get a chisel and hammer out of my van. I can break the lock."

"No. We can't. We shouldn't damage it. After all these years—to abuse the last belongings of Hanna, I won't allow it. Her memories will not be violated anymore, not as long as I am alive. Her secrets have waited this long, they can wait until we can get a locksmith out here."

I reminded myself that the contents of Hanna's suitcase had waited over a hundred years for its release; I could wait twelve hours more to see what Hanna had placed carefully away.

"Tomorrow will be soon enough."

A Voice from the Grave

The next morning, I drove to Peggy's house to meet with the locksmith that Max had called. Max told me that Superior Locksmith Company was the one and only locksmith in Milledgeville. The owner, Mr. Pennywood, would be there by 10:15 a.m. Max quoted Pennywood, saying, "If it can be opened then I'm your man for the job."

I said a silent prayer driving over to Peggy's house. If Pennywood couldn't unlock Hanna's suitcase, we would be forced to resort to Max breaking the lock. The alternative would be to take the suitcases back home unopened and find another locksmith there, an option that was unacceptable to me since I certainly wasn't going to let anyone in Havenridge know about the suitcases, other than Betsy. If anything got out about abandoned suitcases, or about Hanna Brewer not dying from an illness in a Milledgeville hospital, then there would be no stopping that tidbit of information.

I chose to think positive. After all, I had been lucky, to have John Fleming on my side, not to mention that Peggy had insisted on sending Max to help me. In addition to the pure luck of Max not having any painting jobs booked during a normally busy time of the year. He also told me that he was available to help as long as I needed him. Yes, luck and good people were on my side.

It was ten o'clock on the nose when I pulled into Peggy's driveway. She would be at work and later would go for her evening visit with Sadie, so we wouldn't see her until much later. I saw Max's van parked near the back. Our appointment with Pennywood was at "ten fifteen, or thereabouts," as the locksmith told Max. I've learned that *thereabouts* is either a Georgian or a country way of keeping time, which I'd never heard before I had moved to Havenridge. Nevertheless, it would allow me time to tell Max about what Betsy found out from her connection with the Historical Society.

I knocked and entered the house after I heard Max's voice call out to come in. A delicious aroma spilled out from the kitchen. "Pumpkin muffins are cooling and the coffee is hot," Max said.

I followed Max's voice to find him in the kitchen in a ruffled pink apron. "Well, you look good in pink," I said, smiling as he placed two plates on the table.

"Peggy threw my apron in the washer and forgot to dry it. It is a confident man who can wear pink, you know. Can I get you some muffins and coffee?"

"Just coffee," I said holding back a giggle. "I have information from my friend Betsy about how possibly we can fight to get the rest of the suitcases."

"I hope it doesn't have to go through the court system there because Harwine folks are all related to each other, as in any of the law enforcement officers and the only judge. They will fight you as much as that Reed guy."

"Well, I think they just might be a little wary of fighting the Governor of Georgia. It appears Betsy's friend on the Historical Society Board of Directors has a cousin whose daughter just married the Governor's grandson last spring. Betsy said that if we have official documents pertaining to patients' history, like doctor reports or even personal items like letters or diaries that date back fifty or sixty years, we might have a chance. And the Central State Hospital Museum might be interested in getting involved, too. And guess whose new bride is the museum's curator?"

"Mrs. Grandson of the Governor," Max answered with a big grin.

"Bingo!"

Max slammed his hand down on the table and laughed. "That'll teach Reed, *Mister I own this property,* jerk, to think twice about who he picks a fight with."

"We shouldn't get full of ourselves, not until Betsy gets some answers, but it is encouraging. The problem is, we need more than old suitcases filled with old clothes in them. We need to get our hands on written documents with dates, reports, or hospital records, even admission paperwork to help build a stronger case. And Reed is not about to let us back on "his property" to get that."

"He doesn't have to. When you went out front to talk to Fleming, I noticed two boxes marked CONFIDENTIAL MEDICAL RECORDS. I figured there could be valuable information in them so I put them in the van. The boxes had been collecting a lot of cobwebs. Apparently, Reed didn't need paperwork from a hundred years back and wasn't interested in them, but I figured you might be." He shrugged his shoulders and an impish smile spread across his face.

"My gosh, Max! You're . . . you're a genius! Or at least, the most lovable thief I have ever known."

"Genius works for me."

With that, we heard a knock on the screen door in the front of the house. "Hello, Mr. Pennywood here. You called for a locksmith? Anyone home?"

Unlocking more Secrets

After letting Mr. Pennywood in, Max introduced me as a friend of Peggy's from her college days. Max said that I was passing through after a family reunion, where I had acquired some old stored-away family suitcases.

The name Pennywood seemed to fit the man, in my mind that is. He wore a white dress shirt, bow tie, and a vest, looking as if he had stepped right out of the turn of the century.

"I hope you can unlock them. I guess they were used to store things inside," I explained. "Although, I can't imagine why someone would use a suitcase for storage and it's not like any of my family ever had anything of importance to save. Maybe family photos—probably Aunt Gertrude just put string in them—she used to save the string that the newspaper was tied in. Who knows why, she never threw anything out."

I hoped I wasn't overdoing the details. Pennywood stared at me as I babbled, then he said, "Yes, old man Edwards was our town's string collector. When he passed, they found near two hundred balls of string in his attic."

"Really," I answered. Country ways still seem to catch me by surprise.

Max went to get the suitcases while Pennywood and I spoke. As Max returned carrying three suitcases with the name tags pulled off but none looked like the one that had the name Brewer on the tag. He must have grabbed three randomly in a rush to return. Mister Pennywood spotted them and chuckled. "Oh, for goodness' sake. You got yourself some old ones."

"My cousin got tired of storing them after my aunt passed away and he said I could have them . . . or burn them," I shrugged, "because he didn't care. Said they smelled of mothballs."

I was getting into my story but thought I might be overdoing it, so I forced myself to stop talking. Then I waited for Pennywood to speak.

He bent down and ran his palm over the outside of one of the cases, almost caressing it like a long lost object. "Would you look at this—my, my, my," he said as if he were thinking out loud and not speaking to me directly. Then he added, "Dad had a suitcase like this. Loaned it to me and the Missus to go on our honeymoon."

I looked at the relic of a man. I had a hard time imagining a younger Pennywood walking down the aisle to a waiting bride, let alone him in a honeymoon bed.

"Do you think you can get them open?"

"Been a locksmith for some sixty years, little lady, don't you worry. The older the locks, the less complex." He opened the metal box he had carried in with him and grabbed a huge ring of keys, thumbing through them one by one, until he had inspected around a dozen.

"Eureka," he said, holding up a long key with a metal square tab at the end. "Good old skeleton key usually does the trick."

Max and I were wary of allowing Pennywood to see all of the suitcases. We definitely didn't want to ask him to open more than three cases. The country-bred man surely would question why we had more than three suitcases if we reveal all of them. Most folks around here, especially the older generation, didn't travel so they had no need for luggage; one or two to a whole family was standard.

When Pennywood unlocked the last suitcase, he started to pull the top open. I stepped in quickly and pushed the lid down. "Thank you. We don't want to take up any more of your time. How much do I owe you?"

He pushed himself up from the floor, letting out some groans on the way up. Then taking out a raggedy handkerchief from his pocket, he wiped his face. "Got plenty of time on my hands, no need for locksmiths around here much. Can't rightly charge you for unlocking something with a key."

"But I want to thank you for your help; you should be paid for your time. Maybe I can buy one of those skeleton keys from you."

The air grew still. He narrowed his eyes at me and asked why I would need a key. He had unlocked the suitcases.

"I figured it would be good to have—handy. You know, in case of any future lock problems."

I explained that getting the old family cases had piqued my interest and perhaps I could find things people were getting rid of that were locked in boxes or suitcases. I could inquire about the countryside and it would be like a treasure hunt. It sounded like a reasonable excuse to me and we most certainly couldn't drag out all twenty-eight suitcases for him to unlock.

Max turned toward the old man and whispered that I lived in Florida as the reason for my strange way of thinking. It seemed to appease him and he slipped a skeleton key off from the large ring, I paid him and Mr.

Pennywood left, mumbling to himself about crazy Florida people.

In the guest room where Max and I had quickly piled the suitcases the night before, we started to search through the disorganized mess. Reading the tags of the remaining suitcases for Hanna Brewer's name, however, after about five minutes we hadn't found it. All of a sudden, from across the room Max yelled, "Got it!"

My heart pumped hard as I followed behind Max as he dragged the suitcase out into the sunlit living room. My hands were shaking too much to work the key so Max took over. His big, bulky hands worked the lock, and with a gentle twisting motion, the key turned, unlocking Hanna's suitcase.

Max stood back and said, "Stephanie, you should be the first to see what's in this." With excitement and a bit of trepidation, I pushed open the top. Inside were three white blouses with lace around the edge of the collars. They were discolored by age. Four dark navy skirts and some personal items like slips and panties and a beautifully tooled silver hairbrush. I carefully lifted the clothing out to take a deeper look inside.

Max watched in silent reverence as I handed him the other items to free my hands, I noticed there were a pair of delicately knitted pink baby booties. As I lifted them to investigate, I saw that beneath them sat something wrapped in tissue paper. Inside was another soft yellow knitted item. The color hadn't aged but appeared deep and brilliant like the sun on a summer day. The wrapping must have protected it and kept the original color intact. I held it up so the folds fell free, revealing a beautifully knitted women's shawl with delicate seed pearls sewn around the edge. A note tucked in the shawl floated into my lap. I opened the folded paper and recognized Hanna's handwriting immediately. It read:

My dearest husband,

If this letter reaches you that will mean I never returned home and the hospital staff has returned my belongings to you since I have gone home to my Lord.

Please give the shawl to Mabel, tell her that I always loved her and that I had yearned to come home to you both.

It has been a year since the last letter from you. You had written that Mabel went to her first dance. I knitted this shawl in hopes that she could wear it. However, there will be many dances in our daughter's future. You must allow her the freedom a young woman needs. You wrote of your worry and suspicions that Mabel was secretly meeting a young man. My dearest husband, please don't follow the strict footsteps of our parents with Mabel. It will only cause her to keep more secrets and pull away from you. You must trust her. She has a good father, who is a loving man, to set an example and guide her when choosing the man she will love and share her life with. She will choose wisely.

For me, I feel that my mind is cured and I am strong again. My dark moments have gone. I no longer hear the voices. Please rest your mind from worry; I know my sickness does not run in my blood. My recovery and wellness proves this. Mabel is strong and well. Trust me when I say that you have raised our daughter well and she is safe from madness.

You have been a good husband. I know of your love and devotion to me. There must be a good reason for your long stay away from me. I have learned that our letters have been intercepted by the staff here. They think I do not know about letters not getting delivered. For that reason, my darling husband, I am hiding this last letter to you in the shawl for Mabel. They allowed me to go to the shed to pack the shawl with my other belongings.

There are some good nurses here but bad things are happening without their knowledge. The doctors allow trustee patients to guard the rest of us. Unbeknownst to the doctors, the trustees pleasure in tormenting the patients they are in charge of. The trustees laugh and tell me that you have disowned me and that you have stopped coming because the shame of my illness is too great for you. I don't believe their lies.

I hear news about home from a patient here. She is from Havenridge and she shares things from back home. Her name is Frances Swain, you know her husband, Elmer. He committed her because she spoke against him. The night they came for her. Elmer got drunk and grew into a rage. He confessed that he had arranged for her to be institutionalized. He said that he hoped she would die there just like Cain Brewer's wife did. Frances argued and said that I died of consumption and he laughed. He claimed that was a false story but that I had died after living many years in an asylum, the same one she was being committed to. I wonder now if you think that I am dead and this is why you stopped coming. The night they came for Frances, she saw Elmer pay the men money. She suspects he pays the doctors to keep her locked up here.

Frances had not been ill like I was. I know now that you sent me here hoping I would get better and not to lock me away from you and Mabel. One of the guards says no one ever leaves here. I know now this might be true.

There is another patient, a German-speaking man, who digs the graves. The guard says a grave digger costs a lot of money and the German man's labor is free as a patient. They will never let him go. I write to you about these things not to haunt you but so you will understand that you are not to blame for what has happened to me. I am at peace knowing the truth and that your love never wavered. I have Frances to talk to about our daughter. She says she has grown into a beautiful, young woman.

It did weigh heavy on me that Mabel believed that I died when she was a baby. I hope you find a way to tell her about me someday. Let her know she has nothing to fear about my illness coming to her. The doctors were wrong when they said I had bad blood. Mabel is safe and can know the truth.

Frances also spoke about Mabel and a man named Jacob. What you suspected is right about Mabel sneaking off to meet this drifter. Frances' son Clarence claims he has followed Mabel when she goes to meet a lover at Blue Lake. The rumors are true. Frances said that you watched our daughter more and more closely as your suspicions grew. Your actions remind Frances and me of how our parents tried to keep us apart.

Do not fear, I think this someone will be right for our Mabel and has good intentions. One day, Frances overheard the drifter named Jacob telling a shopkeeper in town that he needed supplies because he was leaving to seek work on the docks in New Orleans. However, he declared he planned to return.

The only reason for a drifter to pull up stakes and seek different work is if he needs a larger amount of money because he has plans for the future with a woman. For this reason I am confident Jacob will return with money to ask for Mabel's hand. When that time comes, find in your heart a way to accept him. If I am right, Mabel will need your love, and if I am wrong and Jacob does not return, then Mabel will need the comfort of her father.

Your loving wife always,
Hanna

"Max, this is it. Hanna *did* know about Jacob. I've found what I was looking for—Jacob went to New Orleans. Hanna was lucid. She didn't need to die in that horrible place. We may never know what terrible things happened to those patients but this was during the time Sadie talks about the Lost Fifty. This confirms they did exist and Hanna must have been one of them."

"That's great, Stephanie," Max said. "What happens next?"

"For now, I must find out what happened to Jacob and follow his trail to New Orleans. But I'm not going to close my eyes to the patients who experienced the cruelty that Hanna did. When I get back, I'll find out who the rest of those suitcases belonged to and get some answers about the Lost Fifty.

I looked inside Hanna's suitcase. One item remained—a leather journal similar to the old journal I had found from Cain Brewer in the wall back home in the old Brewer house.

"Max, I'm going to take Peggy's offer to leave the suitcases here for a few weeks."

A squeak from the screen door opening interrupted us. We turned to see Peggy entering. "I had to come home from work for an early lunch to see if the locksmith got the suitcases opened."

She stopped dead in her tracks. "Well, Hell's bells! You got them opened! Glory be."

Returning Home

I told Peggy that I needed to get back to Havenridge. It had been three days. Betsy had to open and close the store by herself and I felt I had abused her good-hearted nature for too long. After all, we were partners and shared the load of our shop equally. Peggy said Betsy sounded like a wonderful person and she hoped to meet her someday.

I decided to take Hanna's journal home with me, that way Betsy and I could go through it together. After I shared this information with Peggy, she called her work. She said that she wouldn't be coming back in today, something had come up.

Peggy told me it worried her about me driving home on the deserted country road between Milledgeville and Havenridge because of what had happened in Harwine. Max was concerned, too. We talked about possible options to ensure my safety. Max and Peggy came up with a plan, in case someone from Harwine had been waiting around until I was alone to start trouble. I had to admit that the road between Milledgeville and Havenridge would be a perfect place for trouble.

Peggy's plan was ingenious. She insisted I wait while she wrapped Hanna's journal in an old pillowcase and put it in the bottom of a brown grocery bag. Then she placed some daffodil bulbs she had dug up to dry and rest before next year's fall planting. She had stored the dirty mess in a brown paper bag and placed them in her garage. After retrieving them, she placed a few bulbs in another small bag, which fit nicely inside and on top of a half dozen gardening magazines. Then topped everything with a few of her hand-sewn potholders, three red-and-white checkered ones, one blue, and two cheery yellow ones and on the very top she added a bag lunch with two sandwiches for the road. That way if someone from Harwine did stop me on the road and searched the car, they probably would give up thumbing down through bag after bag before getting to the journal at the very bottom.

"Anyone looking in the bag will think it's just gifts from a friend you hadn't seen for a few years," Peggy said. "Georgia women don't let a guest go home hungry or empty-handed."

"I'll come back soon," I told Peggy. As I hugged her goodbye, Max put the bag in the back seat on the floor. "I'll let you know what we find out from Betsy's friend as soon as I hear something."

I felt as if I were a spy going through enemy lines, transporting top-secret papers. Max repeated his warnings that Harwine people were dangerous and that this was no game, and told me to be careful.

"I'll be careful," I promised. "Thank you. You've been wonderful; the both of you. I cannot help feeling bad for poor John Fleming. The fear in his eyes when I left him was so obvious. He's terrified of his stepson. I hope he doesn't suffer from our actions."

"Some people are bad clean through," Peggy said. "That Reed man is no good."

"I suspect John Fleming has been suffering from Reed's intimidation for some time now, long before we showed up," Max said. "Stephanie, you need to worry about yourself. Keep your eyes open on the drive home. Reed will fight back with force, if not on your drive back then sometime later. Violence is how Harwine people handle things."

"Well, I'm not a frail old man. Reed may not know it yet, but I'm a fighter. His intimidation won't work on me. If he wants a fight, he'll have one."

"Okay, but not on a country road," Max said sternly. "A right time to fight him will come and I guarantee that there will be a way to get the rest of those suitcases."

"I hope so."

I had been driving for about thirty minutes and had seen neither a car nor a truck for quite some time. I don't know which of my feelings were greater, my excitement that I knew where Jacob had gone, or the optimism I felt that I'd finally get the answers in New Orleans.

But there are still the suitcases. I must not forget about them. The people who owned those suitcases weren't heard in life, but their lives will be acknowledged and valued now.

I glanced in my rearview mirror. There was something on the road behind me, a dot on the horizon—too small to be a car. It appeared to be advancing with great speed. Seconds passed and it became clear that it was a motorcycle. Far behind me, too far to actually hear the motor, but there it was, and it was rapidly approaching. It seemed to come out of nowhere.

I watched in the rearview mirror and realized there were two motorcycles. The whole thing was strangely eerie. Max's warnings about Harwine people echoed in my mind. And then my skin went cold as I remembered something he said the night before: "Most often, you won't even see it coming. Backwoods folks have a way of sneaking up on you."

You won't see it coming. My mind raced and my throat tightened. Max's words echoed, *You won't see it coming.* I gripped the steering wheel tight. A planned ambush. I wondered if one got in front of me and one in back, what I would do.

It was just what Peggy had been worried about. A deserted country highway, a woman alone, unprotected. I heard the motorcycles' roar coming in range, a low growl building stronger and menacing—louder with every second. They were coming fast, so fast I was afraid they would crash into me as I watched them in my mirror.

Close enough now that I could see the dark clothing they wore and their helmets, with full face shields that were tinted an opaque onyx, making it impossible to see the faces of the drivers.

Max was right. Reed's power and influence does reach far from Harwine.

I sped up and glanced at the road, but kept my eyes fixed on my rearview mirror. The motorcycles swerved recklessly about the road behind me. Thoughts crept into my mind. A man like Reed relies on others to do his dirty work. It isn't Reed I need to be wary of—*Harwine people take care of each other.*

The distance between my car and the motorcycles shortened, making the black-clothed thugs so close to my bumper that I was afraid they would ram into me and crash. The roar of their engines seeped through my car's window, like a poisonous gas seeping in through the crack I left open for fresh air ventilation.

The road ahead curved to the right, so I smashed down on the accelerator and took the curve so fast that I almost lost control of my car. I straightened out and kept from skidding out of control, and quickly looked into the mirror. It seemed I had left the motorcycle-riding devils behind in my dust. Relieved and feeling a bit victorious, I still knew it was crucial I get home as fast as possible. At home, everything would be okay again.

I had just relaxed my grip and was working on slowing my breathing down when . . .

Brr . . . ummm.

Please, no. Not again.

One glance in my mirror confirmed my fear. They were back and closing in on me at an extreme rate of speed. The two-wheeled followers barreled around the bend; advancing so swiftly that I thought they might go airborne. In seconds, they were on top of my bumper again. There were no side roads to pull off onto, and the sandy terrain on either side of the road made it impossible to pull over and stop. One cyclist, riding a black motorcycle with yellow painted flames on the tank, pulled out ahead. He rode next to my car for a minute or more, and then the driver lifted the wheel in the air and vaulted forward. The second motorcycle, which was solid black, stayed behind me so close that I could not see any road between me and his vehicle in the rearview mirror.

I was boxed in. I had no choice but to wait for their next move.

Suddenly the motorcycle at my rear bumper darted out and moved to the side of my car. He turned his head, peering in at me from behind his protective armor of black. Then he sped up, joining his riding partner, and both disappeared up the road as fast as they had come.

I loosened my grip on the steering wheel again. Every muscle in my body was tight and ached. My heart was thumping so hard my chest hurt. I took a deep, calming breath. *I'm getting paranoid. Motorcycle people ride the open country road so they can speed. They weren't after me, they were just hot-dogging on their bikes.*

Forty minutes more and I would be in Havenridge. This trip really was triggering my imagination. Let's face it, I wasn't a spy on a mission. I wasn't even a good amateur sleuth. I wouldn't have found out anything if it hadn't been for all the people who had helped me along the way.

I truly was looking forward to getting back home to the boring, sleepy town of Havenridge.

Home Safe Home, or Not

After the motorcycle incident, the remainder of my drive was rather uneventful. Agent Stephanie Oliver and her secret package of daffodil bulbs would make it safely to Havenridge. *Talk about having an overactive imagination!*

The two motorcyclists must've been freaked out by my erratic driving. They probably sped up in order to pass me and put as much highway between them and *the crazy, racecar-driving lady.*

There were no hitmen out to get me. Although Phillip Andrew Reed no doubt would've delighted in that concept. This wasn't a movie. The only danger for me on the road was in my imagination.

What president was it who said, *the only fear is fear?* or was it, *we fear ourselves?* I think it was Roosevelt—yeah, him. The one that was in the wheelchair.

My mind wandered, battering around images of motorcycles, Evel Knievel, and Steve McQueen's cycle jumping the fence in the movie, *The Great Escape.* Until I noticed, my speedometer had climbed. I needed to concentrate on my speed. The last thing I wanted was a speeding ticket to end the day.

Time to focus. *Take slow, easy, cleansing breaths, Stephanie.* I took in a slow breath, paused, and let it out like the movie stars showed on television when they talked about Transcendental Meditation. TM for short.

It worked! After taking ten breaths, my nerves seemed back to normal. Or maybe it was that I was nearing home and the serenity of Havenridge. I passed the sign saying I was entering my county. In less than five minutes I'd pass by my house and in another twenty I'd be at the store but my eyes were growing heavy. I blinked a few times but the road blurred. My plan was to go straight into town to relieve Betsy at the store, but my head jerked forward, jarring me. I blinked several times and opened my eyes wide.

Wake up, I silently commanded myself. Seconds later, my head jerked again. I couldn't keep from nodding off.

Man, I can't stay awake. The last few days apparently had taken its toll on me. I saw my house ahead and decided to stop and splash some cool water on my face before driving further. I'd unload the car, wake myself up, and call Betsy to tell her that I was on my way.

Once inside my front door, I set down my overnight bags and the brown paper grocery bag with the daffodil bulbs disguising the rest of the contents. I made a quick bathroom stop and returned downstairs, and picked up the phone to dial the store.

Betsy answered on the first ring. "Good afternoon, Stephanie and Betsy's Gathering Spot."

"Betsy, I'm in Havenridge but I needed to stop at my house first. I'll be there in twenty minutes so you can go home."

"You don't need to come in. You're probably tired from the last three days. I'll close up tonight, and tomorrow I'll take the whole day off."

"But you've opened and closed for two days straight," I weakly said. "You must miss seeing Joe. I'll come in."

"It's okay, Joe said this morning that he'd double-up his work today so he can stay home tomorrow the whole day with me. He'll be all mine . . . just after he feeds the chickens, of course. Farmers never truly have days off."

"Are you sure?" I asked.

"Yes. I'm looking forward to a whole day off with Joe. How did it go with the locksmith?" Betsy asked. "Did he get the suitcases opened?"

"Yes. I've got lots to tell you. We now have evidence that Hanna transferred from the mental hospital in Milledgeville to Harwine."

"Then the trip was worth your time?"

"Definitely, and like I told you the other day on the phone, I couldn't have done it without Peggy and Max's help. But there's more. In Hanna's suitcase, there was a journal of hers. I brought it home with me."

I heard a familiar *yoo-hoo* in the background. "Is that Gladys?" I asked. "It's not church-shopping day."

"Yes, it's her. And no, it's not church shopping day," Betsy whispered into the phone. "She got wind that you went out of town and *Miss Snoopy-nose* is dying of curiosity. She's been in every day since you left, using lame excuses for stopping by to quiz me, hoping for some new gossip." There was a pause and I heard Betsy call out, "Hello, Miss Gladys."

Betsy lowered her voice again. "Stephanie, I have to go. If she hears you're on the phone, she'll grab the receiver and start drilling you for information."

Betsy hung up in the middle of my goodbye. *Poor Betsy. But I am glad it's her dealing with Gladys and not me.*

Now that I didn't need to go to the store, exhaustion took over me. I couldn't keep my eyes open any longer. Even though it was still light out, I decided I'd go upstairs and lie down for a few minutes.

When I woke, what I had planned on being a thirty-minute nap had turned out to be much more. Outside the sky was an indigo blue color, with several stars piercing through. I stumbled to get up and felt around for the table lamp next to the bed, found the switch, and turned it on.

"Man, I wonder how long I slept," I mumbled to myself.

The long and taxing drive left me with a sticky, dusty feeling. A leisurely bubble bath would wash away the day and any residue of stress, so I went to run the bathwater. While the tub filled, I undressed and grabbed a towel and wrapped it around myself.

As I pulled out my favorite nightgown from my dresser drawer, I noticed through the open drapes a flickering light off in the distance. It looked like it probably was on the other side of Blue Lake, off the highway, which I had taken to come home. Why I had never realized that the same highway I used to go to Milledgeville was the same that the Boy Scouts did their roadside cleanup, I don't know. Nevertheless, it took Rick Strafford's visit the other day for me to realize it. Who knows if I would've ever put two and two together if he hadn't stopped by to ask me to call if I saw any campfires.

I looked out the window to the familiar surroundings. Leave it to Havenridgers to expect to keep a beautiful lake all to themselves. Apparently, keeping the state highway and its right-of-way clean and the town's grip on having Blue Lake exclusive to them, had been a rising problem. And the people in town, of course, expected the deputy to do their dirty work by pulling good people out of tents in the middle of the night and ordering them to pack up and move on. I nudged closer to the window for a better look.

Poor Rick. Trying to appease everyone in town is impossible. But he tries so hard to keep from overstepping his authority. I wondered if building a campfire really could be illegal.

I stared out of the window. The flickering light sure looked like a campfire. I tossed the idea around about calling the deputy and then I glanced at the clock. It glowed nine-thirty. A call would probably be useless because by the time he could get out there; the would-be campers probably would've dowsed the fire out and gone to sleep.

Better to let sleeping dogs lie. I'm the only one that can see it, anyway. I pulled the drapes closed, went to take my bath, and hoped that the campers didn't burn the woods down. If the woods did burn, I'd have the wrath of Gladys to answer to if it got out that I saw a campfire and didn't call in the cavalry.

After indulging in an hour-long bath, I slipped on my nightgown and went back downstairs to fix a late-night dinner. A half-hour later, my empty plate sat on the coffee table as I pulled my legs up to settle back on the couch with Hanna's journal to read. That's when I heard a creak outside on my front porch. I stopped and listened. There was another, louder noise. Someone was out there. I jumped when the knock on the door came.

"Who's there," I yelled.

"It's Betsy."

Whew. I let out a heavy sigh. "Coming,"

When Betsy came in she looked at me, frowning. "What's the matter? Why'd you snap at me like that?"

"Sorry, you just startled me. How come you're here?"

"I couldn't wait until tomorrow. I'm just dying to know what's in the journal you brought back," Betsy said.

"Give me all the details of your trip, don't leave out anything. I had to stop on the way home from the store, besides there's no need to rush home since Joe will already be in bed." She chuckled. "I've already heard Joe's snoring, it's not that exciting."

Not Crazy

Betsy left close to 1 a.m. Once I locked the door after her, I took a seat on the couch to read more of Hanna's journal. The next thing I knew, I woke up with a stiff neck caused by my scrunched up position on the couch. I lifted my head from the arm and found the journal resting between my knees. I had pulled up my legs close to my body and rested the journal there for reading. My watch sat on the coffee table where I placed it after taking it off.

Eight fifteen! Late as usual. The excuse for my tardiness was reasonable; I hadn't been able to stop reading.

Poor Hanna. The last five pages of the journal answered all the questions Betsy and I ever had about Hanna and Cain Brewer. The era they had lived in, and the attitudes toward mental illness and how to treat it allowed their tragic story to unfold. Hanna and Cain had fallen victim to her mental breakdown and Cain's fears sealed their fate. Added to the toxic mix were the unethical doctors who saw an opportunity to pilfer Cain's money and preyed on his and Hanna's helplessness. They hadn't stood a chance for a normal life.

Ironically, the story that the Havenridge community believed about Hanna taking ill from complications of childbirth and dying turned out to be somewhat true. However, her death came years, not months, later. The complication had been a mental breakdown, a little more serious condition of what older generations called the "Baby Blues." Cain tried to nurse her back to health at

154

first while keeping her mental situation a secret with the neighbors. Conversely, she worsened, downward-spiraling to the darkest and most severe condition. Hanna's deep depression continued and ultimately Cain realized he was not equipped to handle caring for her alone. Institutionalizing Hanna seemed his only hope. He tried to take care of the household chores while tending to a newborn baby and working to earn money to feed his family and pay doctor bills. He did the best he could.

Hanna's journal divulged evidence that she eventually pulled out of what she wrote was *her long journey to Hell and back*. She wrote that she had been crazy for years; actually her exact words were *completely mad*. This explained the letters sent to Cain. Her irrational and bizarre writings, mixed with other, normal, letters. All written in the same hand but not composed by the same mind.

Those letters sent to Hanna's husband spanned her one-year journey but then they had abruptly stopped. Letters that Cain kept (the ones written by a madwoman and yet others written by a loving wife) all tied together with string and safely hidden in the wall of my home where Cain had placed them before his death.

The letters by crazy Hanna had me believing that she had been insane. I shivered remembering Hanna's letter to Cain about the mouse that would come through the stone walls at night to warn her of her husband's plan to kill her. The mouse was a witness that Cain would sneak into where Hanna slept to slip poison into her food. The paranoia had gone on for pages.

How awful it must have been for Cain. His last few contacts with his wife were those awful letters. No one could blame him for believing Hanna was insane.

Through the grace of God, Hanna recovered and remembered it all. All the insane moments and the accusations she made against Cain gave her strength to persevere and write the truth in her journal for Cain to have later. But she didn't stop only with her story. She investigated the stories of other patients, their wild allegations. She understood what it was like to not be heard when people thought you were mad. She found the truth and documented it. She was not the only sane patient locked away in the asylum. The stories about what went on inside Harwine were accurate.

Of course, there must have been ill patients there. However, once Hanna could think straight, she wrote about the treatments and the conditions there. It was all documented in her journal. The insane world of ice water baths, electric shock treatments, leg chains, and iron locks on the doors for those who argued about their sanity. A wide-awake nightmare located in a snake pit world of what asylums were like at the turn of the century.

Hanna wrote about her demanding the staff to release her to go home. Her handwriting was flowing but not graceful in those entries, and she apologized for the untidiness of her script. The reason for her shaky hand was that her unbending proclamations of her good health had resulted in additional "therapy treatments."

It was somewhere around those entries that she noted that she had realized that the people who were in charge of keeping the patients under control were patients themselves. It was indeed common practice to entrust keys (of the inside doors) to the more manageable patients. A practice widely used back then that created new and different problems. Experiencing and observing how these trustees treated those who spoke out, Hanna wrote that she decided she must gain the trust of the doctors so she might convince them that patients should not be shackled like wild animals. Still, some passive patients were not chained but allowed to work in what was called the safe areas where the doctors and nurses walked about freely. Hanna commented that rebelling was not an answer; she needed to work in that area of the hospital where the sane worked and the windows didn't have bars.

She documented that she became a model patient and had been assigned to work in the hospital offices. She eventually had been trusted with keys to the head doctor's office door and the file room. One day she noticed a stack of boxes in the corner of the file room. Her supervisor told her they were waiting for pick-up to go to a storage building. Once alone, she found the courage to examine the contents and look inside one of the boxes. It contained files of deceased patient records. Thumbing through tabs on the folders, she recognized the German name of the man who dug the graves. She wrote about not understanding why the doctors would have packed his file away as deceased. He hadn't died! Nor had he been released. Hanna thumbed through more folders, reading more names of living patients, and then she found a file with her name on it.

The file contained doctors' notes, her shock treatments, everything, all the truth about her stay there. One of those boxes waiting for storage contained financial logs. An expense log recorded the medical bills submitted to the state with reimbursement forms filed for the medicine. There were records of paid salaries of maintenance personnel who didn't exist for doing jobs like digging graves, which the German patient did regularly without pay. Another set of logs for income showed checks received from families of the patients. The deception was easier with the group of patients that had been transferred from Milledgeville since they had no family on the outside asking about their recovery or return home. Being well enough to work committed the patients who should have been released, committed for the rest of their lives. Using patients' free labor for the hospital saved hundreds of dollars a year.

Hanna was the only patient from that group who had any connection to the outside world. Hanna noted that one year checks from Cain were logged in to her account. Then she said that she found a letter from Cain saying; *I will be stopping my monthly checks and will take care of my wife myself. I cannot live any longer without her. I will come for my dear Hanna by the end of the month.*

The hospital would no longer receive Cain's money and he more than likely would believe his wife when she spoke about abuse at the hospital. How the hospital would handle this problem with Cain was answered in the next entry.

The next paper Hanna found was more horrific than anything she had seen. It was a condolence letter to Cain about his wife's sudden death, followed by Hanna's death certificate! This explained why Cain's letters had stopped coming to her.

Hanna's journal documented everything. The well patients who came from Milledgeville were valuable assets for the hospital. Releasing them had never been an option. After finding her file and death certificate, Hanna entered in her journal that she knew she would never be released.

She had to be very careful documenting the abuse and violence inside the asylum's walls. Her very life depended on it. The hospital had nothing to lose if she died, except for the work she performed. After all, they already had her death certificate.

On the second to the last page of the journal Hanna explained her plan. She had to safeguard the journal so Cain could receive it later. She decided that she would enlist the help of a nurse who had befriended her after she started working in the office. Hanna asked the nurse to take the journal and pack it away for her. She had no choice but to trust that she wouldn't read it. "I don't need it now," Hanna told the nurse. "It's only the writings of a crazed woman who used to talk to a mouse. I want to pack it away in the suitcase that I brought when I was sick."

"Please don't read it," Hanna had begged. "I'm embarrassed about the things inside. I wasn't in my right mind then. If I get well enough to go home one day, it will remind me that I must always trust what my doctors tell me."

Hanna didn't get home nor did her journal make it to Cain. Everything made sense to me now. All the dots were connected, except for Mabel and Jacob.

The entry that weighed heaviest in my heart was when Hanna's breakdown started. The entry documented Mabel's birth. The same night Mabel took her first breath; her twin brother exhaled his last breath, cradled in Hanna's arms.

JOURNAL ENTRY:

I'm a mother of two babies. Blessings from God. My son I had for less than five minutes until he was taken from me. My daughter was taken, too, and kept from me for years. I write down my memories of the night for my loving husband. The night I held my babies, and then, went mad.

"You have a baby girl!" my midwife said. She placed my beautiful Mabel in my arms. Moments later, the pain came again. This time it was almost unbearable. I remember screaming and asking what was happening. The midwife snatched Mabel away from me and called for my husband.

"Take her away," she yelled, pushing my baby into his arms.

Cain stood, looking uncertain.

"Now! Take her, take the baby away!" she shouted at him.

The pain felt like my body was tearing apart.

"There's another baby coming," she said.

Moments later, I saw my son. His skin was blue, not pink like Mabel's. A scream forced past my lips as I was blinded with more pain . . . then blackness fell over me.

When I woke, I saw the midwife holding the baby upside down. "Breathe." The baby made no sound. Slap . . . slap. . . . "Breathe."

My mind blurred with the scene in front of me. Then I heard the cry. Low, small puffs of cries. Weak, very weak, cries.

"It's a boy," the midwife said, turning to me.

She placed my son in my arms. I looked down at my dear Nathanael.

"Say your goodbyes to him before he dies. The priest won't get here in time to bless him. The Devil will come first and take the baby's soul."

I shivered and felt the same sadness that I'd felt last night when I read Hanna's account of that dreadful night. I couldn't stop thinking about it. Hanna suffered not from "baby blues" but from post-traumatic stress, just like the soldiers who suffer after horrific battles, from the death of her newborn baby.

Hanna wrote that Cain came in and took his son's lifeless body to go and bury him as ordered by the midwife. Hanna wrote that she believed the Devil walked beside Cain, whispering in his ear. A hallucination from the trauma.

My heart ached for Hanna . . . and Cain. *It could easily have been me. Not so long ago, I felt like I was going crazy. After my Lily died.*

Hanna's pain from the grief of losing her son was beyond her limits. The darkness I had felt after Lily's death had almost broken me. The difference was my journey to Hell didn't have unethical and greedy doctors waiting on the dark side.

I had teetered, holding onto life, and cursed the insanity of grief that beckoned me. Purchasing the old Brewer house and finding Cain's journal had been the lifeline I needed to grab hold of and pull my way out of the darkness. My connection to Mabel and Jacob, and Cain and Hanna became stronger than ever.

I went upstairs, once dressed, I pinned my hair up in a makeshift bun since I neither had the time nor the patience to curl it. Then I pushed my feet into my shoes and headed downstairs.

I couldn't comfort Hanna now but I could give her journal the respect it deserved and not leave it carelessly on a coffee table. I picked up the journal, grabbed my keys, and paused at the front door, glancing back. The Brewer home had held both happiness and misery inside its walls. It was time to correct history. *To hide the truth can only do harm.*

Game Plans

Driving to the store, I couldn't get the journal out of my mind. My commitment to rectifying the wrong inflicted so many years back on the Lost Fifty was not wrong, but I had lost too much valuable time in the pursuit of Jacob. Although Phillip Andrew Reed's name was on a long list of people who were instrumental in the abuse at the asylum in Harwine—now deceptively called a boarding house—bringing him to justice would have to wait for a little bit.

My publisher had been relentless in hammering me for the first draft of my story of Mabel and Jacob. I couldn't stall them or my agent much longer. Hopefully, the historical society would be able to find some legal ground to seize the suitcases in Harwine, and I will be able to pass the gauntlet to them to ensure the voices of the Lost Fifty will be heard.

For now, all I knew was that Hanna's journal gave me the direction of where to go next for the answers about Jacob—New Orleans. Thank goodness there were only a few asylums near Havenridge for husbands to send their wives and Frances Swain was sent to the one Hanna had been committed. If she had not shared information about Jacob and Mabel to Hanna, I would've hit another dead end.

I turned my car down Main Street and passed by Gladys hurrying down the sidewalk in her usually determined fashion. I waved and turned to go behind the building just as I noticed two out of place, dark motorcycles parked at the curb in front of the barbershop.

"Well, I guess they didn't burn down the woods around Blue Lake."

EARLIER THAT SAME MORNING-
MILLEDGEVILLE, MAGNOLIA BREEZES NURSING HOME

Sadie slipped on the navy blue blouse. It was one of her favorites because of the pearl buttons. She paused to think about her visitor from the other day.

I don't think Stephanie Oliver believed me about Hanna being in the Harwine asylum. Sure, she listened politely, but that's what people do now.

Sadie's trembling fingers struggled with the pearl buttons on her blouse. *I'll never get used to being seen as an old lady! They look at me with skeptical eyes when I talk. Like I can't distinguish between reality and fantasy.*

The horrible part was that she knew exactly what would happen. It was already starting to happen, the memory loss and the confusion. The lines of reality blurring.

It would start sporadically at first. She'd not know if she needed to go to the hospital for her nursing shift, or was she retired and living at Magnolia Breezes Nursing Home? Slowly, yes that was how most of her elderly patients experienced it. More often their mind, and now hers, would ever so gently slip into the past for brief moments and stay a bit longer each time. It was as if who she was, who she had been, was disappearing like a flickering candle. Soon her light would burn out.

Not today, I'm not burning out today! I know who I am. I've got my mind back for a reason—to finish what I started years ago. Today, I'm getting ready to talk to my daughter Peggy. She'll help me. I'm a nurse. As long as I have my mind I can keep the oath I took.

Sadie had her crisp thinking and logical mind still. For how long, she didn't know. She realized that for whatever reason, her disease had stopped advancing. The strangest thing was her mind seemed to be sharper than before the onset of her dementia. There was no time to waste.

Sadie picked up the hairbrush and pushed the bristles through her silver hair as she thought about the patients from her nursing career who suffered from dementia and Alzheimer's. She understood now why they acted so unruly when she tried to calm and hush them. The staff at Magnolia Breezes now dismissed her when she was outspoken, the same way she had done for her patients. She hated being a failing old lady who was ignored. Her anger mounted; however, her irritation deflated, replaced by unsettling frustration.

Alone in her room, she looked into the mirror at her unfamiliar image and mumbled, "But the symptoms of my illness have stalled out."

She shook her head to cast out her doubts as her mind traveled back to her last battle to halt the abuse in the Harwine asylum so many years ago. *I've dealt with Phillip Andrew Reed; that sweet Stephanie has no idea what's ahead of her. She not equipped to fight him.*

She felt a connection with Stephanie. Sadie's younger self had been just like Stephanie Oliver who had come to visit her. They had a lot in common. They were both idealistic and believed in justice.

"Justice is only served in the movies." Sadie's agitated voice bellowed. "In the real world cheaters win, unless you can fight dirty," Sadie said, defying the ghosts of her past who'd come forward to argue with her. Looking into the mirror with determination, she smoothed her hair and straightened her collar. "I may have turned old but I have years of experience on my side."

She knew that telling the doctors about her remission would be useless. They wouldn't listen. Tests or lab reports were the only things doctors paid attention to and dementia remissions didn't show up on lab reports. Even nurses were leery of patients' recovery testimonials. After all, how many times had one of Sadie's patients claimed, in a clear and steadfast voice, that they were "of their right mind" only to go on to warn her of a little green man standing next to her? Yes, Sadie learned quickly not to blindly believe a patient. She was banking on Peggy to believe in her words now.

Sadie looked around the room. "Now, what was it I needed to get for Peggy?" she said with one hand covering her mouth as her brow furrowed. Fear flooded in. She had to fight the disease for just a little longer. Long enough to carry out her plan.

"The plan! That's it! I need to get the doll ready for Peggy."

Target, Jacob, and New Orleans

Before unlocking the front door to open up for business, I scanned the store for a secure hiding place for Hanna's journal. *Well, Stephanie Oliver, you have now joined the ranks of true Havenridgers.* I held back a laugh and mumbled, "Now I'm looking for a hiding place to stash Hanna's journal."

Paranoia aside, I had a nagging feeling that my home wasn't a safe place since Reed and his goons knew me, and finding out my physical address probably wouldn't be that hard. A small country store was not usually a target for a robbery and Havenridge certainly was not a hot seat of crime. The store would work nicely as a hiding place.

After Reed's threat, I feared that my obsession for securing a safe haven for Hanna's journal might be well warranted. Standing my ground with a backbone of steel against Reed, like a true super sleuth, had been only a good illusion. I still shook inside like a scared little child whenever I thought about that day in Harwine. I marveled at Sadie's strength to single-handedly take on Reed years ago.

Where can I hide this that no one will stumble over it? I worried that Reed could have a legal claim to Hanna's journal, as bizarre as that sounded. Over the last few years, I had seen strange things happen and the strangest always seemed to be connected to the law. If asked to produce the journal, I would just claim that I threw it away after reading it. Hanna's journal wasn't going back into his hands if I could help it.

A children's party game, in which partygoers would hide something out in plain sight, came into my mind. It was crazy but even if it lay on a table, clearly visible, everyone would walk past the "hidden" object, not seeing it.

That's when I thought, *under the phone book, behind the counter. Not exactly in plain sight, but who would search under the phone book?* Besides, Betsy and I were the only ones that went behind the counter to the register and if anyone ventured back there Betsy would protect the journal's whereabouts with her life. I placed the trusted journal in the hiding place—safe and sound—then opened the store.

When I pulled the *tea-of-the-week* sandwich sign out to the sidewalk, I spotted Gladys crossing the street and heading toward me. I averted my eyes and hurried inside.

Fifteen minutes and twenty questions later, the phone interrupted us. It was Betsy's friend connected with the Historical Society.

I cupped my hand over the phone's receiver I said, "Miss Gladys, I'm sorry but I have to take this. Business, you know."

Gladys waved a handkerchief at me, accepting my excuse, and left.

Thank goodness.

"I'm so glad you called. Can you help get the rest of the suitcases?" I asked with every hope resting on her answer, but my expectations were quickly shattered.

"Harwine Boarding House is privately owned and located on private property," she explained. "When we get involved in any restoration or a historical find of sorts, it's always been by the owner's request."

She went on saying that she would love to get her hands on the suitcases but there was no legal avenue to pursue. She said in a deep southern drawl, "Even if we knew there was a suitcase with belongings of our brave General Ulysses S. Grant in it, we couldn't legally seize it. Not on private property. I'm sorry, Miss Oliver. I wish I could help you. The only way for anyone to gain access to private property without permission would be if a crime had been committed, and then, it would be the police who would go."

"How would anyone know," I answered, "if a crime had happened if no one can get into Harwine Boarding House to collect evidence? I guess laws only protect the property owners."

Hearing my frustration, she apologized again for her lack of good news.

I thanked her for calling and we hung up. I sat there with my hand on the phone. Reality had hit me in the face. The law was on Reed's side. Blind Lady Justice was protecting the wrong person.

I jumped as the phone rang under my hand and I picked up the receiver to hear Peggy's voice. "I was about to leave to go to see Mother and wanted to know if you've heard anything yet from your friend's contact at the Historical Society."

"Yes, but I'm afraid it's bad news. There is nothing we can do legally. It looks like Reed has won."

"Oh dear, Mother will be so distraught. I don't know how I'm going to handle her. She has been absolutely out of control about this."

"Why are you going to see Sadie now? You don't usually go for your visit until after lunch. Is she okay?"

"She's fine, I guess. She called me and insisted I come over bright and early. I figure she wants to drill me about the suitcases. She's like a dog with a bone."

"Well the problem is, the suitcases are on private property, which gives Reed the legal power. He can keep us off his land, and out of his business. I'm afraid without being able to get on the property, we're operating blind. We can't see what's going on behind closed doors. I'll do everything I can to keep the suitcases I have, barring the threat of going to jail for stealing. Although, I don't know how he could claim that I stole them, but I wouldn't put it past him to do so. John Fleming is too scared of him to help us any further."

"Stephanie, you've done what you could. Poor Mother, I had no idea about her fighting Reed. No wonder she was tortured all these years. I'm angry as hell, and I haven't even battled with Reed like you and mother have."

"I'm open to any ideas, but at some point, we may have to face that a wrong can't be righted."

"I don't think Mother will accept that," Peggy answered.

We stayed on the line in silence for seconds, while the tragic reality sucked the life out of us. Then Peggy spoke. "You've done more than most people would. What are you going to do now about searching for that man? What was his name . . . Jacob?"

"Yes, Jacob Thompson. Getting the suitcases and Hanna's journal was what I was looking for. It told me where Jacob went eighty years ago: New Orleans. I'm going there. I hope to find out what happened to Jacob, or if he left to go somewhere else. I promise, once I'm back I'll come to visit with Sadie."

"Oh, that would be nice. Even if Mother isn't with us in her mind, she always likes visitors. She loves people, taking care of them—it's the nurse in her. It's like breathing to her." Peggy sighed. "I used to be jealous about that when I was little."

"I'll call you tomorrow and see how Sadie did with the news."

"One good thing is she may not even remember meeting you. I'm starting to think her illness is a blessing. I hate seeing her so upset. Her not being able to do anything about the abuse in Harwine is killing her." Peggy paused and sighed. "Listen to me, like my mother and I are the only people with worries. You be sure to drive carefully, Stephanie. Reed may still be a threat; he might want revenge on you."

"I'll be okay." I hung the phone up and heard the roar of the motorcycles outside. Was I going off the deep end with the cloak and dagger talk?

Focus, Stephanie. Come back to center. People ride motorcycles for fun. And camp out in the woods because they like nature. Life can be as simple as that.

Sadie

Peggy walked into the lounge of Magnolia Breezes and approached the nurse on duty. "Good morning, Debbie, have you seen my mother? We're having breakfast together today."

"No, she's probably still sleeping. Miss Sadie usually comes out for our early lunch, not breakfast, around noon."

"Well, not today apparently. She called and woke me up this morning at six a.m. and insisted I be here promptly at ten-thirty. She said we could have breakfast together and talk."

When Peggy's mother moved in, Debbie was designated to be Sadie's nurse and personal life assistant. Every patient had one.

"Sadie wanted you here for breakfast?" Debbie said.

"That's what she said."

At Magnolia Breezes, the nurses' duties went beyond just administrating medicine. They were to help the patients in every way—medically or personally. Therefore, patients, nurses, and family members all became very close. And Debbie knew Sadie's normal routine.

"I can go and check on her for you if you want," Debbie offered.

"Yes, thank you. Mother seemed very anxious. I figured she'd be waiting for me when I got here. Something must've been bothering her."

"I've noticed that the mood swings have been more frequent. Remember, Peggy, that's to be expected with her condition."

Peggy was grateful for Debbie and often said that she was a godsend. The woman felt more like an extended family member rather than an employee of Magnolia Breezes.

"I wished you had phoned after Sadie's call. I could've talked to her and calmed her before you came over so early." Debbie's words weren't scolding but more of a compassionate petition.

"I guess I should've."

"I'll go . . ." Debbie paused and glanced toward the hall that led to Sadie's room. "Oh, here she comes now."

At the end of the hallway, Sadie moved forward with steady determination.

Debbie turned back to Peggy and shrugged. "Sadie is one strong-willed lady. If she wants an early morning visit, she'll get it, one way or another. Well, I guess I don't have to tell you that. You two girls have a good time."

"Good time . . ." With a furrowed forehead, Peggy looked toward the hallway. Not taking her eyes off of her mother, Peggy answered, "Yes. Thank you."

Debbie left, crossing the room toward an elderly woman who was struggling with the lock on one of the wheels on her walker.

Down the hallway, recognition flowed over Sadie, as she noticed Peggy waiting for her. *I must remember to stay focused and not get flustered when I talk to Peggy. I'm the mother here—and an adult. As long as I maintain my parental authority with her, she'll go along with my plan.*

In the crook of Sadie's arm rested a doll. She held her eyes fixed on Peggy while rehearsing what she would say. As she got closer, Sadie saw her daughter's posture collapse. She realized Peggy's eyes were fixated on the doll.

I don't have time for this pessimism today. Sadie knew what it looked like to Peggy. To her daughter, it must've seemed that she had deteriorated to a child-like state. *Relapse will happen soon enough, Peggy—but not today. You can mourn for me later.*

Sadie marched up to Peggy, without any hellos, and mustered up her harshest mother's voice. "Peggy, how many times do I have to tell you to stand up straight! Now come over here, we've several things to discuss."

The old woman took three steps toward the settee in the corner of the room and stopped. Looking back at her daughter, she instructed, "Peggy, pay attention. Time is wasting."

"But . . . but, didn't you want to go for breakfast?"

Sadie looked at Peggy's puzzled look and wanted to wrap her into comforting arms and tell her everything would be all right. But, that was not reality. She fought off her motherly instincts. Lies wouldn't help her daughter prepare for the road ahead. Lies wouldn't make it easier for Peggy when the Alzheimer's symptoms worsened.

"We can have breakfast later," Sadie answered. "I have something of the utmost importance to talk to you about."

Through Sadie's nursing experience, she knew the unexpected and abrupt mood swings were the most difficult for families of dementia patients. She also understood her prognosis. Memory loss, confusion, disorientation, and losing touch with reality. Once the symptoms set in again, her disease could move full force into the final stages. The stages that would rob her of the life she knew. She'd no longer be the independent person who used to care for others. The tables would be reversed and she would have to rely on the care of others. There was one salvation, a gift, per se: Alzheimer's patients are unaware of their loss. In the last stages, Sadie knew she would be wrapped in a safe cocoon of innocence. The disease that steals everything away would inflict the pain of witnessing its merciless theft on Peggy, and Sadie was helpless to protect her daughter from the emotional pain the future would bring. However, Sadie still had time to help the patients in Harwine.

"Come on, dear." Sadie patted the cushion. "Sit here beside me." Sadie's voice was now a softer tone. *If only Peggy were married, then her husband could be there for her when I'm not really here.*

"There's no need to be melancholy, Peggy. We're wasting precious time."

Peggy took a seat next to her mother but her eyes fell to her mother's lap. "Mom, why do you have this doll?"

"Don't look at me like that. I'm perfectly fine. Besides, frowning will give you wrinkles. I haven't regressed to my childhood—not yet."

Undeniably, their roles as mother and daughter would change, but not today. Today Sadie was still the mother. "Listen, Peggy. I want you to hear me out. I need your help with something."

Sadie's hands shook as she turned the doll over in her lap. Her fingers tugged at the buttons on the doll's dress. The more she struggled, the more the task became impossible.

"Help me with these buttons, my hands—these old fingers, they don't work. I can't undo this dress."

"Mother, it's all right." Peggy turned the doll back over and smoothed the long flowing dress. "Let's just visit for a while. Do you want me to go get you something to eat? We can have breakfast here. We don't have to go to the dining room."

"No. What I need is for you to help me with the buttons on the doll's dress." Sadie's patience was growing thin.

Peggy's eyes filled with tears as she stared speechless at her mother.

"Yes, I know it's a doll," Sadie said firmly. "I'm your mother, listen . . . to . . . me. I have something to show you." Sadie thrust the doll toward Peggy.

Peggy dabbed a tissue at the corners of her eyes. She then unbuttoned the doll's dress. As she pulled the dress down, as Sadie instructed, Peggy's eyes widened with surprise. There in the back of doll was a small wooden box, inserted into a hole cut into the plastic.

"I made this box out of balsa wood," Sadie explained. "I used a scalpel to cut a hole big enough to maneuver the box into the back of the doll."

"How did you do . . . I mean it fits so perfectly."

Good. I've got her attention. "You're forgetting that I started as a surgical nurse before I went into geriatrics. I watched hundreds of surgeries. Cutting into the soft plastic wasn't very difficult especially considering that a life wasn't resting on my ability to make a proper incision."

Sadie explained that by leaving out the-bottom of the box, she was able to glue a sack made out of fabric to the top edge. Once the sack was adhered, she inserted the box into the cavity of the doll; the flexible sack could expand and hold many items. It was where Sadie had hidden the newspaper clipping that she gave to Stephanie Oliver.

"You see," Sadie said, "I wanted to stop the abuse in Harwine and that horrible man, Phillip Andrew Reed. I had found some damning evidence and wanted to sneak it out of the hospital, but Reed got suspicious of me. In his office, he kept files of the patients he had used for his sick enjoyment. In those files were the rolls of paper tapes from the electrotherapy machines with the readings of the voltage levels and the length the shocks were administrated to the patients. No ethical doctor would've *ever* used those high levels. And the length of the currents, no one ever should have experienced that kind of brutality."

"But, Mom, back then weren't electroshock treatments considered helpful?"

"Peggy. I was a nurse. The treatments Reed ordered or gave himself could never have been thought of as helpful. Trust me, Reed was not led by compassion. Only a sick and sadistic person would allow voltages what I saw recorded. It was a miracle he didn't kill someone."

Sadie shook her head and then added, "He had to be stopped. I told the newspaper reporter that I'd get the evidence, enough to start an investigation. There was a patient who would carry a doll with her all the time. But she would put it down and forget where she left it and start crying for it. The nurses would have to go looking for it."

Peggy filled in her mother's story and said, "And Reed wouldn't think anything was odd about a nurse carrying that doll."

Sadie answered, "That's right. So I bought another doll almost identical to it and got it ready to hide the tapes."

"This is that doll?"

"Yes."

"What happened to the shock therapy tapes?"

Sadie lowered her head so as if not wanting to look at her daughter in the eye. "I never got back in the hospital. Reed knew I was planning something and he stopped approval for my work requests to Harwine. I never got the tapes out. Reed was too slick. "

"Was that when he threw around the accusations about your competency as a nurse? When he threatened the newspaper with a lawsuit?"

Sadie nodded. "Reed wanted to send me back to Milledgeville, but the hospital was so short-staffed that he couldn't transfer me back without a good reason. It would draw attention to him and the hospital. He didn't know if I had uncovered evidence but he wasn't going to take any chances. He decided to try to scare me, so I would ask to return to Milledgeville. I figured a man like Reed was not above using illegal ways to stop me. I was afraid he'd hire someone to break into our house looking for anything I might have against him."

Peggy touched her mother's arm, "You went through all this? Why didn't you tell me?"

"You were only a young girl when all this was happening. Later on, after you were an adult, I was ashamed that I didn't fight back. You see, Reed found out I had a daughter. One day at the hospital, he cornered me and said it would be a shame if my pretty little daughter got hurt riding her bike home from school. He named your school and mentioned that old, beat-up bike you loved with the daisies you had me paint on the fenders. After that, I took you to school every day and my neighbor picked you up and kept you at her house until I came home."

"Mom, you tried your best. You protected me."

Sadie believed there were still innocent people under Reed's control, even today. Sadie had once had knowledge about the evil that went on in the past and she was certain evil was still going on, as long as Reed was running Harwine Boarding House.

"You *have* to let it go now," Peggy said. Her mother was old and not well. What could she do? "It's all in the past."

Sadie was determined to make Peggy understand. "Reed falsified the charges about my being an incompetent nurse. I was dismissed, pending a State Board of Nursing review. But I wasn't going to stop pushing for a complete investigation of the hospital. Reed wasn't going to scare me, and I thought I could protect you. Then one night he called and said if taking away my professional reputation wouldn't stop me, he would eliminate you from my life."

Sadie took a hard look at Peggy. "Eliminate. That was the word he used. It was then I realized if he could hurt old and helpless people, he could hurt a child just as easily. It wasn't just about me anymore. I couldn't guarantee I could keep you safe. I couldn't keep you inside the house 24 hours a day. You had to go to school—and play outside. You needed a normal life. He had won."

"I understand, but it's over now."

"No, it's not. Don't you see there are still helpless people under Reed's care. A leopard doesn't change his spots. I guarantee he is as abusive now as he was back then, if not more. He's probably intoxicated with the power of getting off scot-free. Stephanie Oliver's visit made me realize that there is still time for me to do something."

"Now is not the time. You're not young. You need to take care of yourself."

Sadie's face turned tight, her eyes focused intensely on Peggy. "Now is my last chance. I swore that someday I'd make him answer for what he did, once you were grown and out of harm's way. That's why I hid away the newspaper clippings, to remind me. But I need your help."

Partners

Sadie insisted Peggy examine the construction of the box that was nested in the doll. Peggy needed to see the attention Sadie had made to small details like adding a metal bar, which held a hinged door securely shut. The box could convince Peggy how plausible Sadie's plan could be. After all these years, the box was still sound. The compartment opening was between 5 to 6 inches long by three or four inches wide. With the small bag made of stretchable material, it could push further in the doll's cavity, making a sizable hiding place. Sadie explained that with the disposable cameras available now, the sack would be big enough to hold one and it made the task easy. The time was right.

Sadie watched as Peggy examined the box and the doll. She was accepting everything she was telling her. Maybe she might help. After all, Peggy had stopped arguing or trying to divert Sadie's focus on gathering evidence against Reed.

So Sadie continued with her arguments, while Peggy had an open mind. "Stephanie Oliver is a nice woman, but she won't stop Reed."

Peggy's attention went back to the doll as she flipped the hook catch. "You know, Mom, I can't believe you kept all of this a secret from me. The newspaper clipping, that you were at that hospital, this doll—all of it."

At that moment Peggy froze, and then her head snapped up. She turned to face Sadie. "You were the nurse informant, the one the reporter keep secret—his *source*. The one he wouldn't reveal—it was you?"

Sadie sat in silence but slowly nodded.

Peggy muttered the words again. "It was you."

"Oh yes, it was me. I had planned to go to the Georgia Department of Regulations and Licensing until the danger to you was a real possibility."

"Mother, listen to me. Stephanie has some of the suitcases from the patients. There could be evidence in them to use against Reed. She's going to New Orleans on business, but when she comes back, maybe she can get the newspaper to write an article again. It could lead to an investigation of the Harwine Boarding House. Stir things up."

Sadie shook her head. "No, that won't work now. Legally there's nothing that can be done. There's no one who regulates boarding houses like hospitals. There are no inspections, no watch guards. Besides, it has been too long, even if we could prove abuse back then. We need to get evidence of abuse going on today. Then the law will be on our side."

"So, nothing can be done," Peggy said. It was more of a statement than a question. "Unless someone dies out there, no one will investigate Reed's actions?"

"I think something can be done before that. I have a plan and if it works we'll have the evidence we need."

"I don't know, Mom. Sounds like the only evidence that would work would be testimony from a patient or someone witnessing a patient being beaten . . . or worse. How can we get that?"

"By getting me inside."

Peggy popped up off of the settee. "What! Oh no. That's not going to happen."

"Please, Peggy, sit down and listen."

Peggy sat and glared at her mother. "I'm listening."

"If Reed is running the boarding house the same as a hospital or a nursing home, like giving patients sleeping pills or other medications and without maintaining the proper licenses and allowing regular inspections, he's breaking a lot of laws. Then we can shut him down. I'll bet Reed is telling the families of the patients he is running a nursing home and *not* a boarding house. That's fraud and if we have any proof, the authorities will step in. And if there's abuse going on, then Reed will go to jail for years."

Laughter spilled into the room as a group of residents entered where Sadie and Peggy sat. Obviously, returning from breakfast. Sadie hurriedly pulled the dress closed and turned the doll over in her lap.

"If we decided to try to get evidence," Peggy whispered. "I repeat, *if*, then I would have to be the one to do it. It's not possible, I'm not a nurse. How could I get inside? Reed's not going to let me walk in and look around the place."

"He most certainly will if you were going to pay to put your mother in the home."

"No. I won't allow it. You're not going into that place."

"Peggy, it's the only way. I want you to put me in there as a patient. I can bring my doll. I'll have it with me at all times, you know, because I'm regressing into my childhood."

"Mother, you expect they're abusing patients. No, you can't ask me to do this. Reed is dangerous; besides, he'll remember you. It won't work."

"Reed won't remember me. I'm an old woman now and look very different. My maiden name was on my nursing diploma. That's the name he would recognize, without that name, and with this old body, he won't make the connection. It's the only way."

Peggy sat in silence. Sadie's daughter was compassionate. She also had inherited her sense of justice. Sadie was betting that Peggy couldn't turn her back on innocent people in need of rescuing.

"Peggy, you have to help me. Please." Sadie looked down. "I've been haunted by this. I could've had the hospital shut down years ago but I didn't. I took a pledge when I became a nurse. An oath to keep for life just like doctors do; nurses are expected to *do no harm*. Back then, I did harm by keeping silent." Sadie looked up with pleading eyes. "You have to help me rectify this."

"How can I? I'll be putting you in danger—you can't expect me to do what you couldn't do to me all those years ago?"

"You were a child. I have lived a good life. I want to find peace in the days I have left."

Peggy gazed at her mother.

Sadie waited for what seemed like minutes although it had been only a few seconds.

"All right, Mom. But we need to have a failsafe plan to get you out if it gets too dangerous."

"Absolutely. I have it all worked out."

Undercover Princess

Peggy pulled up to the old southern building. The once-grand architecture failed to mask the deplorable condition of the house. The four large pillars across the front of the building reminded Peggy of bars on a jail cell. Black mold bled out around all the decorative trim and an abandoned bird's nest spilled off the top ledge of the pillar nearest to the front door. The surrounding grounds were a mixture of dead or overgrown shrubbery. The yard was vacant of grass, with only dirt covering the area.

"Mom, are you sure about this?" Peggy asked, staring at the house as she parked the car.

A sign anchored in the dirt a few feet from the steps leading to house read, *Harwine Boarding House*. At the top of the steps, the front door's paint was a chalky gray color. It appeared as if it had been black to match the window shutters at one time.

"It's not too late to turn around and go back home."

Sadie sat in the car's passenger seat. She grabbed the doll in her lap and reached for the car door handle. "I've never been so sure of anything in my life. It's the only way to know if the people staying here are safe or not, and if they're being treated with the respect they deserve."

"Wait." Peggy's hand grabbed hold of her mother's arm. "What if your mind slips because of the Alzheimer's, and you have another spell?"

185

"Peggy, I can't explain it but I *know* that as long as I'm focused on this one thing, I'll be all right. I have to finish this."

Sadie knew Peggy was strong but she hoped her daughter's sense of justice was just as strong to ensure that she would stick to the plan. "My mind's clear, don't worry. Remember, we have a failsafe plan. As long as I get a confidante inside so that if I lose touch with reality, then the confidant will call you. I'll make sure whoever it is, has your phone number. I can't guarantee I won't have a spell but with the failsafe plan, you will never lose touch with me. Trust me, this is going to work."

"Okay, you're the boss, Mom." Peggy reluctantly released her hold on Sadie's arm. Turning to her door to open it, she said, "Let's go."

Inside the house, Sadie pulled the doll closer to her chest. She grabbed her daughter's sleeve, bunching it into a tight ball with her gnarled fingers, and clenched it tight into her fist. Sadie then nestled her head deep into Peggy's shoulder.

Peggy walked forward into the foyer of the boarding house. The two of them moved in unison as Sadie shuffled and dragged her feet while keeping hold of her daughter's sleeve.

Peggy slowed, hesitating as her eyes scanned the room. The walls of peeling paint, the cobwebs in the corners.

"Peggy," Sadie whispered. "Stop looking horrified. Remember you want to get me out of your hair."

"Right," Peggy said, steeling herself.

A woman in white approached them from a door on the left. "Hello, you must be Miss Hamilton. Dr. Fleming is expecting you."

She led Peggy and Sadie down a dingy hall and into a small office where a pleasant-looking, older man introduced himself as Doctor Fleming. Although he promptly insisted they both call him John.

"I am so glad you have an opening, doctor." Peggy proceeded with the story she and her mother had rehearsed. "I just can't take it anymore," she said as she took a seat in a leather chair positioned in front of the desk where John Fleming was seated.

Peggy fingered at her hair, pushing the curls into place. "I have a life, you know. She needs to be watched *all the time*. The other day, she decided to walk to the store because she wanted a candy bar! The closest store is five miles away. I found her wandering the streets, two miles from the house, walking in the opposite direction of the store."

"Oh, dear. Yes, that is a problem. It must be very difficult for you."

"Difficult!" Peggy rolled her eyes. Sadie had coached her well.

Peggy needed to appear to be a relative that was at the end of her rope, plus give the lasting impression that there would no possibility of her dropping in, or checking on Sadie. If Peggy didn't get that point across, Sadie feared Harwine Boarding House wouldn't approve her admission.

"Difficult is an understatement," Peggy said. She blinked, glancing down momentarily. She smiled and said in a softer tone. "Please, don't get me wrong, I'm not a heartless woman."

Peggy fingered at her hair again. "I need to think of myself. I'm not getting any younger. I have needs, too. My mother wasn't kind to me in my childhood. Life wasn't a bed of roses when I was growing up. She never cared about me. She would go out drinking every night *and now*, I'm supposed to be tied down taking care of her? When is it my time to have a good life? Oh no, I refuse to be shackled anymore."

The man behind the desk appeared to be unruffled. John Fleming sat silent. His posture changed slightly, stiffening, and his jaw tightened. Sadie worried that Peggy might be overacting. Then not missing a beat, he quickly regained his composure like a true professional and his passive demeanor returned.

He said with a kind voice, "It is very difficult dealing with an Alzheimer's patient. I'm sure we can help. I'm glad you came to us."

"Does that mean you will take my mother?"

"Yes, we can admit her. Now, you do understand that we are not a hospital. We can administer medication prescribed by her doctor, but if she needs medical attention for something serious, we would have to transport her to the nearest hospital. I am the doctor on call for small things, like sniffles or bumps and scrapes—things like that."

"Oh, yes. I understand. Can you take her today? I have her suitcase."

Fleming paused, pursing his lips, but then answered. "Yes."

Sadie yanked on Peggy's sleeve several times until Peggy turned toward her and snapped at her in her meanest voice. "Stop that!" Pulling the material out of Sadie's hand, Peggy smoothed it out, but still, the blouse sleeve had wrinkles. "What do you want?"

"I'm going to live here now?" Sadie asked.

"Yes, thank goodness," Peggy answered.

"Sadie," John Fleming interjected. "We would be very happy if you would stay with us for a while. Would you please come live with us?"

"Can my doll live here, too?" Sadie asked.

"Of course. That would be lovely."

Sadie stroked the hair of her doll. "Okay, I'll stay. My doll's name is Mabel, she goes everywhere with me."

As they walked down the hallway, Sadie whispered to Peggy. "Don't worry." At the foyer, Fleming called for the nurse to escort Sadie to her room. Before following the nurse, Sadie discreetly nudged Peggy toward the front door to leave.

Once Sadie was alone in her room, she looked about the small ten-by-ten space. She remembered Johnny Cash talking on television about prison cells being six-by-eight in size. *Not much bigger than Johnny's jail accommodations.*

A twin-sized bed was pushed against the wall on the left and a single chest of drawers sat across the room. Between the two pieces of furniture was a small window with a pull-down shade. The only nice thing was the private bathroom. However, it was only big enough to step in, turn, and sit on the toilet, then pivot to the sink to wash your hands. The nurse told her that the showers were down the hall but if she wanted to use them, a staff member needed to accompany her. It was for safety purposes, of course. Then the nurse left without saying another word.

Well now, time to explore. Sadie headed toward her bedroom door that opened to a community hallway. *Let's see what kind of supervision there is around here.*

Before leaving, Sadie picked up her doll, but felt something on the doll's back give way. Peggy had been worried that Sadie wouldn't be able to get to the hidden box and insisted on leaving the doll's dress unbuttoned, but unbeknown to Sadie, she also unlatched the door on the box. Gravity and the weight of the small disposable camera tucked inside caused the door to slip open, which now threatened the camera's possible escape. If this happened at the wrong moment, it would expose her and the whole plan would be ruined.

"My, I can't have this," Sadie mumbled, and hurried back over to the bed and took a seat. She fumbled with the dress, opening the back, and latched the box. "Peggy worries too much. I can handle the slide latch, it's the buttons I can't do." Once everything was secure, she hurried out of the room to investigate.

There were eleven guest rooms upstairs, excluding Sadie's room. Downstairs, there were eight rooms for guests who were 'not to be disturbed' as the nurse had told Sadie when she asked if the doors down the hallway had toys in them. "Are there any little girls in the rooms?'" Sadie asked, "Maybe they'll want to play with my doll."

The nurse tersely answered, "No, they can't play. Those guests stay in their beds at all times. End of discussion."

Sadie explored the entire upstairs without anyone intervening. All of the rooms were empty except for the room three doors down from hers.

Entering that room, Sadie saw a man sitting in a chair at the window. "Oh, sorry, I thought this was my room."

"That's all right. Come in. You're new, when did you check-in?"

"Today."

"My name's Norman." The man said.

"I'm Sadie."

"Is that short for Sarah?"

"No, just Sadie."

"Good name. The Hebrew meaning of Sadie is 'princess.'"

"Why are you the only one up here?"

"I don't like it downstairs. Too damn depressing. I like to look outside and watch the birds. It helps me forget where I am. Spent most of my life working outside. I was a house painter and made a good living at it. Good enough to raise three sons. But they're busy with their own families now."

"I don't have a chair in my room."

"You have to let them know who's boss around here. Have to stand up for yourself, Sadie. I gave them trouble until they got me a chair so they wouldn't have to deal with me asking every day. Most of the patients here are too feeble to cause any trouble."

"Dr. Fleming says we're guests, not patients."

"Honey, Fleming's a nice man but he doesn't know what is going on here. He's as out of touch as much as some of the . . ." Norman motioned two rabbit ears in the air, "guests." He looked at Sadie, and then he lowered his gaze to the doll in her arms. "What's that?"

"It's my doll. I take her everywhere I go."

"Yeah?" He squinted and frowned at her.

Sadie could tell that he was not a fool. He wasn't buying her childish act. She wasn't sure what to do, so she waited. A few seconds of silence passed.

The old man gave a burst of laughter. "Sadie, honey, your eyes betray you. There's light in them. You're not lost like some of the others. I don't know what's with the act, but I bet you're someone who can see through to the truth. Are you looking for the truth, Princess?"

"You sound like your vision is pretty good, too."

"You got that right."

A small smile escaped Sadie's lips. *I might have found my confidant.*

TWENTY MINUTES LATER.

Sadie left Norman's room to check out the downstairs. The stairs were difficult maneuvering for her. Still, she made it without anyone noticing her. As she headed toward the rooms on the first floor, the ones where the bedridden guests where, a nurse hurried out of a room and almost crashed in to Sadie. The nurse stood with a shocked look on her face.

"Who are you?" the black-skinned woman wearing a white uniform asked. Her blazing green eyes seemed unnatural and made the hair on the back of Sadie's neck stand up.

Time to slip into my little girl character. Sadie hoped Norman's observation was correct that feeble guests were ignored and left alone.

"I'm Sadie." She held out her doll. "This is my doll. Her name is Mabel. Do you want to play with me and Mabel?"

"No. You aren't allowed here." She grabbed Sadie's arm and twisted her around, almost knocking her off balance. "Come on, I'll take you to the general area." She briskly walked Sadie to a large room where other guests sat in chairs at tables. Even more, sat in wheelchairs about the room. There was no television, no checkers, nothing for the people to occupy their time. Some were talking to each other; however, most just sat in silence.

I think I'm not in Kansas anymore, Toto. Neither am I at Magnolia Breezes.

The Big Easy

The month's tea shipment had come into the store and still needed to be put away. I was able to unpack it, log it into our inventory list, and then place the packages out on the shelves all before closing up for the night. Betsy's support has been unshakeable. She has encouraged me every step of the way, and has pushed me to continue on my quest to unravel the mystery that surrounded Mabel Brewer and Leanne's uncle Jacob.

As my first deadline rocketed toward me, my publisher and agent continued to hound me by constantly reminding me of my contractual commitment. The stress was wearing, not to mention the guilt I felt every time I had to leave poor Betsy to man the store by herself. After all, we were partners and I had been failing to hold up my end of the responsibilities. I hated dumping on Betsy, and now Peggy and Sadie were counting on me, too. Although I couldn't let guilt stop my efforts now. Not when I was so close.

Tomorrow morning, I'll get an early start, pack the car, and head out to New Orleans. If all goes well, I'll have my answers and then I can return to write Mabel and Jacob's story.

That would take care of my apprehensive agent and publisher. *One down and a heap more other commitments to go.*

Once I return to Havenridge after my trip I would contact a lawyer to help go after Reed in Harwine. That would take care of the promises made to Sadie and Peggy.

When all of the commitments are dealt with, I'll be able to go back to being a business partner to Betsy. *Two and three down –done and done and the universe will shift back into place.*

NEW ORLEANS

As I arrived in New Orleans, it was not what I expected. What that was, I don't know. Still, this wasn't it. The streets were intimidating, with names like Carondelet and Tchoupitoulas. How do you even pronounce those? The one-way streets made it difficult, and roads where people just parked their car in the right-hand lane, got out to go wherever, was downright crazy! Not to mention the bridges. *I hate, hate bridges.*

After approaching the edge of town and crossing an ironclad bridge, which should've been a short twenty-minute drive to the French Quarter, I found myself traveling in unfamiliar territory. It felt as if I had crossed a border into a different country. One with buildings, roads, and landscapes that seemed the same as anywhere in the USA, but still very different. Oddly, I recognized things. An hour later, I had crossed over the same bridge for the third time and I realized I must've made another wrong turn.

I yearned for the security of my small town of Havenridge, where Gladys jaywalks on Main Street daily, waving her handkerchief at people so they'll stop and visit. For me to like this strange place known as the "Big Easy," I would have to see and learn a lot more before its so-called charm would win me over. It didn't look anything like the glamorized city in the movies or that was presented in travel books.

Getting to the ever-famous French Quarter proved to be almost as hard as tracking down Jacob. After forty five minutes of nomadic roaming, finally, I found it. The streets, although narrow and busy, were somewhat appealing. Now I could see the familiar scenery displayed in movies. Ornate wrought-iron balconies and horse-drawn carriages with the sounds of hoofs clicking on the brick roads added a whimsical charm. *Now, this was what I had expected.*

My reservations were at the Chateau Hotel located on Rue Chartres. I learned that Rue in French means "street" from a chatty Directory Assistance operator when I had called for a listing of a place to stay before I left Havenridge. She had explained that the hotel was a block from Royal Street and two blocks from Bourbon Street, so it would be "perfect for my visit." She probably thought I was the typical tourist. Having never been to New Orleans, but remembering what I had read about the city, the streets Royal and Bourbon had rung a bell with me. I promptly took the phone number of the hotel from Miss Chatty Operator, then had dialed and booked a room.

I managed to find the Chateau Hotel after cruising through the streets. I checked in, took my small overnight bag, and found my room. After freshening up from my long journey, I headed back to the lobby. The front desk manager, Tommy, gave me a map and explained in a genteel southern accent that the hotel was an easy walk to just about anywhere. He suggested I might like to go two blocks down to Jackson Square, where there was always lots of activity during the daytime. It would be a couple of hours before sundown and the clubs did not start "jamming," as he put it, until eight or nine o'clock. After that, the streets would be packed with the party-going crowd until at least two in the morning.

"I'm not wanting to go to the bars. I'm interested in finding out about someone who has passed away—around ninety years ago."

"Oh, then you need to go see Ghistaine. She has a shop on Royal. If you are serious about connecting with someone who's dead then she's the one you'll need. Her place is open until eleven. Don't bother with anyone else, there are lots of . . . ." He put his hands up, moving his hooked index and middle fingers up and down, indicating quotation marks, "*fortune tellers*, but Ghistaine is the right person for you."

I thanked him and left with a map that had the big red "X" mark where Ghistaine's shop was located. The sky above glowed in soft, golden hues. There were puffy clouds scattered about, against the fast-approaching night sky. The shy moon barely visible, not yet bright, announced its forthcoming against the twilight radiance emitting a tranquil beauty.

I walked to Jackson Square first, delaying my visit to Ghistaine. I had been working on getting back to my old, confident self. However, occasionally I would fall back into being Miss Want-to-Please-Everyone Stephanie. This was one of those times. I couldn't face the hotel manager after he was so eager to help me, and tell him I didn't go see Ghistaine. He would surely ask how I made out with her upon my return.

Tommy was right about Jackson Square being alive with activity. Leann would love this. Paintings were propped up, leaning against the wrought iron fencing extending from the top edge of a half-brick wall that surrounded the park square. An array of scenes of New Orleans in oils, watercolors, and acrylics mixed with the nearby artists, musicians, and street performers who meandered about, waiting for passing strangers to stop. Inside the park, I stopped to talk to a food vendor standing next to a red and white cart with a sign that boasted, *Best Hot Popcorn in New Orleans*. He spoke to me while throwing kernels to a flock of pigeons flapping overhead and said that he came to the square every day.

He stopped throwing the corn and said, "Hold your arm out straight with your palm up."

"What?"

"Ya' ain't afraid of birds, are ya?"

"Oh, no," I answered.

"Then hold your arm out straight with your palm up." I did as instructed and he placed a kernel in the middle of my hand. "They will land on your hand, but be ready, they're heavy."

A pigeon landed on my fingertips, the weight of the bird pulled my hand down immediately as it plucked the kernel up and flew away.

The man smiled big, then chuckled and said, "Dere ya go, dat's how you do it." He placed some more kernels in my hand. The next thing I knew, I had two pigeons on my hand, one on my arm, another flapped to my left shoulder, as many flew around me.

"Oh my!" I said. "I guess they like popcorn."

"Yes 'er deedy."

Once the pigeons realized feeding time was finished, they returned to the grassy area to our right. I thanked the vendor and turned to go. Pausing for a moment, I turned back. "Do you know a woman known as Ghistaine? She has a shop on Royal."

"Missy, everyone knows Miss Ghistaine. Someone you know has died and needs guidance?"

"Not exactly."

"Cause some kin don'ts know they should move on and they stay right here—waiting. Miss Ghistaine has the gift. You go to Miss Ghistaine. She'll fix you up."

"Thank you." I left with my curiosity piqued. In the short time I had been here, two people had insisted that I go see this Ghistaine.

The smell of food from the pull-carts and aroma spilling out from the restaurants' open doors made me realize that I was very hungry. It was a little early for dinner, so I stopped at the Café' du Monde for a small something to hold me over. I ordered a chocolate croissant, forgoing the overly sweet-looking, sugary beignets. My chocolate-injected choice was scrumptious. After a few minutes, I figured I needed to head over to Royal to find Ghistaine to discover why everyone thought I needed her.

Royal Street was a mixture of bars, novelty shops, fortunetellers, and stores to buy charms or get readings done. Sprinkled among them were generous amounts of voodoo shops with signs in the windows offering love potions or curses—take your pick. Images in my mind conjured up scenes from old Tarzan movies and dialogue like, "Witch doctor bad. Tarzan don't like." Even though Tommy had said Ghistaine also did scientific astrology charting for people besides her added talent of talking to the dead, the whole Ghistaine thing gave me a creepy feeling. Was she into science or spirits? Furthermore, were the two really any different?

Stephanie, stop being a baby. Don't get creeped out. Ghistaine is just a woman with a gimmick who wants to make money.

Halfway down Royal, curiosity made me stop at a shop window. Big painted letters on the glass spreading across it read: candles, charms, and voodoo dolls. Guaranteed to do the job.

An old woman with wiry gray hair fanned herself as she sat in a small chair that propped the store door open. "You lost, my child?" she asked as her fan kept a steady pace. "Come in and I will help you."

"Oh, thank you. No, I'm not lost. I was just looking." I turned to go in the opposite direction as she spoke again. This time she did not ask a question. "Lost you are, child. Come, let Ghistaine help you."

I spun around. "You're Ghistaine?"

"Yes. I've been expecting you."

The old woman stood, took two steps toward the doorway, and then paused. She looked back over her shoulder and repeated firmly. "Come!" She turned, departing into the store with her purple and gold floor-length skirt trailing behind her.

I followed, thinking that Tommy must have called her and told her I was coming.

Inside, a collection of smells assaulted my senses as I looked at the things around me. Some odors were nauseously sweet, others earthy, but all very pungent. Candles were burning throughout the store. Dolls and animal figures were displayed along with statues of various Catholic saints.

A younger woman pushed through a curtain of multicolored beads that hung in the doorframe behind a counter. "Good, you've come in. I'm going to leave now, Ghistaine. Do you need anything before I go?"

"No. I'm just going to talk with this young lady. She's come a long way and needs my help."

Danger Speaks

"Tommy, the hotel manager from the Chateau, must have called you," I said. If she knew I wasn't going to fall for her little sham, maybe I could get out of there quickly.

The woman frowned as if she didn't understand what I was saying.

That's good, look confused. You have no idea what I'm talking about, right? I'm buying that.

"I sense you have unanswered questions," she said, ignoring my comment. "Answers are close to you. Welcome and open yourself to the good energy around you."

"I am very sorry, but I am not interested in any charms or . . . er . . . ." I looked over my left shoulder where assortments of human and animal dolls were stacked on shelves. "Or curses. I think Tommy misunderstood. And I'm not paying for any of your services either. I was just looking."

"Curses?" Her eyes gazed over to where I had looked. "Oh, you've misunderstood. My partner, the young girl who just left, is the one who is the ordained priestess, not me. I don't practice voodoo. But then that is not what you seek."

"I told you, I am not *seeking* anything." I turned and headed toward the door. I wondered what I was doing here, because of a hotel manager's suggestion. Every time I turn back into old, weak Stephanie who worries about what people will think, it's a mistake.

202

When I get back to the hotel, I'll set the record straight with Tommy. I'm not interested in any of this mumbo jumbo.

In my hurry, I tripped on the threshold and stumbled out onto the sidewalk with Ghistaine hot on my heels.

"The energy around you is female. Listen to her."

"Yeah, okay," I yelled over my shoulder as I kept walking.

The Wrong Place

I hurried down the sidewalk, furious with myself. Over the last year, I had found the person I had once been. I was no longer the Stephanie that obeyed and didn't step out of line for fear of what others would think. Moving to Havenridge had been a start to gain back my old confidence. I was strong again. I realized that it wasn't bad to focus on my needs and what I wanted. I was comfortable once again to speak my own will.

How did I slip so easily back into "Old Stephanie?"

I straightened up my posture, willing myself to walk with the confidence of character that I had reclaimed.

I looked back at the Voodoo store. Ghistaine was standing at the doorway, shaking her head with a dismayed look on her face.

I glared at her but kept walking. Then she turned and went back into the store.

"Jeez. What a kook," I muttered as I turn forward.

I had walked a couple of blocks when I heard the thumping of running steps approaching fast behind me. "Great. Now what?"

As I turned, halfway expecting to see the gray-haired witch galloping after me. Before I knew, I was struck full-force as a powerful body hit me, not Ghistaine, but a man. His hands locked around my arms as he pushed me into a small alley.

"What are you doing?" I screamed. "Stop it!"

Once in the alley, he slammed me up against a wall with such blinding speed and pinned my body between him and the side of the building. I instinctively turned my head sideways seconds before impact, thank goodness, but I still scraped my cheek hard into the cement.

Dazed, my vision failed me briefly, but not my sense of smell. The alley reeked of rancid garbage.

"Shut up." His hot words spat at my face.

Paralyzed for an instant and out of breath from the collision, I gasped in a deep breath. I opened my mouth to scream but my assailant clamped his huge hand over my entire jaw and mouth.

"You women are all alike," he said, pressing his face against my cheek, which prevented me from seeing his face. "You're nothin' but trouble makers—and teases."

The smell of stale cigarettes mixed with a strong onion odor hung in the air. "Don't mess with me or you'll be sorry;"

I struggled to break away but he was too strong. A muffled scream worked its way up my throat. His hand held tight against my mouth.

"I said shut up, bitch!" He puffed heavily as a hot burst of breath spilled out on me. His rough hand squeezed between us, worming its way under and up my blouse. Scratchy tentacle-like fingers crawled up to my left breast and then he worked his hand across my chest like a giant spider, scratching and groping at me.

I struggled against him as I tried to free any part of my body to fight back.

"Women need to know their place. You're not calling the shots. Be still and enjoy this."

His breaths increased as he tore at me. He moaned as he continued raking his free hand across my skin. He pressed hard against my body, rubbing himself up and down against my body. I was trapped.

Stop. Stop it. I screamed in my mind. My arms were pinned between us. As he pulled away to grope at me some more, I worked my right arm free just before he shoved his body back toward me. As he pressed forward, I balled my free hand into a fist and flung it toward my back, swinging wildly. I somehow made contact as my fist hit him in the small of his back with a forceful thump.

"Ow!" he wailed. Onion smell, cigarette odor, and spit droplets blew across my face as his hand moved off my mouth and he arched his back in pain. I pushed sideways to escape, only to be slammed back as he clamped his hand back cross my mouth. But before he made contact, I opened my mouth wide, biting at his hand when we connected.

He let out another shout of pain and yelled, "Bitch!"

My head jerked back as he grabbed hold of my hair. Blinded by the shooting pain, I feared he would pull my hair out by the roots. His hand held firm but I didn't release my bite. He pulled me away from the wall, my feet barely touching the pavement, and then threw me forward. Still tied together by relentless force, my biting, and his hold of my hair and body, we spun around and fell together to the ground. We hit hard. He lay on top of me with a crushing weight. I could barely breathe.

He's going to kill me. I'm not going to get away.

Somewhere behind us, I heard a frantic voice yell, "Someone's coming. Let's get out of here."

The weight eased off me, but he didn't let go as he lifted me by my hair.

He's taking me with him so he can kill me later, after he . . .

My mind raced with fear as images of my body being found in a swamp swirled through my brain.

As he pulled me only halfway up, he stopped, then smashed my head back down onto the road and let go. I lifted my head, putting my hand to my forehead. It felt warm and wet, as the liquid slid down over my eyebrow. My eyes fluttered, things blurred. Then my world went black.

Not Giving Up

I woke up with my head throbbing, along with the sensation of movement. Arms—strong arms—wrapped around me, carrying me off. Blinking, I tried to focus but the sun blinded me. I couldn't make out his face; he was just a shadow in front of streams of strong rays of sun. I screamed and kept screaming as I swung my fist at his face, shoulders, chest—any part of his body I could hit. I kicked and kept kicking my legs in an effort to get away, causing him to slow down.

"Stop," I heard him shout at me. But I didn't. "Wait a minute," he commanded.

I ignored him again, wiggling, kicking, and screaming. He stopped dead as I felt my body slipping from his strong grip.

"Stop it," he repeated.

I wasn't about to stop swinging my fists and fighting him. There was no way my body would be fed to the gators in some Louisiana swamp.

The ground seemed to come up to meet me as my feet made contact with it but my knees buckled. He grabbed me by my shoulders and caught me.

"I'm a cop. The guy who jumped you is gone. You're safe now."

Although things were spinning, I could make out his face now. I looked at what he was wearing. No uniform. No badge. I pulled away and stiffened my stand. "No. You don't look like a cop. Get away from me."

"Plainclothes. I'm a detective. Not all cops wear uniforms."

I stared at the dark-haired man before me. "You, I mean, how did you know I was being—wh . . . what happened?"

I could barely focus. The ground seemed to be rocking and the sky wouldn't stop whirling about. His hand reached out for me as I teetered. I slapped it away, almost losing my balance.

"After you left Ghistaine's store," he said, "she sensed you were in danger. She went back outside to call for you but didn't see you anywhere. Then she heard you yell to someone to stop."

"Rrrright." I glared at him. "And how do you know this?"

Dizzy. The spinning in my head was getting worse. The sun suddenly darkened and blackness poured over me. I felt myself going down and he scooped me up into his arms. My head was exploding.

"Look, lady, I'm a cop. Accept it! I'm taking you back to Ghistaine's place."

This time I didn't fight him but held my head, muttering, "My head, it hurts." I wrapped my arms around his neck, laid my head on his chest, and held on.

The familiar bell over the door chimed as we entered, followed by Ghistaine's strange accent. "You found her."

He lowered me down and I opened my eyes to find I was on a small couch.

"Her head is bleeding, Tony. I knew it was bad. I didn't know which way she went. Then I heard her scream."

In front of me was the doorway where the colored beads hung that separated the back of the odd store from the front area, where I had left minutes before the attack. It appeared I was in the back area now. My stranger, who claimed he was a cop, had taken me back to Ghistaine's store. Thinking about the voodoo dolls and candles just a few feet from us didn't make me feel much safer, but it was better than that horrid alley.

The gray-haired gypsy woman hurried over, carrying a bowl filled with clear liquid and put it down on a table next to me. As she dipped a cloth into it, she said, "I am very sorry, Miss. She didn't tell me which way you went. She just pushed me out the door into the street."

"Who? Who spoke to you?" I asked.

She ignored my question and continued patting my head. The water turned a darker red each time she rinsed and wrung out the rag. Dabbing at my forehead again, and again, "Thank goodness I knew Tony was down at Cajun Jack's for lunch." She turned to the man who had carried me in. "Tony, did you see who hurt this poor girl?"

I pushed the cloth away and sat up on my elbows. "Stop poking at my head and answer me! How did you know about the man attacking me? Who spoke to you?"

I turned to the man—the cop, or plainclothes detective, or whatever he was—and said, "I think it's rather strange that she . . ." I motioned to Ghistaine, "says she knew I was in danger before I even got mugged. Don't you?"

He grimaced and moved between the strange woman and me. Then he placed his hands on my shoulders and eased me back down. "You need to lie down, Miss. You were unconscious when I got to the alley and your head is still bleeding."

He took the rag from Ghistaine and waved her away. "The cut is deep," he said, looking more closely at the wound. He put the rag to my head and applied pressure to stop the bleeding. "You might have to have stitches. You need to go to the hospital to make sure you're taken care of properly."

I pushed his hand away and demanded, "I want to see your badge."

"Okay. I can see you're thinking clearly now." He stood up, took a wallet out of his jean pocket, and flipped it open, exposing an official-looking badge with the Louisiana state seal on it. Through blurred vision, I read his name, Tony De Luca.

De Luca . . . a good Italian name. I relaxed and he continued dabbing at my forehead with the rag.

The cool rag felt good against my forehead. *Wouldn't you know I would get rescued by an Italian—in New Orleans!* Any Italian that I ever have met, either wanted to feed me or take care of me.

"Did you see who jumped you, Miss?"

"No, he grabbed me from behind, pushed me into an alley, and slammed me up against the cement wall."

I paused as I watched the dark-haired man. He pulled the rag away and examined my forehead again.

"It happened so fast," I explained. "He said some awful things, then he hit me. I guess I blacked out because the next thing I knew you had me."

He stopped dabbing the cloth and a serious look came over his face. Still focused on my care but different than before. "I can call a policewoman for you to talk to," he said softly. "So you can feel more comfortable. I mean, if there is more you need to tell us about the attack."

"What?" I touched my fingers to where the blood had been coming from and looked at my fingertips. No red. It must have stopped bleeding. Then I looked at the man in front of me. He was tan, had wavy hair but his eyes betrayed his tough, professional exterior. His eyes revealed a tenderness to him. He sat looking at me, silently waiting.

"Oh," I said drawing out the word as I realized what he thought. "No, that's not necessary. A woman police officer, that is. He didn't . . . I mean . . . nothing happened. Uh, other than I got the tar beaten out of me. But I don't need to go to the hospital for . . . you know. I'll be okay."

"Well, this was a little more than a snatch and run." He looked at my head, examining it even more closely. "It stopped bleeding. That's good. I guess I could fix you up with a few butterfly bandages."

"I have some, Tony," Ghistaine said. "I'll go get them."

"Are you staying with someone in town? You shouldn't drive, Miss."

I explained that I just arrived in town and told him where I was staying. He bandaged my head and asked more questions, like my name and address back in Georgia, making notes in a small pocket notebook. When we were finished, I said I wanted to go to my hotel.

"I'll walk you."

I shook my head, "No, I'm fine. Thank you." When I stood up though, all the blood seemed to drop to my feet. I wavered, felt lightheaded, and sat down again.

"Miss Oliver, you've had a traumatic ordeal. If you insist on refusing medical attention then you really should not go back to your hotel room. You may have a concussion. You need to stay awake. When was the last time you ate?"

I thought back. "I got in town late. I had been on the road so I skipped lunch. I did get a croissant right after I got here. What time is it?"

He looked at his watch. "Eight."

"I guess that I had the croissant almost three hours ago. I *am* hungry. I'll get something to eat before going back to the hotel."

I stood again and the room began to darken. I wobbled a little and he grabbed my arm, bracing me. "You shouldn't be walking alone. Look, I'm off duty and if you're not going to the hospital, I would feel better if you let me buy you dinner. I know a great place two blocks over from here. Away from the noise of the bars."

He did have a point about having a possible concussion and not sleeping. I was still very wobbly and didn't really want to walk alone, plus I was hungry. "Well, all right. A police escort to dinner would be nice."

Survival Basics

"Welcome back, Miss . . ." Tommy, the desk manager's pleasant voice stalled out. The smooth-talking manager at my hotel suddenly lost his verbal abilities and southern charm. His body immediately morphed when he saw Detective De Luca walking in next to me.

"Miss Oliver, is there a problem?" I heard more trepidation in Tommy's voice than concern for my well-being. The genteel, southern-mannered man vanished. His smile disappeared and his body took on the rigidness of a soldier. Perhaps he thought I was in trouble with the law.

"Everything is fine, now," I answered. "Nothing for you to be concerned about, thank you."

The detective at my side jumped in to fill the awkwardness. "Hello Tommy, it's been a while. How's your mother doing?"

Tommy's eyebrows squished together, as a worried frown formed. He stared speechless at my face and then slowly his eyes moved down to my chest. I looked down and saw my blood-covered blouse.

"Oh, I had a little run-in with a mugger. The good detective wanted to walk me back here to make sure I arrived safely. We're going to go get something to eat after I get cleaned up."

The detective turned toward me and said, "You know, I really would feel better if you had a doctor look at your head."

"I'm fine. Why won't you believe me? " *Boy, you're cute, but you're not going to let go about me going to the hospital.*

My Supercop gave an accepting smile, along with a disapproving shrug. With a shake of his head, he said, "Have it your way." Then he turned his attention back to Tommy. "Your mother must be getting up there. How old is she?"

Tommy's eyes retreated away from my chest. "Eighty-five. She's still doing all her charity work and is as finicky as ever."

"Excuse me, while you two catch up I'm going to go upstairs and change into some clean clothes."

"Wait." Tony grabbed my arm and glanced at the desk manager. "You still have those paper laundry bags in the rooms for your guests?"

"Of course, we do," Tommy answered with a slow New Orleans-style drawl. *And the Southern gentleman reappears. I'm back in New Orleans again.*

My Supercop leaned in and whispered, "Miss Oliver, please don't wash your clothes. Put them into the laundry bag—they're evidence—and bring them back down to me."

UPSTAIRS IN MY ROOM

I pulled out a light blue cotton dress and threw it on the bed. Picking white sandals to go with my new outfit, I dropped them to the floor beside the bed. I couldn't stand having the bloodstain blouse on any longer so I stripped down to my panties and bra. There was no time to shower with my Super Cop waiting. Still, I needed to take time for one phone call. I grabbed the phone and dialed Peggy.

I felt uncomfortable about leaving Sadie and Peggy waiting for me to deal with Reed and the suitcases. But I had no choice. I had to stay focused and remember why I had even agreed to see Sadie. My purpose was to find Jacob. There would be plenty of time to deal with Harwine later. Unfortunately, time was a luxury that Sadie didn't have. The hourglass of time was running out for her. It pained me to let both Peggy and her mother down. The least I could do was give Peggy a quick call before going to dinner.

Peggy answered, but with a strange sound to her voice. The hello that came through the phone had a distant and detached tone to it. It was as if my call was as welcomed as an irritating salesperson's call wanting to get her to sign up for the weekly paper. Something was different.

"Peggy, I wanted to let you know I arrived in New Orleans and have checked into my hotel. However, I stumbled into a bit of a problem."

"Thank you, you're kind to call. You caught me home because I'm not going to visit mother tonight."

"Peggy, the problem was that I was attacked. He pulled me into an alley."

"I drove mother to another nursing home today."

Suddenly, I felt my throat tighten and it was difficult to breathe. It was as if an invisible weight pushed on my mouth and I thought I smelled cigarette smoke. I turned my back toward the wall the bed was pushed up to and watched the locked hotel door.

"I fought him off. He said some vile things. His hands . . . he . . . I got a little beat up."

"Mother insisted I stay away for four days. That should be enough time."

"What? Peggy, did you hear me? I was attacked."

"Yes, that's awful. Four days, don't you think that's too long to stay away?"

Peggy wasn't listening to me. But then, I wasn't in the mood to listen to what was happening with her right now but I needed to try. "No, it's not that long," I answered.

I guess neither one of us needed to update each other since apparently, we both had things going on at the moment. "I might have to stay longer, especially now that I have to deal with the mugging. I'll have to file the police report and go through mug shots. Anyway, I wanted to check in and let you know. I need to go now; it's been a long day."

"Okay, thank you for calling, Stephanie. Be careful, I hear that New Orleans has some crime in the French Quarter. I'll let mother know you called . . . when I see her. Four days seems way too long to me . . . Goodbye."

That was strange.

I returned the phone to its cradle and grabbed the laundry bag from the closet and stuffed my bloodstained clothes inside. The smell of cigarette smoke was creeping me out. I slipped on the fresh outfit from the bed and crunched close the bagged evidence tightly in my hand capturing the smoke, blood, and evil inside. Then pushed my sandals on and hurried out of the room.

Trapped but in Control

HARWINE BOARDING HOUSE

Sadie made her way down the hall to an alcove where a tiny wooden table sat with just enough surface space to hold the large black telephone. With the tenderness of grabbing a butterfly by its wings, she lifted the receiver up to her ear with her right hand; she inserted the index finger of her left into the small circle-shaped hole for the number nine. She pulled the dial around, and it slid back, and she continued dialing: 5-5-1-1 . . . However, a mechanical voice buzzed in her ear before she finished dialing the number. "Enter your security code to place a call."

She pulled the phone away from her ear and stared into the receiver. *What? Peggy's number isn't long distance. Why should I need a code?*

She hung up the phone and stood frowning. She looked around to make sure no one was nearby and picked up the phone and tried again. Once again, before she finished dialing the voice commanded her to enter her security code.

Sadie placed the receiver into its cradle. It took a few seconds for her to pull from her memory her nursing days in the state hospital. The patients would have made calls to China if the hospital hadn't put a locking system on the phones. Each staff member had their own assigned code,

218

which they had to dial so they would receive a dial tone to be able to make a call.

Sadie made her way back upstairs and noticed the door to Norman's room was resting halfway open. If anyone could be able to confiscate the security code for the phone, it would be Norman. Sadie knocked on the door.

"Dag-nab-it! I'm going to be bald before I'm through."

"Norman?" Sadie called. Then she heard an explosive string of cuss words. She pushed the door open. She burst in to see Norman standing in front of a mirror in a thin-strapped undershirt with a towel draped over his shoulders. In his right hand was a pair of scissors.

"Norman, what is going on? Was that you talking?"

"Who the hell else would it be!" he shouted. He spun around. His eyes widened when he saw Sadie and stood speechless. When he focused on her, a smile grew across his face.

"Oh, it's you. Sorry, Princess. This salty dog left the Navy years ago but a bit of a sailor's mouth stayed with him."

"What are you doing?"

"I'm giving myself a haircut. My son is supposed to come this weekend, but he probably won't. In case he does, I don't want to look like a vagabond." He held out the scissors and asked, "Do you think you can help a clumsy old man out, Princess?"

Sadie smiled, turned, and closed the door. She walked over and took the scissors and ordered Norman to sit in the chair. "I used to cut my husband's hair. He was a gifted surgeon but when it came to cutting his hair, he was all thumbs."

Sadie cut while pumping Norman for information. *Was his son coming on Saturday or Sunday?* Norman answered he didn't know, could be Saturday. Could be Sunday. Could be neither, like usual.

She asked if his son called him regularly. Norman spat back, "No. Too busy."

Sadie combed and cut. "Norman, do the patients here get regular visitors each weekend?"

"No," Norman replied. "Most of the patients are alone in the world. Except for me."

He added that it seemed like the staff had been anxious at first about his son coming to visit regularly, but when his son didn't, the staff stopped fussing and checking on him. After that, they settled into ignoring him just like the rest of the patients who live there.

Norman had quizzed them why they were concerned about his son visiting. What did they have to hide? *Nothing. The staff said. His son could visit as often as he liked.* Which turned out not very often.

Norman mocked, "My son is a big-time businessman, too busy to visit an old man who only has stories to tell of *his* life."

Sadie cut with the precision of a skilled barber. Suddenly Norman grabbed her hand, making her stop as he turned and looked at her. "Say, Princess, you've got a lot of questions today. And I see you don't have your doll with you. Have you stopped talking to her? Or is that act just for Nurse Green Eyes?"

Sadie leaned in close and whispered. "I think you're a man who can keep a secret."

"Your darn tootin', I can. The Navy trusted me during the war to keep some big secrets. Old Green Eyes isn't as tough as those Japs. They didn't get anything out of me even when they threw me in a hole they dug in the ground. Lived in that damn ground with every crawly thing that slithered into that pit for five long months. If you have a secret, I'm your man, Princess."

"I need your help. I tried to make a call—"

"No way, it can't be done. They have them phones blocked. Can't make any calls, not without the code number."

"Do you know it?"

"Hell, no. The staff here is too smart to write down any codes. Told my son that we were trapped here like penned animals, but he didn't believe me. Thinks I'm imagining it. Probably thinks I'm remembering the days from WWII, that I believe I'm back in that hole."

Norman pulled Sadie closer. "You need to be careful, Princess. Green Eyes is like those Jap guards, she's a mean one. Like one of the Japs who guarded us: he was mean, too. He liked to knock a tree limb into a pit that held a new prisoner. Then he would turn his back so the prisoner would try to escape. He enjoyed catching him so he could dole out punishments. He had a hunger for inflicting pain. Green Eyes has that same cold look in her eyes like that Jap guard. Trust me, Green Eyes has a hunger for watching people suffer, too. Don't get caught by her or you will pay the price."

Norman and Sadie talked for over an hour. After hearing Norman's suspicions and listening to what he said that he'd seen and heard, Sadie was certain that her fears of abuse happening was valid.

He told Sadie that the patients on the first floor were the weakest and had no way to protect themselves from harm. All were bedridden and some were even comatose. He had heard cries of help, which most of the time went unattended to, in the late at night. The worst was watching from the staircase when an attendant *would* go down the hall to a patient who was screaming in pain. From the stairs, he'd hear the shouts to shut up, and then the silence would follow. Norman tried to get help but the few people he could tell didn't believe him. It tortured him wondering what silenced those patients he heard crying for help.

Minutes before Sadie left Norman's room, they both agreed that as a team, they would get the evidence to shut down the boarding house or die trying.

Garage Seating

We walked and talked. Detective De Luca said my case would be turned over to another detective who worked tourist-related robberies. Even though nothing had been taken, it was assumed the intent was to rob me but it had gotten out of hand. Since violence was involved, it was classified as an aggravated robbery. Once Detective De Luca had turned in his report, he was no longer officially connected to my case. Since now he was "off duty," he insisted that I call him Tony. I agreed. It felt natural.

The conversation was easy as if I'd known him forever. Maybe it was the Italian thing going on. I always had been a pushover for Italians. *Tony, I like the name.* It seemed to fit him as gently as his easygoing nature came across.

He stopped in front of a weathered green door that screamed for a fresh coat of paint. "This is it."

The name "Nick's Place" flowed diagonally across the door in a flowery script. "Mostly locals only know about this place. Nick doesn't advertise. But somehow, it's always packed. We might have to wait, but it's the best food in town."

He opened the door as I took one step up, and walked inside a small room. "Wow, I would've never known there were this many people in here," I said as I scanned the shoulder-to-shoulder crowd. "From the

223

outside, it looked like one of those narrow houses between the shops."

The room was about the size of a small bedroom. I only hoped that the dining room would be larger. "Where are they going to seat everyone?"

Tony laughed. "That's the charm, or the curse, of the French Quarter. Buildings go back, long and narrow, and up when possible. I guess that's why Nick's remains kind of obscure to most people passing by. This building goes back a full block, and Nick makes every inch of it count. He puts the people next in line to be seated in the garage at the rear. At least once you get there, you're not packed in like sardines. You get a folding chair and get served a glass of wine."

"You don't say." I gave a half-smile, trying to make every effort to be polite. Still, the tightness of the room made the temperature seem to be at least 100 degrees. My skin had that clammy feel to it like it gets just before fainting. Maybe coming here hadn't been such a good idea.

Tony's eyebrows pinched together in an upward slant. "You're not looking so good."

"Thanks, just what a girl likes to hear."

"This is the locals' number-one spot to eat but I forget that Nick can pack in 300 to 400 people in here on a good night." A slight smirk formed as he said, "Don't let the Fire Marshall get wind of that. It gets like this because the business out-of-towners who come regularly to town keep finding out about the place. It used to be a nice quiet restaurant—when only locals came."

"Darn out-of-towners," I said lightheartedly.

Tony's face again grew a concerned look. "Coming here probably wasn't the best choice considering the crowd and all." He looked around the room. "Nick and I've been friends for years, I'm sure he'll get us a table quickly. Your color isn't looking good. I need to get some food in you."

"It's okay, I'm fine." However, I could feel the blood rush from my face and I felt queasy.

"Tony," called a man from across the room. He was dressed completely in white with ash-blonde hair. Made me think of a young, good-looking Colonel Sanders.

He crossed the room, squeezing through the crowd. "You finally made it. Roffy has been here for three weeks, cooking up a storm. Where the hell have you been? I was afraid you'd miss seeing him. He'll be leaving soon. Guess you're getting too busy for your old friends."

"Of course not," Tony said and he turned, facing me. "Stephanie, this wickedly successful man is Nick."

"Finally you bring in a date." He extended his hand. "How do you do? Tony doesn't share well, especially when he's out with a ravishing woman."

"As you can see, Nick is quite the charmer," Tony said. "Nick, this is Stephanie Oliver. We met today. She had a French Quarter experience *unbecoming* to our good city. She was mugged. Do you think you can get us a table without a wait? She's still a little woozy."

Nick looked at my forehead where the butterfly bandage was over my eyebrow. "My, that looks nasty. You poor thing, are you okay?"

"Yes." I shot a disapproving look at Tony.

He shrugged and said, "Hey, anything to keep us out of the garage."

"You're not going to the garage. I'll be right back," Nick said and promptly disappeared.

Taking this opportunity before Nick returned, I wanted to make it clear to Tony that he had stepped over the line. "I really don't need you announcing about my getting mugged to everyone. And would you explain to me why the garage would be used for prime seating? Sounds a bit weird."

"It's the French Quarter, what can I say? Nick's place is unusual. Most places don't have garages. Hell, no one living in the French quarter owns a car. It's too hard getting around, so you walk. Nick uses his garage for restaurant customers."

"Very enterprising."

From across the crowd, Nick waved and called to us. "Tony, Stephanie, come on. I have a table for you."

Tony looked at me. "See, it worked like a charm." He extended his arm, parting the crowd for me to move forward. "Our table awaits."

I whispered to Tony as I passed by him. "Well, maybe this one time you're excused for playing the *lady was mugged* card. I do need to sit and food sounds good, too."

Magic Soup

We were barely in our seats when a squatty man came barreling toward our table. Immediately, panic washed over me. The pounding steps of my attacker replayed in my head. I blinked back the feeling of Déjà Vu. The man had one of those long kitchen aprons that hung past his knees. The apron strings scarcely made it around his waistline with barely enough left to tie a small knot. His round body gave an impression of a bowling ball with two legs propelling in a blurred image of motion. New Orleans had already guaranteed the most unique people I've ever seen. Havenridgers were unique, but they didn't hold a candle to these people. I felt I'd fallen down Alice's rabbit hole.

"Stephanie, your luck is about to change," Tony said with a chuckle. "This remarkable man who you are about to meet will be the delight of your trip."

"Tony," the man said in an excited voice. "Nick told me you were here. I was beginning to think you were mad at me." His smile seemed to glow. It was only dampened by the twinkle in his eyes. He turned to me. "Who is this gorgeous creature with you? Aren't you afraid I'll steal her away from you and whisk her off to the Keys with me when I go back home?"

Tony looked at me with a twisted face. "Stephanie, the minute Nick and Roffy get together they compete to see who can be the best charmer." Tony turned back to the man. "Don't bullshit the lady; she's not your type. Besides, you have Robin waiting for you back home."

"A man can be in a committed relationship but it doesn't make him blind to beauty."

"Stephanie, this is my friend, Roffy. He works magic in the kitchen and is the best chef in the country."

The plump little man leaned over to me and brushed away my hair to examine my forehead. "My, that is a whopper. Nick told me about your encounter." I immediately moved my hair back over my wound.

After a few pleasantries, Roffy said he had a special sweet potato soup that would wash away any memories of my unfortunate day and he'd whip up some appetizers to go with it. Then without another word, he hurried off to the kitchen.

"I truly don't appreciate all this attention about me getting mugged. It's a private matter." Handsome Italian or not, I was getting very miffed about the way this whole dinner date was unfolding. "And another thing, you may be into that whole mumbo-jumbo thing that Ghistaine is selling, but I'm not buying any of it."

"Whoa, Ghistaine was trying to help you. And I didn't tell Roffy about the attack. Don't blame me for that one."

"Well, whom do you think the blame should go to then?"

Tony motioned a "T" with his hands as if calling a time out. "Can we back up and start over? Nick and Roffy are nice guys. I've known them for years. I just wanted to get you something to eat—and this is the best restaurant in town. Besides, it's quiet here in the dining room and I figured you probably wouldn't be up to bar hopping."

I looked into his eyes and had to smile. "No. Bar hopping is the last thing I'd want to do." He was so handsome, and those eyes of his, they held a genuine kindness in them. "You're right, I'm not feeling well. My head is splitting. But, it is true, I don't believe in psychics. I know some people do. That's evident by how many people recommended Ghistaine today. But trust me, I'm *not* a believer."

"I know where you're coming from, I didn't believe it either. Until she saved a little girl's life because of her visions."

I couldn't ask what little girl, because Roffy returned to our table with a young man trailing behind him, balancing a large tray on his shoulder. The man pulled the tray down to hip-level as Roffy grabbed a platter from it and placed it in the middle of our table. The platter held an assortment of munchies. He then lifted a bowl from the tray that contained a creamy pumpkin-colored soup with a dollop of sour cream in the middle. "Here's my Magic Soup, guaranteed to soothe and chase away any bad . . . er . . . bad energy."

After serving me the soup, he placed another bowl in front of Tony and then looked back at me with a concerned look. "Stephanie, I'm sorry if I was too forward when we met. I can be overbearing sometimes. Really, I'm adorable once you get to know me. I hated hearing about your . . . uh, episode today."

Tony was right. Roffy did seem like a great guy. I told him everything was fine and that I was upset that I had acted rudely toward him.

Once Roffy retreated to the kitchen, Tony and I started in on the appetizers. They were amazing. After one bite, I realized that I was famished and I devoured most of them, not leaving much for Tony. They were breaded chicken poppers topped with cheese, bacon, and garnished with fresh sprigs of herbs. Next, I attacked Roffy's *Magic Soup*. It was to die for. With my nerves soothed and my pounding head quieted, I said in between sipping my soup, "Tony, tell me about Ghistaine saving a little girl."

"She didn't physically save her. It was her insistence with my captain that made him send my partner and me back out to Manchac to check things out. That resulted in us finding the missing girl. It happened five years ago. The whole city had been alerted about a six-year-old girl who went missing. Her mother was a real doozy. She lived in a shack out on Manchac Bayou outside of town. Bayou people are different—private and secretive. They don't depend on the police for anything. Who knows why it was different with little Emmie Lou, but we got this anonymous call about her being missing."

"How long was she missing?"

"Three days. We didn't get the call until the second day. The Cap sent me out 'cause I was partnered with Laurent, who was born and raised on that bayou. People trusted him, as much they can trust someone who leaves the bayou and becomes a cop. We did our investigation, spoke to locals, searched the homes that we were allowed into out there, and came up with nothing. Zip. It was as if little Emmie Lou had just vanished. Bayou folks would rather depend on Sister Ezora, a voodoo priestess who lives out there, than outsiders or city people. Laurent and I went back and told the Cap that we couldn't get anywhere. All we had was a pink plushy toy pig that Emmie Lou's mother gave us. Said her daughter never let it go, not even when she was eating. Her *mother*, and I use the term loosely, said that the Devil must've taken Emmie

Lou, so she didn't want the toy around anymore because it had bad vibes. If we found Emmie Lou, she said she wouldn't take her back—since the little girl had been touched by the Devil. Can you imagine that, a mother who doesn't want her daughter? All that woman worried about was getting us out of there fast before we found the still she kept in the backyard. Laurent said bayou people kept her rich by buying her moonshine."

"People still make moonshine?" I asked.

"Yep. Laurent had heard about Emma Lou's mother when he was a kid. He said that it was her *shine* that was his first introduction to alcohol at eleven years old."

Tony shook his head. "Eleven years-old, yes, bayou people are a rare breed." He continued, "Emmie Lou's mother was so wasted she never recognized Laurent. Hell, she wouldn't have recognized Jesus Christ if he had walked in the door and handed her own daughter to her. Poor little Emmie Lou probably would've been better off with the Devil."

"How did Ghistaine get involved? Did she live in the Bayou then?"

"Nope. You see, Ghistaine has intuitive powers. She is an empath."

I couldn't help rolling my eyes. "Yeah, I was in her voodoo shop."

"No, you have it wrong. Ghistaine doesn't have anything to do with voodoo. That's Jasmine, she rents out part of Ghistaine's shop. It's purely a business decision to help with finances."

"Okay, so tell me about the missing girl case."

Tony grimaced. "Really, Ghistaine is not a nut job. Believe me, that was my first thought, too. She came into the station not long after Laurent and I got back from the bayou. She said that Emmie Lou was alive but wouldn't be for long. Then Ghistaine grabbed at her chest and started gasping for breath. Said we needed to act quickly."

"So why didn't you question her as a suspect?" I asked. "That sounds like a threat. You know, like, you need to listen to me or the little girl will die."

"Right, that was my thought, too. But before I could say or do anything, Ghistaine spotted that pink pig on my desk. She grabbed it and her eyes glazed over. Her breathing got even more labored and she started describing a shack that was adjacent to the little girl's home. Since Laurent and I had just got back from out there, we knew what she described was correct. Ghistaine said the house had this funky metal roof with a hammered half-moon and blue painted stars all over it. I'd never seen anything like it before going out there but she described it perfectly."

I finished my soup and pushed the bowl away, and wiped my mouth. "Well, all the more to be suspicious."

"Except, then Ghistaine says Emmie Lou is in a canvas sack under the steps going up to the front door. She cried out, *you have to hurry, Emmie Lou is dying.* Then she collapsed."

"I'm sorry, Tony, but it sounds like an Oscar Award-winning performance if you ask me." I could envision the gray-haired woman in her purple skirt collapsing to the ground, and I wasn't even a psychic. "Don't tell me your captain bought into her act."

"That's what I thought when he sent Laurent and me back out there. Cap said we couldn't wait to question the psychic and risk a child's life. I was sure it was some kind of scam. When we got to the house, the guy who we spoke to earlier was still there. I'll never forget the skull tattoo on the side of his neck. He came out on the porch—a real swamp dirtbag—but this time he acted real jumpy. That's when we heard this whimpering from under the steps. The guy took off running. We let him go; hearing the muffled crying coming from under the steps, we had probable cause to break through the wood lattice nailed around the steps. After crawling under, we saw it. The canvas bag, lying in the black, mucky ground. Stenciled on the outside of the bag in green letters was the feed store's name that Ghistaine said would be on it. The bastard had put Emmie Lou in the bag and threw it under there, leaving her to die. He had bound her hands and mouth but she was still breathing. Emmie Lou's little fingers were bloody from clawing at the bag to get out. The doctors confirmed that she wouldn't have lasted another night."

"Ghistaine could've made that anonymous call and when you didn't find the girl, she decided to come into the station. Maybe she was part of a kidnapping plan that went bad."

"You would think, but if you're going to kidnap someone, they wouldn't be from the bayou. They don't have any money to pay ransoms," Tony said. "Later on, I investigated Ghistaine. I wouldn't let it go. I found out that Ghistaine had never been in the bayou or within a hundred miles of the skull tattoo guy, or Emmie Lou. She checked out at every turn. Come to find out three years earlier, Ghistaine had helped find a cop in Arkansas who had been kidnapped and tortured. She's the real deal. We've asked her for help for close to ten or eleven cases in the last five years but every time it takes a toll on her. An empath physically feels what the victims go through. It's very traumatic. However, Ghistaine says that she can't ignore someone in need."

"What happened to the man who took Emmie Lou? Did you catch him?"

"Yes. The judge gave him a life sentence, but he didn't last long. Another prisoner killed him in jail eight months later. Emmie Lou's mother died the next year and the little girl went into foster care. A wonderful couple adopted Emmie Lou."

"I guess maybe I owe Miss Ghistaine an apology."

"She doesn't want apologies or thanks. She says that she would rather lead a quiet existence, but victims and spirits won't leave her alone."

Mind Terror

Norman ran the comb through his hair one last time and checked the mirror. "Not too bad for an old man, if I do say so myself." He left his room, went straight to Sadie's door, and knocked.

Sadie opened the door. "What do you want?"

"I've come to escort you to the dining room for breakfast."

"All right, let me get my doll. Wait here." Sadie returned holding the doll in the crook of her arm. "I'm glad you came. I have difficulty getting down the stairs."

"You don't have to worry as long as Norman is here."

"Who?"

He frowned for a moment and then answered. "Norman, that's me. You forgot my name already, Princess?"

She muttered to in a low voice. "Norman. I know that."

"Good. I do my best to be unforgettable."

They climbed downward with caution. Sadie's eyes focused on each step, her body stiffened and she stopped dead. "No, no, no. Not now!"

Norman turned, not knowing what to do or say. What had gotten her so agitated?

Sadie took in a slow, soothing breath. "Norman. Please, I have to tell you something. Remember yesterday when I told you that it was easy for my daughter to put me here in this so-called boarding house because of my medical condition?"

"Princess, at our age we *all* have medical conditions. Stick with me and it won't be that bad."

"But, my medical condition is important because there are strings attached to them. I have to keep it under control until I accomplish my task of finding out if there's abuse going on here."

"I told you, I'd bet my life there's abuse. At the very least, patients are not getting the proper care. And I guarantee the word *abuse* is Nurse Green Eyes' middle name," Norman added. "If we could get rid of her, and that Reed fella who owns this place, things would change."

"That's why it is imperative that you know everything about me so you can be my backup if something goes wrong. I have some kind of dementia or Alzheimer's. The doctors can't seem to agree because my symptoms vary too much. Whatever it is, my memory slips. I'm not sure how long I'll be able to hold it together. It's important for you to stay close and make sure any evidence that I uncover gets to someone who can shut down this place."

Norman patted her hand. "I'm not going anywhere, Princess."

Sadie ignored him. Sympathy wouldn't help her. What she needed was an ally who didn't wear rose-colored glasses. "You see, my mind gets lost."

He looked intently at her: he was listening now. Sadie explained. "It's like a stuck door, keeping me in the past. So far, I've been able to unstick the door and come back into the present, but one day it won't open and I'll be gone. I've got to do this one last thing, gather enough proof of patient abuse here, before my mind is locked away for good."

"Together," Norman said. "We'll do the job together. We're a team." He leaned over and kissed Sadie's forehead. "Now, come with me to breakfast."

When they got to the bottom of the stairs, Nurse Green Eyes was there talking to another nurse. She paused and looked at them. "Oh, lookie here, if it's not the high and mighty Norman Miller. So, you decided to grace us with your company for breakfast. Or did you come down to complain about something and stir up more trouble?"

"No complaints. I've turned over a new leaf, Mercy. I just want to get along. No trouble here."

"Now I've seen everything," she purred. "You've mellowed out 'cause yous got a girlfriend?"

"Please, we're not making any trouble." Norman pushed past the two nurses. "Come along, Sadie."

Inside the dining room, Norman and Sadie sat at a table. Soon one of the male kitchen helpers brought two plates of runny scrambled eggs, cold hash brown potatoes, and four slices of half-burnt toast.

Norman looked at Sadie twisting her napkin. "Don't let Mercy bother you."

Once their server was out of earshot Norman spoke in a low voice. "I have an idea, how we can get around the green-eyed devil-woman. I've been watching her. Mercy always works Saturday nights. She's not happy about it because she's gotten herself a boyfriend. I've been suspecting she's been overdosing the patients at night to keep them still so she can slip out to meet her new fella."

Sadie perked up and looked at Norman.

"I've heard her around nine-thirty, dialing the phone. Then he pulls up outside, she runs out the front door, and off they go. I'm not sure when she comes back . . . haven't been able to stay awake that long. Sometime before sunrise, I suppose. That's when the day nurse comes in for the shift change."

"I could go into the patients' room on the first floor at night when she's gone," Sadie said. "Take some pictures, check the IV's, and their charts. Being a nurse for so many years, I haven't forgotten my training. My long-term memory is clear as a bell."

"That's good. You see, it's all working out. And when Mercy places the call to her boyfriend, she'll have to enter the telephone code. All we have to do is come halfway down the staircase, she won't notice because that area is in shadow even when there's a full moon shining in the front windows. When she dials the code, we can write it down on a piece of paper."

"Norman, I can't manage those stairs."

"You don't have to, I'll do it. After all those years climbing up and down ladders on my painting jobs, stairs are a piece of cake for me. Besides, I have perfect vision since my cataract surgery. I'll be able to see the code she dials to get through to an outside line. Then whenever we need the cavalry to come to the rescue, I'll be able to call."

"You'll call Mable?"

"Mable? You told me your daughter's name was Peggy. You wrote it down on a piece of paper with her telephone number for me. I hid it my shoe so no one would find it. Who's Mable?"

"I told you about Peggy?" Sadie asked, then her eyes clouded, not focusing on Norman or anything in particular. She mumbled as if talking to herself. "Her birthday was last week. I got her that bike she wanted. I had to wait until Friday for my paycheck to have enough money to buy it."

Norman sat silently, looking at Sadie and waiting. Realization washed over her face suddenly and she dropped her fork on the plate. She grabbed her hands together and wrung them.

Tears welled up in her eyes. In a shaky voice, she said, "No. That's not right. She's not a little girl anymore. Peggy came up with the failsafe plan. She is grown up now."

Placing a hand over her mouth, Sadie's face held a look of terror. She whispered through her gnarled fingers. "No, not now. My mind has to work for a little longer."

Norman put his arm around her. "It's okay, Princess. Your mind is still here. A door just got stuck for a moment."

Creole Nights

Tony and I walked, still chatting away. Two hours had flown by at Nick's. Now, our conversation had spilled outside without any pause or break as we walked back to the hotel. Strolling through the darkened streets of the Quarter, I didn't have a care in the world. My Supercop, along with Roffy's Magic Soup, had washed away all the bad memories of my attack. I felt safe and content with Tony beside me.

I looked at him while he was telling me about a night he, Nick, and Roffy had unsuccessfully tried to talk their way out of a bar fight. His eyes sparked with a life that Daniel's eyes only displayed when he shared something that he had discovered in his lab. Test tubes, Petri dishes, cell division, and growth, that was Daniel's life. I had willingly joined his quiet and unspontaneous world so many years back that remembering it was like thinking about a movie where two strangers played us. Life had no room for impromptu actions, like fights in biker bars. No, my life had followed a predictable path, which started when I married Daniel right after graduating high school. That's when I fell right into step as the dutiful, good wife.

I smiled at Tony as he was so animated telling his story. He held so much passion for life. *How can two men be so different?*

"I swear," Tony said, holding a hand up as if taking an oath. "Being around Roffy can be dangerous and life as his friend can be unpredictable." He shook his head and chuckled. "So, there we were in this biker bar and some guy said that hogs—" he paused to clarify for me, "Harley Davidson motorcycles are known as hogs. He said hogs were the only bikes to ride."

No, Tony was wrong. Being a friend of Roffy had nothing to do with it. Tony was a man who went after life and took hold of it, like taking a bull by the horns. *He reaches for the golden ring; that's what made his life unpredictable and exciting.*

Although my ex-husband had many golden rings in life, it was not from taking chances or living life with zest like Tony DeLuca. Yes, Daniel had his so-called "golden rings," but the difference was they were given to him. He never had to fight for them. He never knew the excitement or passion of living life to the fullest. Work was Daniel's passion. Three months after our wedding, the reasonable and customary length of time to start a family, Daniel suggested we have a baby. One year later, Lily was born. Life had always followed a logical order with Daniel. One step after each, predictable step, after another.

I knew Daniel had loved me and Lily, but we weren't part of his world. We could only watch from the sidelines. My husband, the "boy genius," had always been compared to all of the Einsteins of the world. In Daniel's scheduled life, his logical order of things, there was no room for the unexpected bar fights. No time to experience the real world or life in general.

As Daniel's wife, his superior status in the medical field provided a comfortable life for me and Lily. I never had to face any financial difficulties like *normal* people. Life was safe, secure, and consistent, until when Lily was four. That's when everything changed and my life turned upside down. Safety and security left, along with Daniel.

Tony's voice interrupted my wandering thoughts of the past. One of his hands was stretched high over his head. "Well, this mountain of a man with a tangled beard that made him looked like half-man and half-grizzly bear continued to insist that no other bike could live up to Harleys. He made his claim one too many times and my roly-poly friend, Roffy, says that *The Indian* was far more superior to anything Harley Davidson ever produced."

"Oh no, he didn't," I said. "In the bar that you said had about twenty-five, Harley Davidsons parked out front?"

"Yeah, that bar."

"What happened?"

"Pow!" Tony punched the air as he pantomimed the action. "The guy swung a fist so fast it seemed to be a blur, but Roffy was faster. He ducked," . . . Tony ducked . . .. "And instead of making contact, the dude spun in a complete circle."

Tony shook his head. "You wouldn't think a little round chef could move that quick."

We both laughed so hard that tears formed in our eyes. It amazed me that this man who I had just met knew how to live life with a zest that most people only read about in books. I could tell Tony led with his heart; another difference between him and my ex. Logic doesn't fit with the emotions of the heart. If my brother met my Supercop, he would say that Tony's life was all about the journey.

"Pow!" Tony threw one last punch in the air. "Fists flew that night for sure. Jeez, that was one helluva night. N'awlins is filled with all kinds of people, but they're good folks for the most part. That bear of a guy turned out to be one of the good ones. He's a regular at a great local honky-tonk outside of town. He goes by the name of Banjo, 'cause that's what he plays."

"Tony, you have some great stories about living here. Sounds like you have a lot of friends and people you care about. But earlier tonight you shared that you were thinking about moving. I can't believe that you would want to pack up and leave here."

"Yeah, other places don't have what we have here. But finding a new place with its own special beauty is right for me now."

"But, you've been here for ten years, love your job, and say New Orleans is home. Why leave now?"

"Don't really know. It's just time."

"You're widowed, could it be that there are too many unhappy memories here?" My question poured out of my mouth without any hesitation. I felt closer to him in these few hours than I had felt to Daniel in our entire marriage. Still, my question was maybe too personal. "I'm sorry, that was rude of me to ask."

He stopped and turned to face me. A tender smile spread across his face. "I don't mind. The subject of losing my wife and her illness had always been off-limits. Of course, my friends all *know* about it but not all of what I went through in the year and half of her illness. They came to the funeral, but we never talked about it then, or even now. I've kept it to myself. Strange thing is, I'd like you to know. You're so different from my wife, but I think you and she would've been friends."

He was silent for a moment and then took my arm and wrapped it around his and started walking again. "Maybe, it's because of my losing my wife . . . maybe not. I guess I'll never know for sure. What I do know is there's a season for each moment and a time for each season. Maybe, this is the right time for a move. It's different now, *I'm* a different person. Like talking about it to you, it's okay. It seems natural. It doesn't seem personal; it's as if I'm sharing my history. That's all. I was married, my wife died, and I'm back to being *just Tony*."

"It took me over a year to get back to being *just Stephanie*. I do understand about loss. After my divorce, moving to Havenridge helped me but there was more to it than that."

I sighed. "You see, I had a little girl. Her name was Lily but she died suddenly. It was a reaction to medicine—medicine I gave her. I guess no matter how someone dies, there are feelings of guilt because if you loved them, then you should've protected them and kept them safe."

"I'm sorry. I can't imagine having a child die."

"Yes you can, Tony. Losing someone you love hurts, no matter if it is a wife you vowed to protect or a baby you held in your arms and promised to keep safe."

We walked without saying anything more. He broke the silence a few minutes later. "I found out that I like fishing. That's part of the new Tony. I've thought about maybe moving out to the country. I've done some camping out your way, in Georgia."

"Really? Ever drive through Havenridge?"

"Once. I remember there was a lot of open land around there. Seemed like a nice little town. Quiet. A good place to find yourself."

Peace flowed over me. Supercop Tony made the world seem safe and at the same time, intoxicatingly exciting and wild. Yes, Tony wasn't anything like Daniel.

When we entered the hotel lobby, Tommy was sitting behind the counter reading a newspaper. He looked up and asked, "How was your dinner?"

"Great," I answered far too quickly. My mother taught me to maintain an air of uncertainty on a date. *Never appear too pleased, or too impressed*, she would say. But then, I had to remind myself that I was not on a date.

"Tony, I have a message for you." Tommy shuffled some items around on the desktop and plucked a pink message form up. "Here it is, your partner Laurent called. He wants you to call him immediately."

Tony took the message. "Thanks. Can I use your phone?"

"Sure thing."

Tony said he would only be a minute as he dialed the phone. "What do you have for me?" He smiled and gave me a wink.

I motioned to the overstuffed chair across the room and I mouthed, *I'll wait over there*. I heard Tony as I took a seat. "Georgia, huh. Same county?" His eyes glanced over in my direction. "Yeah, she's still with me."

I didn't felt guilty eavesdropping on his conversation since obviously, the call involved me. His partner must have uncovered something about the men who attacked me.

"Okay." Tony straightened up and looked like he was about to end the call. I diverted my eyes when he glanced over. "See if you can find out where they are now, Laurent."

He looked away, pausing. I stared back at him. His posture seemed to change when he was Supercop rather than when he was just cute Tony. "No, don't get a warrant. If I know that kind, they are still here. Probably hold-up in one of the bars, drinking since the incident. Start looking on Royal first. They gotta be pretty tanked by now. When you find them, just pull them in on a public intoxication charge. I'll come in early tomorrow morning to question them."

Tony hung up and walked over to me.

"Was that about the men who mugged me?"

Tony glanced over to Tommy, who had been busily straightening magazines as he craned his head toward us and seemed to be fixated on the corner where we were located.

"Let me walk you to your door," Tony said as he extended his hand to escort me. "We'll walk and talk."

I waited in silence as we rode the crowded elevator to my floor. When the elevator doors opened upstairs, we exited, and Tony spoke as we walked down the hallway. "Laurent has been doing some snooping around the Quarter while we were at Nick's for dinner. Come to find out, a few people noticed two black motorcycles parked near the alley where you were attacked. Close to the same time of the incident, the shopkeepers next to the alley reported hearing your scream and within seconds they heard motorcycle engines gunning up. Then they saw the black cycles zoom past their store windows."

"Did they recognize the men?" I knew I couldn't identify them since the attack came from behind. An eyewitness was our only hope to catch the men.

"No. Even if they did, it would be a cold day in Hell before anyone would talk to the police. Laurent is a different type of cop; he has a unique talent for establishing trust. People who live in the French Quarter don't see him as a cop, but as just another person on the street. I don't know if it's because he's creole, or that he speaks Y'at. Whatever it is, he's the best out there to get information. That's why I called him to check things out. Still, having witnesses testifying or answering questions at the station is a whole different ball game."

"But, the shop owners certainly don't want criminals attacking people on the street. That's not good for business."

"You'd think, wouldn't ya? People in the quarter have a *live and let live* attitude. Anyway, black motorcycles stand out, especially if they aren't from around here. Storekeepers were happy to report that the cycles they saw had Georgia plates proving that the crime wasn't from any locals. Could you know of someone who wanted to even a score with you, or give you a scare? Maybe someone from back home."

Tony's question echoed in my mind. *Even a score?* My drive back from Milledgeville buzzed in my ears as I remembered the sound of the cycles on the highway when they passed my car.

"The cycles were totally black?" I asked.

"One was, but the other had yellow flames painted on it. Do you know them? Anything at all would help to establish a thread connecting them to you. Perhaps you have an idea of a motive for the drivers who attacked you. We might nail them if you could share some info that could lead us to them."

At dinner, I had told Tony about getting the suitcases in Harwine from the old storage building on the same property of the Harwine Boarding House. I also shared about my scare with the two hot-dogging cyclists when I was driving back from Milledgeville to home.

"I can't believe anyone would hire hitmen to scare me." I imagined the secret henchmen who existed in Italy, who threatened people by putting the mark of a black hand on doors. I had learned about them from an elderly Italian neighbor back in Florida.

Tony laughed. "Hitmen? No, just people who live by different rules than most." Tony stood silently waiting. It was apparent that he expected me to have information."

I took a breath and recounted the whole nasty scene with Phillip Andrew Reed. How it unfolded with me and Max narrowly escaping with the vanload of suitcases. "Tony, it still seems a bit far-fetched that Reed would send someone after me here in New Orleans."

"It happens every day. A good, law-abiding citizen crosses the wrong person. There's a whole different world of people who think nothing of doing something less than legal or moral. Those kinds of people and their friends have the same moral code. And friends think nothing about helping by putting the squeeze on someone who crossed a buddy of theirs. The good people, the Average Joe or Jane, will cave easily because they don't have experience with that other world of people. A lot of members of that world get their kicks from bullying or terrorizing people, it's a power trip for them."

"Nice." The hairs on the back of my neck stood up from just thinking about people like that. Reed definitely lived in the world Tony was talking about. "I guess Max was right. He said the fight wasn't over. He warned me that Reed's reach went far. Said, someone from Harwine might threaten me. Max even had a name for them, goombahs."

Tony chuckled. "Sounds like a wise man. But, don't you worry. Max isn't the only one who has dealt with *goombahs*. I've seen a few of my own, Nola style. They're all the same. I can handle them."

Tony paused, deep in thought. I could almost hear the cop's gears turning. Too bad he was ready for the next stage of his life. Supercop fit him.

After a few seconds, he said, "I never thought your attack was a mugging. It didn't feel right. Plus they didn't steal anything, so you can't really call that a mugging."

His expression changed. Supercop disappeared as the kind and tender Tony reappeared. He gently swept my hair back, exposing the bandage near my eyebrow. "I should've insisted on you going to the hospital."

"Stop it." I pulled his hand down. "They would've put a butterfly bandage on my head and charged me three hundred dollars. You took care of me and I got dinner, too. I got the better deal."

"Okay. Just the same, it probably would be best not to go to sleep for another couple of hours."

"Did I understand you correctly? Your partner doesn't know where the two men are? They're still on the loose?"

"For right now, but Laurent will track them down if they're still in the Quarter. Don't worry."

"What good will *that* do? I can't identify them."

"Not a problem. I'll run a check on them. People like that usually have a record. Trust me; I'm good at my job. I can be very persuasive and when I'm finished with them, they won't bother you anymore. They'll probably want to get out of town as quickly as possible."

I shrugged. "If Laurent finds them, that is."

He looked at me, his eyes filled with warmth. "One thing good came out of the attack."

I rolled my eyes. "What's that?" I just wasn't up for a pep talk.

"I met you."

How can he do that? Melt my heart with his words? That safe feeling washed over me again. "Dinner was perfect. Roffy's magic soup was incredible."

"Yeah, leave it up to Roffy to even make soup special."

"How long have you known him?"

"About eleven years." He put his hand out, palm up. "May I have your key?"

I looked at him, dumbfounded. "Wh . . . what?"

"Your hotel key."

Not knowing exactly where this was heading, I dug inside my purse, following orders like a starry-eyed teenage girl. I found the key and handed it over. He took it and opened the door. "Stay here," he said, stepping inside my room without any hesitation.

I watched him as he hit the light switch on near the door and swiftly moved to the bathroom. Then, he flipped the bathroom light on and disappeared into the bath area for a few seconds before he reappeared. He proceeded to move toward the bedside table lamp and turned it on. He turned and scanned the room once more.

"Looks safe and secure," he said as he walked back to me. I was still standing in the hall doorway. Then he handed the key over to me. "Can I stop over to see you tomorrow? I mean, so I can update you on the investigation."

"I'd like that. I thought I'd check hospitals and the courthouse records for Jacob tomorrow. Maybe I'll go talk to Ghistaine. She might know where I should look for someone who lived here over ninety years ago."

"She could be of some help. You never know."

Tony turned to leave and I grabbed his arm. "Tony."

He turned back. "Yes."

"Thank you for tonight . . . and the room check."

"Of course, a gentleman makes sure a lady who's in his company gets home, or to her hotel room, safely. Goodnight."

I grabbed him again, but this time I didn't want to waste time talking. Pulling him toward me, I kissed him on the lips. He kissed me back. Then stopping, he pushed back and stared at me with an inquisitive look.

"I'm sorry," I blurted out. "I shouldn't have done that. I know this wasn't a date. You must think of me as forward. I'm not, it's just that you were so, uh, sweet and made me feel . . . safe."

"Shhh." He pulled me to him and kissed me. Two long kisses. Then he stepped back, holding me gingerly by my shoulders. "I would like to call tonight a date—if permitted—our first date."

"Okay," I answered.

"I'm not glad about the way we met, but I am glad for tonight," he said. "Goodnight, Stephanie Oliver. I'll see you tomorrow."

I watched him retreat down the length of the hallway. Then I stepped into my room, closed the door, and chained it.

Post Attack

The warmth left me immediately once I was alone in my room. All of my safe feelings vanished. A flood of fear crashed over me and memories of the attack thundered back. The charming restaurant, Tony, and the evening spent together—all the happy moments—gone. Gone, replaced by the thoughts of the alley tumbled into my mind. Those awful minutes when evil pushed its way into my life, now controlled my thoughts.

I hurried over to the window and pulled the drapes closed. My heart pounded as unreasonable paranoia ruled me. I grabbed the cushioned chair in the room, dragging it over to the door that led to the hallway and wedged it under the doorknob.

"There, that's better." I took three, deep, cleansing breaths. My body relaxed back to a normal state. However, instead of having the feeling of Tony's embrace return, my skin crawled with the residue of the man in the alley. All I wanted was to take a shower and scrub away the feeling of my attacker's touch. I imagined the odor of stale cigarettes and onions. Was it imagination? Or did it lie in my hair? On my skin? Strange, I hadn't noticed the smell on me before.

I stripped down to my bra and underpants and grabbed my pajamas from my small travel bag that I had brought. Then, I headed into the bathroom and turned on the water in the shower. Flashes of images of a knife from the shower scene of the movie *Psycho* with Janet Leigh after she had checked into the Bates Motel sped through my mind. I pushed Janet Leigh and the horror movie away but it only made room for another thought to creep in. *There was another door in my room!*

The closet was an open wall space without a door. Still, I was sure there had been another door in my hotel room. With the water running, I reentered the bedroom where two double beds were located. I scanned the room where there was one small round table, the television, and a dresser.

There! Next to the double dresser was a door. *It must adjoin the room next door to mine.*

With great care not to make any noise, I unlocked the deadbolt and peeked inside to a dark, vacant space. It was approximately two and a half feet square. Just big enough for a person to stand and wait for the occupant of the room to fall asleep. Of course, the door that connected the two rooms didn't have doorknobs on the inside of the space. The only feasible access to my room would be if I left my side unlocked and open—unless, as Tony said, there are all kinds of people in the world and I'm sure some of them would know a way to open a door without a handle.

I closed and locked my connecting door. Getting the only other chair left in the room, I carried it over and wedged it under that doorknob. I realized my actions were absurd but I couldn't help myself. I thought if someone tried to get in, at least with my makeshift alarm system in place, they would make noise doing so.

I wasn't my normal Stephanie Oliver. Paranoia ruled inside my hotel room. It felt like I was in a scene from a horror movie in slow motion, and someone was about to shout, *look out behind you!*

Looking at the second door with the chair, I took a breath and tried to get a grip. "That should do it," I said again as if saying the words out loud made it more logical.

Approximately five minutes later, I sat on the bed with red skin from the feverish scrubbing of my body that I endured in the hot shower. However, an elusive odor of cigarettes and a faint smell of onions still lingered in the air. It was apparent to me that tonight I would get very little sleep. Especially, since I decided to leave all the lights on in the room for added security. The clock in the room confirmed that forty minutes had passed since Tony had left me alone.

Will I ever sleep without fear again? I thought. Then I remembered I hadn't called Betsy. She had me promise to call her upon my arrival into town. Talking to her certainly would calm me. She had a way of soothing my nerves. I dialed the phone and she answered on the second ring.

"Stephanie, I thought you were going to give me a call around five o'clock." I could hear the concern in her voice. "Did you have car trouble?"

"No, no car trouble."

Betsy worries far too much but I couldn't keep what had happened to me from her. "But, I did run into a different kind of trouble."

Ready, Set, Saturday Go

With painstaking care, Sadie finished buttoning her blouse and slipped on a light sweater. Then she folded the pajamas that were lying on the bed in front of her and carried them over to the dresser. The top drawer was resting partially open. Waiting for her on the dresser top were three items; a scarf, a small black comb, and her doll, all sitting in a perfect row.

After putting the pajamas away, she began her morning ritual. With the scarf in her hand, she said, "This is my daughter, Peggy's scarf. She is all grown-up now. Blue is her favorite color. She is helping me here."

Sadie's eyebrows furrowed. "Helping me? Helping me . . . helping me how?"

Without an answer coming to mind, she laid the scarf down and touched the object next in line. "This is Norman's comb." She smiled. "He calls me Princess." Her faint smile grew. "That's it! I remember."

She put the comb down and grabbed the scarf again. "Peggy insisted on a failsafe plan. Norman will call Peggy if I need help. Peggy will come get me."

Sadie's eyes sparkled as she placed both the scarf and comb away in the drawer and closed it. Then she picked up the doll. "This is my doll. I call her Mabel but no one knows that Mabel was my *real* friend—except for Norman and Peggy. They know that the doll is part of the plan."

Leaving the room, Sadie walked the few feet to Norman's door and knocked, clutching the doll to her body. He opened the door, holding a hairbrush in his hand. "Morning, Princess. Come in, I'll be ready for breakfast in a jiffy."

Sadie took a seat in Norman's chair by the window as he brushed through his hair. "Craziest thing, my comb is missing," he said. "I hate brushes."

"Don't worry, it will turn up somewhere," Sadie said with a knowing smile. "I was thinking you're probably right about Mercy drugging us. I haven't been swallowing my evening pill; the one she says is for my arthritis. I've been putting it against my cheek and holding my tongue back to hide it when she makes me open my mouth to see if I've swallowed it. I spit it out after she's gone. Since I've stopped taking it, I'm more alert in the morning. Not sleepy and my memory is getting better again."

Norman turned to Sadie excited. "I knew it! That's why I refuse any medicine at night. I take my blood pressure medicine in the morning. They wanted me to take other pills but I told them no. Don't believe in vitamins and I don't have arthritis. After a while they stopped insisting that pills had to be taken at night because they work better. They know not to argue with me anymore."

"I did notice that they do seem to leave you alone. Another thing I was thinking about, why can't we move our plans from Saturday night to Friday night? You said Mercy goes out both nights. The sooner I get into the patients' rooms, the sooner we can get evidence and can shut this place down."

"No, we need to stay on track. Saturday is the big party night and Mercy usually stays out longer than on Fridays. Besides, I think she and the boyfriend have been fighting. I heard her talking to the other nurse about him. The boyfriend slipped and called her Latisha."

"That's not good. Maybe she won't go out at all."

Norman turned to Sadie and said, "Don't worry, Princess, old Green Eyes likes going out." He turned back to finish brushing his hair. "The way I figure she might make him sweat it out until Saturday but she'll forgive him. She likes going out too much. By Saturday he'll be prime pickins' for flowers, dinner, and dancing—the whole nine yards. They should be out until the cows come home."

"I bet she's steaming. How stupid can one be, mixing women's names up?"

"You got that right. So we need to give Mercy time to calm down. Let the boyfriend patch things up and by Saturday night he'll be in high gear with romancing her. We'll have plenty of time to do what we have to do."

"What if they break up?"

"Then it will happen on Friday and Green Eyes will be back early. Either way, we can't risk having her catch us in the act. Who knows what would happen? Mercy is dangerous. Let's stick to the plan."

"All right. Then Saturday night it is."

The Empath

I must have fallen asleep sitting up sometime after 4 a.m., so I woke up late with a bit of a stiff neck. The phone rang on the bedside table as I was putting on my shoes.

When I answered, I heard a familiar voice say, "Mornin'. I'm surprised you're still in your room." The friendly and gentle voice was Tony. "You said that you had a full day ahead of you last night."

"Good morning to you, too. I do have a lot of things to do, but I slept in. I guess it was Roffy's Magic Soup." I was too embarrassed to tell him about my plunge into insanity last night. I had a new understanding of the fine line between real and imagined. The mind *really* is a fragile thing.

"I was hoping you would call. Did your partner find the men who jumped me?"

"Yep, and they're from Harwine. We held them overnight. But before sending them to lockup I told them we had enough to put them away for years. New Orleans doesn't take to people coming here and causing trouble. Especially messing with pretty little ladies who are visiting our French Quarter."

"Put them away for years, is that true?" I asked.

"Naw. A crime like this could get them a few months. But without a definite ID, even that would be hard to get, although, they don't have to know that. I finished by saying that I didn't want to put you through the months of a trial just for a sentence of 5 to 10. I suggested that if they would leave town immediately and never bothered you again, I'd drop everything."

"Tony, I know you're trying to make me feel good, but I'm not naïve enough to think that words are going to scare them. Have they been released?"

"A few hours ago, but trust me, they won't bother you. I followed them to the state line. Scumbags like that are loyal only until that loyalty gets in the way of their freedom. Words may not scare them but those two have a history with the law. They know the next time they get arrested it won't be easy to squirm their way out of a long sentence. The courts get tired of seeing the same faces. Your trouble with them is history."

"I appreciate all that you've done . . . but I don't want you to jeopardize your job. Threatening someone, even scumbags, I'm sure isn't part of standard police procedures."

"Don't worry about it. I know what I'm doing. Also, I called that Reed, the one you said owned the boarding home in Harwine where you got the suitcases from. If I'm not mistaken, he'll be watching over his shoulder for a while. I put the fear of having a New Orleans cop on his heels, he'll probably be careful from now on."

"That might help me more than you think since I'm planning to hire an attorney to see if I can get the rest of those suitcases. It might just take some fight out of him. Until then, I'm not stepping foot on his property again. No telling what he's capable of."

"Smart lady. More things go on in the backwoods of America than people know about. People can disappear. Stick with the court system. As flawed as it is, it's the safest way to deal with places like Harwine."

As much as I wanted to help those poor people under Reed's control, I was glad that I didn't know anyone living at his so-called boarding house. At least, that was one less thing for me to worry about.

"Uh . . ." Tony said.

I waited during an awkward silence to see what was on his mind.

"I was calling about something else. Remember that honky-tonk lounge I told you about? The one where my friends and I hang out at and play music. It's the best place to hear real Cajun-style music on this side of the Mississippi. You can't leave without experiencing it. Saturday night is the best time to go. I could pick you up after you finish with your day. It's a ways out of town but worth the drive. How about it?"

"Like a date?" I asked. "Officially my case *is* closed, right? So you wouldn't be breaking any rules."

"You get right to the point, don't you?" Tony chuckled. "Your case is not officially closed but it's icy cold." His voice was light and he didn't wait for any response. "I guess I am. I'm a little rusty on dating etiquette since I haven't asked anyone for a long time. But yes, I'm asking you out on a date."

"Don't worry, I'm rusty too. I'd love to go out on a date with you. I've never been to a real live honky-tonk—Cajun-style or any other style."

Tony said he would pick me up at the hotel by seven-thirty. It would give me enough time to do some shopping and research. The first stop would be to make a visit to Ghistaine's. We hung up after agreeing on a time to meet in the hotel lobby.

I took one last look in the mirror to check my outfit. I wouldn't have time to change before meeting Tony. My white peasant-style blouse would be cool during the day, paired with basic jeans; the outfit would work for daytime shopping or a night of dancing. I was excited about our evening plans. The reflection of me in the mirror was okay, but not really right.

I need something to dress up my outfit.

I went to my small cosmetic traveling case where I had packed my lingerie and makeup. In the zipper compartment was Mabel's locket. I put it on and moved back to the mirror. "That's perfect! Just the finishing touch the outfit needed."

I threw my purse over my shoulder and hurried out the door. I had a lot of territory to cover before my date tonight.

After leaving my hotel and a short walk, I entered a small shop obscurely nestled between a bookstore and an attorney's office on Chartres Street. I would have passed by it without noticing it, if not for the hand-painted lettering on the window that read, Antiques to Newly Vintage Items. Seemed like an oxymoron, what does newly vintage mean anyway?

It looked small from the outside, but once inside it went back forever. Tony was right about shops being long and narrow. Browsing down a narrow aisle, I searched for something—but what, I didn't know. Then I saw it. A porcelain mustache-shaving mug with a brush and an ivory-handled straight razor. A chip was on the rim of the cup near the handle. What appeared to have been a white glazed mug at one time had aged a dull yellow with an infinite amount of crazing. This obviously was one of the antiques and not a newly vintage piece. Cradling my treasure in the bend of my arm, I weaved my way down the aisle and up the last one. A few feet before getting to the front counter of the store, I spotted an old, silver dresser brush. That completed the items I needed.

The man at the check counter loved to talk. No doubt, not many people found their way to his little part of the world. He rambled on with details about the razor's possible age.

"The new razors use plastic handles," he said. "Young kids don't know the difference between plastic and ivory but there's a big difference. You have a good eye for antiques, missy." Never skipping a beat, he continued. "Did you know these shaving brushes are made of badger hair? The good ones are, that is."

I hurried him on with my purchase by handing him a fistful of cash. I didn't want to labor the conversation anymore, not wanting to make a lasting impression. Outside the shop, I removed the items from the paper bag and pulled out the scarf I brought in my purse. After wrapping the items carefully, I threw away the paper sack and placed my treasures deep into my purse.

Now if Ghistaine was at the store, it wouldn't be long until I'd discover if she really possessed a sixth sense or not.

I cut through Jackson Square and then walked down a cobblestone passageway known by locals as, *Pirate's Alley*, which I had read about, to get to Royal Street.

If Ghistaine is the real deal as Tony insists, I'll get some answers, when and if she connects with Jacob.

Jacob's Message

I approached the shop. It seemed odd that if Ghistaine owned the shop that she would rent out space to a Voodoo Princess when she didn't believe in voodoo. Although voodoo apparently was as common in New Orleans as peaches and pecans were to Georgia.

Another déjà vu hit me when I saw Ghistaine out on the sidewalk, sitting in a chair that propped the shop door open. Her wiry, gray hair matched her strange gypsy-like attire that was so familiar to me, only today her floor-length skirt was green.

"Hello," Ghistaine said. "I'm glad to see you're looking well today." She stood and I noticed that her skirt entailed many pointed layers, like overlapping scarves with gold metal beads sewn to the hem of each layer. I couldn't help to wonder if her style of dressing was all part of a great marketing scam. Tony believed deeply in her powers and I hoped for his sake, and mine, that he was right about this bizarre woman's sixth sense.

I answered her, "Yes, I'm feeling much better than the last time I was here. I wanted to come and thank you for everything you did for me yesterday."

"It wasn't me. The spirit who walks with you told me you were in danger. She's the one to thank."

"You see spirits?"

"No. When I do connect with a spirit, I *feel* them. Not all clairvoyants' abilities are the same. I'm an empath. I don't see spirits—just sense them. It's much like tuning into a radio station. Some spirits come through strong and clear, and others just barely. It depends on the emotions that the spirit brings with them and their energy state. If I connect during a time of trauma, the feeling can be very powerful."

"I understand." What I understood was a con artist when I saw one. "Ghistaine, I'd like your help. Can we go inside?"

"Of course, my child. I knew you were coming yesterday for my help, but you left so abruptly. Your mind was not open for my help then."

She stood and walked into the shop with the beads on her skirt tinkling ever so faintly, like tiny fairy bells. She glided as if floating off the floor through the store, heading toward the doorway with the beaded curtain. Once in the back area where Tony had brought me after the attack, Ghistaine and I sat at a small nearby table.

"Tony said if you had an object that belonged to a person who had passed, that it could help you connect."

"Sometimes," she answered.

"I have some things with me." I dug the scarf out and unwrapped the items, then placed each in front of Ghistaine.

She studied them without saying a word. Then she took the silver brush into her hand saying, "The spirit around you is a female." Ghistaine held it close to her chest and closed her eyes.

She sat for several seconds not saying anything so I prompted, "Do you feel anything?"

"Shhh. I must concentrate. Spirits live in an alternate world. They communicate from another plane. It's difficult to tune in to the frequency that the spirits communicate from. We must be patient."

I sat in silence, feeling rather guilty of my deception. However, if Tony was right about Ghistaine, she would pass my test.

"I feel a woman. She wants you to help her."

Ding, ding, ding! Failed. She took the bait.

"The energy I feel is around you but not from this object." She placed the hairbrush down on the table. "The female spirit near you is connected with her heart to another. Stephanie, you do have a bond with this female spirit. But, I feel that you're not interested in connecting with her. Your energy is focused on another one. A male spirit."

Did I speak about searching for Jacob sometime and not remember? Perhaps Tony was right. Why did I need to play games with Ghistaine? Perhaps I needed to trust what Tony believes about her. It was on record—she was responsible for saving Little Emmie Lou. What more proof did I need?

"Maybe a different object?" she asked. I pushed the shaving mug, brush, and razor forward. Ghistaine looked at them and then held her hand over each piece as she closed her eyes. First the razor, then the brush, and last the mug. Her hand wavered in the air above the pieces, traveling back and forth for several minutes. She removed her hand from the air, dropping it to the table beside her. Exhaustion permeated her face.

"I'm so sorry, Stephanie, but I'm not feeling anything from these pieces." She looked at me and touched my hand. "I'm getting interference from the spirit around you. As if she is pulling me away from the objects—toward you."

The sorrowful look on her face made me ashamed. I was the only fraud at this table.

"I can't help you." Ghistaine pulled her hand away and winced. Pressing her fingertips to her temple, she said, "I don't know what you want me to do." No one was with us in the back area, not physically that is, but still I knew she wasn't talking to me.

Ghistaine pleaded to the invisible person. "Please stop, you're hurting me. Slow down and speak softer. I don't understand." She frowned, keeping her eyes shut, she pressed hard at her temples as if in great pain. She opened her eyes, glaring at me. "You want me to use Stephanie as the channel?"

I watched her in horror. Her face contorted. Was Mabel really with me? Or did Ghistaine suspect I had been deceiving her? Could she be throwing my deceit back at me to trick me?

"Ghistaine, what's going on?"

Could it have been Mabel who pushed Ghistaine out into the street as I was being attacked? Living in the old Brewer house, I had felt a bond with Mabel. I wondered if Mabel really could be here with us.

Ghistaine said, "The spirit says you are wearing Jacob's heart."

I gasped and my hand immediately grabbed the locket around my neck. Remembering Jacob's words in his note to Mabel, "You possess my heart." I had my proof. Ghistaine could talk to the dead.

I pulled the locket off. "I think Mabel wants you to hold her locket to connect with Jacob." I placed the locket into Ghistaine's open palm.

Death Knocks

Ghistaine's hand clenched around the locket and pulled it close to her chest as her shoulders bowled over in a slouch. Her breath slowed. "This woman's jewelry has traces of a man's spirit."

"Yes. Inside is a lock of hair from the man that I'm searching for information about, I want to know how he died and where. Can you tell if he was in New Orleans?"

"Yes. He's here now."

I told Ghistaine that Jacob vowed his love to the woman whose spirit is around me. "Jacob never came back for Mabel. Did something bad happen to him here—was he murdered? Is that why he never returned?"

"Shhh." She held her palm up, signaling me to stop talking. Beads of sweat formed on Ghistaine's face. "The spirit experienced something dreadful—immense pain but it was not bestowed by another person."

As her body began to shiver, a muffled moan expelled from deep inside of her. "Child, get a piece of paper and pencil from that drawer." She pointed to a small chest in the corner. I did as I was told. When I returned to the table, Ghistaine had slumped over, her head resting on the table in front of her.

"Place the pencil in my hand."

I did so and put the paper under her hand. She held on to the locket with her other hand and closed her eyes. She lurched back into the chair and then her whole body bent and curled inward as if someone had just punched her stomach. She moaned again. "He's here."

"Who?" I asked. I needed clarification.

"Jacob."

Ghistaine opened her eyes and starting writing as her lips quivered. The whites of her eyes were a dark yellow color.

"You're ill," I said. "You need to stop."

Ignoring me, she spoke with a labored voice. "So very, very tired . . . in much pain. He's afraid that he'll die like the others. Many, many dead. The families carry the bodies to the cemetery gates and leave them there. Piles of the dead."

Ghistaine scribbled, *Althea R*, but then her hand slid, trailing a crooked line across and off the paper's edge. She moved her hand back to the paper and wrote *O*, then *S*, but stopped as a scream of pain forced its way out of her mouth.

"That's it. I'm getting help," I said. As I rushed out of the backroom, I crashed into Miss Voodoo Princess.

"What going on?" she demanded.

"We have to call for an ambulance."

Ghistaine lifted herself from the chair. "No. Get Tony, I need to see him. A doctor can't help."

The other woman grabbed Ghistaine seconds before she collapsed. Between both of us, we managed to get her to the couch to lie down. She lay grasping the locket with one hand and the paper and pencil with the other.

"Go get Tony," the Voodoo Princess said. "I'll stay here with her."

I ran to the street and turned left. Scanning the sidewalk. Across the street, I spotted the restaurant he spoke about at dinner. The one he said he usually ate lunch at and ran in its direction.

Entering the restaurant I yelled out like a crazy person, "Tony—Tony Deluca!" A waiter looked at me, wide-eyed. "Is he here?" I asked.

"N-no. He doesn't eat lunch until around two."

I raced out into the street and looked up one end and then down the other. I spotted him. "Tony!"

He turned. I waved frantically and ran toward him. When I got to him, I was out of breath but managed to say two words, "Ghistaine—sick."

He grabbed my hand and we ran toward the shop together.

Inside the shop, Ghistaine was rolling from side to side, with her arms pulled close to her body. Tony knelt down and felt her head. "She's burning up. How long has she been like this?"

"It came over her almost immediately. She was connecting to . . . to Jacob's spirit."

Ghistaine held out the paper. "Give her this. It is what Stephanie needs." Tony snatched it and threw it down to the floor. He glared at her other hand curled into a fist at her chest. "What do you have here?" He unfolded Ghistaine's clenched hand, which held the locket. "What is this?"

"I gave it to her. It's Mabel's locket. Inside of it is a lock of Jacob's hair."

Tony grabbed it and shoved it toward me. "This is what is making her ill. Get it out of here before it kills her!"

"I didn't know. She was fine. I thought it would help . . ."

I turned and ran out of the store with the locket. Outside on the sidewalk, I paced back and forth.

She really has the power. Please, don't let her die like Jacob.

Tears streamed down my cheeks. It *was* real. Ghistaine had felt Jacob's pain. The pain that had killed him!

A Believer is Born

I'd calmed myself and stopped pacing. Being out of control wouldn't help anything. I sat in Ghistaine's chair outside the shop entrance. Tony needed an explanation from me. There had been no way for me to realize the extent of Ghistaine's powers. Coming up to speed with everything and accepting new ideas quickly wasn't my strong suit. My stubbornness and my determination to test Ghistaine's skills before believing in them had put her in danger. For that very reason, I didn't know if Tony would forgive me.

My ex-husband had left me because I had turned into a weak person. My marriage had morphed me into a shell of the person that I had once been. Now that I had found the strong Stephanie again, would that strength be too much for Tony? Would it push him away?

Things were happening so fast. Changes had been hurtling at me at rocket speed. I'd never believed in ghosts, but I truly felt Mabel around me. And Ghistaine having powers? Now I *do* believe that she is an empath. Would Tony ever understand my stubbornness? But he too had to have her powers proven to him. The difference was when I set out to prove her skills it might've killed her. Although it had only been less than 24 hours since I'd met Tony, I wanted him to be a part of my life. I hoped that I hadn't crushed that possibility.

Tony emerged from the store. He looked as if he had just left a battleground.

I jumped up and moved toward him. "How is she?"

"Better. Her color is back to a natural rose. I never saw anyone look so jaundice." After a slight paused, he asked, "Was she like that when you got here?"

"No. She was fine when I got here. It wasn't until . . . ."

Tony nodded his head. "Right. The locket. She connected to that guy, Mabel's lover, through the locket and that's when things went sour?"

"Tony, I'm sorry. I didn't know."

I had to explain and make him understand. I couldn't lie, no matter what. Strong-headed and stubborn, I question things I don't believe in; that's who I am. I couldn't change and go back to weak Stephanie ever again.

"I stopped at an antique shop and bought some things," I confessed. "I wanted to test her to see if she would tell me she felt Jacob through them."

Tony looked confused. "What? You believed she was a fake, so you were baiting her?"

"It... it wasn't like that." But that was exactly what it was, I baited her. "She didn't feel anything and then she said something about what Jacob had written to Mabel. I knew then that she was real. I was wearing Mabel's locket with a lock of Jacob's hair inside it, so I gave it to her to hold."

I started to cry. Not out of weakness but because I was so angry at the thought that my independence and being strong could cost me this man, who had become important to me. The tears flowed like a water leak from a dam. Trickling, one, two tears at first, and then an uncontrollable stream of them. The tears were more from anger than anything else. I was angry that I, or any woman, was forced to make a choice between being true to who she is, and remaining whole, or molding into something different to keep a man.

Tony pulled me into his arms. "Don't cry. She's going to be all right. As soon as you took the locket away, she started to come around." He pulled away to look at me as he wiped my wet cheeks. "You didn't believe my story about her finding the kid in the swamp? So, you decided to test her and prove that she was a fake?" He shook his head as if in disbelief. "Incredible."

"I'm sorry. I hadn't planned on giving her the locket. I figured she'd pretend she felt something from one of the things I bought, the phony items, and I'd have proof it was all a charade. I'm sorry that I didn't believe you. I put Ghistaine in danger. I'll understand if you don't want to have anything to do with me."

"What! Are you kidding? You did what I had wanted to do when I met Ghistaine. I'm glad, not that she had a bad spell, but glad you were gutsy enough to find out for yourself and not take my word for it. If you didn't you would've rated me in the nut category along with Ghistaine."

He pulled me back into his arms. "Oh, I almost forgot. Ghistaine was adamant that I give you this." He pulled out the paper with Ghistaine's writing. The words were broken up and trailing down the paper but it was readable if you linked the letters together: *Althea Ross, 3-15-651, Little Palermo.*"

"Althea Ross? I don't know who that is—and Little Palermo— is that a person or a place?"

More mysteries. I either hit dead ends or receive more questions.

This time I broke Tony's embrace and asked, "Did she tell you who these people are? And the numbers. What am I supposed to do with them?"

"She didn't explain. She probably doesn't know. When she connects to the spirits, sometimes she sees things, like messages. She passes them on to who they are intended for, but as she has explained to me in the past, many times only the person who the message is intended for will understand it."

"Great, I don't know what this means. What am I supposed to do now?"

"Don't know. All she said was Stephanie needs this to find Jacob."

"Perfect!"

Tony smiled and looked at me. "You know what I think?"

I stared at him with frustration that immediately dissipated when I saw his face. A strong jawline, a sign of confidence and wisdom, gentle and caring eyes. *How can I feel like this? I just met him.* Still, it's like we were in sync.

"I think," he said, "that you look beautiful and every man tonight will envy me when we walk into the room. How 'bout I finish up my work. I've got to write my daily report, then I can clock out. It shouldn't be more than thirty minutes. I promised to take you out tonight and I'm a man of my word. Hope those pretty shoes of yours are dancing shoes."

"A night out at the honky-tonk involves dancing?" I teased.

"You better believe it."

Kingdom of Evil

Phillip Andrew Reed had moved to Harwine after his mother's death. His intention had been to lay claim to his stepfather's money. He had been determined to get his hands on the money, which he did, and then leave town—but he never left.

After years of growing up dirt poor, Reed knew that happiness required money—lots of it. Childhood memories of going to bed hungry and listening to his parents' violent arguments about bills taught him that money mattered. Other kids he knew didn't go to bed hungry. They had Christmas presents under beautifully decorated trees, bicycles to ride, and parents who didn't fight. The way he had figured it, he must have done something bad to make God so angry and want to punish him with his childhood situation, but he didn't know what it was.

Although by the time Reed was a teen, he stopped blaming God. He saw the real reason for his unbearable childhood: it was his father's drinking. Memories of him returning home late in the night, drunk and penniless. Many nights the young Reed had woke in the middle of the night to his mother shouting about not having food, and his father yelling back, to *shut the hell up*, those were Reed's childhood memories. The mental anguish of beatings and defending his mother by blocking his father's fist with his body stayed with him as an adult. The physical scars had faded over the years; however, the mental scars remained open and raw.

Looking in the mirror, Reed straightened his tie as his mind wandered to a time when he was ten years old. His father had been more violent than normal that night. When you're ten years old, a boy feels like a man and wants to protect his mother so he ran to the kitchen where his parents were fighting. His mother lay on the floor, bloody and beaten. His anger swelled; he wanted to kill his father. He charged at his father, swearing his hatred for him, and shouting that he'd kill him.

Reed's father just laughed, and then backhanded the small boy, striking Reed and leaving a large gash across his son's eyebrow from the Garret ring he always wore. Blood poured down Reed's face. It was more than his ten-year-old strength could bear, and he cried.

The adult Reed's anger swelled even after all the years that had passed. However, the anger was not at his father but toward his mother. He stared into the mirror, visualizing the scene from so many years ago, as his mother grabbed and spun him around. She had told him to go get a rag to stop the bleeding. She was angry at him! Not glad or proud that he came to her rescue.

Reed could almost feel the warmth of the blood on his face now. That was it, his mother had been angry. She didn't thank him for his heroic actions. Nothing Reed had ever done was ever good enough. Reed shook his head, pushing away the memory. "Humph, a mother is supposed to protect her child," he muttered.

Haunting memories, even after all these years, would sneak up on him, back into his mind like trickling, burning lava.

"At least God released me from that drunk," Reed said firmly.

That was not the only bad memory that haunted him. At nineteen, the death of his father from a late-night car crash seemed as if God had answered his prayers. But, instead of an answer to his living nightmare, things got worse. His mother couldn't find work and soon the bank foreclosed on the house. Reed's mother moved in with a friend and slept on their couch. Since there was no room for Reed, he found out what it was really like to fend for himself.

He found work and rented a room in the flophouse in town. That's when he decided that God wasn't going to help him, if God even existed. At nineteen, Reed surmised that the only thing that made any difference in life was money. Money made happy memories with Christmas trees and presents underneath, childhood birthday parties, and food on the table. That's when he stopped praying. If happiness was out there for him, it would be up to him to fight for it. Reed learned to be a survivor. It made him strong . . . but bitter.

Reed crossed the bedroom floor to his walk-in closet. He pushed the button for the motorized tie rack and selected his favorite tie. The ties and rack cost more than a week's pay at Reed's first job. He walked back to the mirror and pulled the tie around his neck. He looped it into a Windsor knot, which he had learned how to do from reading the men's fashion magazines. He wanted to forget how his mother had struggled after his father's death, but she hadn't struggled for long, not like Reed had. His mother met a soft-spoken man named John Fleming not long after being widowed. He took her to fancy restaurants, while Reed worked as a laborer with a construction company.

A few months before Reed's twentieth birthday, he read in the newspaper of their wedding announcement and about the lavish wedding plans. The article said the couple was to honeymoon in Hawaii and that the future groom was rich. In fact, it said he was the richest man this side of the Mississippi. Certain that his mother would welcome him back into her new home, Reed called her.

Can I come live with you? Reed asked. But the answer was no.

His mother explained that she couldn't ask her new husband to support a son from another marriage. *You'll be fine. You are young and strong.*

Love, happiness, and financial stability came to his mother but not for him. Reed didn't call again. Ten years later, John Fleming called Reed with the news that his mother had died. That's when Reed traveled to Harwine, vowing that he would take what was rightfully his and claim his fair share of the Fleming estate.

Reed stared into the mirror at his tie. *Perfect,* he thought. He slipped on his jacket and checked his image. His suit, the tie, everything was perfect, just like the models in GQ. The three-hundred-dollar suit showed the world that he wasn't poor anymore. He grabbed the diamond tie tack off the top of the dresser and pierced the black silk material, adding the final touch.

Reed was finally a rich man. He owned John Fleming's entire estate. He schemed away everything from his passive stepfather; the money, the land, and the buildings. What once had been Fleming's family-operated hospital, Reed renamed Harwine Boarding House. He owned it all, now.

Reed headed out of the bedroom and paused at the door. He glanced back to the open closet and smirked. Hanging inside were six suits and four, sports jackets spaced three fingers apart—just the way he demanded from his housekeeper. Harwine's population consisted mostly of farmers and moonshiners. Most of the men in the county didn't even own a suit to be buried in when the time came. Poverty was a way of life there but not for Reed. His money ruled Harwine, and it made him the king there.

Reed walked to the kitchen where Bobbie Sue was wiping the spotless countertop.

"Good morning, Mister Reed."

The poverty of Harwine didn't bother Reed. He could manipulate the poor and weak, like his housekeeper. Reed only had to show his disapproval and she would cower. Her life was similar to Reed's childhood; she too received regular beatings at home from an abusive husband just like Reed and his mother had.

"Morning. Have you made the coffee?"

"Yes, it's hot." She opened the refrigerator and pulled the crystal pitcher out that held the cream for his coffee. "I've chilled the condensed milk just the way you like it."

Reed waved a dismissing hand at her. "That will be all. You can go now to make my bed and clean the other end of the house."

Bobbie Sue left Reed pouring his coffee.

Just like a king, Reed didn't mix with the common people. He maintained his level above the hired employees the same as a monarch who reigns over the soldiers who guarded the kingdom.

Reed walked out of the renovated kitchen to the adjacent sunroom at the rear of the house. It had a huge bay window that overlooked the boardinghouse, which was a quarter of a mile away.

The clients living at the boarding house signed over their Social Security money to live there. Add to that the Medicare payments received for nursing services, which they never received, plus of course the boarding house fees; all of Reed's careful manipulation paid off. The boarding house and its clients generated an income of thousands of dollars. Between the patient's money and fraudulent invoices, which he pushed through different state department offices that paid money out to businesses that helped with the care of the elderly, and the funding for medicine from government agencies; it was as if he had captured the *Hen that Laid Golden Eggs*. Any medicine they did buy for patients with the money received was reduced to half-doses or none at all. The orders to the staff were to sedate the difficult patients. It made sense, heavily sedated patients required less staff to manage them. Reed had derived a business plan and operating system that worked well. It was a win-win situation with a constant flow of money coming which kept Reed wealthy beyond belief. Harwine Boarding House was better than a dozen hens laying golden eggs.

Reed not only ruled over Harwine Boarding House but he controlled the entire county. He had Pete Newman, who was the vice president at the local bank, and the Sheriff in his hip pocket. No one would stop him. Reed controlled everything and everyone within a hundred-mile radius.

His house was a mansion beyond anything he had ever dreamt of owning. It cost next to nothing since it originally had been one of the abandoned buildings on the property. The renovation was done with overflow money from the boarding house and laborers who he could blackmail with something he knew about them.

Reed sipped his coffee and looked out the window to admire his kingdom but a loud noise cut through the air, disturbing his peaceful world. Seconds later, he saw the two black motorcycles speeding down the dirt path toward the boarding house.

"Shit! Why are those two morons going to the boardinghouse? I gave them one simple task to do. They must've screwed something up."

He hurried out of the house and jumped into his car. Reed reached the boardinghouse right as the two men were entering the front door. Reed followed them. As he stepped into the foyer, he heard an argument taking place.

"I'm telling you that we need to see Reed. We're not makin' no appointment," shouted the tall one. He was looking down at the nurse in front of him. "You just go fetch him now, girl."

The Jamaican woman did not back down. "Mister Reed isn't here. Like I said, he only sees people by appointment."

Reed could count on Mercy, she stood strong when handling difficult people but best of all she closed her eyes to questionable things about the boarding house. She followed orders, did whatever was needed, and would never ask Reed about characters like Bubba and Charlie who came around. However, she did this not out of loyalty but because Reed knew things about her. Reed could have her deported anytime he wanted. To Reed's surprise, Mercy had become his most dedicated worker and she had come to be his right-hand person. Their relationship was a symbiotic partnership of sorts, and it worked well for Reed.

Reed slammed the door. All three heads snapped around to see him standing there.

"Mister Reed, I tried to stop them," Mercy explained. "They just burst in here yelling."

Reeds eyes glanced over to see several boardinghouse residents huddled together at the dining room doorway, gawking at the scene unfolding.

"That's all right, Mercy. Please go take care of our guests, take them back to the dining room. We need not upset them."

Reed waited patiently while glaring at his two hired guns. Mercy approached the group where Norman stood in front, with Sadie peeking out from behind him. Mercy pushed the crowd back and steered them all into the dining room.

Reed moved around the back of the two men, grabbed each by an arm and scurried them outside. "What the hell were you two thinking coming here!" he hissed. "I told you to put the screws to that Oliver woman so she'd stop snooping around here. You've really stirred the pot. I had a New Orleans detective call and threaten me. What happened? Why were you in New Orleans?"

"That cop called you?"

"Yes, Bubba. That cop called me."

Reed turned and looked at the other man. "Charlie, I didn't expect your brother to use his head, but I anticipated better from you since you're the *brains* of the family. Now, not only do I have to deal with that Oliver woman, I have a detective's radar on me from another state. What happened?"

After listening to Charlie's slanted details and rambling excuses, Reed held his hand up. "Stop, I've listened to all the rubbish that I'm going to. Let me get this straight. You two followed her to New Orleans and thought that force would fix everything. Don't you know that if you threaten someone like this type of woman, it'll make her even more determined? The best way to get a woman to do what you want is to find out if she has a kid and then, threaten the kid. That'll stop the gutsiest of women. I *know* from experience."

"But, Boss, we staked out her house in Havenridge. She lives alone," Charlie said. "There were no kids anywhere around. Then she headed out of town, so we followed her."

Bubba added, with a look of achievement on his face, "I jumped her and dragged her into an alley. I told her to mind her own business or she'd get hurt." Continuing to defend his actions he said, "I didn't say anything about you. Believe me. You told us to put the pressure on her."

Reed scratched his head, taking it all in. They had been told to stop her. If that meant getting physical, so be it. Reed looked at the two. *Country bumpkins.*

"You were hired to scare her," Reed said. Although Reed tried to distance himself from violence, he understood the power of it. He also knew Bubba's mentality. "Not to get your jollies molesting her. Now get out of here and lay low until I know the heat is off."

"What about our pay?" Bubba piped up.

Reed shot him a hard look.

Charlie grabbed his brother, pulled him, and mumbled, "Later, we'll get our pay later. We need to go."

The Unexpected

Norman inched his way down the staircase, stopping halfway. Below, Mercy put her finger in the dial hole on the phone for the number five. The dial spun back as Norman wrote down the first number of the code. He watched as she finished dialing the other two numbers to get an outside line. Norman quickly wrote 5-2-7 on the paper.

Norman looked at his scratchy handwriting and made sure it was legible. He smiled. *Easy peasy, they can't outwit me.* He shoved the paper with the prized code numbers into his pocket along with the pencil and carefully backed up the stairs and out of sight.

He had the security code; it had been the only thing that stood between him and the outside world. Possessing the code provided the lifeline that Sadie needed to stay safe. If anything went wrong, now he could call Sadie's daughter as he had promised. Norman wouldn't let anything happen to his princess.

Mercy's voice echoed as she spoke to someone on the phone. "You can pick me up now."

Norman stopped in the shadows on the stairs to eavesdrop. Old green eyes was predictable but not stupid. He knew if they underestimated her cunningness it could be very dangerous.

"They should all be asleep now," she said. With a tone of repulse, she added, "except for that obnoxious old man, Norman Miller."

Norman's eyes narrowed as he stood still in the shadows, listening. *Just wait, Green Eyes, you haven't begun to see obnoxious yet. You'll get yours. Just wait.*

"Don't worry, he'll be no trouble. He stays in his room usually." A moment of silence passed as Mercy tucked the phone between her cheek and shoulder, holding it there to free her hands. She opened her purse and pulled out a mirror and a lipstick. "What? No, you don't listen to me." She paused, still cradling the phone, while she uncapped the lipstick.

"I told you, he only comes out in the morning, for breakfast. He's started coming down to the dining room with the new woman. Her name's Sadie." Mercy twisted the lipstick up and smeared more of the fire-red stuff across her lips. She smacked them together. "Boy, they're a real trip. She's looney tunes and he thinks he's Macho Man."

Admiring her image, Mercy pursed the painted lips into a kiss and then returned both mirror and lipstick into her pocketbook, snapping it closed. "Yes, come now! That's if you don't have to stop by to see Latisha first."

Norman slapped his hand over his mouth to hold back his laughter. *Just like a woman. She's goin' to make him pay for his mistake for months, no doubt.*

"Okay, okay. Yes, I believe you. You're not seeing her anymore. Just hurry up and get over here. This place is creepy at night. Besides, I'm ready to go dancing."

Five minutes later Norman saw the headlights of a car through the side panel window on the front door. Mercy was out the door in a heartbeat and the taillights trailed off in the distance, down the path leading away from the boarding house.

Once Mercy was gone, Norman climbed to the top of the stairs. Sadie peered out from the slit opening of her bedroom door.

"The coast is clear, Princess," Norman said.

Seconds later on the staircase, Sadie maneuvered the treacherous steps with the aid of Norman's helpful arm. In Norman's free hand, he held Sadie's doll. When they reached the bottom, Sadie took the doll.

"I've already unlatched the door of the compartment in the doll's back," Sadie said. "The disposable camera is hidden in there. Remember? I showed you." She didn't wait for his answer. "I'll be okay from here. Keep a lookout. Reed lives on the property somewhere close. All we need is for him to see Mercy leaving and decide to come here to wait for her to return."

"He hasn't noticed her leaving yet, I think we'll be fine. I'll keep my eyes open just the same. Call me if you need me."

"Norman, I'm perfectly capable of gathering evidence. Besides, you wouldn't know what to look for in the charts, I do. You act as my eyes, as a lookout. Once I've finished, I'll need your help going back up those horrible stairs. My legs don't work so well anymore."

Sadie wandered down the darkened hallway toward the rooms where the incapacitated patients stayed. The first room was vacant. At rooms two and three, she went inside and took photos of the deplorable conditions the patients were forced to live with. Open bedsores, the stench of unsanitary conditions, and malnourished bodies, all were evidence of abuse and neglect. The patients' bodies resembled more like concentration camp survivors rather than those of persons living today in America. Sadie hated to invade their personal life's torment, but the damning photographic evidence was the best way to expose the conditions here. One woman was so emaciated that Sadie couldn't believe she was still alive.

In the fourth room, the patient's chart provided the most incriminating evidence. The only possible reason for the elevated dose of medicines being administered to him would be to keep the patient in a continued vegetated state to eliminate the needed care from staff. There was nothing in the chart to indicate any medical need for the strong medication.

Sadie aimed the camera at the chart. The flash lit the room with a quick, burst of brilliant light. This room had a window that faced the front of the building. She prayed that, wherever Reed's house was located, he couldn't see the boarding house from there. With no moon tonight, a sudden flash of light would catch anyone's attention.

Seconds later, Sadie's eye caught a flash of light. There were headlights coming down the dirt drive, approaching the house at a rapid speed.

"Sadie . . . Sadie! Where are you?" Norman yelled from the hallway. "Someone's coming."

Sadie hurried to the door, opened it, and crashed into Norman as she was leaving the room.

"We've got to get back upstairs, Princess." Norman put his arm around Sadie's waist and all but dragged her toward the staircase. "Hurry."

"Norman, we've got them. Those poor people. Death would be a blessing." She stuffed the camera back into the doll and latched the back as they moved down the hallway. "Did you hear me? We've got them."

"I heard you. If we don't get back upstairs, they will have us."

When they got to the base of the stairs, a car door slammed outside. There were voices shouting as another door slammed.

"Ah, come on Mercy. Don't be like this."

"Don't be like this? You're a lying, no-good, womanizer! Stay away from me."

"Ah, baby. We're good together. Come on back and give me some sugar."

Thunderous footsteps stomped around on the other side of the front door as Norman and Sadie struggled to climb the stairs.

"Where are my keys? I'd rather keep company with the old geezers than you."

"You don't mean that, baby. Why, take a look at this fine, fine body. I can give you what you need, girl."

Inside, Norman pulled Sadie's shaking body up the stairs, stepping onto the fifth step. "Princess, come on. Just lean on me. We can make it."

Sadie's legs shook uncontrollably, like a jackhammer. "I can't do it. I'll fall. My legs won't hold me, they're trembling too much." She pushed the doll into his hands. "Take the doll and go."

"I'm not going without you. Come on, try." Then they heard the key enter the lock.

"Go, I'll play my disoriented act. I'll be okay. I'll say that I was hungry, and was trying to get to the kitchen. If you're with me, Mercy won't buy the story. She'll know we were up to something. You are putting us both in danger by staying. You must get to your room."

Norman stared at her.

They heard Mercy's irritated cursing outside. "Damn key won't turn." Then the jammed doorknob twisted, rattling back and forth without opening.

"Please, Norman." Sadie looked at him with begging eyes "The only way you can help me is to go. Give me the doll back. It goes with the act. It'll work. She'll believe that I was going to the kitchen. Trust me."

Norman's eyes welled with tears. Sadie pulled the doll out of his hand and said firmly, "Go."

Norman turned and charged up the stairs, leaving Sadie behind.

In Search of Food

Sadie held onto the banister to steady herself, while the doll lay in the crook of her free arm.

The front door flung open with Mercy still holding onto the doorknob as she stumbled forward over the threshold. Outside on the stairs leading to the porch was a silhouette of a broad-shouldered tree of a man.

Viewing the two figures made Sadie realize for the first time that the woman she feared was not tall. Sadie pictured her own daughter Peggy's petite stature. Mercy appeared about the same size. Unlike Peggy's small but stout body, the nurse's thin frame gave the image of height, which had made her seemed menacing to Sadie.

Mercy righted herself and straightened her twisted skirt, turning around to face the shadowed man. She yelled, "I mean it this time. We're through! You better get your sorry ass out of here before I go get my gun."

"If I leave, don't think I'll come back. At least Latisha knows how to treat a good man."

Mercy grabbed a vase off of a table next to the door and hurled it outside.

The man ducked. "Okay, you crazy bitch. I'm leaving."

"Good riddance!" she screamed, as she slammed the door. Mercy twirled around, took two steps, and stopped dead when she saw Sadie standing halfway up the staircase. "Wha . . . what do you think you're doing up there?"

"I was hungry. I wanted to go to the kitchen, but I got lost in the dark. Can I have a peanut butter and jelly sandwich? I like peanut butter."

"Noooo, you cannot have a peanut butter and jelly sandwich," Mercy said in a whiny and irritated voice. She headed up the stairs toward Sadie, talking all the way. "Does it look like I'm running a restaurant here, you old bat? Yous need to get back to your room."

At the top of the stairs, Norman held his door open a crack, just enough to watch the scene unfold. He didn't want to let Sadie go it alone but he saw that she was doing fine. He chuckled and said in a low voice, "Princess, you're really something. You should get an Oscar for this performance."

Below Sadie held out her doll, "Mabel is hungry, too. Why won't you help us find the kitchen?"

Norman closed the door. *I hate that nurse. Even if Sadie is playing a part, I'll not be a witness to Green Eye's verbal abuse of her.*

Sadie waited on the stairs for Mercy's next move. She marched up stopping one-step below her. Their eyes met. Mercy looked Sadie square in the face. "I don't care if you're hungry. You stupid, old woman—go to your room!"

The nurse's golden Jamaican skin had darkened with anger, probably partly from hearing Latisha's name. Now her body quivered with fury at the senile old woman who wanted peanut butter. Sadie had pushed her too far. Mercy grabbed Sadie's arm, pulling her hand away from her grip on the banister. Then, she spun her around to face the top of the stairs.

Sadie wobbled.

Mercy put her hands on Sadie's back and shoved her. "Upstairs, now! Get moving."

Sadie's legs crumbled under her with the force of the push. Her fragile body fell forward, crashing to the steps. As she struck the steps, Sadie felt an internal snap. A scream escaped her lips as intense pain and a burning sensation surged down her leg. As everything darkened to black, she heard a door bang open in the distance.

Soon, Sadie's vision came back and she realized that she was lying on the stairs with her face teetering on the sharp edge of one of the steps. In the background was moaning, seconds later she realized the moaning was coming from her.

"Look what you've done now," cried Mercy.

Pounding footsteps on the stairs thundered toward them.

"What happened?" Norman shouted.

Mercy looked up as Norman vaulted toward her.

"She fell."

"Princess, what did she do to you?"

Mercy glared at Norman. "I did nothing. She fell. I told you."

Norman eased down on a step near Sadie. "Princess, I'm here."

"I'll take care of her," Mercy spat. "I'm a nurse, you're not needed. Best you go back to your room."

"The hell I will, you old witch." Norman remained on the step next to Sadie. "Don't move her."

Sadie's sobs and moaning were increasing. She tried to control her outburst of cries that came whenever a new stab of pain shot up her leg. Looking past Norman for the doll, she saw it three steps above them. "I fell just like she said. It was my fault. Norman, see if Mable is hurt?"

Norman frowned. "What?"

Sadie looked hard at Norman and then moved her eyes toward the doll. "Mabel and I were hungry but we fell. See if *Mabel* is hurt."

Norman looked at Mercy. She wasn't listening to them as she moved Sadie's skirt to examine the injured leg.

"Oh, right. Mabel," Norman said. "Right, I'll check on her." He looked around and saw the doll lying face-down with the hidden door bulging under the doll's dress.

Norman leaned forward and grabbed the doll, tucking it under his arm. Sadie screamed out in pain as Mercy touched the bloody part of her leg.

"Her leg is broken," Mercy said. "There's a lot of blood, the bone must have pierced the skin."

"We have to call for an ambulance." Norman insisted.

"Ambulance?" A deep voice came from behind them and demanded, "What's going on here!"

Norman and Mercy turned around to see Andrew Phillip Reed standing in the front doorway.

Help Arrives

Reed took the steps two at a time. When he reached Sadie's crumpled body, he looked at Mercy. "What happened?"

"I found her wobbling on the stairs, talking about her and her friend wanting a peanut butter sandwich," Mercy answered.

Reed looked at Norman. "Why would you take this poor woman downstairs in the dark?"

"No, he wasn't even here," Mercy said. "She's delusional. There's no friend. It's all in her mind. He came down after she fell."

Reed studied the woman lying face down. Was she dead? He hoped she was only unconscious from the trauma. "Let's turn her over."

Norman placed the doll down on the steps above where Sadie lay, in order to help. The three of them gently turned Sadie over and she started to whimper. There was blood on the steps. Reed ordered Mercy to get a gurney since the only way to stabilize the old woman would be to get her lying flat, instead of being crumpled on the uneven staircase.

When Mercy returned with a gurney, the three of them decided how to move Sadie. Reed would lift her, cradling her torso in his arms as Norman and Mercy would hold her injured leg steady so it wouldn't move and cause further damage. Sadie's crumbled fragile body probably only weighed eighty-five pounds was now completely vulnerable.

As soon as the three lifted her, Sadie let out a scream. Reed's eyes quickly scanned the upstairs floor. All the doors remained closed. The dose of meds handed out every night was working, at least for the rest of the residents. The three moved in unison, creeping gently down the stairs with Sadie toward the waiting gurney.

"Tell me why this woman was wandering around," Reed asked. "Why didn't you give her the medicine ordered for sleep?"

Norman spoke before Mercy could answer. "Some of us don't take to being drugged. That's why."

"I did give her a sleeping pill," Mercy said defensibly. "She must've spit it out after I left."

"Ha!" Norman croaked.

"All right, you two. What's done is done. Once we get her on the gurney I need you, Mercy, to go call John."

"No," Norman said, not taking his eyes off of Sadie. "She needs us to call for an ambulance."

"I know but not . . ." Reed stopped and asked. "What's your name?"

"Norman Miller."

"Norman. I understand you're worried about her. So am I. But the worst thing for us to do right now is put her through more trauma. I'm afraid she can't make an ambulance ride in her condition. She needs immediate care. My stepfather is a doctor and can be here in minutes. He can give her something for the pain, then he'll decide what to do next."

They were at the bottom of the stairs and eased her onto the gurney. Although they were gentle, as they moved their hands out from under her body, Sadie screamed out in pain again.

Norman leaned over to her. "Hold on, Princess. They're calling a doctor. It won't be long and you'll get medicine for the pain."

EIGHT MINUTES LATER

John Fleming entered the foyer where Sadie was resting.

"Oh, dear me." John looked at Reed. "What happened?"

"She wandered away from her room and fell on the stairs. I was afraid to traumatize her further with an ambulance ride, so I had Mercy call you."

"That was a good decision. Elderly people are very fragile." John whispered to Mercy to go get a syringe and morphine, instructing her of the proper dosage to pull from the locked medicine cabinet. He moved toward the gurney and met Norman's frightened eyes.

"Well, hello Norman," John said.

"She's hurt real bad, doctor," Norman said.

"Don't worry, we'll take care of her." John looked at Sadie and took her hand. "Hello there, my dear. I remember when you came to my office with your daughter, but I can't remember your name."

She looked at him with tear-filled eyes and struggled to force a smile on her face. "It's Sadie."

"Oh, yes. How could I forget such a pretty name? Well, Sadie, I'm going to take good care of you so don't you worry."

Mercy hurried to John's side with the morphine.

John took the syringe from her. "Now Sadie, I'm going to give you a shot. It'll be a small sting and then the pain will go away. Is that all right with you?"

"Yes, thank you."

John gave her the shot and then he turned to Mercy. "Her hands are cold. Get some more blankets. We need to make sure she doesn't go into shock."

Reed stepped up to John and asked, "What about an ambulance? Can we keep her here?"

"I believe so. The break is not a compound fracture like Mercy thought. Sadie's skin is so thin from her age that it tore from the fall. It's not from a bone piercing it. The medicine Sadie is on thins the blood and any little cut bleeds as if it's a major wound."

Reed's eyes kept moving from John to Sadie and back again. His mind was spinning with the conversation that had unfolded in front of him between John and the old woman on the gurney. A frown deepened on his forehead.

"Her name is Sadie," Reed said slowly, more as if a statement than a question.

"Yes," John said, He shook his head and frowned. "I should've thought about her wandering those stairs when I checked her in. She's got dementia."

Mercy came back with the additional blanket. Sadie had her eyes closed and was quiet, tears still wet on her cheeks. Norman was still at her side.

Reed told Mercy to take Norman back to his room, then he pulled John Fleming away from the gurney. "Look, John, I don't want to call her family in the middle of the night."

"We have to call her daughter. Her mother has had an accident."

"I don't think it would be wise to frighten the woman by waking her in the middle of the night."

299

Mercy had Norman by the arm, leading him toward the stairs. Reed paused and reached out to grab Mercy by the arm. He whispered something in her ear and she nodded. Norman was still, his face expressionless, like a soldier after a bloody battle. Mercy led Norman up the stairs without him objecting.

Reed looked back at his stepfather. "John, you haven't even set this woman's leg and you want us to call her daughter? What are we going to say, 'look your mother has broken her leg but we haven't done anything yet? We wanted to wake you up first and tell you we know nothing.' Yeah, she'll be tickled pink to hear from us."

John didn't say anything for a few seconds. "I suppose you're right. Her daughter didn't seem like a Worrying Nelly. I guess it won't hurt to wait until the morning."

"Good," Reed said. "I'll call her tomorrow. You don't have to worry about it."

"But I'm her mother's doctor."

"And I'm the owner of this facility. I'll make the call."

Doubt

Norman and Mercy climbed the stairs. A few steps up, Norman paused and bent down to pick the doll up. Before moving farther, he glanced back downstairs to see John Fleming holding Sadie's hand and talking to her. Reed pulled the side railing up, and then they pushed the gurney with Sadie down the hallway.

Norman's image of John had always been that he had no backbone. He saw almost daily how John allowed his stepson to push him around. Reed controlled John like a puppet master. That weak image of John Fleming seemed inaccurate after what Norman had witnessed tonight.

John Fleming was more complex than the timid, humble man who insisted everyone call him by his first name. Norman had agreed to call him John after multiple requests from him, but it just wasn't right. Doctors should be shown respect. Calling a doctor John undermines his authority. There were protocols. However, tonight John Fleming came in and took charge with confidence and authority. He handled the emergency with the levelheadedness of . . . a skilled doctor.

When Mercy and Norman reached the second-floor landing, Norman took one last look at Sadie's gurney disappearing down the hallway. *You're in good hands with Dr. Fleming, Princess.* It was evident that John Fleming was very competent.

"Now, Mr. Miller," Mercy said in her usual condescending tone. "You mustn't worry."

She opened his door and stood to the side for him to enter. "I want you to go straight to bed. We don't want you to take ill from lack of sleep."

"No one ever got sick from lack of sleep!"

"No? Where did *you* get your medical degree?"

Norman glared her. *Probably the same place you got your nursing degree.*

"Go on." Mercy waved her hand at him. Her long, curved fingernails clattered as she wiggled them in the air.

"I'm going. Stop waving at me." *Nurses don't have spiked fingernails, you Voodoo Woman.*

"Hurry up. Get in there. I've gots to get back to help the doctor."

Norman entered his room and turned to face her, one hand on the doorknob and one holding the doll. "What happened here tonight is not finished. Mark my words; you'll be going back to whatever jungle island you sprouted from before this is all over."

Mercy opened her mouth to say something but then Norman slammed the door. He hurried over to his dresser and knelt down. Opening the bottom drawer, he pulled out a sweater and two shirts, leaving an empty space big enough to hide a doll. He placed the doll inside and covered it with clothes. As he patted the sweater down to fit, he heard a loud click.

Norman pulled himself up from the floor and went to the door. He turned the knob. It only turned halfway until it snapped to a dead stop. Old Green Eyes had locked him in the room.

Maybe he and Sadie weren't out of danger yet.

Honky Tonk, 'Nawlins Style

Before calling Betsy, I had tried Peggy's number but there was no answer. Sadie and Peggy had been on my mind ever since Ghistaine's episode. The suddenness of my attack made me dreadfully aware of how life can change in a flash.

New friends and the things important to me were so very different now. Peggy had become a dear friend. Sadie was part of that package. She had squeezed her way into my heart as well.

Betsy answered on the third ring with a gentle, "Hello."

"Betsy, I only have a few minutes but I wanted to check-in."

"You have good news, I hope. Did you get information about Jacob?"

"Yes and no." I got information—actually more than that. I got a lead. But the question was what to do with it. Maybe, I had reached another dead-end. Again.

I explained, "I saw Ghistaine. You remember, I told you about her?"

"Yes. How could I forget? She sounds like quite a character."

I didn't know how Betsy felt about Ghistaine's powers. Was she a believer or not? I realized that whenever I had called Betsy, I was so busy telling her my beliefs

303

about fortunetelling that I'd never asked her opinion on the topic.

"Ghistaine gave me information from Jacob to help me in my search," I said. "But I don't know what to do with the information, or where to go from here."

"Can't Ghistaine help you?"

"No. She says that she's just a messenger and doesn't have answers. She gave me three things. Three sets of numbers, a woman's name, and some Italian name. She wrote them down listening to, I think, the ghost of Jacob. I'm supposed to know what to do with it. But, I'm clueless. I've got the paper Ghistaine wrote on in my purse."

The Betsy then told me a story. "My grandmother kept seeing her dead sister in her bedroom late at night. She kept telling her to clean under an old trunk. My grandmother thought her sister was tormenting her until she finally moved the trunk to wash the floor and found an envelope of money. I don't know why she couldn't just say, 'there is an envelope of money under the trunk.' Ghosts don't communicate well. Anyway, there's a reason for you to have this information, Stephanie. Don't worry. When the opportunity presents itself, you'll know what to do."

"I suppose so."

After my call ended with Betsy, I felt better about tracking Jacob down. Talking to Betsy always had that effect on me because she usually was right with her advice. Like she said, I'd realize the opportunity when that door opened for me. Still, I had an uneasy feeling that lingered on. I couldn't stop thinking about Sadie and felt the uncomfortable feeling was connected to her somehow.

No doubt, all of the ghost talk and seeing into the future had a subconscious influence on me. I had to remind myself that Sadie was old and not in good health, it was as simple as that. I'd never had a sense of urgency regarding my promise to her until now. It sat heavily on my shoulders. Perhaps Sadie's youthful spunkiness and sharp, no-nonsense mind gave me a false sense of never-ending time. However, a diagnosis of either Alzheimer's or any other kind of dementia indicated that time was indeed slipping away for Sadie. Now not being able to get ahold of Peggy put me on high alert, but I couldn't do anything about it.

For right now, I needed to get going and stop worrying. I had a date waiting.

When I exited the elevator, Tony was in the hotel lobby. He said we needed to take his car to go to the Honky-Tonk because it wasn't located in one of the wards near us. I didn't bother asking him to explain what a ward was since by now, I had grown to accept that I'd only understood half of what people were talking about here. New Orleans had a unique language all of its own.

While driving out of the French Quarter, Tony commented that I looked pretty. I thanked him and tried not to blush.

"I stopped in to check on Ghistaine before picking you up," he said.

"How is she doing? She really frightened me."

"She's fine, acted like nothing ever happened. You have to realize that when she connects to a spirit, once the connection has been broken, everything stops. She doesn't worry about what happened to her during the connection. To her, it's over and done with."

"But, she was so bad. I thought she was dying."

"Yeah, it was bad this time. And don't get me wrong, when it's over, there's a residual effect. If the spirit has experienced trauma in its life, or maybe died violently, Ghistaine feels it. The worse the trauma, the harder it is for her to recover later. It's not like getting over a bad cold. It can take a long time until she's back to normal. When we rescued Emmie Lou, Ghistaine had breathing problems for weeks afterward."

"Tony, that's just it. You rescued Emmie Lou."

Tony put his blinker on and turned onto a ramp to enter a highway. He frowned and said, "What are you getting at?"

"You got to Emmie Lou in time. She lived. Jacob is dead and I don't know what killed him."

In my mind, I feared the worst. Nothing would've stopped Jacob from returning to Mabel. "I think Jacob died here in New Orleans. If Ghistaine's powers had connected her at the time of his death, and you hadn't taken the locket away from her, who knows what would've happened. What killed Jacob could've killed her, too. You even said so."

"Look, Stephanie, I told you the locket was killing her, but it was in the heat of the moment. It's one thing to connect to a ghost, but what you're thinking is impossible. Death can't be transferred from another dimension, or through a ghost and kill a person living in the present."

"I don't know." I couldn't push away the thought that I could have killed Ghistaine. Besides that, I couldn't believe I was arguing semantics about ghosts. "I'm not willing to find out who's right about this. I'm not asking Ghistaine for help again. I've got those names and numbers here," I patted my purse. "I'm just going to have to ask everyone I meet if the message Ghistaine wrote for me means anything to them."

"Ah-huh. So that's your plan."

"That's it for now. End of discussion. So, tell me what's on the agenda for tonight."

"Okay." Tony smiled. "You're going to meet my partner, Laurent. He plays in a band every Saturday night."

The lights of the city were disappearing behind us as we headed for one of those long, two-lane highways with the cement guardrails. In the dark, I couldn't tell if we were traveling over water or dry land.

"Laurent can be your first person to ask to decode Jacob's message," Tony said. He chuckled and added, "That is, if you leave time out for dancing. Laurent loves dancing. He won't do any talking if he hasn't danced first. The man can swing, that's for sure."

Snap Beans

We drove into coal-black emptiness. The half-moon occasionally peeked out from behind the clouds casting ghostlike shadows across the road ahead of us. If I hadn't been with Supercop Tony, it would have completely creeped me out.

Tony rolled his window partially down. A symphony of sounds poured into the car from night creatures. I figured we had driven far out of the city, to the surrounding swampland of Louisiana. The city noise was replaced by the deafening serenades of the things that slither and crawl in the night. The loudest was the croaking of frogs. There was another sound of a low, grumbling growl that moaned out from the darkness. Blanketing all the noises were the chirps of the crickets.

"Where are we?" I asked.

"Different landscape than the French Quarter, huh?" I was uncomfortable somewhat even with Tony, looking into the black outside and listening to all the unknown sounds. Tony seemed to read me the way couples do after years of being together. "That's what makes Louisiana unique. It has so many variations to it. It's more than Mardi Gras and food. Remember, Stephanie, I promised you that tonight you'd experience something the average tourist doesn't get to see. But there's nothing weird or dangerous out here."

"Sure. I can tell that by the sounds out there." I waved my hand out the open window.

"Sorry," Tony said sheepishly. "I forgot how spooked I was the first time I followed Laurent out here. Trust me, you'll enjoy yourself. There's no werewolves or vampires, the folks out here are good people."

I forced a smile. Off in the distance, I could hear the faint sound of music. As we continued to drive, the music became louder. Soon, it became so loud it almost drowned out the sounds of the night creatures, and ahead in the darkness, there was a soft golden glow.

"We're almost there," Tony said.

We went around a bend and a wooden building came into view. Around the edge of the roof hung multicolored lights. The music thundered from inside. At the front of the wooden building, nestled near the peak of the roof, hung a wooden sign with hand-painted letters, spelling out *Snap Beans.*

I couldn't help but gape in utter surprise; it seemed to appear right in the middle of nowhere.

Tony pulled up next to a pickup truck and turned the engine off.

As he got out, I called to him, "It's amazing. What . . . what is that music?"

Tony ran around to open my door. As I stepped out I said, "It's not bluegrass. It's jazzy, but it's not blues-jazz. "

"Zydeco," he answered.

"What?" I asked, cupping my hand around my ear to capture his words as the music blanketed me.

Tony yelled, "It's called Zydeco music. It's a little of this and little of that. Mix Creole with Cajun, and splash it with a bluegrass sound, and you have Zydeco."

We climbed up the steps to an open porch, where a few people were smoking and talking. I could feel vibrations from the music on the porch's wood plank floor. Tony opened the screen door and the excitement indoors drew us in.

Tony grabbed my hand and led me through the crowd to a bar on the right. Spotlights focused on the stage, where a man stood front and center, playing a fiddle. Beside him, a man with dreadlocks rocked out on an electric guitar. To the left, slightly back near the drummer, was a dark-skinned, string bean of a man with a ribbed piece of metal hooked on his shoulders that lay flat on his chest. He raked a square-shaped wire comb over the metal in rhythm with the music.

Tony squeezed in at the bar. "Hey Randy, give me two Snap Bean Fizzes."

He turned to me and smiled. I think that was when I realized my mouth was open in awe. I closed it quickly and smiled. Tony paid for our drinks.

I glanced over to the dance floor. *How do you dance to that kind of music?*

Everywhere I looked people were moving to the rhythm of the music—fast, faster, and lightning speed, their feet barely touching the floor. The whole place was hot with music and a passion that seemed contagious. The floor overflowed with dancers, wet with sweat.

"Try this," Tony said. "This will get you in a dancing mood." He handed me a tall, thin glass. It contained a whitish concoction with a slice of orange at the rim, topping it off.

I sniffed the drink. It had a slightly sweet smell but I couldn't even guess the ingredients. Then I took a sip, "Wow! What's in it?" It had a kick. I swallowed down a bigger sip. Strangely enough, the second taste had a smooth and intoxicating blend of flavors.

"Whoa, be careful. Snap Bean Fizzes can creep up on you."

"It's good."

"Yeah, it's Randy's specialty. It's similar to the Quarter's Ramos Frizz with some other secret ingredients. I thought you'd like it."

I took a third sip to decide. "It's different. Gets better with every taste."

"Glad you like it. Better take it slow though, the night's young." He pointed to the stage. "See the tall guy playing the washboard in the back near the drummer?"

"Yes, who is he?"

"That's Laurent."

"You said washboard? As in laundry."

"Yep. Zydeco has to have someone on the washboard and a hand accordion, or better known as a squeezebox. You should recognize Roffy. He's on the squeezebox. And that's Eugene on the fiddle."

I noticed that the bartender was entering the right side of the stage with a guitar in his hand. He walked over to Laurent and spoke into his ear.

Tony watched. "Oh, now what are you up to, Randy?"

Randy propped the guitar up next to the drums and exited the stage.

Laurent stopped playing and put his arms high in the air, moving forward. He yelled, "Stop the music. Stop the music, guys."

The band stopped playing, but the dancers kept moving. It took a half a minute before they slowed to a stop and looked toward the stage.

"Everybody, you might have noticed that Tony just walked in, but I've been told he doesn't plan on playing with us tonight. Now, we can't let that happen, can we?"

The crowd roared. "No!"

Laurent called out. "Tony DeLuca." He put his hands to his forehead, shading his eyes from the bright lights. "Where are you? You've been made, man. These good folks aren't going to let you get out of playing with us. Are you, folks?" He started clapping and chanting, "Tony, Tony, Tony."

The crowd joined in.

Tony looked at me. "Sorry."

I smiled. "Give me your glass." I waved him away "Go."

I worked my way to a table to listen while Tony tuned up and started to play. He was really good. After ten minutes, I'd finished my drink plus Tony's. I noticed Laurent unhooking his washboard then leaving the stage. He moved through the dancers toward the bar. Randy handed him a yellow can. They spoke and Randy pointed in my direction.

Uh-oh. Now I've been made.

Laurent walked up. "So, you're Stephanie."

"Yep, that would be me. Would you like to join me?" I motioned to the tall chair across from where I was sitting.

Laurent gulped his drink down in one swallow, wiped his mouth with the back of his hand, and then slammed the beer can down on the table. "Naw. I wanna dance and you, dawlin', been sitting too long."

He pulled me off the chair and looked down at me. "Well, now, ya a little thing." Then he said, "Come on."

I barely had time to put my glass on the table. The next thing I knew we were on the dance floor. He twirled and swung me, in and out of his arms like a ragdoll. We whirled around like the swing dancers of the '40s but the lightning speed of Laurent's steps and kicks were closer to jitterbugging.

Then he broke away and kept moving. Without him leading me, I couldn't follow his moves. I froze.

"I . . . I don't know how to dance like that."

"Jest feel the music, dawlin'. Feel the music and ya can't stand still."

I followed his moves and went with the rhythm and he was right. The music took you.

"Dat's it. Yeah, you rite, dawlin'."

I don't know how long we danced. It was so much fun. I had never been to a place so alive.

When the music changed, Laurent looked at me and shook his head. "Whew, ya dance like ya one of us. I'm worn out. Let's take a break."

I pushed back my wet hair and told him I could use another drink.

"You rite. Come on."

Laurent headed to the bar, while I grabbed my purse back at the table where I'd been sitting. After I returned to Laurent, he handed me a drink that looked like the first two I had.

"Randy says you were drinking Snap Beans." He held up a familiar yellow can and said, "I have a personal stash of Dixie beer behind the bar. Want to step outside where it's cooler?"

Cool air sounded like heaven to me so we headed toward the stage and out a side door. Laurent waved to

Tony and he nodded back. There were tables outside, but no people. Laurent said the area was for the band to take breaks.

"So Stephanie, you seem to be occupying a lot of Tony's time. I'm glad he brought you here. I was wondering; what are your plans once you are finished with your investigating?"

All of a sudden, his grammar was perfect. I could understand every word he said. He said "you" not "ya," and not once did he call me "dawlin'." I didn't know what kind of game he was playing.

"Your *accent* is gone. I don't get it. Inside you were a different person. What's the deal? I think you need to explain before you start asking *me* questions."

He gave a big belly laugh. "Now I can see why Tony likes you. I talk Y'at when I'm around most people. Being a cop makes people uneasy, so talking the same as them makes everything cool. You know the saying, when in Rome. But when I'm with friends or co-workers, I don't have to play the part. But . . ." He crooked two fingers in the air to make his point, "*Ya rite.* I can understand your suspicion."

"It was weird and I know when I'm being conned. I'm not stupid. This whole trip has been strange."

"I can't imagine anyone thinking you're stupid but there's no con. Tony's a good friend. He's been through some bad times, so that's why I wanted to ask you about your plans."

"He told me about losing his wife."

Laurent looked surprised. "He told you about his wife and all?"

"Yes," I answered.

"He wouldn't talk to any of us at the time; Tony kept all that to himself. It was obvious he was hurting. Still, he wouldn't let anyone see him grieving. It didn't fool any of us. Tony jumped back into life as if nothing had happened."

"Everyone handles grief differently," I said.

"You've got that right. Tony started dating—a lot after she died. I figured that maybe he was feeling the emptiness of his loss and that he just needed to fill it. Then the women stopped, perhaps that's when the healing started."

I nodded. I had heard about others going through the same process after being widowed.

Laurent added, "Then he meets you. This is the first time he's ever brought a date here. So, you see, that's why it was a surprise."

We sat for minutes without speaking. I sipped my drink and he gulped his beer.

Laurent spoke first. "After I pulled those two guys in that jumped you, when Tony arrived at the station, he was really boiling. I never had seen him so mad. I thought he was going to lose it when he saw the two lowlifes sitting there, but he held it together."

He stopped and looked at me with wide eyes. "I'm sorry about what happened. We do have crime, just like any other place, but our city has good people living here. When Tony called Georgia and it wasn't even his case, I knew that something was different about you. Then he brings you here." Laurent shrugged. "I know it's none of my business."

"I understand," I quickly interjected. "You're his friend. Losing his wife, he's vulnerable. But only Tony can work his way through that. I've had my own losses, so I know. Tony and I've talked about it. As far as my plans . . .

I don't know. Tony's a great guy. Everything has been so strange; I feel like I've known him forever."

We sat in awkward silence. Laurent asked if I liked the French Quarter, jokingly adding, "When you're not being mugged."

"Everyone should visit the French Quarter once in their life," I answered. "It's definitely unique. Ghistaine is on top of that list. She gave Tony a paper for me with the name of someone on it. Like I'm supposed to know what to do with it. Also, there were numbers and the name Little Palmero. She said it was a message from a spirit. I don't understand any of it."

"Well, Little Palmero is easy."

"You know who he is?"

"It's not a he, but a place."

Supercop, Super Guy

The door behind me opened. Music from inside boomed out at us. Tony's shadow filled the doorway for a brief second before he stepped outside where Laurent and I were sitting.

"How's it going?" Tony said as he closed the door, trapping the music back inside. "Sorry to desert you like that, Stephanie."

"I understand. Your public beckoned you."

Tony laughed and took a seat next to me. "The band's taking a break, but I won't be joining them when they go back on stage. I'm all yours now." He winked at me.

As lousy as it might sound, although I was totally attracted to Tony and he was charming, all I could think about was Little Palermo. *Why did the band have to take a break now?*

"I saw you two dancing." Tony took my hand in his and looked across the table. "Hope you aren't trying to steal my girl."

Without skipping a beat, Laurent responded, "Sorry, man. You could always see through my plans." He stood and gave a nod to me. "That's my cue to leave. It's been a delight being your dance partner, Stephanie. Enjoy the rest of your evening."

"No! You can't leave." I blurted out.

Tony looked at me with one eyebrow raised. "He can't leave? Did my friend steal my girl when I was off playing the role of a rock star?"

I could feel my face flush. "No. Laurent was the perfect gentleman. Besides, I always leave the dance with the person I came with." I motioned to the chair. "Please Laurent, sit back down."

He did as told.

"Tony, I was telling Laurent about what happened today with Ghistaine and the message she got from Jacob's spirit. I mentioned that I didn't know who Little Palermo or Althea Ross was, and I didn't know what to do next. Laurent said that I didn't need to look for a person but a place."

"Really?" Tony looked at Laurent and waited.

"What I said was," Laurent corrected, "Little Palermo wasn't a person. I don't know who Althea Ross is."

"Okay," I said. "But you do know something about Little Palermo."

"Sure."

Tony seemed intrigued now and jumped in. "So, give it up. What's the scoop? Anything you know could help Stephanie."

"Well, what I know about Little Palermo is because of my grandma."

"Miss Marguerite?"

"Yeah." Laurent explained that Miss Marguerite was his grandmother. "Tony's been over for Sunday supper at my grandmother's house often. She always says, *Sunday supper is a time for friends and family*."

"Okay, now that Stephanie knows I take advantage of free food from Miss Marguerite, get on with it," Tony said.

Laurent waved his hand at Tony, "Hold your horses, I'm getting there."

Laurent turned back to me. "So, one day I stop in to see my grandmother in the middle of the week. I walked into a henhouse full of clucking women. Meme, that's what I call my grandmother, was having a meeting of the Historical Society. She's a very active member. There were all kinds of stuff spread out on the dining room and kitchen tables. Books, maps, papers, photographs; there were piles everywhere. My grandmother told me they were organizing and cataloging information into record books about the history of the French Quarter."

"What about Little Palermo," Tony asked.

"I'm getting there," Laurent answered.

I prompted, "Did your grandmother speak about Little Palermo to you or say where it is?"

"It's in Louisiana."

"No kidding." Tony glanced over to me and saw that I was about to burst with anticipation. "Okay, go on." Tony motioned for Laurent to speed it up.

Laurent leaned forward. "So, I picked up an old picture of what looked like one of our courtyards in the Quarter. In the photo, there was laundry strung out across on lines from railings on a building on one side to another building's railing on the opposite side of a courtyard. There were people standing around, adults and children of all ages, all of them dirty and in rags. There must've been ten or twelve families living there, packed in that small place. I commented that it looked like the slums of a third world country and Meme hit me upside of my head."

"That's Miss Marguerite, for sure," Tony said.

"Yeah, Meme will wallop you if she thinks you're being disrespectful." Laurent continued. "She told me it wasn't slums of a third world country but this city. The photo was taken in the French Quarter at the turn of the century. There was a big population of Italians who had immigrated to our port and moved to the Quarter, but there was not enough room for so many. Families were packed in, and it was the way the immigrants had to live at first. In fact, there were so many that a designated area of the French Quarter was dubbed as *Little Palermo* since most of the people living in that area had come over from Palermo, Italy."

Pay dirt! Laurent was who I was supposed to connect with. Betsy was right. The door of opportunity did appear for me.

"Laurent," I asked, "can you call your grandmother and ask if I could talk to her?"

"About Little Palermo?"

"Yes. And tell her the other name that Ghistaine wrote down, Althea Ross."

"Sure." Laurent stood again. "I need to go; I hear the band tuning up. Tony, I'll call you tomorrow and let you know what time you two should come over to Meme's house. I'll meet you there."

"Okay," Tony said.

I copied the message I had in my purse for Laurent on a napkin and handed it to him before he left. With any luck, maybe his grandmother would know what the numbers meant and who Althea Ross was, too.

Laurent went inside and I was finally alone with Tony. He put his arm around me and we listened to the music together.

It was several hours later when we left Snap Beans. We arrived back at my hotel and Tony walked me to my door. It was very late, too late to call Betsy to let her know what had developed that night. Besides, I was more interested in connecting with Tony than talking about connecting the dots of the past with Betsy.

Tony unlocked my hotel room door and handed me the key. I thanked him for a great evening and said how much I enjoyed the music and his friends—and—well, everything. Tony kissed me goodnight. I looked at my watch and said it was too late for him to drive back home and suggested he stay.

He paused, then looking at me, he asked, "Do you have a couch in your room where I can sleep?"

I kissed him again, then said, "No, but my bed is big enough for two."

Exposed

Reed finished maneuvering the gurney down the hallway into a vacant room. His stepfather was on the right side still holding Sadie's hand, which had put most of the work of steering onto Reed. Carrying the full load, fixing, or steering difficult situations into safer positions, was the story of Reed's life. His life had always been threatened by other people's mistakes that he needed to manage. Why would tonight be any different?

"Now Sadie, we need to set your leg," John said in a calming but firm voice. "The shot you received will help some with the pain but it's going to hurt. I can't give you any more morphine because you might not wake up from it. You understand from your nursing days that we need to be very cautious with how much morphine we administer."

Sadie didn't open her eyes when she answered. "I understand, doctor. Morphine can be fatal."

Reed had been listening to and watching John. When Reed heard John say 'nursing days' he snapped his head back toward Sadie and studied her face. *She had been a nurse. Could she be the person who threatened to. . . ..*

Reed thought back to the newspaper fiasco and that meddling nurse from so many years ago. Although it worked out that the threat of an investigation helped him coerce John Fleming to sign over everything, it could have

322

gone much worse. If the private investigator he hired hadn't found out that the nurse had had a child . . . *what was that kid's name?*

"John, what's Sadie's last name? I need to pull her file."

"Campbell."

"Are you sure? Not Hamilton."

"No, Campbell. Sadie Campbell."

Mercy came into the room pulling a stainless steel pole with an IV bag filled with clear liquid on the hook at the top. "Doctor, I have the saline."

Reed asked Mercy, "Is our other guest in his room?"

"Yes, he's secure in his room like you requested."

"Hurry up, nurse." John's voice was sharp but with an urgent tone. "We need to get the IV in and set this woman's leg immediately. You can address those other matters later."

"Yes, doctor."

Reed watched the two moving around the gurney with precision. He had never seen his stepfather working in a doctor's role, let alone during an emergency situation. He realized John was competent, which could be a major obstacle if Sadie was who he thought she was.

"I'll get her file. John, it's in your office, right?"

John Fleming didn't raise his head; he was focused on his patient. "Yes, yes, the large file cabinets on the left," he answered. "Go get it. I'll need the file later to make my notes."

Reed hurried out of the room. He wanted to get that other file, the one with all the details of abuse that the nurse had given to the reporter. Reed's attorney had confiscated what he could and gave those papers to Reed without looking at them. They were locked in his private safe. If that old woman was who he thought she was, then the danger from the past had come back and he could lose everything he had worked so hard for. The years of worry about the past returning was real and it was in the form of an old woman lying in a room down the hall with a broken leg. Reed just knew that it was her, and old or not, she could destroy him.

Once he had the old file with the name of the daughter in it, he left to go to John's office to compare the information. In his stepfather's office, he rushed to the left side of the room, where the wide medical file cabinets sat. They were the kind used in hospitals or doctor's offices that slid out huge open trays, sectioned off with wire that held the exposed files. Reed frantically thumbed through the sections: A, B, and then finally, C. His hand shook as he pulled out Sadie Campbell's file, and then he rushed over to the desk.

Reed flipped the file open and started to read. The first page had details like her diagnosis of dementia, medications, and that she was transferred from Magnolia Breezes in Milledgeville.

Why would she transfer from there? Unless she's started snooping again. It's got to be her.

He scanned each page and found nothing concrete to link her to the Sadie who had opened the abuse investigation on the hospital years earlier. Then he came to John's notes from the day of the old woman's admission:

THE PATIENT EXHIBITS A CHILDLIKE MENTAL STATE. SHE APPEARED AFRAID AND CLUNG TO A DOLL THAT SHE CALLED

MABEL. ONCE I ACCEPTED HER WORLD TO BE TRUE, AND I ASSURED HER WE WOULD TAKE GOOD CARE OF HER DOLL, THE PATIENT RELAXED. THE PATIENT EXHIBITS TO BE A HAPPY PERSON WITH NO NEGATIVE OR AGGRESSIVE BEHAVIOR.

THE PATIENT'S DAUGHTER, PEGGY HAMILTON, ADMITTED HER AND INSISTED THAT OUR FACULTY TAKE OVER TOTAL CARE OF HER MOTHER. WHAT I FELT STRANGE WAS BEFORE LEAVING MISS HAMILTON TOOK ME ASIDE AND STATED THAT HER MOTHER HAD BEEN A CAREER NURSE AND KNEW EXACTLY WHAT MEDICINES SHE SHOULD OR SHOULD NOT TAKE. I ASSURED HER THAT OUR STAFF WAS PROFESSIONAL AND COMPETENT AND THAT WE WOULD ADMINISTER HER MOTHER'S MEDICATION PROPERLY.

Reed stood motionless. Then he reread, the patient's daughter, Peggy Hamilton. He opened the investigator's report from so many years back and thumbed through it until he saw:

. . . THE SUBJECT HAS A SIX-YEAR-OLD DAUGHTER NAMED PEGGY. THE SUBJECT UNDER SURVEILLANCE IS AND HAS BEEN A CAREER NURSE FOR MANY YEARS . . .

"Sadie Hamilton. You've come back!" Reed hissed.

Getting the Story Straight

It was almost 4:30 a.m. when John left Sadie's room. His face was taut and worry reflected in his eyes. It had been years since his days as attending doctor in an emergency room. Maybe that was reason enough for his stress and deep concern.

"She's stable," John told Reed. "Mercy is going to monitor her for the next few hours. I've instructed her to call me if anything changes. I mean *anything*. I expect you to acknowledge my authority here, as the doctor in charge. Is that clear?"

"Of course," Reed said. "You look exhausted, John. Everything is under control here. Why don't you go home? We'll call if there is any change."

John looked hard at his stepson. Maybe he had been wrong about him. He rallied in tonight's emergency and even showed tenderness toward Sadie when she screamed out in pain. His stepson had been even worried about the trauma of an ambulance ride, and rightfully so. Many elderly patients died in transport—too weakened and traumatized to survive the shortest of drives. He looked into Reed's concerned eyes and wished his dear wife had been alive to see the compassion her only son had shown tonight.

"You're right. I am exhausted. I'm too old for this kind of upset." John headed toward the door, then paused and looked back at Reed. "You did good tonight, son."

Reed watched with relief as the old man walked out the front door. *John never called me son before.*

Reed stood, momentarily pondering. Life would have been so different if only his mother had married John first, and not his father. The first time he met John Fleming was after his mother's death and they started off on the wrong foot. Tonight Reed saw what his mother had seen in his stepfather. His stepfather was not weak, as he had always thought him to be. John Fleming was not driven by financial gain; he didn't fight for prosperity like most people. What Reed had seen as weak was compassion. Tonight John Fleming showed herculean strength when it came to his patient. And he was an honorable man. It was that honor above everything that Reed didn't understand. That honor was the wedge that came between Reed and his stepfather. Now John Fleming's honor could be the most serious threat to Reed since his stepfather could always see through his lies and deceptions.

Reed stood staring at the front door John had gone through. It's too late for a stepfather and stepson relationship. Reed's entire life and what he had built rested on keeping John Fleming away from that old lady for the next day or two.

But tonight, John called me son.

Then Reed shook his head, returning to the matter at hand. He walked down the hallway where John and Mercy had rolled the old woman down to a room. Stopping at the door, Reed poked his head into the room where Sadie was sleeping. Mercy sat sentry by her bedside.

"Mercy, step out for a minute," Reed whispered. "I need to talk to you."

Outside in the hallway, Reed kept his voice low. "We have a problem to deal with."

"Mr. Reed, I did nothing wrong. She fell, that's all."

Reed nodded his head. "I believe you, but no one else will. Trust me; my only concern now is protecting you. That old woman doesn't have but a few months to live at the most and now after falling . . ." He shrugged, making sure to play the concerned role to the ultimate level possible. "I don't want to see this accident ruin *your* life. You know if there is an investigation—and there will be an investigation—you'll be deported."

Mercy started to cry. "Please, help me, Mr. Reed. I can't be deported."

"I don't know . . . ." He posed the best-concerned look he could muster and stood in silence, hoping he would pull Mercy into trusting him even more. "A lot has happened here tonight."

"Please, I'll do anything."

Reed rubbed his chin as if he was thinking. "It would be different if she were to die from the trauma. The death certificate would say she died from natural causes."

"But, her vitals are strong. Doctor Fleming thought if they stay the same throughout the night that we could have her transported to a hospital in the morning."

Reed looked directly at Mercy. "Don't most patients die within twelve hours of a traumatic injury—like an elderly person breaking a bone?"

Mercy paused as if to reflect on what Reed said. After a few seconds, she nodded her head in agreement with his unspoken suggestion.

Reed had a plan to resolve the situation. He instructed Mercy that they had to smooth over any suspicions that the old man, Norman Miller, had after being locked in his room. They had to act quickly. Mercy was to go upstairs and quietly unlock Norman's door. When he wakes up in the morning, his door would be unlocked. If he asked why Mercy locked his door, she should say he was confused that when he tried his door, and it didn't open, it must have been stuck—not locked.

Reed knew that John was wiped out from tonight's episode. If they didn't call him as instructed, he would oversleep. That would give them enough time to inject Sadie with a high enough dose of morphine that she would be lulled into a coma and die—never waking up.

At 7 a.m., Mercy should check Sadie's vitals. Reed explained to her that they will be dangerously low and she should then call EMTs. Afterward, she should make a frantic wake-up call to John, but it will be too late by then.

"Sadie will be pronounced DOA when the ambulance arrives at the hospital," Reed said in a matter-of-fact tone. "One of the hospital doctors will sign Sadie's death certificate, thinking that it was another elderly person dying after a fatal fall. It happens all the time and you will be free and clear. By tomorrow noon, this whole nightmare will be all over."

Emergency Call

Norman had barely secured the doll in the bottom drawer of the small dresser when he heard the lock on his door click. In his younger years, he would not have been fooled. Now he couldn't protect his Princess; he couldn't even stop a small, devil-like woman with green eyes from locking him in like a caged animal.

They won't get away with this. He went to the closet and grabbed a wooden box from the shelf.

In the box were two items. A framed picture of his wife taken as she held their newborn baby son, the other item was an envelope marked; "For My Son, after my death." He took the envelope out and put the box on the bed. He opened the envelope and pulled out a folded paper that bulged from what was wrapped inside. The sides of the paper were secured with staples.

They're messing with the wrong man. I may be old but I still have some tricks up my sleeve.

He ripped off one of the stapled edges and tipped the envelope to pour out what was inside. A Swiss Army knife spilled out into the palm of his hand. *Norman Miller knows to be prepared for anything.*

At the door, Norman began working at the hinges. He had never learned how to pick a lock, not even with the aid of a Swiss Army knife, but if he could get the pins out of the hinges then he could wedge the door open from the opposite side of the doorknob. He'd be free even with the locked knob still in place.

He worked feverishly at the hinges and pins. Soon, after working at the top and bottom he realized neither one of the pins was budging. Whoever had painted the interior of the room had painted the door and the old hinges too, instead of replacing them with new ones. Even though he had chipped away most of the paint, the hinges were stuck tight. He needed something to loosen the rust underneath the paint before there would be any hope of removing the pins. If only he had some WD40 or some kind of oil, any kind. Thinking for a second, he got up and hurried to the bathroom and opened the medicine cabinet. There had to be something in there that he could use that would be oily enough to loosen the rusty pins. Then he saw the tube of Brylcreem.

"A little dab will do ya," he muttered, remembering the jingle from the old television commercials. "I'll use more than a dab. Sure hope it works," Norman said to himself as he grabbed the tube.

His son was constantly telling him to use hairspray, instead of that greasy stuff. *Stop being so set in your old ways,* his son would say. Now Norman was glad he'd never listened to him. Hopefully, those old ways would be the answer to his escape plan.

Back at the door, he first warmed the cream by rubbing a quarter-size dab into his hands. After working it almost into a liquid state, he slathered it over the rusted metal of the lower hinge and pin. He picked up the Swiss Army knife and got to work again.

Downstairs, Mercy pulled herself together and promised Reed that she'd do as he had instructed.

The plan was that Reed would leave to go home and return in a few hours, sometime before 7 a.m. By then, Norman would find his door unlocked and the rest of the guests would be starting down for breakfast, or already in the dining room.

Reed had it all figured out. Mercy would go to do her morning check on Sadie and find her unresponsive. The guests entering the dining room would witness Mercy rush out into the hallway to the phone. She would be frantic but still focused on saving her patient. She would dial the phone to call for help.

If Norman came downstairs before then, insisting that he wanted to see Sadie, even better. Mercy would lead him to see Sadie, only to find the poor woman in a coma. Norman would witness Mercy's heroic actions to save her patient.

Mercy patiently waited in Sadie's room for morning to come. A few times, Sadie woke and the faithful nurse had patted the old woman's forehead with a damp cloth. "Go to sleep, everything will be all right in the morning," Mercy told Sadie as the old woman drifted in and out of sleep, never knowing what fate lay before her.

5:30 A.M. SUNDAY MORNING

Mercy unhooked the saline bag and left Sadie's room to get another full bag. At the foot of the stairs in the foyer of the house, she paused to think. *I better go up and unlock the old geezer's door before I forget.*

As she climbed the stairs, she heard tapping from somewhere above her. At the top landing of the stairs, she walked softly to Norman's door and pressed her ear up against it to listen. The tapping had stopped. She put her key in the lock and twisted it, unlocking the door as quietly as possible. After that, she retreated downstairs for the new saline bag and a syringe with the fatal dose of morphine for Sadie.

SECONDS EARLIER, FROM INSIDE THE ROOM

Norman heard Mercy's footsteps in time to stop working on the door hinge. The lower hinge, the first one he had started working on, only moved a fraction of an inch in the hour and a half he had been working on it. He didn't know why Mercy had unlocked his door, but he didn't care. He knew that this could be his only chance to get to the phone downstairs and call Sadie's daughter.

His knees hurt from kneeling at the door for so long but he ignored the pain. He waited for Mercy to get back downstairs, and then he opened the door. Norman hobbled toward and down the stairs, making his way to the phone without running into anyone. He watched for Mercy as he dialed the code for an outside line. Mercy was nowhere to be seen.

The phone rang six times before a woman picked up. Her soft voice answered in a groggy, "Hello."

Norman whispered into the receiver. "You must listen carefully. Get dressed right away."

"What? Who is this?"

"Don't talk. Just do what I say. It's a matter of life and death."

"Look, whoever you are, no one is getting dressed or undressed. Stop calling women and trying to scare them. Just rent one of those porno movies and quit calling people."

"No, don't hang up. Sadie is in danger."

"What—who is this?"

"My name is Norman. I'm at the home with your mother."

Norman explained what had happened and told Peggy to call the police and get to Harwine as quickly as possible. As soon as he hung up the phone, he heard footsteps. He ducked down in the shadowy nook of the staircase just as Mercy passed by, carrying an IV bag and disappearing down the hallway.

Seconds later, Norman slipped out of the shadows and unlocked the front door, opening it a crack for Peggy. Then he moved down the hallway, looking in each room for Sadie. The hair on the back of his neck told him that he couldn't wait for Peggy. It was up to him to save his Princess. When he found the room where Sadie was, the Jamaican nurse was standing to the right of the bed. Sadie had her eyes open and was talking. Sadie's shaky voice was thanking Mercy as she hooked the new saline bag on the pole.

"No need to thank me, Miss Sadie. I'm a nurse, this is what I's do. You rest while I go get you another shot for your pain." Mercy headed toward the door.

"No, I'm still woozy from the last shot you gave me," Sadie called after her. "I've had enough. I don't want to be overmedicated. I'll let you know if I need anything." But Mercy didn't answer or turn back. She kept walking, out of the room, and down the hall.

Norman ducked into an empty room to hide as Mercy passed. Once she was out of sight, he slipped out of hiding and entered his Princess's room.

Sadie's face lit up. "What are you doing here?"

He put his finger up to his lips. "Shhh."

"Why do I have to be quiet? How did you get to the hospital? Who drove you?"

"Hospital, is that where Old Green Eyes said you were?"

"Yes. What's going on?"

"I'm not exactly sure, Princess, but help is on the way. You're not at the hospital, you never left the home. There's not enough time before Old Green Eyes comes back so when she comes in, just play along with her. Don't let on that you know where you are. If you can hang on a little longer, Peggy will be here."

"Peggy. You called her? They suspect that we're investigating them?"

"They suspect something, that's for sure. I've been locked in my room all night until about twenty minutes ago."

"They locked you in?" The effects of the pain shot seemed to not have worn off yet. Sadie had some trouble processing what Norman was saying. However, she still had her wits enough to realize the situation was dangerous. "We need to get out of here."

"I can't get you out of here by myself. Besides, we don't have a car. The way I figure it is, they're going to make a move soon. They can't risk anyone finding out what happened last night or having an investigation opening up on this place. I called your daughter and she will be here soon. I'm sorry, but you need to hang on for a few more minutes. Right now, I need to go before Old Green Eyes comes back."

"Norman, wait. Do you have the camera that I put in the doll?"

"Right here, Princess." Norman patted his pocket and then slipped out the door.

Dead Evidence

Norman saw headlights approaching the house. It was 6:45 a.m. and Mercy had been in and out of Sadie's room for the last ten minutes except for the last time when she stayed in there.

Something was happening, he just knew it. If the car coming up the driveway wasn't Peggy's, he decided he wouldn't wait any longer. He just would have to force his way past Mercy and get Sadie out somehow. He wasn't going to leave her alone, like last night. Besides, soon the day duty nurse would start her shift and who knows what Mercy would tell her. The woman followed orders like a robot. He'd get no help from her.

Norman sat on the stairs, ready to move if that car wasn't Peggy's. The front door opened slow and easy. A woman with flaming red hair poked her head in and Norman rushed over to her. "You're Peggy?"

"Yes. Are you Norman?"

"The one and only," he said. Norman grabbed Peggy's arm and pulled her toward the hallway. "Hurry. You've got to get her out before it's too late."

He stopped and pointed down the hallway, indicating which door to find Sadie behind. "Mercy, a so-called nurse, just went into the room where they took Sadie. Tell her who you are and that you're taking your mother home. You'll be able to handle her as long as you maintain your authority."

"What are you going to do?" Peggy asked.

"I'll keep a lookout for Reed. I think we'll be okay as long as he doesn't show up."

"Do you think my mother will be able to walk with my help?"

"Your mom could walk on hot coals if she had to. She's one strong cookie."

In Sadie's room, Mercy approached the bedside and took a syringe out of her pocket. She inserted the needle into the port near the top of the bag, right as Sadie opened her eyes.

"What are you doing?" Sadie demanded. "You just gave me morphine minutes ago. I told you then I didn't need it. You . . . you can't give me more now. It's too . . . too much." Sadie's words slurred. Her eyelids fluttered closed, then they flashed open again. "I don't need anymore. Stop!"

"It will be all over in a few minutes," Mercy said. "Now close your eyes. You brought all of this on to yourself. We can't let you live now."

"No, stop. You won't get away with it."

"No? Just watch me, you old biddy."

Mercy pushed the syringe and released the morphine. Half of the liquid had emptied into the tube when a voice called out from the doorway.

"You heard my mother. Stop!"

Mercy removed the needle, placing it on the table; she turned to face the woman in the doorway. "Your mother has broken her leg. I'm taking care of her."

"The hell you are," Peggy said. She moved forward, pushing Mercy away from the bed. "I'm taking her out of here. She needs to go to a hospital."

"She can't be moved. You don't know what you're doing."

"Well, maybe then, I need to listen to a professional nurse."

Mercy smiled and moved forward. "That's more like it."

Peggy pushed her back, stopping Mercy from moving forward. "I mean a *real* nurse," Peggy said. Then she bent over Sadie and asked, "Do you need help?"

Sadie nodded her head.

Peggy stood up straight and glared at Mercy. "Stay away from my mother or I'll break *your* leg!"

Peggy bent over Sadie again and asked, "Mom, how do I take the IV out?"

"Remove the tape on my hand where the IV tube is." Sadie's voice was weak. "Pull the needle straight out."

Peggy did as Sadie instructed. Once the needle was out, she pulled her mother up to a sitting position and turned her legs to the side of the bed. The cast on Sadie's one leg would help hold her up and Peggy would be her anchor on the opposite side. Peggy pulled Sadie to a standing position.

"Mom, lean on me. We're getting you out of here."

An awful commotion echoed from the hallway. Peggy heard the loud voices of two men yelling. The shouting grew louder and louder. Then the door flew open and Reed entered the room, with Norman on his heels.

Norman yanked at Reed's arm and shouted threats at him. Reed jerked his arm out of Norman's grasp, ignoring his angry words.

Reed looked at Peggy and Sadie next to her with her arm draped around the woman's neck. "Madam, what do you think you're doing?"

Peggy held Sadie by the waist and stood tall. "I'm taking my mother out of this place."

"You can't. We're responsible for her safety and you are putting her in danger. She stays here."

"Over my dead body," Norman shouted from behind Reed. "Peggy, I've got a wheelchair in the hallway. Bring her out there."

"You stay out of this," Reed said, pointing to Norman. He turned back to Mercy, who stood frozen beside the two women. "Nurse, put your patient back in bed."

As Mercy took a step and Peggy warned, "Stay away from us."

Peggy pulled Sadie forward, making her take a step. "Mother, please try to walk."

Sadie's eyes were dull and half-opened. She blinked, focusing on Reed. Recognition seemed to spark in her eyes. Then her eyes widened with a fearful look. Sadie stopped and pulled back.

"Mother, keep walking," Peggy pleaded.

Sadie's free hand, that had been resting on her waist, fell limp at her side. Blood ran from the back of her hand where the IV had been and trickled down her fingers. It dripped off of her fingertips and blood started to puddle on the floor. Then Sadie's body slumped over.

Peggy pulled her up. "Walk, mother!"

"Peggy, it's too late." Sadie's voice was barely audible. "I can't make it."

"Yes, you can. Try."

Sadie looked at Peggy. "It's all right, we've got them. There'll be evidence. You need to demand that the coroner run a toxicology test. My autopsy and the test will be our evidence."

Peggy looked at her mother in horror.

"My death will shut this place down."

"No!" Peggy screamed. "You're going to the hospital. You're not going to die."

Sadie's eyelids flickered as her eyes began to roll back into her head. The weight of her body pulled down on Peggy's arms, almost causing both of them to fall to the floor.

"Mother!" Peggy heaved Sadie's body up, holding her tight. "Mother, you have to *walk*."

Sadie opened her eyes and forced her foot forward, taking a step.

In the distance were sounds of sirens approaching.

Reed looked out of the window as state police cars and an ambulance sped up the drive. He moved forward and grabbed Sadie, lifting her. "Nurse, get the wheelchair. We need to get this woman to the ambulance."

Mercy stood paralyzed as Norman rushed out of the room. He returned seconds later, pushing a wheelchair. The three of them, Norman, Peggy, and Reed helped put Sadie in the wheelchair and rushed her outside.

Reed called to one of the paramedics. "Thank goodness you're here. This woman is going into shock. She needs immediate attention. Please, come quickly. My nurse put an IV in her before we realized that she needed to be moved to the hospital. We need your help."

Road Map to Jacob

I woke up to find myself stretched diagonally across the queen-size bed. My head rested near one corner and my feet were at the opposite end. It took me a few seconds to realize I wasn't in my bed in Havenridge but in New Orleans.

Last night I slept better than I had in months, maybe years. Contentment flowed through me. Memories of nestling my head in the crook of Tony's arm put a smile on my face. Sharing my bed with his body resting next to mine had felt so natural.

Although before we were entwined together, and before the lovemaking, things hadn't gone so smoothly. I had insisted on talking between his kisses, saying I had feelings for him but that it didn't mean anything. We were free agents.

Free agents. What was I thinking? To say it was not my best moment would be a monumental understatement!

Once that hotel door closed last night, my modern woman's confidence crumbled. I started babbling, saying things like his staying over didn't come with any strings. I went on and on. Obviously, I was a little rusty on dating etiquette and not *that* modern.

Finally, I'd stopped my childish chatter. The modern woman was back and I took the lead. I moved my hands down Tony's chest, my fingers stopping at the buttons on his shirt. In the heat of the moment, I tugged at them, trying to unbutton the shirt. Giving up, I just pulled, eager to get at his naked chest, then I felt the shirt release. A button—may be two—popped off and went flying, landing somewhere over to the right side of the room.

Now in the clear morning air, the memory of my performance was more than I could bear. Wanting to forget last night's awkward moments, I reached across the bed, swiping at the sheets to feel for Tony. All I felt was emptiness.

My eyes flashed open. I was alone. Laurent's statements about Tony's months of dating a different woman every week buzzed in my head. Tony was definitely more experienced than I.

I scared him off on our very first date. My words from last night rushed back. Somewhere during my appalling foreplay performance, I said that I didn't expect a commitment in exchange for the invitation into my bed.

"Ugh." The involuntary response escaped from my lips as if to purge every unthinkable blunder from my head. I put my hand over my eyes and turned over on my back.

"You're awake," I heard Tony's voice say cheerfully.

Removing my hand, I opened my eyes to see him sitting at the small table on the left side of the room. His shirt hung open and he had a newspaper spread out in front of him.

Guess he's not a love-'em-and-leave-'em kind of guy. Why do I overthink everything?

Men are just different than women. Sex fixes everything with men. On the other hand, with a woman, if she is widowed or going through a divorce, sex is the last thing she wants. However, I had taken celibacy to a new height. Thank goodness having sex is like riding a bike. There may be mishaps at first, but it all comes back to you.

"You seemed to have slept well," Tony said. "Want some coffee? We have a 4-cup coffee pot over there. I saved you a cup."

"Only one?"

He shrugged. "What can I say? I'm a coffee drinker."

I brushed my hair away from my face. "That's okay." I gave a small laugh and said, "I'll have the cup later when I'm getting ready for you to take me out for breakfast."

That was the moment when I realized that today was another new beginning for me. I had a man in my life. Although strangely uncomfortable, it seemed at the same time extremely comfortable. Whether Tony would be here for one day, two, or more, only time would tell. I lifted myself up on my elbows and asked, "How did you sleep?"

A half-smiled formed on Tony's face. "Better than I've slept in years."

"I was afraid I might have pushed you out of bed."

"Nope. I'm just an early riser. You stretched out after I got up. "

"I'm not used to sharing my bed," I admitted. "It took me a long time after my divorce before I stopped sleeping on only one-fourth of the mattress. Now I take the *whole* bed up."

"Yeah, I hugged my side of the bed for 8 months after my wife's death."

I couldn't help but smile as a realization washed over me. *I guess there isn't that much difference between men and women after all.*

I got out of bed, walked over to Tony, and gave him a hug.

He looked confused. "What's that for?"

"Just because," I said. "After the way I babbled on about things last night, you must have thought I was a nut case."

Tony shrugged again and shook his head. "I thought you were talking because my technique was crummy."

"Your technique was fine." I giggled, and then added, "Except you're not any better with buttons than I am."

"It's not my fault. Women's jeans shouldn't have buttons. Snaps belong on jeans."

ONE HOUR LATER

We decided to grab coffee and beignets to go and we took them over to Jackson Square, the park in the French Quarter where I had fed the pigeons on my first day here. It'd be a nice way to kill time until Miss Marguerite's church service ended. That's when I told Tony his dear friend Laurent had shared all about Tony's dating escapades.

"You see, the blame for my nervousness last night was mostly because of Laurent," I said. "My image of you suddenly changed from cop to playboy. Laurent said, and I quote, *you had dated 75 percent of the available women in New Orleans.*"

"Remind me to have a long talk with him. Laurent needs to get the facts straight. I only dated 50 percent of the women."

We laughed and I offered up a story from my past. "After my divorce, I thought that I couldn't wing it alone. After all, Daniel and I had gotten married right out of high school. In a weak moment, I decided to track down this old boyfriend I had dated before I met Daniel. Actually, I dumped the guy to date Daniel. I fantasized that my old boyfriend had been pining away all those years that I'd been married, and he was patiently waiting for me to come back to him."

I finished telling the story, explaining that he still lived in town and I'd found his number in the phone book. I called him and we had agreed to meet for lunch. When he showed up, he had his wife with him—she was eight months pregnant. Tony said he couldn't top my story, that I took the prize for embarrassing moments.

A few minutes after we'd finished sharing war stories of bad dates, Tony said we should head over to Miss Marguerite's house.

Thirty minutes later, we pulled up in front of a white frame house, modest in size, with green shutters. There was a low wire fence surrounding the property and a tidy garden of zinnias in the front yard. The flowers gave a welcoming appearance and added a burst of cheerful colors of bright yellows, oranges, and reds. Laurent was sitting on the porch in a wooden rocker. He jumped up to meet us as we pushed the gate open.

"Glad to see you," Laurent said. "Meme brought someone special home from church to meet you, Stephanie."

"Me? Who is it?"

"A lady from the Historical Society."

Tony smiled big and took my hand in his as we followed Laurent into the house. "Laurent, you really came through. This almost gets you out of hot water for dubbing me *Tony Playboy Heffner DeLuca* of New Orleans."

Miss Marguerite's home was furnished with a French influence. The small living room had a red velvet couch and matching drapes. As Laurent's grandmother approached to welcome us, she reminded me of a black version of Peggy. Although Marguerite had a stronger personality than that of Sadie's daughter, still Peggy had the same tender, motherly manner about her like what I saw in Laurent's grandmother.

"Stephanie, Boo told me all about you and the man you're trying to track down information on," Miss Marguerite said. She turned and started walking toward another room while she continued talking and waved to us to follow her.

I turned to Tony and mouthed, *Boo?* Tony leaned in and whispered in my ear, "That's Laurent. It's a Creole thing. An endearment of sorts, like calling someone kiddo."

A woman was sitting at a round table in what appeared to be the dining room. In front of her sat a china cup and in the center of the table was a small plate of cookies. When we entered, she took a final drink of the tea and placed the cup on the saucer, and looked toward us with a broad smile.

Miss Marguerite said, "This is my friend from the Historical Society," motioning to the old woman. Then turning to us, "Stephanie and Tony, may I introduce you to Althea Ross."

Althea versus Ghistaine

My eyes grew wide and I stumbled as I rushed over to the elderly woman. Snatching her hand up, I pumped it with excitement. "You don't know how glad I am to meet you. I've looked for so long. Been through so much." I turned to Tony, nodding to him for his confirmation. "Isn't that right?"

"Yes, Stephanie has been searching for a while and it hasn't been easy for her. She came from Georgia, hoping to get answers."

"Yes, that's right. And here you are," I sputtered with the excitement of a six-year-old on Christmas morning.

The woman's face contorted into a frown as she stared at me. I realized I was still shaking her hand. Her dark, chocolate-colored skin had a cross-stitched pattern of deep wrinkles that mapped across her face. Her age conveyed an illusion of wisdom, like an ancient guru.

I released her hand and took a seat. "I'm sorry for my excitement." Not having anything to do with my hands, I smoothed the pressed tablecloth in front of me. I added, "It's a pleasure to meet you, Miss Ross."

"Everyone calls me Miss Althea, child. Tell me how I can help you."

"Okay." I forced myself to stop fidgeting with the tablecloth and look at her. "I'm not sure where to start." My head was spinning with questions. "You see, I'm trying to track down a person that I believe passed away 75 or 80 years ago."

"Why don't you check the death records?" Miss Althea asked. "That's where you need to go. The state capital has those."

Tony tried to help by clarifying. "She has checked death certificates at the capital in Georgia. That's where the man lived for a while but there were no records of his death."

"His name is Jacob Thompson," I added. "He lived in Havenridge. That's where I'm from. He never owned any land. We've—my friend, Betsy, and me, checked property records. We've also contacted numerous courthouses in surrounding towns for any records, as well as checking churches for death records, and there was nothing. I finally was able to get ahold of letters and a journal that said he came to New Orleans but I can't find evidence of his existence here. I believe he died here. When Ghistaine gave me your name, I didn't know who you were or where to look for you. So you can understand when Miss Marguerite introduced you . . . well, that's why my excitement overtook me."

The old woman's face puckered up as if she had just had bitten into a lemon. "Ghistaine! You mean the Star Lady? The one who is friends with that voodoo, devil girl."

She waved her hand in my face and said, "You best be on your way, child. I won't have anything to do with her and her devil's workers." Althea got up and started to gather her purse and Bible from the table.

Marguerite stepped forward. "Now just a minute, Althea. You call yourself a Christian woman?"

Althea stopped dead and glared at her friend. "I do. You know I am!"

"Doesn't the Bible say you should help anyone who is in need?"

"Yes, but . . . but, Ghistaine. You know she has that voodoo shop in the Quarter."

"No, she doesn't. That young girl who rents a spot there is the one who has lost her way. And if she came to you for help, even she should receive help from a true Christian. Only the Lord should judge us. So sit down and listen to Tony's girlfriend."

Althea stood firm for what seemed like a century, then put the Bible and her purse down and took a seat. Looking at me, she asked, "The star lady told you I could help you?"

"Yes, she did. The man who I am searching for information about, his name is Jacob Thompson. Can you see if you can find him in your records?"

She exhaled a frustrated breath and rolled her eyes upward. "We at the Historical Society don't keep peoples' names in a log. Our records are of *historical value*. They're not yearbooks of the community. Did Jacob fight in a war? Or was he a government official?"

"No, nothing like that. He was an ordinary man, never owned anything, and wandered the country. Still, he was important. Important to the woman he loved and to his family."

"I can't help you."

Tony said, "There has to be a reason why Ghistaine gave Stephanie your name." I tensed with the mention of Ghistaine. I didn't want Tony to set her off again, but she just listened to him as he continued. "You must have some record of him—somewhere."

The old woman put her hand to her face, tapping her fingers against her lips as she looked off in the distance, deep in thought.

"Maybe he didn't do anything important," she said, "but was in New Orleans during an important time. What year was he here?"

"I'm not sure," I said, "sometime around the turn of the century. I have numbers that Ghist . . . uh." I stopped myself, so not to mention Ghistaine's name again. "I have numbers written down. Maybe they are index numbers listed in one of your historical documents."

I dug into my purse and pulled out the paper with the penciled scribbling and gave it to Miss Althea.

She looked at it. "Child, this could be grave mapping numbers."

With that, Laurent pulled an empty chair to the table, sat, and leaned in as he looked over Althea's shoulder. "I didn't think of that," he said. "The sets of numbers are right. Can I see the paper?"

Miss Althea handed it to him as she got up from the table. "Marguerite, where is the box with the grave documents and death rolls of 1906?"

"Over there in the corner, sister." Marguerite pointed to the far side of the dining room. The two women headed over to the corner. "I'll help you find them. We need to look in the documents for deaths from Little Palermo. Boo told me that Ghistaine wrote that down on the paper."

Althea stopped midstep and turned toward Marguerite. "You knew the star lady sent her to me?"

"Sister, the box." Marguerite prompted.

The old woman glared at her friend, then turned, and started walking, while continuing to talk. "I know what box to look in. The child gave me the paper. *I can read,* you know."

Laurent said to Stephanie and Tony, pointing to the paper, "You see, these numbers could identify the location of a grave. Here in N'awlins, we bury our kin above ground in tombs to avoid problems because the water table here is just a few feet below the surface. Don't want our dearly departed uncle Louis to float away." He paused and pointed to the paper. "If this is map coordinates of a grave, then 3 stands for the third aisle in a cemetery. The 15 is the row number, and 651 identifies the tomb or crypt."

Althea and Marguerite returned to the table with armloads of books, papers, and what appeared to be folded maps.

The older woman spoke first. "What I think is, if the man you're searching for . . ." Althea paused and asked, "What is his name?"

"Jacob Thompson," Tony, Laurent, and I said in unison.

"Yes, your Mister Thompson probably was here in 1906."

Marguerite jumped in. "That year fits and would be the most logical reason for us having records of your Mister Thompson. As sister said, The Historical Society doesn't keep personal logs of people or records of their death unless their passing was connected to something of historical significance. And we've been working for the last six months on what happened in 1906. It was yel—"

"Yellow Fever," Althea interrupted, followed by a big Cheshire cat grin. She was obviously hooked now on the mystery and wanted to maintain her ranking as top-sleuth on the team. "If Jacob Thompson was here, and if he lived in Little Palermo, he probably died of yellow fever. Those numbers you showed me resemble the combinations of group numbers that we have been recording in the burial books for the gravesites."

Marguerite stood and unfolded a large paper, placing it across the table. "This is a map of the graveyard where most of the yellow fever victims are buried. A team of people helped with the restoration of aging and decaying headstones. Also, they worked to recover unmarked graves of yellow fever victims for their inclusion in this graveyard. Althea and I have been working on the record books. We matched grave and death records by logging every bit of information uncovered during the last five years of the project."

"The boxes here are only part of the work," Althea added. "We have everything cross-referenced now. If Jacob was a yellow fever victim, he'll be here."

I felt the weight of the tragic event. I looked at the boxes and boxes piled in the corner. The two lovers were torn apart in so many ways, but it seemed ultimately they were separated by a devastating plague that touched many.

"Ghistaine said Jacob was in pain and afraid he was going to die like the others," I said.

Nodding, Althea didn't denounce Ghistaine's words; instead, she seemed to accept the confirmation of the yellow fever connection. "To die from yellow fever was a painful death. Over 12,000 people died of yellow fever in New Orleans. If your Jacob worked the docks, more than likely he would have been exposed. There were big water barrels on the docks, which continued to breed the mosquitos that carried the fever. Even though Louisiana was plagued with yellow fever, Little Palermo had been hit the hardest because the people were packed in the housing where many of the dockworkers lived. The immigrants living there were afraid of the doctors, afraid to say they were sick. The death toll there was huge."

"Jacob told Ghistaine that there were piles of dead bodies," I said. "I couldn't imagine what he was talking about."

"Yellow Fever, that's what he was telling her about," Marguerite said. "There were so many dying that the people started burying bodies on top of each other."

"There is only one way to find out if your Jacob Thompson died of the fever," Althea said. "Where're those numbers the star lady gave you? I'll look them up."

Ghosts and Graveyards

Althea opened a large logbook with the listing of all the grave marker numbers that the Historical Society had of the yellow fever victims.

"Everything is cross-referenced," she explained "Those numbers you have will be the best place to start. The name logs are not accurate because of spelling. An Italian man named Joseph could be listed under G since Giuseppe is Italian for Joseph or under the J's for the American spelling. It all depends on how they documented the death. It gets even more complicated on account that some patients were so sick they couldn't speak. In those cases, the nurses and medical staff would give them a name to identify them instead of saying, the patient in bed one. It also meant that when a patient died they wouldn't die nameless and be buried in an unmarked grave like discarded rubbish. So you see, you're very lucky to have those numbers. Without them, it would be near impossible to track down your Jacob if he was one of the ones too sick to give his name."

She trailed a boney finger down the page until the end, and then turned to the next page, stopping halfway down.

"Here," she said. Then as if scolding herself, she mumbled, "No, that's not it."

Her finger continued moving on down each page to the bottom, then flipped the page to the next one. Page after page. By the fourth page turn, her finger trailed three-quarters of the way down and then jerked to a halt. "Here!

Three, fifteen..." she read, pausing to wet her wrinkled lips, "six hundred and fifty-one."

"That's it," Laurent said. "That's the number 3–15–651."

"That's what I just read, Laurent." She glared at him as she grabbed for another book. "Now we need to see what graveyard that marker belongs to so we can cross-reference the graveyard to the patient death records. The hospital records will have the name listed with the name of the graveyard the body was sent to and we'll see if they have the name Jacob listed. Maybe there'll be some personal information listed, too."

"Personal information?" I asked. "What kind of personal information?"

"Well, you see, the hospital and neighborhood clinics were so overworked that it was all they could handle to keep the patients comfortable. However, some Good Samaritans who lived in surrounding neighborhoods would come with wagons and take patients to their homes. There the family members who lived in the house would care for the yellow fever victims until death came.

"Mine you, not many families did, because most were afraid of catching the sickness, but there were some. If your Jacob went to one of those homes for his care, he probably would have gotten more than just nursing needs. Many good-hearted family members read to the patients or wrote letters for them, while they were there."

"I didn't find any letters from New Orleans," I said.

"That doesn't mean they weren't written," Althea corrected me. "When the patient passed away, the hosting families would send notice of death back to the hospitals. In case a loved one came to the hospital looking to claim a body. Some of the hosting families felt a duty to store the personal items of those who had been in their care. They informed the hospitals in case someone came looking for the belongings. When we announced the Society's plans to record the deaths of yellow fever patients, the Good Samaritan's living relatives brought us boxes that had been collecting dust in attics for years. The donated items were given to the Society for historical significance. I suppose the families were relieved to finally get rid of the boxes with a clear conscience and not to have thrown them away after being in their care for generations."

I could hardly believe my search might be over. Althea kept explaining details about what the Historical Society had learned and the things they had been trusted with to identify, mark, and catalog.

"Yellow fever brings a painful death. Often the patients requested for their final words be taken down in letters to loved ones. But the patients either didn't have addresses memorized or were so delirious with pain the families had nowhere to send the letters. I'm guessing once a letter was written, it brought comfort to the dying patients. It must have allowed them peace, thinking they wrote to their loved ones before dying."

Marguerite said, "Some of the older family members remembered hearing elderly relatives tell the stories about the times when the fever hit. Later, those living relatives of the Good Samaritans came forward and relayed what they heard growing up. We have tape-recorded the oral histories from them."

"That's right," Althea said. "This has been a massive project that has gone on for years."

Marguerite crossed the room to look in one of the boxes for the cross-reference book.

Althea called out to her. "We need cross-reference Ledger 4113."

Marguerite dug through the box, pulling out books. As she pulled another book from the box she called out, "I have it here, sister." She walked back and placed the book on the table in front of the old woman.

Althea opened the ledger and thumbed through the pages until reaching a section identified as Fayette. "Fayette is the cemetery where the body 651 was buried." The ledger lay flat, exposing the section marked with a big letter J in the upper right-hand corner.

Althea pointed at the letter J and said, "You see, Stephanie, we started logging by the last name but found out right away that it wouldn't work. Many victims' names were noted only by a first name. Either the last name wasn't available, or they didn't know the foreign spelling of the last name."

She spoke while searching down the columns. "Well, glory be! Here's your Jacob. He stayed at the Basile Plantation home until his death."

"You've found him," I said in disbelief. After all, it was hard to believe it was that easy to find Jacob. "Maybe it's another Jacob. What else does it say?" I questioned. "Is there a last name?"

Marguerite looked over Althea's shoulder, smiling and then answered, "Thompson. It's *your* Jacob, my child."

"It's noted here as his original home," Althea added, "was Havenridge." She pushed up the reading glasses resting on her nose. "There's another note. It says, 'All belongings to go to Mabel Brewer, of the Brewer family in Havenridge."

"Jacob did love Mabel." I couldn't hold back my tears. *He loved you with all his heart, Mabel.* I hoped Mabel could hear my thoughts.

The message was clear in our findings. It confirmed what Mabel believed her whole life, that he did love her. *Jacob's death was the only thing that stopped him from coming home to you, Mabel. You were right to believe in his love.*

Althea and Marguerite located the box that contained Jacob's personal items. All those years, the Basile family had stored them in the attic of their home, waiting for someone to request them. Now the box was in the care of the Historical Society to preserve it for history, logged into yet another ledger. The items were one gentlemen's cap, a pair of workman's gloves, a man's money pouch with some paper money and several old coins, and one gold pocket watch with the inscription. *Safe travels, all my love, Mabel.* And a letter.

Althea handed me the folded letter, which had turned yellow with age. She read from the ledger, "it says here in the record notes that the only daughter of the Basile family had nursed and comforted Jacob in his final days. She wrote that letter for him on his deathbed."

My hands shook as I opened the letter and read Jacob's final words out loud.

My dearest Mabel,

I know now that my body has become too weak to fight this sickness. I fear my death is near. My last request for you is to be happy and know that I love you now and forever.

Jacob

Saying Goodbye

Tony and I placed the bouquet of zinnias at the base of a simple stone marker with the name Jacob Thompson chiseled in it. Otherwise known as yellow fever victim number 651.

I unclasped Mabel's locket from my neck. Holding it in my hand, I turned to Tony. "Do you think Mabel's here?"

Tony's brow furrowed.

"I know it's ridiculous," I said defensively, "but Ghistaine said there was a woman's spirit with me. I want to leave the locket here—it belongs to Mabel."

Scanning the cemetery grounds, I explained my concern. "I don't want anyone to take it. Jacob and Mabel have had too much taken from them."

Tony nodded and pulled out a knife from his pocket. He opened it and knelt next to Jacob's marker as he cut a patch of grass. Pulling it up with dirt clumped beneath the blades of green, he dug a small hole in the dirt. Tony looked up at me, raising his open palm. "Give it to me."

I placed the locket in his hand. He carefully set the locket into the hole and gently pushed dirt over top of it. Then he returned the patch of grass and stood, tapping the grass with his foot until it was secure. "It's safe. No one will know about it except Jacob and Mabel."

We walked hand-in-hand back to the car in silence. Tomorrow I'd return to Havenridge. I had kept my promise to Leann—and I guess, even an unspoken promise to Mabel. It was time to keep my commitment to my publisher. Once in Havenridge, I'd call my agent and inform her that I had solved the mystery of Jacob. Next, I'd work to honor my promise to Sadie and help the patients in Harwine. The battle with Andrew Phillip Reed hadn't ended, it had just been delayed.

The ride back to the hotel was quiet. Tony and I both knew that today closed a part of my life. With any closure comes a new beginning. What that would be was unknown.

"You did something good here, in New Orleans," Tony said. "You're a remarkable woman."

"No, I'm not remarkable. I've made so many mistakes in my life."

He smiled. "We've all made mistakes in our lives. Still, because of you, Jacob and Mabel are at peace now. That's not bad."

Thirty minutes later, we entered the lobby of the hotel. Laurent was there, standing in front of the television with Tommy. When Laurent saw us, he came rushing over. "Tony, I've been waiting for you. The guy in Harwine who you had me run a check on, Andrew Phillip Reed, he's been arrested."

"What!" I said, "What did he do?"

"The news doesn't have the whole story yet, Stephanie. But the place is hopping with State police, news crews, and ambulances."

We hurried over to the television as he updated Tony. "The local police have been removed from the investigation of the boarding house that Reed owns because of their possible involvement. The reporters are going wild. They said IA was called in to investigate the entire Harwine police department."

"Sorry, but what's IA?" I said.

"Internal Affairs," Tony said to me, then looked at Laurent. "Go on."

"Well, the morning news has been recapping everything that happened but now they are running the special report. Reed has been charged with conspiracy to commit murder, plus a butt load of other charges. Neglect, abuse, you name it. One old lady was rushed to the hospital, probably won't make it . . ."

Tommy called, "Hurry up; they're playing the film from the raid again."

As we joined Tommy, I recognized the front of Harwine Boarding House as the footage played on the television screen. There were lights flashing from at least twenty police cars parked all around the front of the dilapidated building.

The camera panned to a news reporter standing near the front steps. "We're outside the boarding house, where many senior citizens lived. An urgent 911 call brought the police here in the nick of time to stop the murder attempt of an elderly woman."

"Sadie was right about Reed," I said. "Thank goodness someone finally stopped him. Those poor people who had lived there."

The camera panned back to the house as the reporter continued telling the details.

Reed came into focus as the camera zoomed in as he helped wheel someone outside. A woman followed along the opposite side of him, helping the injured person. I couldn't see the woman's face but I caught a glimpse of the familiar flaming red hair. *It can't be. That looks like Peggy.*

"Tommy, please turn up the volume," I said.

One of the paramedics stepped forward to the wheelchair and scooped up the limp body. The blanket was wrapped around her tight, blocking the view of her face. He gently placed the body on a stretcher.

"Looks like she's dead," Tommy said.

"Shhh," Laurent said. "We haven't seen this footage before."

The camera panned back to the reporter.

"We've been told the woman you see being put in the ambulance will be transported to the hospital in Milledgeville. Additionally, we have found out that she came to Harwine Boarding House less than a week and a half ago. In that short time, she received a broken leg, multiple lacerations, and an attempt on her life. The victim's name is Sadie Campbell."

"No!" I screamed. "What was Sadie doing there?" I looked at Tony. "Can you call the hospital and find out more about her condition? You're a cop, they'll talk to you. Please. She can't be dead."

"Calm down. Yes, I'll call."

After about ten minutes on the phone, Tony found out that Sadie had made it to the hospital but she was in critical condition. He got through to the nurses' station and had someone get Peggy on the phone so I could talk to her. Peggy shared a few sketchy details about Sadie's undercover plan to get evidence against Reed.

I couldn't help but blame myself for not staying there to fight Reed, instead of Sadie. If I had, then maybe Sadie would not have talked Peggy into this dangerous plan. I had underestimated Sadie. She was a small old lady, but she had guts.

Peggy said the doctors advised that the next 72 hours were critical. Sadie wasn't out of the woods yet, she could still die.

I hoped that Sadie's strength had not been used up in Harwine. I told Peggy that I would be praying for Sadie.

Peggy remained hopeful and said her mother had always been a strong woman. Before hanging up she said that I could come to visit Sadie once she was better and had returned to Magnolia Breezes.

I couldn't help but think, *that is if she ever returns to Magnolia Breezes.*

The next morning I packed, fighting off the guilt that I had let Sadie down. As I drove back to Havenridge, Tony's words played through my mind. 'You're remarkable.' I didn't feel so remarkable.

Why hadn't I focused more on helping the living, instead of the dead?

Magnolia Breezes

I waited in the foyer as Debbie, the nurse, instructed me. I looked into the familiar sunlit room as she walked over to the white wicker settee. There was Sadie, sitting between Peggy and Max.

Debbie said something to Max. He looked toward my direction, then nodded and stood. As he approached me, I couldn't help but watch Sadie in the distance. I noticed how well she looked. It appeared that the only remaining evidence of her ordeal was a plaster cast on her leg.

"Stephanie," Max said cheerfully. "Peggy and I are so glad you were able to come and visit with Sadie."

"Wild horses couldn't keep me away. She looks great," I said as I watched Sadie and Peggy laughing. They were going through an album-sized book, flipping the pages and stopping to point at things on the page. They continued to chat and laugh as they turned the pages.

"I'm surprised to see you here, Max. Did Peggy realize that her mother should finally meet the man in her life?"

"No . . . not really. That's what I needed to talk to you about before you go in. Sadie recovered physically from what happened in Harwine but the Sadie we knew died on that night. Mentally, that is. You see, Sadie thinks she is twenty years old and has never been married. She doesn't know that she has a grown child."

He pointed to the two women sitting together on the settee as they giggled like schoolgirls. "Since that night, Sadie doesn't know Peggy. She thinks she's Mabel. Peggy's mother is gone forever."

"Oh, no. How awful for Peggy. I'm so sorry."

Max smiled big. "Don't be sorry. Peggy isn't. You see, she told me that she dreaded the time when her mother would go away. Peggy said that she used to feel Sadie's Alzheimer's was a curse. Now that it's taken over and stolen Sadie away, Peggy says the reality is that it's been a gift."

"A gift? I don't understand."

Max pointed to the two women on the settee. "Look at them. They're like this all the time now. Laughing and enjoying each other, not fearing the future. Peggy claims that not many daughters get a chance to get to know their mother as a young girl. How many daughters get to share their mother's dreams they had when they were a young girl?"

I smiled and understood. Sadie was happy, and Peggy was able to be part of that happiness.

"You know what they are looking at in that book?" Max asked me.

I shook my head.

"They're looking at pictures of Mabel and Sadie. It doesn't matter that some of those pictures are baby pictures of Peg. Sadie thinks they're *her* baby pictures that Mabel kept. Peggy brought me to meet Sadie one day, not knowing how she would react. Sadie jumped up and hugged me. Then said, "Jacob, you've come back.""

"You don't say. She thinks you're Jacob?"

Max nodded. "Peggy is getting to share things she never felt comfortable to share with her mother before. They're girlfriends—it's a gift, not a curse."

Endings and Beginnings

So much had happened since that day I visited my friends at Magnolia Breezes. Peggy and Max got married, with Sadie as Maid-of-Honor. Sadie's dementia hasn't changed much, although Peggy says her mother tires more and is declining, little by little. Some days, she doesn't even recognize her as Mabel. Still, Peggy says that each day she has with her is a blessing.

I chose not to attend Peggy and Max's wedding since my last visit had confused Sadie. It was as if, somewhere in the echoes of Sadie's memory, she knew I didn't fit into her new world, where Mabel and Jacob lived.

Tony and I talk twice a week on the phone. He finally was content with the decision to retire, which he did last month. Laurent and Miss Marguerite threw a New Orleans-style celebration with "all the fixin's," as Tony told me. He said it was the right time for him to say goodbye to work and farewell to friends and memories of the past and start his new life.

I wrote 200 pages of my book, *A Love story in Havenridge.* I put it in the mail yesterday to TopHat. The writer's block everyone talks about isn't a problem for me anymore. Whenever I sit at the typewriter, the words flow.

Leann and Steve put their house up for sale. I'll miss them, but things change. My brother got a fantastic job offer in Atlanta, so they decided to take it and move. The regular salary will come in handy because Leann is pregnant. Their house sold last month but the tenant couldn't move in until this week. Leann said that she met him and he'll be a good neighbor. She made me promise to take him a plate of homemade cookies from her recipe and insisted he would love them since he was a bachelor.

The timer on the stove buzzed and I hurried to the kitchen. The cookies smelled great. After I placed the last cookie on the plate, my phone rang.

I answered it and heard Leann's voice.

"Yes. I just pulled them out of the oven," I answered.

"No, I didn't forget. I would be delivering them now if I hadn't been stopped to answer the phone."

Leann claimed that she wanted to make hot homemade cookies a tradition for moving to a new home. She said she took a plate over to her neighbor's when she moved to Atlanta.

"Don't you have the tradition a little backward?"

Leann said the move-in tradition could go either way.

"Okay, have it your way, Leann. I suppose you're right and yes, good luck can travel both ways—that is, when following traditions."

Leann seemed to be carrying this tradition thing to extremes by having me take cookies over to the person who brought her house. Although, I think tradition might be just an excuse so she can play matchmaker.

I wanted to talk more with my sister-in-law, but she insisted I take the plate over while the cookies were still warm. We said our goodbyes and I hung the phone up.

Outside, the day was bright and clear. The sweet fragrance of magnolia blossoms was in the air. Minutes later, I approached the front door of the house on the hill.

I saw that the new owner had kept the hand-painted welcome sign Leann had left in the garden. It was still stationed between the spider jasmine and the blue hydrangea bush.

I climbed the stairs and knocked on the screen door. I could see moving boxes inside and a voice called out that he'd be there in a minute. The sun streamed inside, creating dark patches in the front hallway. I could only see a shadow of a figure approaching, but the gait to his step was familiar.

The door opened.

"Leann said to expect you," Tony said.

I stepped inside and thrust the plate forward. "I brought warm cookies."

Tony smiled and took the plate from me, and placed it on top of a box.

"Good. I love cookies." Then he wrapped his arms around my waist, pulled me toward him, and kissed me.

Author Note

In writing, *Finding Jacob, Book Two of the Havenridge Mystery Novels*, the storyline was clear to me. I knew the focus of, Stephanie Oliver, my protagonist. I would have much more mystery in book two and continue with the dark history of the Brewer family.

Delving into the time period of generations of the Brewers showed how our country's attitude was toward mental illness in the first novel, *Secrets of Havenridge*, and it would continue in-depth in, *Finding Jacob*.

My original research of the surrounding areas gave me the true history of those decades to build my fictional story in both books. Thank goodness I decided to make a family tree for the Brewers, going back three generations, which gave me a road map, so-to-speak, for writing book two.

The picturesque, Norman Rockwell-like town was so powerful with its far-reaching effects on the protagonist that it was obvious that it would be the nucleus of many stories to come, thus the Havenridge Mystery Novels were born.

One of the most interesting historical detail that I had uncovered in my research for book one was the real nearby town of Milledgeville. It had been the location of one of the largest and oldest asylums, dating back to 1842.

In *Finding Jacob*, Stephanie would follow the thread of Mabel's mother (Hanna) and grandmother (Josephine) to Milledgeville, and then, to Harwine Hospital (a fictional institution). Cain Brewer's fear of tainted blood being passed on to his daughter was very much an intricate part of the story.

However, I realized, after writing several chapters that Stephanie's grueling search for Jacob needed something more. Tracking the past in the 80s before Google, was monumental for her and to keep her inspired, as well as help her with the investigation, she needed a new connection other than her friend, Betsy. That was when another character spoke to me, Sadie Campbell.

Sadie was such a strong, important character that I had to let her follow an investigative path of her own, paralleling Stephanie's.

Traveling from Havenridge, Milledgeville, Harwine, and New Orleans allowed the readers to visit fresh locations as the two parallel tales of mystery, intrigue, and danger moved forward.

New Orleans brought new characters like Ghistaine (the empath) and Detective DeLuca.

Harwine introduced Norman, nurse Mercy (Green Eyes), and the vile, Phillip Andrew Reed.

Story elements included things like; the suitcases found in Harwine, which was fashioned after the real suitcases found in a storage area of Willard Mental Hospital in New York before its demolition, and the rescue of Emmie Lu, a character adapted from the true crime story about a little girl who was snatched from her Florida home and murdered by the convicted killer, John Couey.

Since the story's strength was ultimately a love story that stemmed from the legend of the Lovers at Blue Lake, and all about Mabel and Jacob, it seemed only fitting to add some romance for Stephanie with a handsome Super Cop.

Havenridge has become a favorite place for me, even though I can only visit it in novel form. The people are good and the town is a step back in time. I hope you will enjoy the Havenridge Mystery Novels as much as I have enjoyed writing it.

Your Author Friend,
Chris Coad Taylor
www.chriscoadtaylor.com
amazon.com/author/chriscoadtaylor

www.ingramcontent.com/pod-product-compliance
Lightning Source LLC
Chambersburg PA
CBHW020323180626
46812CB00001B/33